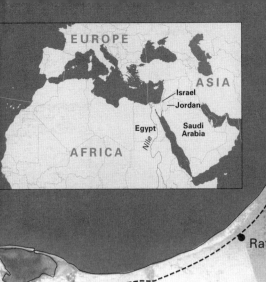

EUROPE

ASIA

Israel
Jordan

Egypt
Nile

Saudi
Arabia

AFRICA

Salt Sea

• Rafa

—— Way of Horus

Wadi Arava

Nakhl •

Timna •

trade route

Naqab •

ETHAM

Wadi Masri •

Baal Zephon

TIH PLATEAU

Red (Reed) Sea

RY

OCT / V 2006

SEVEN DAYS

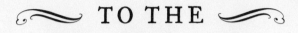

TO THE

SEA

An Epic Novel of
THE EXODUS

———

REBECCA KOHN

RuggedLand

RUGGED LAND | 401 WEST STREET · SECOND FLOOR · NEW YORK CITY · NY 10014 · USA

RuggedLand

Published by Rugged Land, LLC

401 WEST STREET • SECOND FLOOR • NEW YORK • NY • 10014 • USA

RUGGED LAND and colophon are trademarks of Rugged Land, LLC.

LIBRARY OF CONGRESS CATALOGING-IN-PUBLICATION DATA

Kohn, Rebecca.

Seven days to the sea : an epic novel of the Exodus /

Rebecca Kohn.-- 1st ed.

p. cm.

LCCN 2005028665

ISBN 1-59071-049-5

1. Bible. O.T. Exodus--History of Biblical events--Fiction.

2. Miriam (Biblical figure)--Fiction.

3. Women in the Bible--Fiction.

I. Title: 7 days to the sea. II. Title.

PS3611.0368S48 2006

Book Design by

JOOYOUNG LEE

RUGGED LAND WEBSITE ADDRESS: WWW.RUGGEDLAND.COM

1 3 5 7 9 10 8 6 4 2

First Edition

FOR LEAH

You are not obliged to complete the task,

neither are you free to refrain from it.

Pirke Avot 2:21

And He said to Abraham,

"Your seed will be strangers in a land not their own and

they will be enslaved and oppressed four hundred years.

But I will bring judgment upon the nation for whom they slave,

and afterward they will come forth with great wealth."

Genesis 15:13-14

PROLOGUE
OUTSIDE CAMP
Miryam

These are the hands that Yahveh gave me. Once they kept the cleanest home in all of Egypt. With these hands I welcomed Aharon's sons into the world. They fed my brother Moses and all our family. They baked the first bread of offering for the Tabernacle. From childhood my hands never lay idle. They always knew how to set everything right.

These are the hands that helped build a nation.

Look at them! White with the scales of tzaraat. I strove for purity with every breath, with every fiber of my being! Now I am tainted and unclean.

Foul with this dreaded disease, banished from camp into the barren wildernesswhat use am I?

I, who never cried, can not stop the flood of tears.

Yahveh! I tend the Children of Israel as if they are the fruit of my own womb. Make me whole again for their sake!

The prayer weeps from every pore. Does He hear?

The water in my goatskin does not refresh me. The beauty of the blue sky against the yellow sand and red rock eludes me. The midday heat glides over my garments without penetrating. Only the horror of my punishment touches me. I have never been so alone.

I am condemned to this isolation for seven days—as long as our flight from Egypt to the sea. In those seven days we began to shed our slavery. The waters parted. We crossed into Midyan as a nation reborn.

We sang and danced with joy. Tzipporah took the timbrel from me. She touched my hand. Our eyes met. In that moment, by the edge of the sea, I recognized how much we shared—I saved Moses soon after he came into this world and she saved him when he stood on the threshold of greatness. We each had our purpose, our part to play in history. In the shadows of my heart I must have known that Moses needed her as much as he needed me.

What became of my heart?

What will become of me in these seven days?

I stare into the wavering horizon. The glistening sun deceives me. A shadow flutters. The figure draws closer. The Angel of Death.

I rise in fear.

PART

I

EGYPT

ONE

Miryam

EVEN as a young girl I always saw the truth before me—how my mother longed for more children, how my father loved us with quiet devotion, how my brother Aharon sought to please everyone. As I grew older, my vision grew wider. I saw my people's weakness for the fleshpots of Egypt. I saw through falsehood and deceit. I saw good and evil struggle in the same person. Wherever I looked I saw room for improvement. If something lay amiss in my father's household—crockery in uneven stacks, a chipped brick on the stair, a tress fallen loose from a friend's braid—I fixed it without delay. Some things I could not repair: injustice, sloth, cowardice, the corrupting influence of the Egyptian gods.

For nineteen generations the Children of Israel prospered in Egypt. Under the tyrant Rameses we came to know oppression and hardship. Every year in Shomu—the dry season—I watched the pharaoh's army march into Goshen. They went into our homes, our fields, and our workshops to seize men for compulsory labor. I saw them beat those who tried to escape. Once a man tried to disguise himself in his wife's wig and dress. When the soldiers discovered his ruse they castrated him. After that, no one dared to evade the soldiers.

They sent some of the Israelites to work on temples far upstream. Most of our men remained in the Eastern Delta—a short walk from Goshen—to build the new capital, Pi-Ramesse. Of all the pharaoh's many ambitious projects, nothing compared to the obelisks, pylons, temples, and palaces of this extravagant city surrounded by rivulets.

From a young age I understood the fate of those who labored under Rameses's foremen. Year after year I saw them return broken and weak. I heard how they spent long hours in the withering sun, how they received the whip by day and nothing more than a little bread at night. Life was short for the poorest, both Israelites and Egyptians—few lived beyond the age of twenty-five. Pharaoh's heavy burdens struck down rich and poor alike. The canals of Egypt flowed with the sweat and blood of our men.

I might have turned a blind eye to all the suffering—I counted my own family among the lucky few untouched by Pharaoh's harsh rule. My father, Amram the vintner, learned winemaking from his father who learned from his father, generation after generation all the way back to our forefather Levi son of Yaakov. Father did not rush his wine to market. He often waited as long as three or four years for a vintage to mature before he added spices and honey. Those sealings went for the highest prices and found great favor with Rameses himself. The royal household enjoyed my father's wine so much that Father and his workers, including my younger brother Aharon, remained exempt from all conscripted labor.

Many of my friends and acquaintances envied our good fortune. I took care never to speak of it. I did not allow myself to rest content in the shadow of my people's suffering. I learned to be solicitous and helpful. I brought baked goods and words of comfort to our neighbors. In the marketplace the women of Goshen welcomed my sympathetic ear.

I took my place among these women earlier than most. My mother, Yoheved—who loved her family with a sweet and generous heart— had little skill for housekeeping. By my eleventh birthday she filled my eager hands with work. A servant helped me with the cleaning, but I did all the cooking and shopping. I always looked forward to seeing my market friends. We exchanged gossip. We shared recipes and remedies. We advised each other on the day's best stalls for fresh produce or meat. Despite my young age, many sought my company. I took a lively interest in everyone.

My friends could always count on me to know the palace news, the weather predictions, and the matchmakers' latest triumphs. In return for everything I told them, they often teased me about Nunn, son of the jug maker.

I was a girl of eight and Nunn a young man of thirteen when he began to deliver jugs to the vineyard for his father. I liked him from the first. He spoke to me as an equal. He never tired of my questions. He seemed patient and kind with everyone. Once he gave me a little jug no bigger than my fist. I liked it so much he made several more for my next birthday. I filled them with oil and fruit juices. I smiled every time I saw them on my kitchen shelf.

As the years passed, Nunn matured into a handsome and energetic man. To some women he might have looked like any Israelite, with his dark hair shaved close to the head and his body dressed in a linen loincloth with a linen apron over the front. But I saw how his passionate brown eyes opened wide whenever he spoke with fervor, as he often did. I found myself drawn to his exuberance.

Nunn tended to forget details or overlook them altogether. He did not seem much aware of his surroundings. In this we stood as opposites. Yet he admired my neat and orderly ways. He did not object when I suggested a better method for stacking the wine jugs in the storage cellar. He never complained when I straightened his cloak or retied his sandals. He seemed to enjoy my hands fussing over him. He responded with good humor when I advised him to clean his nails with more care. We laughed at each other as brothers and sisters do.

Nunn and I often discussed the injustices around us. We scorned the Egyptian nobility who spent their wealth building magnificent tombs for the hour they rose from the dead. We mocked the pharaoh who imagined himself a god.

Nunn's fury with the pharaoh grew even greater after his first season on a labor gang. He returned thin and weak. I vowed to secure his release. He shook his head with disbelief.

"What can a twelve-year-old girl do? What can anyone do? Even the God of Father Yaakov can not save us."

Like all our people, I prayed to the gods that our ancestors brought with them out of Canaan into Egypt—El and his consort, Lady Atirat of the Sea. But I put more faith in the power of deeds. I wanted to save Nunn. I would find a way to do so.

The task proved easier than either Nunn or I anticipated. On the very evening of my promise, as Father and Aharon returned from the vineyard, I realized that Father had the means to release my friend from servitude.

I pleaded with Father to take Nunn into the winery during the dry months as an apprentice alongside Aharon. Nunn did nothing to advance his own father's business while he labored for Pharaoh's glory. Why not ask him to work for us instead?

"It is for your benefit as much as his," I argued. "Aharon is yet young. You need more help in those months when you are moving heavy jugs. Nunn can haul the wine to market. He will take more care than hired help."

Father saw the wisdom in my words. He declared that no more sensible or persuasive girl lived in all of Egypt.

The next morning my father arranged matters with Nunn's father. From that day forward Nunn looked at me with different eyes. He grew more tender and attentive. He brought me pretty flowers and sweet, ripe fruit. My height—even at twelve I stood taller than most men—had always embarrassed me. Now I began to feel conscious of my physical self in other ways. When I sat near his strong, broad body, my flesh tingled. I grew shy in his presence. I came to anticipate our meetings with both excitement and apprehension.

In a few short weeks my steady, sisterly affection for Nunn grew into the fluttering, hope-filled love of a young woman for a man. I prayed that Nunn also wanted our friendship to become something else. I knew my parents would approve. Nunn was a good man from a good family. He respected his elders. He cared about our people. He worked hard. He would never sit idle with his cup of beer if I needed help. Nor would I linger in the market if I could be of service to him. Our partnership would be joyful and productive.

But as the weeks passed without a word from him, I grew worried and skittish. I began to fear that he did not share my desire.

Even under Pharaoh's oppression our people multiplied. We looked forward to a better time when once again our people could dwell in the land with honor and dignity. We told each other that our situation could only improve.

We soon learned otherwise.

One morning in the twenty-eighth year of Rameses's rule—my thirteenth year of life—I stood in the marketplace hot with embarrassment as once again my friends teased me about Nunn.

"He has shoulders broader than an ox!" one girl announced.

"Have you seen his massive hands?"

"But such a slender waist!"

"He should wrap his loincloth tighter!"

"The way he stares at Miryam!"

"Like a hungry young dog."

"Stop it!" I laughed. "I have known him since I was a little girl. We are friends."

"*Good* friends," another tormentor said as she tilted her head toward a woman with an enormous pregnant belly.

"You are all cruel," I complained as I burst into laughter again. I stopped short when I noticed a palace messenger mounting the box in the center of the marketplace. I welcomed the distraction.

"Look!" I pointed to the man. "Let us listen to the announcement."

We drew closer. He opened a scroll and began to read.

"The Pharaoh Rameses II, ruler of the two Egypts, beloved of Amun-Re, Seth, and Thoth, declares that all male children born to the Israelites between today and two years hence will be put to death. Any who seek exemption will themselves be put to death. He further declares that midwives are ordered to carry out this edict as soon as a child emerges from the womb!"

As the terrible words entered my ears, all other sound ceased. I scanned the crowd in disbelief. Their contorted faces matched the horror in my heart.

The messenger stepped down. Cries of mourning rose from the crowd. I ran from person to person to see if I could learn the reason for this gruesome edict. A cloth dyer told me he had heard that Pharaoh's horoskop—a priest who read the stars—had predicted that a male child born among the Israelites in the next twenty-four months would rise up one day to overthrow the dynasty.

"May the slaughter of innocent children seal his fate," the man said under his breath.

"Let it be so," I whispered.

I ran home to tell my parents of the decree. My own mother, barren since Aharon's birth ten years before, had nothing to fear. That did not relieve our family from suffering. We loved our people. Their grief and ours were one.

The midwives refused to act on the order of death. They claimed that Israelite women, strong and quick in labor, did not require their services. I admired the courage of these defiant women. But I could not rejoice as others did. I knew that Pharaoh would not permit a few midwives to thwart his purpose.

A week after I heard the edict in the marketplace, Pharaoh's soldiers marched into Goshen. I watched as they invaded our homes. They snatched every newborn boy from his mother's breast. They did not bother to check the child's age. Sometimes they did not even determine the sex. Later I heard that mothers had offered all their jewels and gold in exchange for their children's lives. Some had even offered themselves. All proved futile. The soldiers took the bribes and the babies too.

I stood on the edge of the River Nile as soldiers emerged from several homes with wailing infants tucked under their arms. Mothers chased after the men with wild fury. Their anguished pleas filled the air. Other soldiers beat back the desperate women with the blunt ends of their spears. Some of the mothers managed to follow their children into the water. I too plunged into the river. I did not stop to tell myself what I already knew—the effort would be hopeless. It did not matter. I could not stand by while the infants drowned.

I clung to a half-dead baby—whose child I did not know—with all my strength. I pulled myself onto the riverbank. I lifted my feet to run but, a soldier caught sight of me. He held his spear across the road. I did not notice it fast enough. As I fell onto my face, he forced my arms apart.

I closed my eyes. I covered my ears. When I looked up again, soldiers lined the river to prevent further rescue attempts. Many other Israelites sat on the ground beside me, wet and defeated.

As I limped home I vowed revenge on Pharaoh and all his army.

The soldiers returned every fourteen days to search from house to house. Our council of elders advised all the Children of Israel to refrain from marital relations until Pharaoh lifted the edict. Some did not heed the warnings. Those who gave birth to girls knew the joy of a newborn at the breast. Those who had male children were not so lucky. None of the newborn sons survived.

In these dark months I found comfort in the company of my family and Nunn. One afternoon, several months after the pharaoh's death decree, Nunn and I sat under the shelter of an olive tree in the grove near the vineyard. We often stole a few minutes together while his father and mine settled their business.

"Is my face fresh enough to kiss today?" he asked. He pointed to his smooth-shaven cheek.

"No!" I laughed. I gave his shoulder a gentle push.

He snatched my hands. I had neither my mother's beauty nor her skill at grooming. I had no patience for the trouble of long hair, cosmetics, or elegant clothing. Jewelry interfered with my household duties. I did not take the time to rub rhinoceros fat into my chafed skin or stain my fingernails with henna. When I caught a glimpse of myself in Mother's copper mirror, I saw Miryam as she was inside and out—a clean, plain, practical young woman. I marveled that Nunn seemed to find me as pleasing as I found him.

Nunn began to stroke my arm. I liked the way his fingers felt on my skin. They made my body throb with a strange and pleasant yearning.

"I have spoken to my father." The words rushed out of him as if he had held them inside for too long. "I know you are young, but I want to settle things between us before someone tries to take you away from me."

I loved him. Now I knew that he loved me. We belonged together. My heart grew so full I could not speak. He read my answer on my glowing face, in my joy-filled eyes.

For a moment I almost forgot the decree, the infants in the river, the pall of mourning that hovered over our land. All of it came rushing back to me.

"It is a dark time for our people," I murmured. "Not the time for a union."

"We should not make a formal arrangement now," he agreed. "But we can look forward to sweeter days. My father will propose a betrothal to take place next year when the decree is lifted, and a marriage to follow no later than your fifteenth birthday."

I nodded. My heart pounded. My lips parted.

He leaned closer. He took me in his arms. I liked the smell of him. I let him kiss my mouth. His lips lingered. I pulled away with reluctance.

"I must return to the house."

"And I to my father."

We rose to our feet. We stood for a moment in awkward silence. In days past I had always embraced him at parting. Now every fiber of my being longed to feel his arms around me once again. But I knew how one thing would lead to another. I would not allow myself to give in. I did not want to shame my parents or his.

"The air has turned cool," I said. "Wear your cloak tomorrow."

He smiled. "What would I do without you to look after me?"

I took the long route back to the house, through the olive grove rather than along the canal. My feet grew so light I feared I might float away. I forced myself to count off all the tasks I had yet to accomplish that day: clothes to wash, bedding to air out, an evening meal to prepare. I added the chore of cleaning the stable—my least favorite—in hope that the prospect would bring me back to my familiar, practical self.

Nothing could distract me from the excitement of Nunn's declaration. I began to run.

After a few minutes I stopped to catch my breath. I closed my eyes for a moment to calm myself. A wind came up. It rattled the olive branches just coming into full leaf. Whispering filled my ears.

"Miryam! Miryam!"

I opened my eyes. Ahead of me in the olive grove stood a single ancient tree that shone like the sun itself. I shielded my eyes.

"Miryam, Miryam!"

I fell down in fear. The light lifted me. It wrapped me in its loving hands. Its warmth and brilliance penetrated my skin, my muscle, my bones. It filled every crevice of my being. It lifted my heart away from my flesh, as if on eagle's wings. As I left my body behind, I soared above the world of men to a still, silent place. The small voice echoed everywhere— in the olive branches, in the sky, on the ground, in my heart. It told me of a mission far greater than that of daughter, wife, or mother. It told me of my true destiny.

TWO

Miryam

AFTER my God came to me the world seemed brighter. My eyes saw everything with startling clarity. The empty sky, the fallow fields, even the dust on the ground beneath my feet seemed to glitter with color like jewels. I felt His presence in all I beheld. I felt my heart swell with love for Him until I thought it might burst.

As I passed over the canal near our home, a vision of His words flickered before me. Wherever I looked, I saw it. When I closed my eyes it remained—a pale and lovely woman, my mother Yoheved, with a beautiful boy at her breast. The light of God surrounded the child, the same light I had seen in the olive grove.

My mother had not borne a child since Aharon. Year after year she grieved for her barren womb. She never spoke of it in words. I saw it in her eyes each time she had news of a friend's pregnancy. I saw it in her trembling lips whenever she held another woman's baby. Over time the sorrow settled in her heart. It made her weak and frail.

Now my parents would give this child life. Despite Pharaoh's edict the baby would survive. When he reached manhood he would rise up to save us from Pharaoh's tyranny.

God had called upon me to deliver this message. I prayed for Him to make me worthy of His choice.

Joy carried me home. But when I reached our courtyard gate a cloud fell over my heart. I could not enter. As I stood with my hand upon the iron latch, a multitude of doubts assaulted me. Would my parents accept this prophecy without other witnesses? None had prophesied among the Israelites for generations. Why would our God come to me, a mere girl? I did not even know His name. Was it El who had spoken to me, or another? What if it proved to be the ruse of a demon who meant to hurt us? What if my words served no more purpose than to remind a barren woman of her empty womb? I would rather die than inflict such suffering upon my mother.

Perhaps, I reasoned, I should say nothing at all. Let the birth happen or not, as God wills it.

I took a deep breath. I dragged my heavy burden through the gate.

I tried to distract myself with preparing the evening meal. I traded a small jug of wine with a neighbor who had a goose to spare. I butchered the bird. I stuffed it with almonds, pomegranate seeds, dates, and leeks. I placed it in a deep pot that I buried in the ashes of a low fire. I worked as if in a dream.

During the meal I remained silent. It seemed as if the prophecy held my voice hostage. My parents appeared too absorbed in each other to notice. Some news must have made them happy. I did not have the heart to inquire.

When we finished eating, Father sent Aharon to feed the donkey. As he left, my parents exchanged yet another knowing smile.

"Nunn's father and I have reached an understanding," Father announced. His face beamed. "Our families will be united."

"You will have the finest wedding clothes!" Mother exclaimed. Her eyes grew bright. Patches of color blossomed on her pale cheeks. "A sheer linen night dress, a close-fitting, pleated white dress, and a sheer, white linen robe with blue lotus flowers embroidered on it! We will call on the dressmaker tomorrow."

My limbs began to shake. My heart filled with fear and uncertainty.

Should I speak of the prophecy? Should I keep it from them? I knew I must say something. I loved Nunn. I wanted to be his wife. But I could not rejoice in my future happiness while this burden lay upon me.

"Nunn is a good man." My voice sounded parched and insincere.

The color drained from my mother's face.

"Does the prospect of a marriage to Nunn not please you?" Father asked.

"He has always been her favorite!" Mother cried out. "A wedding in the house would be a blessing on us all."

I saw my mother's fragile happiness shatter. I buried my face in my hands.

"What troubles you?" Father urged.

The truth lodged in my throat. Other sounds formed around it. "I do wish to be united with Nunn. But how can I consider my own happiness in these times when our people suffer so much?"

Father smiled at Mother to reassure her. A faint flicker of a smile reflected back at him. "The edict ends in another eighteen months. A child conceived a year from now will be safe enough."

A mist fell over my eyes. Once more I saw my mother's child. I could almost feel him in my own arms.

When the darkness lifted I saw God's grace on my mother's worried brow.

The prophecy could gain truth only after I delivered it. I must speak.

"I had a vision," I confessed in a whisper. "In the olive grove this afternoon." As I said these words I felt God's light return to my heart. My flesh tingled with the happiness of a young bride.

My parents leaned closer to me. Father's cheerful face turned serious. Mother looked like a child, wide-eyed with wonder.

"I saw a baby at Mother's breast. A beautiful child. I saw that our God, the God of Yaakov, will send you the one who can save us. You are destined to give birth to another Yoseph, a man to take our part at court."

My mother became very quiet. Tears formed in her eyes. She began to weep. In an instant her grief turned to anger. "I have prayed these ten years to all the gods. Every morning and every night I have prayed. This is a cruel god if He intends to open my womb now, when all the newborn sons of Israel are slaughtered. I will not honor such a god."

Father looked with helplessness upon her boundless sorrow. He could not comfort her.

I held out one hand to my father and the other to my mother. I clasped them tight. I felt God's strength flow through my veins. I would protect my mother. I would save my brother. I would bring light to my father's household.

"Our God will not abandon us," I promised.

In less than a month God's promised miracle came to pass. My mother did not bleed. Her breasts began to swell. She felt a fullness in her lower abdomen.

The pregnancy transformed her. Her face grew round and soft. Her dull eyes glistened with tenderness. She cast aside fear for happiness. She rejoiced that after so many years she could still carry new life within her. She clung to my promises of God's protection. Together we prayed to Him each night.

Father insisted that for my mother's safety we must tell no one of the prophecy, not even our closest family and friends. Mother and I agreed without reservation. My mother allowed her friends to thank all manner of fertility goddesses on her behalf. None suspected the true miracle to come.

God's presence in our lives filled me with goodness. When I looked into a person's face I saw the whole world. I wondered at the beauty of His creation. I felt a surge of love and kindness for everyone I met. I baked cakes and other sweets for all the neighbors and my market friends. I organized a group of women to help look after the bereaved mothers of Goshen.

During this time my love for Nunn lay buried in a quiet corner of my heart. He supposed that modesty kept me from running to him. I did not tell him otherwise. I felt bound to honor the promise I had made to my parents. But I did not plan to keep the secret from him forever. Before long our hearts and bodies would lie intertwined in the marriage bed. When that day came we would share everything, past and future.

My mother asked Shifra the midwife to confirm that she carried a child. Shifra arrived with her nine-year-old granddaughter, Elisheva. The girl's parents had passed away the year before. Now she lived with her older brother and her grandmother. Too young to be an apprentice midwife, Elisheva helped Shifra in other ways. Sometimes she carried towels and water to the birthing room. She ran errands to the market. She also helped her brother's wife with their two young children.

I did not know Elisheva before this day. When my eyes fell upon her at our door I recalled how the gossips had said that she was pretty enough to marry well without much of a dowry. I did not disagree. She had wide brown eyes set an even distance from her thin nose, long black hair, good teeth, graceful limbs, and a shy smile.

While Shifra examined my mother, Elisheva stayed with me in the kitchen. I offered her a drink of pomegranate juice. She accepted with such sweet gratitude, I could not help liking her.

"Does your grandmother make many calls each day?" I asked as I returned to sorting a basket of lentils.

"Often she is out from morning to night."

"Will you be a midwife too?"

"My grandmother hopes I will marry well and not have to work."

I frowned. "A good woman makes herself useful. No matter how great her lord's wealth, she should not sit idle all day."

The girl gazed at me with admiration. She slipped from her chair to help me look for small stones among the lentils.

In the months that followed, whenever Shifra came to visit, Elisheva ran to me. I showed her simple kitchen tasks such as kneading bread and shelling almonds. She did not learn with ease. Nor did she give up. When my patience grew short, she begged me to show her again.

"I know I will never be as good in the kitchen as you," she admitted. "But I want to learn."

I soon came to love her. She had many good qualities—persistence, optimism, grace, and gentleness. She had a full and generous heart. I encouraged her to visit us whenever her family could spare her. She began to spend as much time in our household as in her own.

When my mother's time came, she felt little pain. She smiled as she took her place on the birth stool. Many women—relatives and friends— filled the room with their chatter. They arranged a small shrine to the goddess Lady Atirat in a corner of the room. Some also brought figurines of Taweret, the Egyptian birth goddess who took the form of an upright, pregnant hippopotamus. I did not like to see these in our house. One day, I told myself, the Children of Israel would no longer call upon the gods of our oppressors.

In a short time my mother was ready to push. She rose from the chair to squat. Father's sister held her on one side and I on the other, while the midwife attended to the birth. The other women fell to their knees. They begged the Lady Atirat to grant Yoheved a girl, to spare her child from death at the hand of the Egyptians. I did not tell them what I knew.

The baby slid into Shifra's arms. She announced a son. Cries of woe filled our ears. Only I felt exultation.

I helped my mother back into bed. I watched the midwife's tears spill onto the umbilical cord as she cut it with her sharp iron knife. The women filed out of the room in silence. Their sorrow-filled faces delivered the news to the rest of the family, who waited in the kitchen.

Shifra cleaned the baby. She rubbed salt into his skin, followed by oil. I sensed that Father, Aharon, and Elisheva stood in the doorway, but I could not turn away from the baby to greet them. The truth of God's prophecy encircled the little creature with an arc of light. No one else seemed to notice.

When Shifra finished swaddling him, she offered the bundle to my mother. "Let Miryam hold him first," Mother said.

I took my brother. He did not wail as newborns do. Rather, he appeared calm and content. I saw that he was more beautiful than any infant in all of Egypt. His head seemed to be a perfect sphere, as if he had arrived without pushing through the narrow birth passage. His eyes sparkled.

I stroked his cheek. He turned his head toward me. As I looked down upon him the light in his eyes radiated outward to fill the room.

I sat on the edge of the bed next to Mother. Everyone crowded around me. Through the dazzling light I saw radiant wonder on every face. I knew this light. It had lifted my heart out of the fortress of my body. Now it made me want to open my arms to the heavens, to summon every creature on God's earth to sing His praise.

Words from my heart filled my mouth.

"My brother will live. He will grow to be a fine man. We will gain reprieve by his hand."

"What prophecy is this?" Shifra asked.

"The God of Israel will make it so."

I laid the bundle in my mother's arms. The light receded back into the baby's eyes.

"How will we keep him from death?" Mother whispered. She began to cry.

"Have faith that our God will protect him," I said. I knew no more than that.

Before Shifra left we agreed that the light and my prophecy should remain a secret among us, never to be discussed lest anyone overhear. Shifra and Elisheva gave us their pledge. In this way they bound themselves to our family.

We named the baby Toviah because he was as good to us as all creation. We hid him with my mother in her bedroom. We permitted none to see him.

I attended my mother and the baby almost every hour of the day and night. I eased my mother's burdens with cool compresses for her sore breasts and nourishing food for her hunger. Whenever I held the baby, my heart filled with hope for the future of our people. I loved him as if he was the child of my own womb.

My beloved Nunn came to pay his respects to Mother. I could not refuse him entrance to our house. When I showed him the baby his face grew tight with conflicting emotions. He mourned the birth of another male child condemned to die. At the same time he imagined the happy day that his own child would lie content in my arms.

After a few minutes he rose to leave. Mother insisted that I walk him to the street.

"I fear you wear yourself out with yet more responsibilities," Nunn said as we reached the courtyard.

I smiled. "I shall be well prepared for the day that I have a household and children of my own to manage."

Nunn returned my smile as if he could not help himself. But his face soon turned serious. "I am sorry it is a boy. Do not become attached."

I felt my answer rush out with too much passion. "This child will not die! Our God will save him!" I could no longer keep such a secret from the man I loved. I wanted to tell him everything.

"Miryam." He took my hands to calm me. "Even you can not alter his fate."

"You do not understand..."

"Listen to me!" Nunn interrupted. "You are a woman who demands honesty. You are plain and candid. You must not deceive yourself now. This child can no more stay hidden from Pharaoh's men than all the others."

I looked into Nunn's heart and saw everything as it had always been. I saw myself as he saw me—practical and loving Miryam. He did not know that I had glimpsed the world through God's eyes.

Would my beloved still recognize me if I told him all that I had seen and felt these past months?

My spirit faltered. I had expected the truth to flow easily from my tongue to his ears. Now it seemed to create a terrible rift between us.

He bent toward me. He kissed me on the lips. His mouth moved down to my neck. I shivered with pleasure. He folded me into his arms. He hugged me so close that for a moment it seemed we might become one. I clung to him.

"I am sorry," he whispered in my ear.

I did not want to lose our love. I gazed deep into his tender eyes. Without words I promised that I would find a way to remain his Miryam. I would give him many sons.

We could not hide the baby for long. Every two or three weeks Pharaoh's soldiers invaded our homes in search of newborn boys. It was said that informers lived among our Egyptian neighbors. I waited for God to tell me what to do. How could we save him? Who would care for the child until he grew to manhood? A thousand times I asked God these questions. A thousand times I heard no answer.

I listened in the quiet hours. I lifted my face to the heavens. I felt God's presence everywhere. I could not fathom His silence.

On the sixth day of my brother's life I returned to the olive grove to pray. I fell to my knees.

O God, I will devote my life to Your service. I will show my people the way through You. Teach me to know Your Holy Name. Show me what I must do to save my brother.

When at last I rose to my feet I understood. Just as I had faith in Him, He had faith in me. God had chosen me because He knew I could attend to all the details on my own.

I urged my parents not to circumcise the baby. If he did not look like an Israelite we might persuade an Egyptian family to adopt him. Father could make discreet inquiries among his clients. I would do the same in the markets.

Amram and Yoheved approved my plan. "We will not lose him," I promised. "All will happen as God intends it."

I began to search for a wealthy and upright family in want of a son. With my basket on my arm I wandered the markets of Pi-Ramesse, listening to the gossip of servants and house slaves. One day I asked an old woman who sold fertility potions made of dried dates and rosewater if she knew of a prosperous Egyptian family that might wish to adopt an infant.

"An Israelite baby?" she replied eyeing my stomach.

"No." I shook my head. "A servant in the house of a neighbor. Her mistress does not yet know the truth." The lie came to me with surprising ease.

"Young girls have no shame," the old woman muttered. Then she named two families and told me where they lived.

I dismissed the first family as unsuitable. The old and sour wife of the household beat her servants. I did not wish to leave my brother in her charge.

The lively young wife of the second family seemed more promising. The next afternoon I followed her to a small temple on an isolated branch of the river near the palace.

As soon as my sandal met the shiny white stone floor a sense of calm settled over me. I remained hidden behind a row of wide stone columns along the outer edge of the room. The woman walked forward to the altar at the front of the sanctuary. When I saw a gold-painted sculpture of a frog I knew that I had entered the domain of Heqet, the frog goddess, granter of fertility.

I crept from column to column until I dared go no closer. The lady knelt. She held out a plate of cakes in one hand and a gold chain in the other. A priestess clothed in a white, flowing dress and a high white linen turban stepped out from behind a curtain to accept the offering. She chanted a prayer in a language I did not understand. The priestess placed her hands on the lady's stomach to bless her. The lady bowed. She kissed the priestess's hand. She turned away.

As I drew back into the shadows, I heard a group of women chattering on the stairs outside the temple. They soon appeared in the doorway. Their diaphanous white linen robes and tall black wigs blocked the sunlight.

Thick stripes of kohl rimmed their eyes. They wore strands of lapis lazuli beads around their necks.

The group parted. In their midst, before my eyes, stood the woman who would save my brother. I could not say how I knew with such certainty. But I did not doubt. Perhaps God Himself had chosen her. My heart pounded with excitement.

I stared at the woman. Her companions wore clinging white dresses beneath their robes, but her robe opened at the front to reveal smooth, naked flesh. A thin gold belt emphasized her small waist. Thick gold tassels hung from the belt to cover her loins. A thick collar of lapis, carnelian, and gold lapped at her breasts. She smiled in every direction and laughed with her attendants.

I smiled too. I could not imagine a more beautiful or kinder person to be the bearer of our hope. I felt my destiny linked with hers even before she saw me.

The lady I had followed into the temple fell to her knees before the new arrival.

"May you abound in the blessings of Heqet," the newcomer said in a pleasant voice.

"May Your Highness be blessed a thousand fold," the lady replied.

The woman of royalty—a princess, I assumed—nodded and continued up the aisle toward the altar.

The priestess fell to her knees before the princess.

"Princess Istnofret, I am honored."

Thus did I learn the beautiful woman's identity—Princess Istnofret, daughter and consort of Rameses. The gossips declared her barren womb to be the result of a curse by her own mother, whom Rameses had long since banished from court.

I watched the princess go though the same rites as the first woman. Her offering of gold and cakes appeared to be much larger. She kissed the priestess. When she withdrew she seemed as high-spirited as she had been upon her arrival.

I imagined the wealth and education that would be lavished upon my brother should he be raised in the palace. As a member of the royal household he could gain the influence to save us. I thanked God in His wisdom for leading me to the princess.

I followed Istnofret and her attendants on a footpath behind the temple. After a short time they turned to cross a little bridge over a rivulet. As they continued along the edge of the water I stole from one thicket of reeds to the next. The women made so much noise with their chatter that they did not hear me.

The princess stopped in a clearing on the shore. The high, white walls of Pi-Ramesse rose not too far in the distance, but the spot seemed isolated because no one fished or farmed nearby. One of the attendants waded into the stream as if to check for crocodiles and leeches. When she gave a signal the others removed their clothing and joined her in the water. I crept closer to watch from behind a clump of tall papyrus. The princess's cheerful nature reminded me of Elisheva. She laughed when the others splashed her. She sang. She made a point of including all her servants in her games.

I spied on Princess Istnofret for three more mornings. She bathed in the same place each day. Her character seemed cheerful, steady, and responsible. I saw no reason to doubt that God Himself had selected this woman to raise my brother.

On the tenth day of my brother's life I presented a plan to leave our beautiful baby where the princess would find him. My parents agreed.

My mother and I wove a basket of strong reeds. Father coated it inside with bitumen so water could not seep through. My mother cut a blanket from her wedding robe, a fine, pale blue linen soft on the baby's delicate skin. She grieved in anticipation of losing her child. She took little comfort in my assurances of his future safety and well-being.

When the day came my mother found the separation unbearable. She wept. She moaned. She would not leave her bed. I encouraged her to seek her friends so that everyone might know the child's fate by her grief. "Say nothing of the princess or the prophecy," I warned her. "To you the child is dead!"

I took the baby from my mother's arms and tucked him into the basket. As dawn rose toward us from the desert in the east, I crept out of the house.

When I reached the bathing spot I took a moment to search for crocodiles. Then I waded out into the water. I set the basket in a clump of short reeds that grew in the middle of the rivulet. I bent down to kiss the baby. For a moment I imagined that his bright eyes understood everything.

"We shall not be parted long," I promised as he gazed up at me. I took a little jar of precious bee's honey from my sleeve. I dipped his finger in the sticky substance. I put it in his mouth to suck. When he seemed occupied with the sweet finger, I made my way back to the shore. I hid behind some reeds on the riverbank with a small basket. If anyone noticed me I could use egg gathering as my excuse. I waited for the princess to appear. I did not wait long.

The princess spied the basket even before she entered the water. She sent one of her attendants to retrieve it. I watched her face as she uncovered the baby. The light in my brother's eyes captivated her at once. She gazed down upon him with the love that any woman who longed for a child might feel.

"He is the most beautiful baby I have ever seen!" she exclaimed.

"Probably one of the Israelite children," a handmaiden observed.

Istnofret frowned. She held the baby close to her and covered him with kisses.

"I do not care. I have lived for nothing but my lord's pleasure. I want this child for myself. I will tell my lord that he came to me as a gift of Hapi, the river god."

"What if he suspects the child is an Israelite? Will he not kill it as a precaution?"

Istnofret's face fell.

I emerged from my hiding place with two duck eggs in my basket. I stepped before the princess. I bowed low.

"Might I look at the child?" I asked.

"Who is she?" one of the handmaidens demanded.

"I am Miryam."

"An Israelite?"

I nodded. "I can tell you if the baby is one of ours."

"How?" the princess asked.

"We circumcise our infants. It is a requirement."

"I have heard that," an attendant agreed.

Istnofret glanced from the baby to me. I saw into her heart. She saw into mine. We understood each other.

One of the women unwrapped my brother.

I stepped up to examine him. "Look, his foreskin is intact. He can not be one of ours."

Istnofret smiled upon me with the radiance of the morning star.

"You see," she said to her attendants, "he is a gift of the river god. He is the most beautiful baby in all of Amun-Re's creation!"

The handmaidens crowded around my brother.

"What will you call him?" one of the women asked.

"I name him Moses—son. For he is like a son born to me, though I am barren."

Moses. It would become a name of greatness. I turned back to my egg gathering lest my face reveal too much.

The princess passed my brother from one set of eager arms to the next. When he began to cry, she tried to console him with her kisses.

"He is hungry," one of the women said.

"We must find a wet nurse," the princess agreed. From the corner of my eye I saw her turn in my direction. "Miryam, do you know of someone who has lost a child?"

"If it please Your Majesty, my own mother can serve you," I replied.

"She delivered a daughter not four days ago. The little girl died of a fever yesterday. The milk still flows from her breasts."

The princess showed no surprise. She glanced at her attendants. I did not see suspicion on any of their faces.

I smiled to myself. Had I not shown myself worthy of God's trust? All unfolded as I had planned. The baby would return to our house in royal garb with great fanfare. Few, if any, would suspect the truth. When word spread that my mother served as a royal wet nurse, the gossips of Goshen would keep their mouths shut. They knew that to rouse the displeasure of the pharaoh's consort could cost them their lives.

"Perhaps you should see this girl's mother," an attendant suggested. "The daughter seems clean and well mannered."

The princess nodded and turned back to me. "Bring your mother to my quarters at the palace in all haste. If the woman is suitable I will pay well for her services."

We smiled at each other. In a different world we might have been friends. Perhaps in this one we could yet be.

THREE

Miryam

O N the same day that my mother lost her son, Istnofret hired her as a wet nurse for an infant of the court. All Goshen knew of her misfortune and subsequent employment. They saw me lead my weeping mother through the streets toward Pi-Ramesse. They saw her return in the company of a royal retinue.

I told people lies and half-truths. The soldiers seized my brother early in the morning while Goshen still slept. I wandered along the river in despair. The princess happened upon me. After she listened to my sad tale she asked if my mother would become a wet nurse for an orphan child she wished to adopt. Lest the people imagine that Amram's house allied itself with our oppressors, I stressed the fact that Mother could not decline a request made by the pharaoh's consort.

As I expected, people fixed their eyes upon the trappings of royalty rather than the child. They begged for details about the princess, the palace, and all the fine appointments provided for the baby. The coincidence of timing did not arouse suspicion. Later, when the boy's looks began to reflect his mother's beauty, no one saw past the fine linen dress, the gold-embroidered cotton blankets, and the mahogany crib.

My family, Elisheva, and Shifra kept our secret well. They revealed their knowledge of the prophecy only in the way they looked at me. I saw admiration and wonder in their eyes. I also saw fear and hesitation, as if God's favor made me a stranger to them. They treated me with too much deference. True, God had opened my eyes and my heart. But I loved my family no less. This new distance between us made me sad. "I am still your Miryam," I said to each of them. But my words did no good.

The baby and Nunn helped fill the lonely spaces in my heart. In all of Goshen only Nunn guessed the truth about Moses. He ran to offer his condolences late in the afternoon on the first day of our supposed bereavement. My exhausted mother rested in her room. Father and Aharon attended to some business at the vineyard. I saw the last lingering visitors to the gate. As they departed, Nunn appeared in his soiled work smock and loincloth. He stared at the baby in my arms.

"You have heard of our new charge?" I asked. I did not expect him to recognize the child after a single, fleeting glance the week before. I waited for him to see that I did not grieve.

He looked from the baby to me. I smiled. I clung to the infant as if it were my own. Our eyes met. He questioned me without words.

I replied with a brief inclination of my head. My lips curved upward again.

Nunn shook his head with astonishment. "I fear for your safety," he said in a low voice. "What if the truth is discovered?"

"Istnofret is a friend," I assured him. "She loves the child. She will not let any harm come to us."

"Is there nothing in this world you can not fix, Miryam?"

"The injustice wrought upon the Israelites," I said. "With my brother's birth I feel even closer to our people's suffering. I pray we see the end of Pharaoh's tyranny in our lifetime."

Nunn nodded. We often spoke like this to each other in private. Again I longed to tell him of my new hope, of God's prophecy.

I clenched my lips together. I had made a promise to my parents. But in truth I did not tell him because I feared I would lose him too.

I invited my beloved into the kitchen for a cup of refreshing fruit juice. He drank it down in a few quick gulps. He turned his eyes upon me as if no one else in the world existed for him.

With the baby on my shoulder I could not throw myself into his arms as I longed to do. Nunn snatched my free hand. He brought it to his lips. He kissed the front. He turned it over to kiss the hollow. He touched my breast. I felt the nipple grow hard beneath my rough linen dress.

"We have waited too long," he murmured. "You are fourteen, the edict draws to an end, you have no period of mourning to observe. Let our fathers make the arrangements. Soon you will have your own child to hold."

He drew closer. His voice, his flesh, his eyes—everything about him pulled me into his urgency.

The baby began to cry. His wailing broke Nunn's spell over me. I pulled away.

I rubbed my brother's back. I felt to see if he needed a dry cloth. "Are you hungry, little man?" I asked him. I covered his face with kisses. I cradled him in my arms. I rocked him back and forth. The cries settled into a whimper. I put my little finger in his mouth. He began to suck it with vigor.

As I gazed down upon the sweet little face I felt my chest swell, as if I looked upon my own child. I felt God's grace and favor watching over him with my eyes.

I could not leave him yet. I could not let another child replace him in my heart. God had made a special bond between me and this baby. I could not turn away from him while he still lived among us.

I glanced up at Nunn. He loved me. He would wait for me.

I fixed my eyes upon him. "I must ask something of you," I began.

The disappointment in his face pierced my heart. I could not continue.

Again Nunn took my hand. His jaw clenched tight with resolve. After a moment his face softened. "I will prove myself worthy of you a hundred times."

I smiled at the extravagance of his declaration. "Just this once," I assured him. "Mother is not strong. She needs my help. Give me three years, until the baby is weaned and the princess sends for him to live with her at the palace. After that I will be free for you."

As the months passed Moses grew like any child. He smiled at me, he sat up, he took his first steps, he spoke my name. Each milestone held God's promise of a better time to come.

When Moses passed his first birthday I found that my spirit began to crave activity. I no longer felt content to wait for God's distant day. My hands yearned to work for our people now, to relieve their suffering as best I could until Moses reached full manhood.

I hired another servant to help in the afternoons. I used the time to gather food for the hungry. I called on every wealthy family I knew and all those they could recommend. I called on farmers, cheese makers, orchard keepers. Nunn's father provided a storehouse. I hired two reliable guards to protect the supply from theft. Twice each week I provided an allotment of food to those who needed help.

I saw many women whose men worked on Pharaoh's labor gangs. I saw impoverished widows. I saw righteous men broken by the whips of Pharaoh's taskmasters. I could not understand why no one had provided for them in years past.

As I sought donations for my food project, I spent many happy hours talking with the women of Goshen. I often brought Moses with me. Everyone who saw the child came to love him.

On several occasions mothers hinted at an interest in betrothing their daughters to Aharon. But I had different plans for him. To discourage them I began suggesting other eligible young men. In this way I discovered that I had a gift for making matches. My eyes saw people as if they stood before me unveiled. My heart knew how a person's spirit yearns for another to make it whole. My flesh knew the importance of desire in a bond between a man and a woman. I came to be so successful in my matchmaking that parents began to offer payment for my services. I asked them to show their gratitude with charity to the poor.

While I brought others together in marriage, Nunn settled in to wait for the day of our own union. He helped at my warehouse almost every afternoon. He often brought friends along. They hauled and sorted foodstuff. Sometimes they teased Nunn about the way I gave him orders. He did not let it bother him. "I know you wish she was not already spoken for," I once overheard him reply. I laughed to myself. I could not have found a better match than Nunn.

I took care not to be alone with my beloved lest the urges of the flesh overcome us before our wedding day. Nunn, ever generous and patient, understood. He praised my modesty. He admired my industriousness.

I spent my mornings with my brother in the kitchen. Often Elisheva joined us. Every day brought many reminders that the child would not stay with us forever. We took care to call him by his Egyptian name. We spoke of him as a foster child. We dressed his hair in the Egyptian style, shaving all but the section over the right ear, which grew into a long tress to be tied with a ribbon. Princess Istnofret visited several mornings each week. She hung an amethyst scarab around the child's neck to bring good luck. She posted a notice on our door—a papyrus scroll with the pharaoh's own seal—to identify the baby as protected under her authority.

After a time I saw that Mother grew too used to these reminders to notice them. I feared she would not withstand the separation. I too could not imagine life without Moses. Surely, I reasoned, God did not intend for me to lose all contact with him as he grew into a man. I began to wonder how we might continue to see Moses even after the formal adoption took place.

My mother would have nursed the baby forever to keep him with us. But as his third birthday approached, the princess began to speak of the day she would take Moses to the palace. She told us of the rooms she had prepared for him, the rich clothing he would wear, and the fine education he would receive with the other palace children. Every day she urged Mother to begin weaning him. At last I told Mother that she could no longer refuse. Weaning was the most dangerous time in a young child's life. We knew too many families who had lost their a son or daughter from illnesses that had set in after weaning. But the child was strong enough now to withstand a fever. He craved solid food. He needed it to grow.

When Moses began to eat the food I prepared, Mother lost her appetite. As the day of parting drew near she took to her bed. The bloom of motherhood withered with her dry breasts. She wept to see Moses greet the princess with a joyful face. Many of her friends no longer called upon us; they could not bear to witness her grief.

When Elisheva came to visit I often asked her to sit with Mother who enjoyed the girl's company. Elisheva combed her hair. She brought hand ointment from the market. She told the bedridden woman of all the fashions she had seen and all the birth parties she and Shifra had attended. She took care never to mention deaths, though of course our people endured losses each week—women passed in childbirth, young children from fevers, older children from the flesh-wasting disease, men from crocodiles, illness, and the weakness brought on from laboring for Pharaoh. Father once said that those who survived until the age of thirty often lived to be eighty. But most did not see their thirtieth year.

Aharon also eased our mother's heavy heart. He could console anyone. Our Creator had given him this gift. His large brown eyes seemed to admire everyone they gazed upon. His long, black curls felt soft to the touch. The landscape of his face held our mother's fine features. His work at the vineyard made him muscular and strong. Gentle and patient by nature, Aharon could lift a downcast spirit with conversation and companionship. He could make the plainest woman feel like a beauty. Each day, as the time of Aharon's return home drew near, Mother became animated. He always went straight to her room.

On the day of the adoption Father fled to the vineyard so he would not weep at his son's departure. Mother remained in bed. At midday the Princess Istnofret arrived with all her female attendants, an escort of military men, and a palace priest.

The priest examined Moses. He found the child to be without blemish and therefore acceptable for the princess to adopt. The princess ordered a guard to give Aharon the final wet-nurse payment, a sack of wheat that would feed us for several months.

"Where is your mother?" the princess asked. "I have a gift for her." She opened a small, wooden box. A gold ring glinted in the light.

I smiled at Istnofret. "My mother and all our family appreciate your kindness. She has grown too fond of the child to say farewell."

"She could not help it," the princess replied. She fixed a tender eye on the little boy in my arms. He held out his hand to her. She moved to take him. My heart grew bold. I would not let go.

"Perhaps Your Highness might consent to an occasional visit," I suggested. "It is not uncommon in Goshen for a parent to grant this privilege to the foster family."

Istnofret nodded. Her laughing eyes danced over me. "You are a devoted daughter."

She turned to the priest.

"I see no harm," the man said. "They are an upright family."

I let my breath out in relief.

"The child may visit the family of his wet nurse once each month," Istnofret announced. "Let it be arranged for the second day after the new moon."

The priest bowed to the princess. She turned back to me. I thanked her.

When she took the child from me, he began to cry. He flailed his hands in my direction. "Mi-yam, Mi-yam!"

I kissed him on the eyes. "May you grow to be a brave and righteous man," I said. I choked on the words.

Istnofret handed the boy to an attendant. She put the gift box in my hand. She embraced me. She put her lips close to my ear. "I will take good care of him," she promised. "You will have word of him often."

Her perfume lingered on the air long after her retinue had passed from my sight.

Late that afternoon the southern sky grew dark with an ominous cloud.
The wind died. As I returned from the food warehouse a low rumbling,
like distant thunder, tore through the thick air. The street soon filled with
people rushing to their homes. When I passed into the courtyard I saw
that our donkey ran in circles as if possessed by a demon. Elisheva darted
from the house toward me.

"You must stay here," I called to her.

"Grandmother will worry."

"You do not have time to return to her," I replied. "Come help me."

I closed the donkey into the stable. Elisheva went to sit with my
mother. As the darkness moved toward us I hung heavy cloth over our
windows. When I reached the second floor I almost wept to see how frail
and frightened my mother looked. "Stay with her," I instructed Elisheva.

We had never known a khamsin so severe. All the rest of that day and
night we remained inside while the sand swirled in great clouds over Goshen
and Pi-Ramesse. I could not create a perfect seal with the door and window
coverings. I worked without rest to remove any sand that seeped through.

The next morning—the first without my brother—the sky cleared. I
shoveled the sand drifts away from our gate. Soon Aharon called out from
the other side. He and Father had spent the night in the wine cellar. He
came now only to check on us. Father expected him to return at once. I
convinced him to wait for me to put some refreshment into a basket.

Aharon went upstairs to see Mother. In a moment he came down
with Elisheva.

"She is asleep," he said.

"She lay awake all night while the storm raged," Elisheva added. "I am
glad she can rest now."

Aharon turned to smile at the girl's gentle words. At least once each
day someone asked after Aharon for a daughter or sister. But I knew what
must be done. We would find no better bride for him than Elisheva. She
loved me as a sister already. Anyone could see she would grow into a

beautiful and pleasing young woman.

"Thank you for taking care of my mother," Aharon said to the girl.

Elisheva blushed. Her eyes grew bright. She would require little encouragement to fix her heart on him. Aharon, who seemed to love all women, would need more assistance.

"Brother, I fear brigands will be out after the storm. Will you escort Elisheva back to her brother's house?"

Aharon bowed to my young friend. "It will be my pleasure," he said.

The days that followed Moses's departure seemed empty and dark. At dawn on the third morning I heard a weak knock at the gate. A young girl, no more than eight, stood on the other side. I could see from her fine wool cloak and white leather sandals that she came from a wealthy family. Were it not for the early hour I would have guessed that she wished to inquire about my services as a matchmaker.

"I have a message for Miryam the Israelite," she said.

"I am Miryam. Would you like to come into my kitchen? I can give you a cake."

The little girl shook her head. "I must give you the message and return to the princess. No one knows that I am gone."

My body froze in fear. Pounding filled my ears. I squatted down to the child's level. "Tell me!"

"The princess says to meet her at the river with your basket. She says you will know where."

"Has something happened to Moses?" I demanded.

The little girl looked confused. I realized that Istnofret had instructed her to say no more.

I summoned courage to steady my voice. "Thank you, little maid. You may tell your mistress that you did your job well."

I ran inside the house for my cloak and basket. I flew along the road toward Pi-Ramesse under a rare cloud-covered sky. *Please, God,* I prayed, *do not let any harm befall him. Keep him safe in Your arms.*

When I reached the rivulet I saw that the princess walked alone along the bank. Her eyes, swollen red with weeping, begged my forgiveness before she uttered a word.

"What has happened?" I gasped.

"I know Moses is dear to you," she began.

I felt my chest crush against my heart. The breath in my lungs grew short. A thousand needles stabbed the hollows of my hands. "Tell me!"

Tears filled her eyes. She shook her head with remorse. "He has burned his mouth and lips with a piece of hot charcoal."

I dropped to my knees and buried my face in my hands. My head was a hollow shell upon which the echo of her words struck blow after blow. All of my breath rushed inward to the center of my being and stopped.

"He will recover," Istnofret assured me. She lowered herself to the ground by my side. "The best palace doctors attend him. I have made offerings to Isis the healer and the Great Lord Amun-Re."

I felt my flesh stiffen. What power could her gods hold next to the One who had foretold the birth of my brother?

"I promised to keep him safe...I am sorry."

The suffering in her voice called out to me. She too needed comfort.

I squeezed her hand. "Thank you for calling me," I said at last.

The princess nodded. "When you hear the story you will know the torture I endured, how much worse it might have been."

I waited while she took several deep breaths to steady herself. She glanced around as if to make sure we remained alone.

"He has already become a favorite at court. Yesterday afternoon I brought him into the throne room. He sat on my lord Rameses's lap and they played a hand clapping game. My lord saw that Moses looked at the shining gold cobra of Wadjet on the front of his crown and he removed the crown from his head so the child could touch it. Moses snatched the crown and threw it on the floor."

I could feel my face grow pale. "He is only a child!" I exclaimed. "He did not know..."

"He is only a child," she agreed. "But the high priest of Seth is a cruel man. He accused Moses of treason. He said that the child would grow up to overthrow my lord's reign. Rameses saw no merit in this interpretation, for all young children throw things. But the priest's breath carried poison into my lord's ear and soon he agreed to a test. The child must be offered a plate holding the crown on one side and coal on the other. If he chose the crown it would signify that he was destined to challenge the reign of Rameses and should be executed at once.

"I tried to stop the madness, but my lord would not listen. The priest ordered guards to restrain me during the senseless trial.

"A servant scooped a piece of coal from the kitchens. He did not notice that while one side had cooled, the other still glowed with heat.

"At first I saw the child's little hand move toward the shiny crown. I prayed to the Goddess Renenet, protector of children, to guide his hand away and she did. Moses grabbed the coal by the cool side, but before anyone could stop him he put the hot side into his mouth."

I drew my breath in. I could only imagine the pain that my brother had endured.

"The doctors tell me he will heal. Still I wished you to know from me rather than the gossips. I hope you will find a gentle way to tell your mother. I know her health fails."

I nodded at the princess. I did not tell her that One with far more power and purpose than Renenet had protected my brother.

We rose to our feet. "I will send word tomorrow," she said. "Do not despise me."

I took her soft, bejeweled hand. "You are a good woman, Istnofret. May your gods keep you well."

I returned from the river in a state of turmoil. I felt alone and helpless. I longed to hold my brother. My arms ached to comfort him. I could not imagine how to tell my mother of the burns. What reassurance could I offer if I had not seen them myself?

As I entered the courtyard I heard a voice call me from behind.

"Miryam!"

I turned around. I waited for him to reach me. But I could feel no joy in my heart while my brother lay in pain.

"Peace, Miryam." His smile spread with happiness.

I looked away from his handsome face. I held my arms to steady myself. He seemed too intent on his purpose to notice my misery.

"At last we have cleared the workshop and storehouses of sand from the storm. I can not wait another moment. It has been three years. We can be married in a week if you give the word. Tell me now that you will have me! My father will come to arrange our marriage terms tonight."

I glanced down at my dress, soiled from sitting on the riverbank. Why had he come so fast upon the heels of my meeting with the princess, while my heart yet tore with grief for my brother's suffering?

I turned my head toward the overcast sky. Light streamed through a pinhole in the clouds. I watched the hole open into a patch of deep azure, a portal to God's heaven. I waited for His light to swell around me, to lift me into His arms, to fill my heart with another prophecy, to set my hands upon a task beyond the ordinary, to give me a purpose.

Please, God, return to me. Show me Your will.

"Miryam?"

Fast-moving clouds covered the hole. The stream of sunlight disappeared. I turned back to Nunn. My eyes scanned his familiar, pleasing form. I longed to throw myself into his arms, to feel my flesh against his. What held me back?

A mist of tears filled my eyes. If I could see God's light once more, if I could feel His warm embrace again, if I could know that He had no other mission for me than this, I would be ready to march into the future with Nunn.

I could wait for God or forsake Him.

I stood before this terrible choice. I had no choice at all.

I looked away. I shook my head.

"Miryam!" Nunn's voice cracked with despair.

I could not tell him how my heart broke, how my spirit shattered at the loss of a long-cherished dream to be his wife. I could not tell him that this decision closed off marriage and motherhood to me forever. My own pain could not justify the suffering I caused him.

What could I say to make him understand?

I looked into his anguished eyes. Nothing. I could say nothing.

Let him hate me then. Please, God, let him find another who will give him all her love.

"I no longer feel as I once did," I said. "I can not marry you."

The words tasted like crumbled bricks in my mouth.

FOUR

Miryam

MY brother's burns did not heal well. They left him with an ugly scar on his lips and a speech impediment. Neither did my heart heal. Doubt and regret filled the spaces where Nunn had once dwelt.

In the hours after I sent Nunn away I waited for God to acknowledge my sacrifice. I passed the rest of the day alone in grim silence. That evening I told my parents about Moses's burned mouth. I conveyed Istnofret's assurances. I added my own. Nothing helped my mother. She gave way to unrestrained grief. Father, Aharon, and I took turns comforting her. I sent a messenger to Shifra for a potion to induce restfulness. Elisheva flew to us with a jar. She sat with Mother until they both fell asleep.

When all the family had retired I knelt by my bed. I paced the courtyard. I cleaned the kitchen. I waited the entire night for God to come to me. I imagined the darkness illuminated with His light. I imagined His gratitude. I even imagined Him telling me that I had offered proof enough of my devotion, that I could be both His prophetess and Nunn's wife. I would run to Nunn. He would fold me in his arms. Everything would be right between us.

The first streaks of dawn appeared. I faced the empty day alone.

A month later in the market I heard of Nunn's betrothal to Ahata—a girl I knew by sight. Pretty, slender, graceful, and foolish—she could not have been more different from me. My spirit burned with anger.

After all our years together, how could he have picked a replacement so fast? Then I realized that a matchmaker must have selected her for him. Perhaps he had allowed his family to seal the agreement without even meeting the girl.

My friends surrounded me with questions and concern. I did not accept their sympathy. I would not allow myself to be dishonest. I would not darken Nunn's good name. I assured them that Nunn had broken no formal arrangement, that I had no claim on him, that I had no wish to marry him. Their probing voices felt like arrows piercing my chest. My eyes grew dim. My head began to spin.

I broke away from the group. I ran all the way to the olive grove. I fell to my knees.

"O God! Tell me that I have done right in Your eyes! Show Yourself to me!"

I heard a noise overhead. Hope brought me to my feet. I scanned the upper branches of the nearby trees. I looked beyond the treetops toward the pure blue sky. A bird circled overhead. In the sun's shadow I could not see if it was an eagle or a vulture.

I did not tell my parents that I had refused Nunn. I reasoned that my mother still suffered from the news of my brother's burns. I did not wish to distress her further. When I learned of the betrothal I should have told them. I knew the secret could not last. But still I said nothing.

They soon heard the truth from Elisheva. Mother began to weep. Father grew angry with Nunn.

"It was my choice," I announced. "Mine alone."

Everyone stared at me, speechless with surprise.

Father broke the silence. "Why?"

His question echoed inside my hollow chest. I searched for words to explain. I refused to believe that God had abandoned me. I refused to believe that I had forsaken Nunn for a feeble hope. I knew that I yet had a purpose in this world.

"My mission did not end with my brother's birth. One day Moses will rise up to save our people. I must be ready to help him."

Four faces stared at me as if I had gone mad.

"When did you speak with Nunn?" Father asked.

"Before I told you about the burns."

Mother wiped her tearstained face. She sat up straight with determination. She grabbed my wrist. Her grip seemed too strong for one so frail.

"You must go to him," she insisted. "Go now before it is too late!"

I looked into her watery eyes. I had no gentle words to soften the truth.

"It is already too late."

Pharaoh lifted his edict as promised. Once again the Israelites gave birth and flourished. Ten months after Nunn's marriage, Ahata presented him with a son, Hosea. When I heard the news I hardened my heart against regret. I sent a gift of cakes and a fine linen blanket on behalf of our family. I insisted that Elisheva tell me about the birth party. While she spoke I busied myself in the kitchen. Afterward I swept out the stable. I checked on the supply of grain in our storage closet. I told myself that I felt nothing.

Elisheva and Aharon's betrothal followed soon after Hosea's birth. A year later they married. Their love for each other filled our house. When I saw Aharon gaze upon Elisheva, when I saw him touch her, I recalled my desire for Nunn. I pinched myself to forget. I pinched my arm black and blue.

Elisheva found her purpose in life with marriage and motherhood. In four years she gave Aharon two sons, Nadav and Avihu. I comforted her in the birth room with a cool cloth on her forehead and soothing drinks. I clasped her hand through the long hours of labor. When at last Shifra judged her ready, I helped her rise from the bed. I held her upright as she pushed the baby out. While Shifra attended her I bathed the newborn in clean water. I rubbed salt and oil into his skin. I wrapped him in warm blankets.

During labor Elisheva became a different person in my eyes. I did not see the delicate girl who could not apply enough force on the edge of a knife to slice an almond or who winced when I asked her to punch down the dough. Now I saw a strong and determined woman. No effort seemed too great for the sake of her children.

Elisheva's devotion to her family came to be the ideal against which I measured all other women. She never left her children unattended, unfed, or unwashed. From their first hours she talked to them all day long. She made them smile and laugh. Her own face grew round with contentment. She did not care that her waist thickened. Her affection for everyone grew even more lavish. She always accepted my help with sweet gratitude. "What would we do without Miryam?" she said at the end of each day. I did not disguise the pleasure I took in her need for me.

Elisheva's friends flocked to our home. They brought their young children with them. Every morning a group of women sat with their spindles and their babies in our courtyard. I enjoyed these gatherings from a distance. Often I brought the women refreshment. But I did not make a place for myself within their circle. Nor did they expect me to join them.

For many years the pattern of my life continued unchanged. I took care of our growing household. I went to the market. I collected food for the poor. I marked the passage of time from one month to the next by our appointed visits with Moses.

On each visit he arrived midmorning in a litter with a military escort. He departed before sunset. When he grew old enough to travel the distance on foot I walked with him back to Pi-Ramesse. The guards did not hover too close. I cherished this time with him alone.

As Moses grew into a young prince I saw that my family became uncomfortable with him. His quietness, his formal manners, his rich clothing, his education—all these served as a constant reminder that he dwelt in a world we could not enter. But I did not allow these trappings to put a distance between us. I admired his achievements. I knew that he would gain influence at court only if he appeared to belong. One day we would tell him the truth of his parentage. In the meantime I gave him my love. Our bond flourished.

My brother reached his tenth birthday soon after Elisheva gave birth to Avihu. At ten an Egyptian boy cut his ear lock and started to learn an occupation. How much older Moses looked with his entire head shaven!

He came to the house on the first day of the grape harvest. Father and Aharon could not spare even a few hours away from their work. Moses seemed disappointed to miss them. I suggested we walk to the vineyard.

We passed a group of laborers harvesting a field of wheat. I watched my brother turn his gaze upon the half-naked men drenched with sweat.

"As soon as they finish the harvest they will be forced into labor for the pharaoh." I said no more. I could see that my brother understood the injustice of our situation. He was still too young to help us.

Moses turned his attention from the laborers to a flock of white ibis overhead. The shadow of their great outstretched wings shielded us for a moment from the harsh sun.

When my brother glanced back to me I saw that he wished to speak. As always the words passed through his mangled lips with great difficulty.

"They say that a sighting of the sacred birds of Thoth means a good inundation." His gaze returned to the flock as it disappeared beyond the horizon.

"Those birds come every year," I pointed out with irritation. "We see them pass over us whether the river overflows or runs dry."

Moses shrugged. "I must know the omens if I am to be apprenticed to the priests of Thoth."

"A priest of Thoth?" I repeated in disbelief. God could not mean for this to happen!

I took a deep breath. "Why to that god?" I asked.

"I am a good student in writing, reading, mathem…"

I broke in. "And Thoth is the god of scholars." How could I persuade Istnofret to reconsider? What argument could I make?

"Is this what Princess Istnofret wishes for you?" I asked.

"Merenptah suggested it. She agreed."

Merenptah! Who had not heard of the thirteenth son of Rameses? General over all the armies of the kingdom, Merenptah feared neither man nor god. He conquered the Kushites in the south and the Hittites in the north. He brought home many victories. During the course of his father's long reign, most of his elder brothers had died. Now he stood third in line to the throne. If Merenptah wished to see Moses apprenticed to the priests of Thoth, Istnofret would have little choice but to obey.

I looked into my brother's serious face. Our eyes met. I knew in my heart that the time had come.

"Moses, I have a secret to share with you. Will you keep a secret even from Princess Istnofret?"

He nodded.

"You know that Istnofret adopted you."

He nodded again.

"You do not know this: you were born to an Israelite family. You can not serve the Egyptian gods."

His expression showed more relief than surprise. "Is Amram my father?"

My face flushed with pleasure. "How have you guessed the truth?"

The boy shrugged. "I have always felt it."

My heart ached with happiness. "I am your sister, who loved you even before your birth."

Moses took my hand and led me to a shady spot beneath a date palm. He asked me to tell him the story of his adoption.

I spoke of many things—of Pharaoh's decree and how I had found the Princess Istnofret, of her courage and the very real danger he yet faced. I told him that even Istnofret herself must not suspect that he knew the truth of his own parentage, lest she come to distrust him.

I restrained myself from speaking of God's prophecy. Even as I recalled His light, I said nothing of it. I kept all my hopes for the future of our people hidden in my heart. Only God could reveal my brother's calling to him.

At the end of my story I embraced my brother.

"Be wary of gods who deliver neither justice nor mercy," I whispered. "Heed none other than our God."

"What is His name?" Moses asked.

I could not answer. I prayed that one day He would find me worthy of such sacred knowledge.

I saw that Moses awaited my reply. In an instant I understood what God would have me say.

"When He calls upon you, surely you will know Him."

That night I prayed for God to keep my brother from the priesthood of Thoth. I prayed for him to embrace his mission when the time came. I prayed to be permitted to help him.

The following evening a messenger from the palace summoned me to meet Istnofret at dawn. We saw each other two or three times a year; each time she used a different messenger to arrange the meeting. She always came to me alone.

On this morning she wore a plain black wool cloak. She seemed more nervous than usual. For the first time I noticed how much she had aged— the darkening circles beneath her eyes, the fine lines in the shadow of her lips, the dulling of the skin on her face and neck. I closed my eyes for a moment to recollect Istnofret as she had been when we first met so many years earlier—beautiful, generous, high-spirited. Her father's reign had been no kinder to her than to the Israelites.

I embraced her. "It is good to see you." I handed her a little basket of fried chickpeas and lentils, a snack that I knew she enjoyed. In return she gave me a jar of strong rosewater from the north.

"I have news." She paused to look over her shoulder.

"Should we walk further on?" I asked.

"No, no." She put her hand over her chest as if to calm an unsettled heart. "One of my brothers has become too protective, that is all."

She did not say more. I did not dare probe.

"Can I do something for you?" I whispered.

She shook her head. Her eyes filled with tears. "I can not stay long. I may not see you so often in the future."

Helpless in the face of her trouble, I took her hand. At least I could offer comfort.

"It is time we find Moses a career. He is so inclined to his studies that I wanted to send him to the priesthood."

I nodded. My heart began to pound. "Moses told me."

"There is no profession more noble than that of priest to Thoth. But yesterday the high priest of Thoth turned him away—they fear his imperfect lips will offend the god. I am so sorry."

I glanced from her remorseful face up to the heavens. The clear sky still hovered on the edge between dawn and daylight. My body trembled with a surge of joy. Gratitude flowed through my veins. My spirit rose renewed all the way to God's throne. He had heard me. He had answered my prayer. He held my service dear to Him.

How can I praise Your Name, wondrous God?

I tried to restrain my happiness lest I offend the princess in her disappointment.

"Do not blame yourself," I said. "Neither you nor I can alter a man's destiny."

She offered me a weak smile.

"What will he do?" I asked.

Again the princess glanced behind us. "You know my lord Rameses has always favored Moses," she said in a low voice. "He wishes to see the boy enter the military. He has instructed Merenptah himself to begin the boy's training."

"That is good news!" I exclaimed. Through the army my brother could rise to greatness. The general's attention would lead to honor and respect.

Istnofret did not seem so pleased. Why?

"I must go now," she whispered.

I squeezed her hand.

In time my brother came to be an expert bowman. At thirteen he followed his tutor into battle. Later that year Merenptah's last surviving older brother died from the bite of a sand viper that had somehow found its way into his bedclothes. The general became heir apparent to the throne. Rumors flew through the marketplace: Merenptah sought the reins of power for himself while his father yet lived, he replaced the palace guard with his own men, he took his father's consorts for his own pleasure, he murdered temple priests who would not swear an oath of loyalty to him.

When I heard such stories my heart always turned to Istnofret. Did she find herself caught between her father and brother? Did both demand that she lie with them? I did not know how she fared; she no longer summoned me. I prayed for God to ease her burdens, whatever they might be.

As Moses came to manhood the gossips began to take notice of him. What his modesty held back from me I learned in the marketplace. Skill and courage earned him the respect of his fellow soldiers. Merenptah relied upon him as a clever strategist. The officers trusted him. He earned many gold medals for valor. In my brother's nineteenth year Rameses named him a general. He led the Egyptian army to victory on the western frontier.

Moses grew to be taller and broader than most men. The scars on his lips marred his beauty, but I learned not to see them. His wide, stern brow reflected the light in his deep-set copper eyes. He dressed as an Egyptian prince in a fine, pleated linen kilt with a sheer, long-sleeved outer robe and a gold and lapis scarab seal on his finger. Like all Egyptian nobility, he removed the hair from his body with hardened sugar and shaved his head with a sharp iron knife. He wore a black wig that flowed past his shoulders. He ringed his eyes with thick, black kohl. He held himself with great majesty. Off the battlefield, Moses remained aloof. He grew irritable in the presence of idle chatter. Everyone knew the silent general. People stared in awe as he passed.

My parents took great pride and pleasure in their son's many accomplishments. I saw each honor as a step toward the day when he would become an advisor to the pharaoh, as powerful at court as our ancestor Yoseph had been. He would change our people's condition for the better. Little by little I saw him prepare to lead. I began to hear stories of how he protected those who could not speak for themselves. He objected when other princes beat their servants. He rescued dancing girls who were given to men against their will. He refused a virgin slave that Pharaoh sent to his bed. Every fiber of his being rebelled against the oppression of the weak. I will never forget the day I first witnessed this for myself.

When the army remained in Pi-Ramesse, Moses often visited me. One morning we wandered arm in arm away from the house toward the marshes. Always restless, he preferred walking to sitting inside. Whenever he appeared at our father's door I left my housework to keep him company.

As we walked I spoke of household concerns. I mentioned our mother's continuing poor health. I told him that Avihu would soon begin his apprenticeship at the vineyard. I spoke of Elisheva's desire for a daughter. Moses listened, as he always did, with silent attention.

We reached the edge of the marshes, an insect-ridden, uncultivated area. My brother did not answer when I suggested we turn back for home. Something other than my voice held his attention—an angry man shouting curses just beyond a papyrus reed thicket.

We drew as close as we could without putting our feet into the murky water. Soon we spied a fisherman holding a net attached to a heavy pole. His wild hair, unshaven cheeks, and filthy loincloth identified him as poor and uncouth. Next to him stood a small woman holding a basket that filled her arms. Tears streamed from her eyes. The man raised his pole as if he meant to strike her. She cowered. She had done something to anger her lord; she would pay for his displeasure with heavy blows.

I turned to remove myself from this distasteful situation. But Moses waded into the water. "Do not harm her!" he shouted at the fisherman. Anger made his speech almost as clear as my own.

"Keep to your own affairs!" the man cried. His face turned purple with rage.

The trembling woman dropped her basket. She wore a short, ragged kuttoneh robe—a loose, one-piece sleeveless garment constructed by cutting a hole for the head and sewing each side up to the arms. She tied her matted hair away from her face with a piece of string. Bruises from other beatings marked her arms. I saw that she expected a child.

The fisherman brought his pole down to strike her. As she cried out my brother lunged. He seized his adversary's arms with such a burst of speed and strength that the man could not resist.

Moses dragged the fisherman to the bank. I almost laughed to see the man cowering.

The words stumbled from my brother's mouth. "I am General Moses, son of Princess Istnofret! Tell me your name."

The man seemed too afraid to speak.

"Huyner the fisherman," his wife called out, eager to see him punished. She stood near me, clutching the basket. She smelled of rotting fish and marsh water.

"Where do you live?" Moses asked her.

"Near the lane of the lamp makers in the south market of Pi-Ramesse."

Moses released the fisherman and motioned for him to rise. "I am keeping watch on you," he warned. "Hurt her again, or the child, and you will serve Pharaoh in the western desert. I will take your woman for myself."

The man bowed. My brother offered me a rare smile.

In Moses's twentieth year Istnofret arranged for him to marry one of Pharaoh's daughters begotten on the Hittite princess Maat-Hor-Neferure. I expected no less for a man honored as the bravest warrior in Pharaoh's army. I did not despair that his children would be raised in the shadow of the Egyptian gods. As Pharaoh's son through marriage, Moses could at last begin to hold influence over matters other than war.

Moses invited us to attend the wedding feast at the palace. We wore fine clothing and wigs purchased for the occasion. I allowed Elisheva to dress me. She hung jewels in my ears. She smeared kohl around my eyes. I did not know myself in the mirror. When Elisheva finished with me she turned to help Mother. I caught snatches of lively conversation and a whiff of myrrh behind Mother's bedroom door. At last she emerged. Elisheva's skill with kohl, ointments, and color had recovered a shadow of my mother's youth. For one evening we could imagine what my father had seen on the day they wed.

I looked forward to admiring my brother in his position of honor at Pharaoh's side. I supposed he would be wearing his general's costume with the medals hanging from a thick gold chain around his neck—three gold flies for perseverance in attack and a lion for bravery. I hoped he would recognize me underneath all of Elisheva's improvements.

Nothing came to pass as I had expected. I did not see Moses that night. The men and women feasted in separate parts of the palace. Nor did I see him the following day or the day after that. I tried to call on him at the palace. The guards refused to announce me. I tried to contact Istnofret through a messenger, with no success. I walked along the rivulet at dawn for three mornings. She did not appear.

At last news came to me in the marketplace. My brother's passion for justice had taken him too far. On the morning after the wedding Moses had struck down one of Pharaoh's overseers for beating an Israelite worker near the new jubilee hall. Pharaoh had learned of the murder and sought my brother's life in revenge. No one at court had seen him since.

The story made no sense. Even if my brother had killed a man in a moment of righteous anger, what was the life of one overseer compared to that of Pharaoh's trusted general?

Again I sought an explanation from the Princess Istnofret. Again the guards turned me away. We waited at home for word. Despair crept over our household. Mother lay close to death. I prayed to God day and night.

I continued to go to the rivulet every day at dawn. On the eighth morning after the wedding a veiled woman approached me. With great disappointment I realized that she stood taller than Istnofret.

"Miryam daughter of Amram?"

"I am Miryam." My voice shook.

"*She* asks that you do not try to see her again—for her safety and yours."

"Nothing more?" I whispered. Terror held me frozen.

"Only this," the woman said. She opened her palm to me. It held a golden fly.

PART II
MIDYAN

FIVE

Tzipporah

AT first I did not see the stranger. I did not even glance at the men who idled near the well. As I urged the flock closer, the men began to yowl at me like mating kurta cats. My sisters always hung back when they tormented us, but I did not care. I ignored the rude sounds and laughter. Instead I listened to a blue roller flapping its wings, or a lamb calling for its mother, or cool water trickling down the back of my parched throat. I knew how to open my ears to the sounds I wanted to hear and my eyes to the sights I wanted to see.

The sheep and goats crowded around the trough. Their eagerness made me smile.

"Poor thirsty ones," I murmured. "Your water is coming."

I dipped the skin into the well and began to pour. Not more than a few drops passed into the trough before rough hands reached out to grab me. Water spilled all over my dusty wool kuttoneh and feet.

"Temple whore," a shepherd whispered. His breath smelt of date beer and goat cheese. He dropped the skin into the well and seized my wrist. The other men clapped and cheered. He forced my hand between his legs. I stood, silent and limp, begging the Great Goddess to turn my fingers into a scorpion's stinger.

For a moment I believed She had answered my request, for the man's eyes grew wide with fear. He kicked me away and cried out in pain. I fell to the ground. When I looked up, I saw my tormentor struggle while another man's powerful forearm squeezed his neck from behind like a lion's jaw grasping its prey. The stranger's head and shoulders loomed tall and wide over the shepherd. I glimpsed his head covering—neither a rich man's turban nor a poor man's cloth square, but a dark headpiece that hung like human hair across the brow and down the sides of his face to his shoulders. I had never seen cloth like that of his thin, grey robe. Nor could I see what purpose such a delicate garment might serve. Beneath the open front he wore another strange thing, a pleated loincloth made of the same fabric as the robe. I knew by his feet that he must be a man of means, for only the wealthiest could afford leather sandals and even then none such as these, with thick straps and many laces.

My rescuer flung the shepherd to the ground with great force. The shepherd cowered in the dust like a wounded animal. None of his companions dared come to his assistance.

The stranger extended his hand to me, but I rose without his help. I looked into his eyes, clear pools the color of late afternoon sunlight glinting over sandstone cliffs. I waited for the inevitable fear or revulsion that would follow when he saw the color of my eyes, but his handsome face continued to gaze down on me with a sweet smile. He bowed and kissed my hand as if he took me for the Goddess.

I did not notice the scars on his mouth or the stubble on his beardless face. Later, my sisters laughed about these things and many others. I only saw those beautiful eyes flashing beneath his jutting brow. I only felt his lips brushing against my skin.

He watered the sheep for me. As he lifted the skin out of the well, I could not help admiring the strong muscles of his arms and back. For such a man the Goddess would hasten to renew Her maidenhead in the waters of Her sacred grove. She would come to him in the dark hours and reveal Her charms—Her breasts, white and firm like the eggs of a kudrijje bird; Her neck, smooth and slim as a heron's; Her teeth gleaming like the dew on a cold night; Her mouth tasting of melted honey. She would entice him to the golden altar in Her shining sanctuary and Her pleasure would devour him.

I saw all this before me, more real than the flesh of my own thin arm reaching out to calm an impatient goat that pushed and bit her way to the water trough. I saw the Goddess in Her glory until my demon overtook Her like clouds racing across the full moon on a cold night. I might have gouged my eyes out with a stick to be free of his face stalking me in the shadows. But I knew blindness would not rid me of him. He often came to me in the dark, where his moist breath entered my nostrils and his little black eyes, sharp as flints, flayed me as if I were a hare.

After the stranger filled the first trough, he paused for a moment to watch the sheep and goats quench their thirst. He caught my eye and opened his mouth as if he wished to speak. I looked away.

When we returned to camp, Father emerged from the big tent. I looked at his lined face, stern eyes, and long, white beard. All the softness that his heart had once held had drained away with my mother's life. But I did not remember those days. I only knew the stern man whose passions fixed upon keeping order among his people and serving the moon god, Sinn. As high priest and chief of our clan, Yitro mediated disputes with grim reserve and applied harsh punishments to those he found guilty. Women convicted of adultery, illegitimate children, men caught stealing from another's flock—all faced death on my father's watch. Justice prevailed under Yitro. So, too, did fear.

"You are early," he said.

"A stranger helped us draw the water," Seri explained.

My father raised his eyebrows and looked around.

"Did he refuse to join us for a meal?"

They did not dare lie to Father. No one had invited him.

Seri and Ruda trembled. I stood near them but a world apart. Father's anger could no longer penetrate the sinews of my being.

"You have dishonored my name!" Father's thundering voice brought three other sisters to the entrance of the tent. Only Ka'bu remained inside; perhaps she was nursing her baby.

"Would you let a stranger go hungry?" Father raged.

Ruda and Seri fell at his feet, offering tearful apologies and excuses. I floated away from them, my toes skimming the dry ground. If the stranger yet remained by the well, I would bring him to camp in time for the evening meal.

I found him resting against a palm tree with his eyes closed. The other men had retired to their camps or moved on without offering the stranger shelter for the night—his punishment for defending me.

He had removed his head covering to reveal a downy layer of hair, shorter than a newborn's. I noticed the stubble on his cheeks. Though many travelers passed through Midyan from season to season, in all my fourteen years I had never seen a man without a full beard. He had no animals or goods or even a cloak to keep him warm at night. Where did he come from? I had heard tales of neglected gods wandering among men in search of worshippers. Perhaps he was a god in the guise of a man.

I reached down and touched the skin on his arm to see if it felt like human flesh.

He opened his eyes and jumped to his feet, far too nimble for one of his size.

"Yitro, high priest of Midyan, invites you to his tent." My voice wavered and cracked. I had spoken little in the past few weeks, and only then to the flock.

He nodded and bowed.

Because the clan paid tribute to Father with foodstuff—wheat, barley, dates, even meat—we often had more to eat than most. As befitted a high priest, Father shared this bounty with all who came to us. The fame of Yitro's hospitality spread among the desert dwellers from Tayma in the southwest to the edge of Egypt in the north. And so every evening my sisters and I served many men in Father's tent. After the meal they lit a fire beneath the stars and drank beer long into the night. They did not dare sleep during the darkest hours, when thieves and demons lurked in the shadows. Instead they guarded the flock and told tales.

That evening my sisters took great pleasure in mocking the stranger. They watched him through slits in the hanging skins that separated the men from the women. With one ear I heard them laugh at how much he ate and how little he spoke. He did not know to scoop from the center of the platter with his bread but rather ate out of turn from the side closest to him. The few words he offered—heavy with a strange accent—pushed through his lips with difficulty. My sisters scorned his impractical clothes and supposed that he wore sandals to protect soft feet. They said that the scars on his mouth, which I had not noticed, made him uglier than a hyena.

My sisters did not see his beauty as I did, his godlike stature and quiet strength. They had already forgotten his kindness to me. But I could not forget. While they laughed at his foreign ways, I prayed for Allatimm, the high priestess, to choose someone like him for my dedication to the Goddess. The ceremony would take place on the night that I returned to the temple. I would lie upon the altar and wait for a man to come in to me. The Goddess would bring me pleasure. After that I would join the other girls when they gathered before the men who came to worship. Like them, I would have my pick of those who asked for me. Only Thabis the kitchen slave had no choice. Allatimm forced her to take all the men that none of the others wanted.

I withdrew to a corner and pulled my veil over my face to doze. Some time before the men finished eating, my married sisters must have gathered their children and left for the tents of their lords. I woke alone to Father calling for the finger bowl and pitcher.

Because a priest must be accorded even more honor than a guest, Father washed first. The stranger sat next to him on the lambskin, and when I poured water over his fingers I felt his face turn up toward me. My hand trembled and I let too much water into the red clay bowl.

"Careful!" Father scolded. I walked to the door flap and emptied the bowl onto the ground. I heard the guests laughing at me as if through a thick morning fog.

While I made my way around the circle, Father turned to question the newcomer. Such was the code of hospitality among our people that a guest—whether an outlaw or a prince—must not be disturbed by his host's curiosity until he had eaten his fill.

"Welcome," Father began. "Will you tell us your name, your people, and your purpose, that we may give proper honor to you?"

"I thank your generosity. I am Moses son of Amram the Israelite of Goshen in Egypt."

His tongue became so tangled in his mouth that each word seemed to spew forth in pain. Would any god disguise himself with such a flaw? And so I understood him to be a man. For a moment I pitied him.

Again I felt his eyes on me. I finished making my way around the circle of men and escaped back to the women's side of the tent.

"What brings you to Midyan?" Father asked.

"I wish to begin a new life. Do you have work for an able-bodied man in your camp?"

I wondered at the contrasts in this stranger—his proud bearing and humble manner. Surely Moses had not revealed everything. Secrets dwelt in his heart as they did in mine.

One man suggested that Moses help with the small plots of wheat, barley, and spelt that the women tried to grow on the terraces above the oasis. Others warned that he would find little work in our clan because we were a shepherding people and each man guarded his own flock. The men's voices droned on like locust wings. Soon I heard only my own low humming, a hymn to the Goddess.

Once more Father's call woke me. This time he wished for some dates to share with his guest. The other men had left the tent and sat outside near the fire.

"My youngest daughter, Tzipporah," Father introduced me. He grasped my wrist so I could not flee. He and Moses sat very close, like two men plotting a raid on another's flock. Their shadows flickered against the tent wall in the lamplight. I fixed my vision upon the guest's hands. He wore a large ring on one finger—a blue stone carved into the shape of a beetle.

"She is the last of seven girls my wife bore," Father said. "At least with this one I am spared the expense of a dowry."

I pulled away from him and ran into the cool night air. I did not wish to listen to the tale my father would tell. Whatever he had seen in the sheep's entrails soon after my birth, I knew the truth of my fate far better than he.

SIX

Tzipporah

I LOST my mother almost before my memory of her began. But whenever I leaned over the well and listened to the gentle clicking of the hyena teeth on a string around my neck, my mother's face rose before me in the water. I remembered her in the image of the Goddess she loved: tall, slender, and proud, with flowing hair and a golden crown.

My mother gave me the necklace—a child's talisman against witches—soon after my birth. I clung to it even when I grew older and my sisters began to tease me about it. "You can not protect yourself from what you are!" they laughed. For I was cursed with eyes as blue as a midday sky, the eyes of a witch.

Had I been born to anyone but Yitro, high priest of Midyan, the clan would have severed my head and burned my bones. This and more my father's mother told me when I reached my tenth season of soaking rains. She looked into my terrible eyes and confessed that she had been among those who called for my death.

"We saw that your eyes did not grow darker. Everyone feared that a demon had changed you into a witch at birth. Only your mother pled for your life. She fell to the ground and begged your father to leave the child of his seed untouched. To calm us he made a double sacrifice. He read a favorable future for you in both sets of sheep entrails. 'She will be a blessing for us, not a curse,' he said. Some questioned what he really saw. We all knew he would have done anything for Reema. I never knew a man so devoted to his wife."

I loved to hear the women of our camp talk about my mother. I asked everyone—my sisters, my aunts, my grandmother—to tell me all that they remembered about her. They always began and ended with her voice. When they described my mother's chanting I felt as if an echo of her heart still dwelt within my own.

My mother came from a poor clan who lived in the north near the Wadi Rumm. When stories of her enchanting voice reached Allatimm, high priestess of the Great Goddess Asherah, she offered two sheep in exchange for the girl. And so at the age of thirteen Reema left her family for the temple; she never saw them again.

Women said that no birth chanter ever had a purer sound or a more tender heart. They claimed that Reema's chanting summoned the Great Goddess Herself into the birthing room. When Reema lifted her voice in supplication they felt the Goddess cradle them in Her loving arms until all pain dissolved. Women who labored while Reema chanted always gave birth in joy.

As the demand for my mother's services increased, so too did Allatimm's fee. On days that my mother did not attend a birth, she remained in the temple and chanted the evening star hymns to the Goddess. Allatimm required an offering from those who came to hear her. Men and women flocked to the temple for no other purpose. Reema's voice filled the temple treasury with gold.

Like many men who saw Reema at the temple, Yitro wanted her. He paid the high priestess a lavish sum to keep her for him alone. Allatimm agreed to the arrangement on one condition—the girl must remain at the temple as long as her voice lasted. Four years later Yitro broke his word. Perhaps he suspected the high priestess of letting other men enjoy my mother's favors. Perhaps every other woman he considered for marriage made him long more for Reema. Whatever the reason, Yitro made the five-day journey from the oasis of Madyan to Qurayyah in almost half the usual time. He appeared before the high priestess and announced that he wanted Reema for his wife. Allatimm knew she could not refuse the high priest who represented Sinn, lord of her own Goddess. But she never forgave Yitro for taking her most gifted chanter far from the temple.

At first my father's mother complained about Reema. Girls who came from the temple were reputed to be no better than prostitutes. Yitro assured her that Reema had never known another man. Within a day or two the truth no longer mattered; my grandmother and all the women of the clan had fallen under her spell. Soon they could not imagine life in the camp without her.

Whenever I asked how my mother had felt to leave the temple, they told me that she had returned my father's love in equal measure. I did not believe it. How she could have had any affection for such a grim and forbidding man? But everyone said he had been different in those days. Her death had changed him.

With Reema's arrival, worship of the Great Goddess flourished in the oasis of Madyan. Every evening, when the star of Asherah appeared in the sky, Reema led the women in prayer. She made offerings on behalf of expectant mothers and she summoned the Goddess to their birthings. Because Father did not like her to travel far from us, women of neighboring clans made the journey to her when their time approached. Reema set aside a special birthing tent for these visitors. She never refused help to anyone who asked.

For fifteen years her joyful voice rang throughout my father's camp. Then one day, after a warm, soaking rain, Reema went to the Wadi Abyd in search of truffles for the Goddess. Seven times she had fallen upon her knees to deliver a child and seven times the Goddess had given her a girl. Now, heavy with her eighth child, she made a special offering every evening in hope that this time she would deliver a son.

If she found the truffles that day she never had the chance to give them to the Goddess. A sudden flood swept through the dry riverbed and carried her life away. The next morning a cousin found her broken body far from camp.

No one could believe the news. Reema had done only good in this world. Many people loved and needed her. Why did the storm god, Baal Zephon, send a flood to kill her? Why did the Great Goddess allow her and her unborn child to perish? Even Father, who knew the gods so well, found himself unable to explain this death.

My mother left me at the beginning of my fourth year. I remembered the wailing in our camp, but sorrow did not come to me until later. Perhaps I did not yet believe that she was gone.

Years later my grandmother told me that after the waters of death had receded the wadi had burst into bloom with a carpet of tiny yellow and white starflowers, more luscious than any seen before or since. Sometimes, when my heart ached for a mother's kindness, I ran alone to the place of her death. I lay on the ground, closed my eyes, and imagined that she rested beside me. I saw the flowers all around us, the yellow bluffs on either side, the wide wings of a black hawk against the violet sky. We both floated up to the Goddess, who sat on Her golden throne and welcomed us with Her loving embrace.

When my mother died, Father banned all worship of the Goddess outside the temple at Qurayyah. Evening prayers, fertility and birth offerings, offerings from a girl's first bleeding, birth chanting during a woman's hour of need—all these rites came to be suppressed under the harsh rule of my father's grief. People said that in the early days of his loss Yitro had intended to destroy the temple. But he soon realized that even the powerful high priest of the moon god could not eliminate all worship of his god's own consort. Those who traveled to the temple could pray to Her. He told the other women of Midyan to fix their hearts on Sinn alone.

The women schemed to keep the Goddess among us. We whispered about Her when we knew the men did not listen. We murmured words of praise when the evening star appeared and offered silent words of thanks or supplication as the occasion required. We feared my father too much to violate his order beyond these tokens of worship.

Like my mother, I loved to sing. From a young age, music poured from my heart. After my mother's death the women told me that a girl in mourning could not sing. As I grew older they warned me that because my voice sounded so much like Reema's it would surely reawaken Father's sorrow if he heard it. And so my songs became a private matter, offered to mountains and sand, sky and stars, whenever I wandered alone.

In the years after my mother's death, the animals of Sinn's sacred flock came to be my preferred companions. Their sweet faces did not fear my eyes. They did not tease me. They did not silence my songs. When I wandered among the ewes they nuzzled me as if I was their own lamb. The goats ate from my hand.

As soon as I could walk a distance on my own I followed the flock to its grazing place each day. I watched Father and my older sisters care for the animals. By my eleventh birthday I had long surpassed them in matters of birthing and illness. I knew how to calm a ewe in pain. I could coax a reluctant kid to take its first suck. I could ease a struggling lamb from its mother's womb and breathe life into its nostrils—a gift people saw as evidence of witchcraft. Yet when their own animals labored too long, they did not hesitate to seek my help.

And so my life came to be bound with the seasons of the flock. At lambing time we found good pasture close enough at the oasis of Madyan. When the hot, dry months came, Father and I moved the flock southwest through the wilderness to the well-watered Valley of Gaw below the mountain of the moon god Sinn. While my six older sisters married and gave birth to one child after another, I looked after the sheep and goats.

Soon after my thirteenth birthday—more than a year before Moses appeared at the well—the Goddess called me to Her.

On that morning, my sisters sent me to fill our water skins. In those days I did not like to go alone to the well because I feared the men who lingered there and accosted me with cruel words and ugly gestures. But

I could not refuse my older sisters lest they tell Father and he punish me for disobedience.

At first I had the well to myself. But as I finished filling the last skin, I saw two men in shepherd's clothes—skin loincloths and cloaks and black head cloths secured with leather cords—approaching on the path ahead. I fled from them around the base of a stone escarpment. I climbed up the rough rock until I reached a wide crevice where I could hide while the men refreshed themselves.

I listened to my heavy breath and pounding heart. When I grew calm again, I decided that if the men did not leave soon, I would continue climbing and return to camp across the top of the escarpment. I eased my head back into the open air to listen for the shepherds. A sweet voice sang on the breeze.

Tzipporah, Tzipporah!

"Where are you?" I called out to my mother, across the lonely years.

Tzipporah, Tzipporah!

I forgot everything—the men at the well, my sisters waiting for the water skins, the sheep and goats eager to leave camp for the day's grazing. Nothing mattered more than heeding the call of that voice.

I emerged from the crevice and scanned the steep face of the sandstone wall above me. My eye fixed on a high ledge to my right. As I began to climb, my hands and feet scraped against the jagged rock, but I felt no pain.

When I pulled myself onto the smooth stone shelf, the mouth of a dark cave gaped before me. Etchings of full-horned bulls covered the rock face around this opening. By these I knew the cave to be a sanctuary of the moon god Sinn.

Tzipporah, Tzipporah!

The voice caressed me like smooth sand beneath my feet.

I stared into the darkness. Only the high priest could enter Sinn's sacred dwellings. Father had told us of the terrible punishments that awaited anyone who dared to violate this rule: days and nights of torture deep within the burning center of Sinn's mountain. Yet I did not hesitate. I could not stop myself.

I crept forward, away from the light. The air became thick and my nostrils filled with smoky perfume. As I struggled for breath, the sweet chanting stroked my inner thighs and entered me with a rush of warmth that made my body swell with desire.

I turned and ran, sure that a demon had taken root in me.

That night I slept with more peace than a lamb in the womb. The following morning I woke reborn. My limbs unfolded like the delicate petals of a sweet-scented catchfly flower reaching out of the sand. My flesh glistened with honey. My feet became eagle's wings gliding in the open sky. When my sisters spoke, their words made no more sense to my ears than the squeaking of a jerboa.

I did not care if a demon possessed me. I could not forsake that beautiful voice.

Over the next weeks I returned to the cave several times. At midday, when everyone dozed in the cool corner of a tent or on the shaded edges of a distant wadi, I crept away. I avoided all the well-worn footpaths, the shepherds' routes, and any track leading to the well. Instead, I climbed the steep bluffs and made my way across the scrub until I stood high above the entrance.

I paused to scan the dusty plain below. To the west I had a clear view of the well and the stand of seven palms. To the east I could see the path winding through high, rocky hills and the barren ground below. If no one lingered in either place, I scrambled down the jagged face of the bluff. I soon learned to move with the nimble stealth of a leopard and to listen with its sharp ears. I often heard the voice calling to me long before I reached the entrance.

On my third visit, the voice remained silent. I floated through the dark cave and filled the empty space with my own wordless chant. When the light from the entrance behind me came to be no bigger than my thumb and

I did not dare go any further, I lay down on the cool ground and closed my eyes. I heard a faint echo from a chamber somewhere deep inside the cave. My throat grew tight, but I continued to chant until our voices merged.

That night I dreamt of a tame oryx feeding on tender saltbush leaves from my palm. When I touched her white coat, her tall, thin horns turned to silver. The dry, red earth sprouted around us into a grove of flowering almond trees. The oryx turned and ran from me. I pursued her through the fragrant trees until we reached the cave of Sinn. I knew it to be the same place, yet the rock etchings at the mouth of the cave looked different, for sacred trees replaced the bulls. My oryx stood in the entrance, her body facing inward, hooves poised to plunge into the darkness. As I approached, she turned her soft eyes toward me for a moment. Then she was gone.

I woke weeping for the lost oryx.

I did not need a dream reader to throw his sticks and bones for me to understand the dream's meaning. Even before I rose from my mat I knew that I must seek the oryx in the depths of the cave.

I waited several days until late one afternoon, when Belet went into labor with her second child. The whole camp hovered near her lord's tent. Ka'bu, Ruda, and Ashratum attended Belet in the tent and my other sisters stood watching from the doorway. Father led everyone in a halfhearted prayer to the moon god Sinn. No one, not even Father, believed that Sinn had anything to do with a woman's labor or the delivery of a child.

While the others stood busy with my sister's labor, I stole away with a clay lamp and a flint from Father's tent. In my haste to get to the cave I forsook all my previous caution. I walked along the track to the well. Several men, most of them familiar shepherds, lingered under the palms sharing some date beer.

"Come from casting a spell on your sister's birth tent?" one of them called out. Word of Belet's labor had spread outside the camp.

"When Yitro has a three-legged grandson..."

"The fruit of the witch's own womb!" a third interrupted, referring to me.

A stranger sat among them. He wore a clean, dark kuttoneh and an unusual bright yellow belt. He hid his face in the shadows of his flowing black head cloth. For a moment I felt his attention fix upon me. I looked away and when I glanced back he was gone. I walked around the escarpment and paused a moment to make sure that no one followed me. Then I began the climb to the cave.

I pulled myself up the rocks one-handed, without spilling much of the lamp oil. As I moved into the darkness, I recalled the oryx and her silver horns. But when I lit the lamp, I saw a herd of red ochre bulls—the crescent-horned servants of the moon god Sinn—painted on the gray stone wall. Someone, perhaps my father, had perched an offering dish on top of three head-sized stones at the foot of the largest bull. My spirit sank with disappointment. These drawings looked no different from many altars to Sinn scattered throughout Midyan.

Silence droned in my ears like a flock of blue bee-eaters.

"Where are you?" I whispered.

Tzipporah!

The voice called to me from somewhere deep within the cave. I crept on until the entrance became a tiny shaft of light behind me and then disappeared. The damp stone walls closed in from all sides. The lamp flickered and grew dim. I crouched low to move forward. I turned a corner and entered a large, round chamber with a soft sand floor. The flame in my lamp shot up.

I could see Her as if by daylight.

I recognized the Great Goddess Asherah at once. She had long, curling hair and high, round breasts. She sat on a low throne and held Her golden bow high over Her head. All around Her on the wall naked men and women embraced under sacred trees. Before Her in the sand I saw an offering bowl perched on three stones, perhaps the very bowl my mother had meant to use for the truffles. Since that terrible day, nine long years ago, the Goddess had dwelt neglected in this cave.

I stood before Her image with reverence. I knew so little about Her.

Over the years I had heard snatches of whisperings about Her exploits. She was chaste and yet wanton, able to lie with ten lovers in a night and yet rise a virgin in the morning. Her greed for pleasure inspired wives to submit to their lords. Yet in war none matched Her fury and brutality. It was said that She moved over the battlefield more frenzied than the fiercest warrior. She wore the severed limbs of enemies on Her belt.

Tzipporah, Tzipporah!

How sweet the sound of Her calling, like a precious drop of morning dew shimmering on a scarlet acacia flower. I longed to serve Her like my mother before me.

I opened my voice to the Goddess. Her whispers in my heart told me that I must remove my clothes to honor Her. I admired the shadow of my naked form fluttering in the lamplight next to Hers.

Soon I felt my legs begin to move in a joyous dance. I whirled and swooped like a Nubian roller in flight. My head spun and I grew dizzy, but I could not stop.

One of her lovers appeared, a hooded man whose face I could not see. "You are a sweet fruit ripe for the picking," she said as the man spun before me. She told me to let him have his way. I stopped whirling and staggered. He pushed me onto my back in the sand.

She promised that all the pleasure in the world would be mine if I did not struggle. But I could not help it. I did not like his hot hands on my breasts. His weight pinned my wings to the ground. My flesh burned when he entered me. I cried out to the Goddess to save me.

I opened my eyes and saw Her smiling down upon me. I floated away from my body to embrace Her. Our voices joined as one. I whirled in the beam of Her light and dedicated myself to Her forever.

I shared my secrets with no one. What they learned I did not tell. How I suffered, I could not say. Soon only the Goddess knew the sound of my voice. Only She did not abandon me.

SEVEN

Tzipporah

TEN months after I gave myself to the Goddess, Her priestess came to visit our camp.

When Father received word of Allatimm's approach he seemed surprised and displeased. Although he made a pilgrimage to Qurayyah twice each year to purify himself at the altar of the Goddess and to thank Her for the fertility of the flock, Her priestess never came to us. Excitement flew from tent to tent. My sisters longed for the most important woman in Midyan to admire their beauty. While I turned the flock into the pen, they ran to wash their faces and comb their hair.

Father helped Allatimm dismount from the donkey. As we assembled before the priestess I felt her eyes on me, but I did not dare look at her. I glanced at her face only long enough to see the wrinkled skin that belonged to an old woman. Yet her hands seemed as plump and smooth as an infant's. She wore more cloth than I had ever seen on a person in my entire life. The colors astonished me. Her outer robe—open in the front—was dyed a brilliant azure and crimson, like a bright winter sky streaked with blood. It had long, wide sleeves. Beneath the robe she wore a loose kuttoneh of thin, pale yellow fabric. The black wool veil wrapped over her head and around her neck shimmered with gold beads. Copper bangles circled her wrists and a large gold hoop adorned her nose. Although she stood not much taller than me, she held herself erect with pride. She nodded to each of my sisters in turn but offered no reply to their eager words of greeting.

Allatimm traveled with two attendants, each clothed in a simple black wool kuttoneh much like my own, except longer and with sleeves. One of the women also had a veil, which she draped over her head and across her face below her pretty, almond-shaped eyes. I saw that she used her modest covering to enhance her allure and she turned her gaze upon the men without shame. The other woman wore sadness as her veil. Her eyes remained fixed upon the ground and she stood with her shoulders bowed. Her straight black hair was cut off at the neck and her hands looked red and raw.

When Yitro glared at Allatimm's companions the priestess shook her head and laughed.

"Do not scorn them," she said. "They bring only pleasure."

Father escorted the priestess and her veiled attendant to his tent, where they ate on the men's side as honored guests. The other attendant stood outside the tent as if waiting to be summoned. My sisters and I listened to the lively conversation from the other side of the skin curtain. Allatimm's voice, soft as the leaves of yellow mallow, thanked the men for their hospitality and urged them to pay homage to the Goddess in Qurayyah. They joked and laughed with her. Those men who had occasion to travel through Qurayyah had stopped at the temple to pay homage to the Goddess and to avail themselves of a girl. Seri's lord asked if either of the attendants knew the ways of pleasure as well as their mistress did.

"She prostitutes everyone who works for her," my oldest sister Shapshu whispered. "From the kitchen workers to the weavers."

The conversation of my sisters held less interest for me than the hooting of the owls. They knew nothing of the Goddess or those who devoted themselves to Her. They dishonored our mother's memory with such talk. Once I might have opened my heart to them, but now I did not care to speak. I no longer belonged to their world.

I pulled my veil over my head and turned away.

Some time later, after my sisters had retired, Father called for the beer. I sat up with a start and grabbed the jug. When I plunged into the cold night air I saw that all the men except Father sat outside near the fire. Allatimm's two companions stood away from the men by the entrance of the tent. I motioned for them to enter the women's side. The men whistled and clapped when they saw me with the beer. I shrugged. They knew that they had to wait until Father and his guest had drunk their fill.

I handed the jug to Father. As I gathered up the platter from the meal, Allatimm gestured towards me.

"You have found no man to take her?" Allatimm asked.

"You know I have not." Father's sharp tone surprised me. "Why are you here?"

"To claim what is mine." The high priestess looked at me before she turned back to Father. "It is time you replace what you stole from me."

Father's jaw tightened with anger. "She whom the gods took can never be replaced. You can find girls anywhere."

Allatimm laughed. "Not at so good a price."

Father frowned.

Allatimm smoothed her robe all over. Her hands lingered too long on her breasts. She reclined back on one elbow as if to display every curve of her body. She smiled at him like a woman who knows she has roused a man's lust.

Hope rose in my heart like a glimmer of water at the bottom of a dry well. I belonged to the Goddess. She had already called me to Her service. If Allatimm wanted me at the temple, I would find a way to go whether Father wished me to or not.

After a moment Allatimm spoke. She smiled with every word.

"I am not afraid of you, Yitro. You can not win the favor of the Goddess without me. She is not pleased that you have silenced Her birth chanters for so long. And my income has suffered."

"I will not send Reema's daughter to whore for you," Father said through clenched teeth.

I stood rooted to the ground like a strong tree in a windstorm. I wanted to speak out, to seize my destiny from Father's hands. But my voice lay trapped inside the darkness of my broken spirit. Before I could wet my throat enough to speak, Father cast a frown in my direction and waved his hand to dismiss me.

I fled to the women's side. I almost fell over the sad attendant, who crouched near the tent flap. I realized that she had eaten nothing since her arrival and placed the platter with its few remaining scraps of food on the ground before her. Her eyes widened with surprise and gratitude. The veiled woman reclined on my skins in the corner with her eyes closed. I remained standing and drew close to the curtain, where I could hear the conversation on the other side.

Father's hostile tone continued. "You should thank Sinn that he stopped me from forbidding your whoring altogether."

But the more unpleasant my father became, the harder Allatimm laughed. Fearlessness made her Yitro's equal.

She clicked her tongue against her teeth. In contrast to Father's voice, hers rose loud and cheerful. "You confuse my girls with those creatures who lurk near the temple gate. You know I have nothing to do with them. Tzipporah can tend the animals. She can learn the weaver's art. She can help in the kitchen. Whatever pleases her. I ask for nothing against a girl's will."

"That is your own affair." I heard Father rise.

"Yitro." Allatimm grew serious. Her voice commanded attention. "Give her to me. After all that has happened to her, she has no future here."

Father did not answer. Perhaps he knew Allatimm was right. Perhaps he had known it for thirteen years, since the day he read my destiny in the entrails of two sheep.

Father took the veiled girl, Ahatel, for his own pleasure that night. Though he soon finished with her, he kept her by his side. He sent the other girl to a widowed cousin. The light in my cousin's tent burned all night as the men of the camp took turns with her. When Ka'bu came to complain that the women did not like their men going to a whore, Father dismissed her with rough words. I felt sick in my stomach for the girl. I supposed she must be a slave. I could do nothing to help her.

In those days sleep did not often come to me and when it did I knew no rest. Silence shrieked in my ears. Creatures of the night hovered nearby like vultures over carrion. My own demon invaded every dream. Often I spent the long hours of darkness huddled in the corner of the tent. I grasped the hyena teeth and whispered prayers to the Goddess.

But on this night I felt my mother's tender gaze shining down from her place beside the Goddess in heaven. On this night I would go to Allatimm and seal my future. Nothing could keep me from it.

In the darkest hour, when the crescent moon sank low on the horizon, I crept away from Father's tent to visit Allatimm. Although she sat up in the light of an oil lamp, she appeared to be asleep. I lowered the tent flap behind me.

"Yes, child?" She had been expecting me. Her eyes remained shut, but the warmth of her smile encouraged me to speak.

I knelt before her. "I wish to serve the Goddess at the temple." My voice sounded as hollow as my heart. "She has called me to Her."

The old woman opened her eyes and leaned forward to stroke my cheek. "You will come with me to serve Her."

My spirit lifted like a hawk gliding high over the escarpment, like a young antelope frolicking across a green valley. I fell into Allatimm's embrace.

In the morning everyone assembled to watch us depart. I saw my sisters and aunts, my uncles and cousins. They stared at me as if they looked upon the dead. I did not care. I had left them months ago.

Allatimm motioned for me to share Ahatel's donkey.

"Not enough room," Ahatel called out.

"She is as small as a child," Allatimm replied.

"I will come for her at lambing time," Father said to Allatimm. "We can not do without her then."

Allatimm nodded.

I left camp with only the hyena teeth around my neck, the kuttoneh on my back, and the veil over my head. Had I gone off to marry a cousin, Father would have sent at least three lambs and a goat to help with my keep. But I was unmarriageable now. He gave me nothing.

I gazed down from the donkey at my father. He had no words for me and I had none for him.

After five days of steady travel we reached Qurayyah. I had never seen so many people in one place. We passed several clusters of tents and then a row of mud structures, each large enough to house an entire family. I saw several pottery workshops with large pits for baking clay bowls and jugs. Ahatel greeted a group of women spinning yarn as they sat under a cluster of date palms. She pointed out the market square, where locals sold pottery from the workshops and merchants came with grain, ointments, sheep's wool, and cloth. We saw many traders on the road through town, dusty men leading donkeys laden with perfumes and spices from the south. Each time we approached a man, Ahatel slowed her donkey. Several seemed to recognize her.

"Beauty!" one called out as we passed. "Wet my parched throat before I go back into the desert!"

"All my fortune for a night of your favor!" another one shouted. "Your breasts are as round as two ripe melons."

I cringed at their words, but Ahatel laughed and waved as if she enjoyed the attention. "You know where to find me," she sang out.

As we approached the temple, a bent old man in a ragged loincloth called to us from the side of the road. He held his hand out as if to ask for alms. I wished that I had something to give him. Allatimm told the man to leave us alone. But he must have sensed my desire to help, for he ran up and tugged on my kuttoneh. Only then, as I looked down at him, did I notice the gaping pink hole where his nose should have been. I drew in my breath with horror.

Ahatel kicked the beggar until he let go. She urged her donkey on.

I turned my face away.

"Do not encourage him," she said.

"What happened?" I whispered.

"That is the punishment for stealing in Egypt. No doubt he ran away here to escape the shame. Once I saw a half-dead man with no nose or ears. It seems better to kill a thief as we do in Midyan than leave him like that."

I could not disagree.

The temple seemed a grand place to my eyes. The brick walls rose from the dust and the compound covered far more land than Father's camp. Because the Great Goddess did not require animal sacrifice, Allatimm kept only a few goats and sheep for milk and wool. Even without birth chanters the temple had many sources of revenue. In addition to accepting offerings for the Goddess, Allatimm sold the wares from her weaving workshop. She offered rooms for the weary, plentiful meals, and other comforts, all for a fee. She even required the whores who stood outside the temple gates to pay her a portion of their earnings.

As we entered the courtyard, the women of the temple assembled before their mistress.

"I am returned from the southeast, where the High Priest Yitro is well. He showed favor to Ahatel and she pleased him."

A murmur of congratulations spread through the crowd. I looked at the sweep of faces—young and old, pretty and plain. All the women seemed to revere Allatimm and admire Ahatel.

Allatimm pointed to me. "Yitro has sent his youngest daughter, Tzipporah, to live as a sister among us. Such is his respect for the Goddess and his penance for our losses that he gives up Reema's child for our sake."

As the buzz of voices rose with excitement, the smile on Allatimm's face spread from one ear to the other. I saw that the falsehood in her words had served its purpose—the women honored her even more. But did not serving the Goddess in her temple provide honor enough?

Allatimm turned to Ahatel. "Offer Tzipporah some refreshment and show her where she may rest. Everyone else—back to your work!"

The crowd broke up at once. As I followed Ahatel across the dusty courtyard we passed women weaving on looms in the shade of an open structure. A series of columns held a roof above them. I, who had spent my life in tents, could not take my eyes from it.

Ahatel noticed my wonderment. Her laughter sounded like the song of the black flute-bird. "Have you never seen a colonnade?"

I shook my head. I had never seen a building other than the metal works at Dophka on the way to the mountain of Sinn.

"The breeze blows through the open sides and keeps the weavers cool. In the hot months we like to sleep there."

As she spoke, the animal pen caught my attention. Though the animals seemed to be well fed, their coats looked dull and they stood listless in their own muck. I would soon change that.

Ahatel led me to a long, low brick structure across from the colonnade. She talked about the daily life at the temple, the shared meals and the evening prayers to the Goddess. She warned me to be obedient toward Allatimm and to report all gifts or payments from guests.

"Allatimm always finds out, and then you will not be able to keep anything for yourself. Look!" She held out her arms, laden with four copper bangles, two on each wrist. She lifted her long kuttoneh to show me her leather sandals. "Some people call us whores, but we serve the Goddess and please Her. The Goddess mourns a chaste woman. And Allatimm never makes us go with a man against our desire."

Ahatel seemed to chatter more than my six sisters together.

"Those of us who are not barren take seeds of the wild carrot softened in water to stop a baby. When that fails, Allatimm can give you powdered leaves of the bitter melon and acacia bark. But I saw a girl die from that, so if it happens to you, you should have the baby and sell it. I could not have a child, so I came to serve the Goddess. Did your father send you because you are barren?"

I tried to shake my head, but a shudder seized me. Deep inside my ear an infant screamed.

My talkative guide showed me a cramped room in the low building. Here the temple women slept on mats. The dirt floor felt harder than the floor of my father's tent and the closeness of the stale air made my breath falter.

"We have other rooms for guests," Ahatel explained. "We do not stay with them through the night, even if they ask. Allatimm fears they will become too attached and try to snatch us away like your father did with Reema. She talks about it all the time. Most of us did not know your mother, but they say that she had the most glorious voice, like the Goddess Herself. And now we aren't even supposed to chant at all, but the secret is..." She paused as if to make sure no one could hear her, though the room stood empty but for us. "The secret is we do it anyway. We let women come here for their labor in a special room on the far end of the temple grounds away from the sanctuary, near the weavers. The midwife brings them at their time and we chant. That is my job here. Everyone has a job and mine is to birth chant."

If Father knew this he would sentence the girl and her teacher to death. I turned my eyes, wide with alarm, upon Ahatel. She drew back in fear. Even after almost a week in my company she had not noticed their strange color until now.

"So that is why," she murmured to herself. I did not correct her.

The kitchen building stood near the animal pens. Ahatel resumed her chatter as we stepped over the threshold into a large hall.

"We have three rooms in this building. The dining room is big; sometimes we hold a festival for the Goddess here and people come from all over. For meals we sit together like a family. Now we number twenty-one with you. Some girls ran away from a lord who beat them for no reason. Some faced worse beatings for being barren. That happened to me. My people are not too far from here and I ran to the temple one day with my body so bruised I looked like a bloody sacrifice. Allatimm took me in. My lord declared us divorced, but he got to keep the dowry since I ran away. If I had died, my father could have had it back. I am sure that is what he wanted." Ahatel shrugged and pursed her lips. "I say who cares? I like it here. No one beats me."

The second room held lavish cooking implements unlike any I had ever seen—copper pots and wooden plates, low iron pans and reed baskets, water jugs and brown ceramic bowls decorated with patterns of lines in red, black, and yellow. The last room proved to be for cooking. Two fire pits glowed with charcoal embers. The brick walls had a hole behind each pit for ventilation. Dried herbs hung from the ceiling. Several loaves of wheat bread sat on a high shelf near an open door. Even with Father's bountiful provisions, at the oasis of Madyan we ate wheat bread no more than once in a moon.

Ahatel reached for the bread and held out an entire loaf to me. I tore off a small piece and handed the loaf back to her.

"It is yours," she insisted. "When none of the kitchen girls are here we eat whatever we want." She ripped a piece of bread for herself.

I stared toward the open door.

"The slave keeps a garden out there."

I walked across the room to look out the door. The slave, Thabis, seemed back at work already. She stooped among the plants, picking leaves. She looked up under my gaze and nodded. I watched her eyes move to the room behind me. When I turned I saw that all the women of the temple had left their work again to follow me.

They touched me and told me their names. An old woman, a weaver who squinted from many years of staring at her loom, remembered my mother.

"We used to argue about who could stand near her at prayers. Her voice sent us into the heavens. We felt pure and refreshed after hearing her."

"Will you become a birth chanter like your mother?" one woman asked.

"Hush!" several women called out at once. Yet they turned their eyes upon me as if they wished to know the answer.

"I will keep your secrets," I said. My words came out little louder than a whisper and passed with approval from mouth to mouth until the whole group knew them.

After my mother died, my older sisters often recalled her liveliness. When they marked the time of her passing each year, they said that no one talked as much or with such charm. She made everyone smile. I saw that this was the way of the women at the temple. Ahatel alone filled my ears with more sound than they could take in. As I stood in the midst of twenty talking women, I understood nothing. Only Thabis held her lips together; the others did not count the slave as one of them.

I am sure I disappointed my new sisters, for Reema had drawn people to her. I preferred silence and solitude.

The women soon grew tired of my mute presence and returned to their work. Ahatel left me to rest while she went to gossip with her friends. But I could not breathe inside that room. I wandered back to Thabis, who stood over a pot of boiling lentils. I watched her for some time until she looked up.

"You are quieter than me," she observed.

I smiled. Did she miss her homeland? I had left my father's camp behind only four days earlier, yet already I longed for the high cliffs and the wadis. I did not like being inside a brick structure. I longed for the flock.

"Where is your birthplace?" I asked.

She smiled and lowered her eyes, both pleased to be asked and shy about answering.

"Across the desert in a land called Moav. I have never seen eyes like yours."

"Witches have blue eyes," I replied.

"Are you a witch?" She drew back in fear.

"My sisters say I am."

She broke into a quiet laugh. My heart grew lighter.

I stayed with Thabis until the call for evening prayers. I soon realized that when given the opportunity, she spoke as much as any of the others.

Her father had exchanged her for a cow when she was eight and she had passed from hand to hand until Allatimm bought her. Despite all that I had already seen, Thabis felt that the women of the temple treated her well. But unlike the others, she never wanted a man to take her. Allatimm forced her to lie with those whom the others rejected. Twice she had had to take the abortion powder. The second time she had lain close to death for many days. Still, Thabis insisted that Allatimm had her rights as mistress.

"If she sent those men away unsatisfied, where would the temple be? We can not afford to lose our worshippers."

My heart felt crushed between the walls of my chest. How could I ever accept Allatimm's embrace again? I refused to believe that the Goddess, my Goddess, smiled upon the ways of Her priestess.

"Allatimm is a good and loving mother to the girls," Thabis observed. "As for me, I am better off here than I would have been in many other places."

At dusk all the women rushed across the court to the large sanctuary. We climbed some rising staggered platforms of brick to reach the door. I watched my feet and moved with such caution that Thabis soon realized I had never seen stairs. But that marvel was nothing compared to the main sanctuary itself—a huge room lit with so many oil lamps that it shone brighter than sunlight. At the front of the sanctuary on a granite stone platform, a shining gold statue of the Goddess rose twice as tall as any woman. Her hair flowed down her back and she had the same figure as the Goddess in my cave, with high, round breasts and a slender waist. She held a bow above her head in one hand and a mirror in the other. Jewels hung around her neck and at her waist. I wanted to fall before her, but Thabis held me back.

I stood next to Thabis as many women greeted me. But I could not take my eyes off the golden Goddess and her altar long enough to acknowledge them.

Many small replicas of the Goddess in gold, wood, and clay clustered at the feet of the large statue.

"What are they?" I asked my companion.

"The birth chanters used to take one when they went to a woman in labor," she whispered.

Which had my mother taken? I decided that she must have preferred the little one made of shiny yellow gold.

When I glanced around the room I saw several men off to one side. They reclined on lavish cushions woven with patterns of blue and yellow flowers. I knew that men required the favor of the Goddess as much as women did, but these visitors appeared to be staring at the women rather than paying their respects to Asherah. Their lustful presence tarnished the sacredness of our worship. I frowned in their direction. Then I focused my eyes on the Goddess until the men no longer existed for me.

Ahatel moved forward from the crowd of women and climbed up to the platform. The room grew silent as she prepared to speak. "Let all who bring offerings to the Great Goddess Asherah come forward!"

A young woman with a reed basket moved to lay her offerings on the platform. She kissed the foot of the large Goddess statue. When she turned away I saw that her face glistened with tears.

"Childless," Thabis whispered to me. "Allatimm has already asked her to join us."

I recalled a woman cursed with the same affliction in Father's camp. After two childless years her lord gave her the usual choice—she could return to her father's tent or wander into the desert to die. But neither her father nor her brother would have her back because of the shame her barrenness brought upon them. So she took herself into the wilderness without water. A week later someone found her bones scraped clean by vultures. Yitro forbade us to mourn her passing. Now I saw that the Goddess offered respite from such a terrible fate. My flesh quivered with rage. How many barren women in Midyan did not know they had an alternative to disgrace and death?

I watched the women take their places at the back of the group while several men rose from their cushions to make similar offerings. Whatever they sought—success in war, many sons, the restoration of their vigor— the consequences of an unanswered petition could be nothing like those for a childless woman.

Allatimm entered from a door near a large stone altar behind the Goddess. She wore a flowing white dress and a hand-sized gold medallion hung on her chest. She signaled for the women to move forward. We stood at the foot of the Goddess and began a hymn. I could almost hear my mother—the mournful wail rising into a joyous vibration above the clouds to the stars in heaven, the purity of her high tones like a clear pool in the high mountains after a cool rain.

> *Oh Great Goddess!*
> *You who give us life.*
> *The land is ravaged and you make it bloom.*
> *My womb is empty and you fill it.*
> *May I glow in the light of your beauty!*
> *May I sing your praises forever!*

Tears rose in my eyes. The warmth of the Goddess and my mother's embrace filled me at once. I no longer cared about my disappointment in Allatimm. I would accept her for the sake of the Goddess she served, for the women she harbored, and for my mother whose memory lived and breathed in the very walls of this sacred place.

That night I could not sleep in the cramped room where twenty women's dreams swirled around me. And so in the darkest hour I crept from the building and lay down outside with the sheep and goats.

When a faint first light flooded the sky, I returned to the Goddess in the sanctuary. I knelt at her feet and began to chant without words. I mourned the loss of my mother. I imagined her in those last moments as a torrent of water raced down the wadi and swept her away. I felt the silencing of her voice. I saw the barren women who wandered in the desert and died by the hand of the cruel sun. My wailing fell into the depths of all the pain I had ever known. Then, as the stars rise at dusk, so too did my chanting float upward, carried to the Goddess in heaven by the upper regions of my voice in longing and then in joy. When I finished, it seemed my heart had burst into a thousand pieces and been made whole again.

I heard breathing in the doorway—the women of the temple and Allatimm. How long had they been listening? How long had they been weeping?

"She will be a birth chanter like Reema," someone whispered.

After a moment Allatimm came forward and kissed my cheeks. She looked deep into my eyes. "The Goddess has brought you home," she said.

EIGHT

Tzipporah

THE morning after Moses arrived I woke before dawn. A white half-moon hung in the sky over the western escarpment. I had been back in my father's camp for a full month and lambing was over. Soon I would return to the temple.

I sang a hymn of thanks to the Goddess for Her many blessings. I thanked Her for the safe delivery of all the newborns in the flock. I thanked Her for causing my mother's spirit to inhabit my voice. I prayed that Father would not keep me in camp much longer.

I would miss my beloved animals. But I yearned to return to birth chanting. Allatimm had taught me well. I knew how to modulate my chant depending on the phase of a woman's labor, how to ask the Goddess for a girl or a boy depending on the mother's wish, how to enhance a mother's joy, and how to ease her sorrow when a child died.

Many requested my services. After only seven months I brought in as much payment as Ahatel. The other women of the temple found inspiration in my evening hymns. I satisfied the priestess in all ways but one.

"You can not worship the Goddess with your voice alone! She frowns upon women who refuse the pleasures of the flesh." Whenever she said these words, Allatimm pursed her lips and glared at me. "Even your mother did not refrain."

I saw the truth in what she said. But month after month my reluctance failed the Goddess.

The other women disdained my chastity. Their glances accused me of holding myself above them. Only Thabis did not complain. But I could no longer look her in the eye, for night after night while I refused all our visitors she had to lie with whomever the other girls did not take. Often Allatimm sent her to two or three men before she could retire to sleep.

On the day of my departure Allatimm and Ahatel approached me together.

"Men come to find the Goddess in our flesh," Ahatel said. "Those who withhold themselves make Her angry."

Allatimm grasped my wrist. "She will silence your voice if you continue to shun Her."

I looked down in shame. "I do not wish to shun Her," I whispered.

The priestess tightened her grip. "Then when you return you must take your place with the others."

I nodded my head in agreement.

Now, a month later and the morning after Moses had arrived, I recalled my promise with dread. Allatimm's messenger would come for me that day or the next, and when I returned to the temple I would take my place with the other women each night. I prayed for the Goddess to relieve my dread with joy at the prospect of serving Her.

When I woke, I saw that Father's guest still slept. I took two water skins for the day's grazing and slipped out of the tent. Across the camp I saw Father sleeping on a skin near the flock's pen, where he always spent the night to guard against wolves and thieves.

About halfway to the well I felt a presence behind me. I spun around. The man Moses stood a short distance behind. He wore a frayed black wool kuttoneh that Father must have found for him somewhere in camp and a black head cloth tied with heavy cord around his head. He had removed his sandals. The shepherd's costume did not disguise his height, bearing, or handsome face. Nor could he hide the scar on his lips or the difficulty with which he spoke.

"I will keep the men away from you," he called out. The words took so long to come through his lips that it seemed the dawn would rise in full before he completed his sentence.

I turned and walked ahead without a word or gesture.

Moses remained several paces behind me until we reached the well. Two strangers stood nearby watering their donkeys. By their dress and their gear I knew them for traders returning from Egypt to their home in the south. With Moses at my side they did not dare accost me.

"Thank you," I whispered to him while we waited to use the well.

He gazed into my eyes as if he hoped for something more from me. I looked away. When the men finished using the well, Moses offered to fill the skins. I pretended not to hear.

As we turned back to camp he walked too close to me. I moved away.

"Your father has asked me to accompany you today," he said.

"I can manage on my own."

"I must learn."

I looked up at him with confusion.

"He needs a shepherd. I need employment."

The truth of these words stung me like a swarm of ants. I laughed at myself. Had I expected my place to remain unfilled forever? Father held too many responsibilities to care for Sinn's flock alone. My sisters were busy with their children. None of our kinsmen could forsake their own interests to take care of the sacred animals, which must not be mixed with others. Yet to assign a stranger to the task seemed rash.

Moses sensed my concern. "I am an honest man," he said. "I will work hard."

When we returned to camp I led him to the pen. Before we took the flock out to graze I checked to make sure that no animal had taken sick in the night. As I wandered among the sheep and goats I stroked the young and examined several old ewes whose days must soon end. I remembered helping with their lambs, long since grown with lambs of their own. My heart filled with regret. I would miss these old friends.

Though I did not speak a single word, Moses understood.

"Can you return to visit soon?"

I looked into his eyes. They were filled with tenderness for me, a stranger. I shook my head and hurried to open the gate.

I took my place at the front of the herd and motioned for Moses to position himself at the back. From time to time I stole glances at him. Once he caught my eye and smiled. I grew red with embarrassment.

We soon reached the Wadi Makna, green from the recent rains. The sheep and goats ran to feast on young bean caper plants and Moses sat down under an acacia tree. As I wandered among the animals, I longed to sing a hymn to the Goddess in praise of all the new life around me. But I could not open my mouth in the presence of the stranger whose steady gaze scorched me like the sun on dry earth. I did not look at him often, yet each time I turned to him his attention remained fixed on me. When at last his eyes closed, I walked up to him to make sure he slept. His chest rose and fell in an even pattern and he did not open his eyes. I asked the Goddess to keep his spirit from harm.

I walked back to a cluster of sheep and nursing lambs. I cleared my throat and began my hymn.

Great Goddess who grants life to the mother,
Great Goddess who grants victory to the warrior,
Great Goddess who fills the heart of every woman with love,
Great Goddess who fills the loins of every man with desire,
I sing Your praise! I sing Your praise!

I chanted for a long time, extending the words into sounds that floated from my throat to the heavens and wound around the sandstone cliffs above me like a golden ribbon. I chanted until I became aware that he was listening.

I am not sure how I knew, for his eyes remained closed. Yet his position looked too rigid and his hands appeared tense. Perhaps he had not slept at all. Perhaps he had closed his eyes to spy on me with open ears.

Unsettled by his attention, I ran to the other side of the wide wadi. I did not look in his direction again for the rest of the morning. Yet I could not forget him.

When the sun reached its zenith, Seri brought us a basket of provisions. Moses stood and waved for me to join them under the tree. I hesitated for a moment. But he stood as majestic as an eagle in the sunlight. I could not turn away.

In honor of our guest, Seri spread out a finer midday meal than usual—spelt bread, almonds, and dates. "Did you have great feasts in Egypt?' she asked Moses.

Moses nodded to Seri, but he spoke to me. "Wine, fruit, cucumber, wheat bread, fish..."

"Your father must be a wealthy man," Seri interrupted when she lost patience with Moses's labored speech. She leaned so close to him that they almost touched. "Do all Egyptians eat such things?"

Red streaks rose in his face like flames out of embers. He took a drink of water. When he spoke again I saw the sinews in his neck tighten as if he struggled to restrain himself. "I am not an Egyptian."

"Then who are your people?" Seri asked, popping an almond into her mouth.

"The Israelites."

"Who live in Egypt?"

Moses nodded.

"In Midyan we worship the moon god Sinn. Who do you worship?"

He hesitated. I saw he did not like the question. "My life is here now. My allegiance is to your father."

I knew the hollow voice too well; once it had been mine. His destiny lay hidden deep inside the cave of his heart. I felt it in my own heart and knew what he did not yet know. I could give him hope.

I glanced from the blue beetle ring on his finger and then away to the ground near his knees. "Your God has not yet revealed Himself to you."

Moses started. He gazed at me with wonder. His beauty made my body ache. I looked away.

Seri stretched her arms and yawned. "Do not bother with her. She talks nonsense."

"She has the voice of a heavenly being," Moses said.

I felt my face flush with pleasure.

My sister laughed. A rank wind blew from her throat. "Where she is going she needs no voice at all. Men prefer whores who keep their mouths shut and their legs open."

I rose to my feet and fled my sister's ugly words. I did not care what lies she told Moses. After this day I would never see him again.

In a few moments Moses came in search of me.

"Does she tell the truth?" he demanded.

For many minutes I did not answer. His breath remained heavy with agitation, but he did not rush me. He sat down by my side and watched as I stroked the soft, black coat of a young lamb. When at last words came to me I said them.

"The Goddess has chosen me to serve Her. It is my destiny."

I watched his face twist in pain like a man with a deep flesh wound. He seemed unable to speak.

I looked into his flashing eyes. He understood nothing. Still, my trembling heart whispered that in a different life I could have loved such a man.

Late in the afternoon I left camp to make an offering to the Goddess. When I returned I saw a strange donkey tied to a post near Father's tent. As I drew close, I heard loud voices from inside. I crept up to the open flap. Three men stood arguing: a stranger, Moses, and Father.

No one seemed to notice me.

"She must return to the high priestess at once," the stranger demanded. "Lambing is over." Allatimm had sent him to retrieve me.

"I have made a promise," Father said to Moses.

Moses drew himself up. He stood with his legs apart and though his words came forth with no more ease, he spoke in a commanding tone. "A promise to prostitute one's own daughter can not be binding."

I felt my own face grow hot with anger. By what right did this stranger interfere?

"She is unmarriageable," Father said with exasperation. "None of her kin will take her for a wife. She can not live among us with honor."

Moses allowed his hands to relax. I felt the anger drain away from him. The matter was over; I filled my nostrils with air and exhaled in relief. And then Moses fell on his knees at my father's feet. His voice quivered with emotion and his tongue struggled even more than usual.

"My lord, I am a stranger here. You have been kind and generous. Your daughter is beautiful in my eyes. I beg you. Give her to me. I will take no other wife. I will provide for her and her children."

I could not see. I could not breathe. I heard the Goddess shriek deep in the chambers of my ears.

"She is no good for you," Father objected. "She is not a virgin. She has given…"

"My lord," Moses interrupted. He pointed to the scars on his mouth. "As you see, I am not whole myself. I will honor her as she is."

NINE

Tzipporah

I WATCHED with disbelief as Father gave me to the man from Egypt. Moses kissed my father's hand with gratitude. He handed his beetle ring to Allatimm's messenger as compensation for the priestess's loss of my service. My own loss meant nothing to any of them.

I ran to the flock and crouched among the sheep like a wounded animal awaiting death. How could this stranger wander into camp one day and change my destiny the next? How could he steal my future from me? The Goddess loved me like a mother. She had banished the demons and freed me from the past. Every morning She awakened my voice and brought joy to my heart.

I looked up and saw the face of Thabis projected across the darkening sky. She wore the expression of pain and resignation—a wrinkled brow and dull eyes—that came upon her every night when Allatimm summoned her to the room of a guest. Shriveled old men, traders who reeked of frankincense, men laden with crushing weight—such were the creatures who used her flesh. Had I offended the Goddess by refusing to relieve the slave's burden? Was exile a punishment for my chaste worship?

I prayed for Her to forgive me, to send me back to Qurayyah.

O Great Goddess! Let me lose my voice that I might serve You with my flesh alone! Let me die on Your altar rather than stay here where You are forbidden to me! Goddess, hear my prayer!

A voice called out to me from a distance.

"Tzipporah?"

My heart filled with hope.

"Tzipporah?"

I should have known. It was only Moses in the shadows.

Father gave me to Moses without wedding honors—no feast, no sacrifice, no special prayers, no singing or gifts. My dusty black kuttoneh served as a bridal garment. There was no wedding procession. Instead my sisters and their lords watched in silence as Moses led me to the guest tent.

Someone handed Moses an oil lamp. He held it held high above my head and motioned for me to enter first. As Moses followed me inside, I hid in the darkest corner. Too tall to stand upright, he knelt down and reached behind to lower the flap. We sat alone in silence. I trembled with cold and fear. When he slid near me I shook even more. He draped a sheepskin around my shoulders and sat back away from me. He did not utter a word. I prayed for him to leave me alone.

After a time he began to remove his clothes. I lifted my eyes as he pulled off his kuttoneh and then unwrapped his pleated loincloth. He sat before me wearing nothing but three charms on a gold necklace. In all my days I had never seen a man so uncovered.

I did not want to like anything about him. But I could not deny that he was pleasing to look at, with broad shoulders and legs as strong as tree trunks. The muscles in his arms rippled like waves. Only one thing marred his beauty—the scar that crossed from his right upper lip straight down to his chin. How had he come to be so damaged?

I tried to focus on the imperfection, but I could not keep my eyes from wandering. I imagined what he would look like with long hair and a full beard. Had he been our cousin, had his lips been without blemish, my sisters would have fought each other to be his wife.

He reached for the water vessel, but instead of taking a drink he soaked the edge of his loincloth and began rubbing himself with it. My eyes grew wide with astonishment to see him using water in such a way.

He laughed at me. "You do not wash in Midyan?"

I fixed my lips together. *I will never speak to you*, my angry eyes said.

He poured some water in his hand and splashed it on his face.

I looked away to hide my curiosity.

"No?" he asked.

We washed our newborns and our dead. Between birth and death a rare soaking rain might cleanse us. And Allatimm bathed as part of the yearly sacred rite. This was the only washing I knew.

"Water is precious here," I blurted out.

Moses smiled. "Justice and dignity are precious."

Justice? I shuddered. *There is no justice in this place.*

He finished washing and spread the wet cloth out to dry. The fabric looked so thin and light I wanted to touch it. He covered his loins with the kuttoneh and reclined on one elbow. I hid my face in my veil and turned away. Better to be blind than to look at him.

I felt the hollow of his hand on my head. He offered comfort with tentative strokes.

His touch was sweeter than date sugar.

"You remain with the flock," he murmured close to my ear. "Can you rejoice for this?"

His gentle arms embraced me from behind. His scent, a grove of almond trees after a warm, soaking rain, rose to my nostrils. My taut flesh melted like frost in the morning sun.

"I wish to serve the Great Goddess," I whispered. "I must return to Qurayyah."

He stroked my hair and my face. Desire rose in me like the flutter of a thousand insect wings.

"It is my destiny," I pleaded.

"You are my destiny," he insisted. "I knew at the well."

I looked upon his calm face, his sureness, his scarred lips, the flame of the oil lamp reflected in his eyes. I wanted to lash out at him for his clever words, to shout that he understood nothing.

And I wanted him to love me.

As he took my hand, I noticed the gold cord around his neck and the three charms it held—two flies and a lion. His keen eye caught my fleeting interest. He pulled the chain over his head and put it around my neck.

I gazed upon the man Moses. His beauty and his strength, his sharp eyes, sweet words, soft heart, and foolish beliefs—none of these could keep me from Her. But if I must learn to give myself to men with a willing heart, then perhaps I might begin with him. Tomorrow I would find a way to return to Qurayyah. Tonight I would let him take me in Her name.

He read the decision on my face and leaned back on the mat. He held out his hand to me and smiled with encouragement. I lay next to him and he began to stroke my hair.

"It is so long," he whispered.

I wondered if women in Egypt wore their hair short. I cared nothing for my tangled tresses, but I would no more cut them off than a finger or a toe.

I touched his bristled scalp.

"It will grow back," he assured.

I closed my eyes and he kissed the lids. Tears flowed across my cheeks like the first warm rain after a drought. He pulled me close and began touching me all over through my wool kuttoneh. I wanted to be free of the heavy cloth, to be one with him.

He leaned away from me to blow out the oil lamp. In the darkness I dropped through a hollow infant's scream, back to the moment of my death...

The painted Goddess and Her worshipping couples whirled around me as I turned, faster, faster, faster until I fell flat against the cave wall and spun with them. In the blur of my vision I looked down from the wall and saw a man in a dark kuttoneh, yellow belt, and flowing head cloth. He stared at me in silence. *Has the Goddess sent you?* I asked. My words echoed inside his laughter. He seized my neck and pushed me down to the sandy floor of the cave. My arm hit the oil lamp. The flame kissed my flesh and went out.

I told myself it was Her will.

But the Goddess had not sent him to me. How long had I known the truth? His yellow belt, his sharp eyes staring at me in silence. He had followed me from the well. He and my demon were one.

Moses brushed his lips over mine. A moan rose from deep inside my chest. My bones broke into a thousand pieces and fell away from his embrace. I could not stand his touch. I could not stand anyone's touch.

I crouched in the corner of the tent like a withered thistle, my sharp thorns protecting an empty vessel.

Moses did not reproach me or demand his due as my lord. He wished me good night and said nothing more. In the darkness I could feel his disappointment fill the space between us.

He lay back on the mat and slept. Yet whenever I moved, no matter how slight the movement, he sat up, as if he feared I might run away.

I held myself very still and kept watch over Moses lest a demon enter in place of the breath that left his nostrils. I wondered where his spirit roamed as he slept. Perhaps it returned to Egypt.

In the night I grew cold again and began to shiver. Moses took me in his arms. "We can lie as brother and sister," he whispered. Trusting his words, I curled up like a newborn lamb and slept.

I woke at dawn, my heart as dry as a shallow well in the hot months, my eyes dim, my tongue stiff. I tried to utter a prayer of thanks for safe passage through the night, but my tight throat sealed away all sound. The Goddess was gone from me.

I ran to the flock, my only refuge.

In the days that followed I could not utter a word. I hovered outside my body and watched all that Tzipporah did. She stayed on the edge of camp like a leper forbidden to return. At night she slept with the animals.

Moses continued to treat me with kindness. He brought me food and I ate. I woke on cold mornings covered by a sheepskin that he laid over me. We took the flock out and spent the day in silence. Sometimes I felt his eyes studying my face as if it pleased him. Yet he asked nothing of me other than that I remain with him. He understood that I could not run off in the night and expect to survive. But he never let me out of his sight during the day. Under his vigilant eye I could not slip away to Qurayyah. Nor could I make an offering to the Goddess in the cave.

Moses sat up late with my father every evening, long after the other men went to their wives. My sisters grumbled about the favor Father showed my lord, but the men saw that he had no ambition to be more than Father's shepherd and so they did not trouble themselves about it. When I could not sleep, I crept toward the fire and spied on them. Moses listened to Father speak of justice and judgment. Sometimes Moses posed a question, as if he sought to formulate rules by which Father reached a verdict in a dispute and determined punishments. But most of the time Moses remained silent—because he could not speak with ease or because he preferred to listen, I did not know.

Father never seemed to question Moses about his past and Moses offered nothing on that subject. At first my sisters complained that for all we knew of the man he might be a murderer or a thief. They urged me to find out more about him. But I did not comply and they soon lost interest.

One night Moses asked Father what prevented a stronger man from tyrannizing the weaker in the clan, from stealing his brother's possessions or taking another man's wife. He did not yet understand that we lived in fear of Father and his justice.

"We are one people," Father replied. "We must guard each other from the stranger who would harm us."

"I am a stranger," Moses reminded him.

"You are my son now, though my daughter is no wife to you."

Moses sighed. "She walks like the dead among the living."

"She is as she has always been, and worse. It is not too late to take her to the temple. Your position among us will not change."

Please! Send me home to Her!

"She will return to life," Moses assured him, as if he knew me better than I knew myself.

The hot days fell upon us. I longed to be one with the Goddess again, to sing Her praises and feel Her inhabit me. I whispered to Her in the wadis, at the well, as I fell asleep with the flock at night. I begged Her to call me once again. I begged Her to make me worthy. But still I could not chant. Nor could I give my flesh to Moses. My memories held me back.

In a few weeks my desire to return to the temple fell away from me. I despaired of knowing the Goddess again. The sad eyes of Thabis no longer haunted me. They had become my own.

Every year as the hot days came upon us Father and I gathered the sheep to journey across the wilderness to the mountain of Sinn. There in the uplands of Midyan we found good pasture for the sheep and plentiful water. The days remained cool and pleasant. At the first full moon after lambing, the worshippers of Sinn from all over Midyan joined us to witness the yearly sacrifice to their god, to thank him for the fertility of their flocks. Thousands of men came to sacrifice a lamb and a bull and to partake of a ritual stew—kids boiled in the milk of their own mothers.

Two days before our departure for the mountain of Sinn, Moses offered to help Father get the bull of sacrifice. Its keeper dwelt half a day to the north of us and they would spend the night in his tent. I brought the flock home early that day and ran to the cave.

I stood on the ledge, afraid to enter. Before Moses had come to me, the Goddess had softened the truth with a veil that shimmered like the stars on a clear night. Now I stood alone. Even my own voice abandoned me. I could not enter that terrible place.

I fell to my knees. I wept.

I only wanted to serve You.

The sun slipped behind the western mountains and the moon rose with the evening star—Sinn and the Great Goddess looked down upon me from the same sky. A breeze kissed my upturned face and rustled through the tamarisk trees on the escarpment above. A great yearning filled my spirit. God and Goddess sought to be reunited in the land. How much longer would they have to wait? My heart held no memory of Father before his bitterness; I never imagined he might forgive the Goddess in his lifetime. But surely Reema would have grieved for the exile of her beloved Goddess. Surely Father did not honor his beloved's memory by keeping her Goddess from the women of Midyan.

Perhaps the Goddess intended Moses for me after all. Perhaps he kept me from the temple not to thwart my service but to increase it. Perhaps my destiny lay in returning the Goddess to Her rightful place in our midst.

I opened my mouth to chant a hymn. The words echoed across the escarpment and flew high into the heavens. Soon others outside the temple would join me.

When Moses returned the next day, the whole camp came to see how he mastered the fierce bull with his great strength, quick wit, and gentle, hesitating voice. The men marveled at his courage and Father seemed to look upon him with new admiration. I noticed him for the first time in weeks. His beard had grown in, full and dark. His hair, also thick and black, spread like a soft carpet across his skull. My heart flooded with happiness to see him.

He greeted me by bowing low with his arms crossed over his chest. I knelt and kissed his feet as women of our clan do when their lords have come back from a dangerous journey.

That night I went to him in his tent. He took me in his arms and kissed my neck. I felt his hands rising under my kuttoneh to touch my thighs. I closed my eyes and waited for his desire to wash over me like a warm rain.

His weight bore down upon me. Every sinew of my being snapped. The dead infant lay on a high rock, where vultures pulled out her entrails. I gagged on the vomit that rose in my throat and pushed him away.

"I am sorry," I whispered, my first words to him in many weeks.

He took me into his arms and stroked my hair. I wept for my failure, for the child, for my mother who left too soon. I wept because I knew that however much the Goddess urged me to make my flesh one with this man who loved me, I could not.

He held me and I clung to him. When at last I began to yawn he eased me down upon the mat.

"I am sorry," I said again as I fell asleep.

"I will wait," he replied, close to my ear.

Just before dawn the fluttering tent flap awakened me. Had Moses, always so meticulous, forgotten to close it? I sat up. I heard the light step of the Goddess circle me.

"O Great Goddess, help me with the man Moses!" I begged.

Your love for him will come, She promised. *Each thing in its time.*

TEN

Tzipporah

HE next morning Father, Moses, and I left camp to travel south along the coast and then east through the Hisma—the wilderness of Sinn—to Sinn's mountain. I led the way holding a donkey packed with our tent, provisions, a cooking pot, and a water skin.

Father walked on one side of the flock and Moses walked at the back with the sacrificial bull. At the end of the first day through the high hills we reached Elim, where water from the spring is always sweet, plentiful, and fresh. We did not pitch our tent while we traveled, in case we needed to make a quick escape from thieves or predators. Nor did we light a fire at night. We tried to pass through the land unnoticed.

In the late afternoon on the following day we reached a place where the trail crested over the ridge above the Red Sea. Despite the brackish water at this campsite, I looked forward to our yearly visit. I loved to stare out across the water and watch the white-eyed gulls float on the wind. Sometimes blue bee-eaters and red-throated pipits decorated the jutting sandstone terraces with their brilliant color and filled the air with song. Sandpiper and crab plover ran in and out of the water. But of all the birds, I most loved the long-legged flamingoes. Their graceful necks and pleasing color brought joy to my heart.

I left Father and Moses with the flock at the campsite and ran down the rocks to the shore. On this day I stood for some time without seeing a single bird. I looked for a sign from the Goddess, to assure me that my choice to remain with Moses honored Her. I cleared my throat and chanted a short hymn. I held out my arms in supplication. The sound of the water lapping against the rocks filled my ears. A warm breeze pricked my skin. I felt the storm god Baal Zephon nearby. The Goddess did not dare intrude upon his domain.

I climbed back up the ridge where Moses and Father watched over the grazing flock. The bull stood nearby, tied to a date palm.

Moses read the disappointment in my face and looked at me with concern.

"The pink birds with long necks, " I murmured before I could stop myself. But I did not feel foolish telling him. "Sometimes I see them here."

His whole face smiled at me as if my words brought him special pleasure. "I know them from Egypt."

Moses looked from me to Father and pointed toward the sea.

"Return by dusk," Father replied.

Moses nodded and pulled me toward the trail.

The sun hung low on the horizon and cast a golden glow over the tall sandstone formations jutting into the bright blue water on either side of the beach.

"Come," Moses said. He removed his clothes and his head cloth and placed them on one of the yellow rocks.

"In the sea?" I asked with horror. Even the bravest man never dared set so much as a toe into the water that belonged to Baal Zephon.

Moses laughed as the sea began to swallow him.

"You have not made a sacrifice!" I cried out. "You will drown!"

But it was too late. He waded out as far as his waist and then he disappeared.

I ran to the edge of the water and kept my eyes on the spot where he had gone under. My eyes filled with tears. I did not want to lose him.

Several long moments later his head appeared far away. He waved to me and plunged back into the water again.

"You do not swim?" he called out as he approached me.

I shook my head. I did not know it was possible.

"Come," he gestured, urging me to join him. "I will hold you."

I shook my head again.

"Come come come," he coaxed, splashing the water with his fingers.

I looked at his eyes glinting copper and gold like the setting sun, his eager smile, his gesturing hands. I wondered if anyone had ever refused him anything.

"Turn around," I answered. When his strong back faced me, I removed my kuttoneh and waded into the warm water. *Better to die this way than another*, I told the Goddess.

The sand and stones of the sea floor tickled my feet. I saw little fish in the clear water below me. My legs grew heavy even as the rest of me seemed light enough to float away.

When I reached Moses, I crouched down low enough for the warm water to cover my neck. I tapped him on the back. He turned and looked down upon me with tenderness. He lifted me to my feet and kissed me. His lips tasted of sea salt and date honey. Then he showed me how to climb onto his back with my arms around his neck so I could swim with him.

We glided through the water flesh on flesh. I forgot my fear of the storm god. I forgot my longing to see the birds. I forgot birth chanting and the temple. I even forgot the Goddess.

We swam to shore and lay in the soft white sand. He touched the hollow of my throat. He stroked my breasts until the nipples rose hard under his hand. I felt his desire press against my body and my own desire rise in response.

He would have had me then, as the last rays of light fell into the sea, but Yitro called for us to return. Moses kissed my lips and then my forehead. After I dressed, I still yearned for him between my legs. He rested his hand against my lower back as we walked. I drew closer to him. All the demons of the night and all the gods of sea and land could not harm me in his presence.

That night I fell asleep while the men talked. I dreamt that Moses lifted me to the heavens and we flew above the seashore in search of flamingoes. When I woke in the morning I found two long pink feathers near my cheek.

We traveled down the coast for part of the morning and then turned back to the interior at the Wadi Sadr. Stark red granite mountains loomed to the east and sand soon gave way to hot gravel. The wadi grew still and silent. For much of the day Moses walked at the back of the flock and I took the lead. Though I did not see him, I felt his presence behind me. I smiled when I remembered the water. As I recalled his touch it seemed that all the beauty in the world presented itself for my delight—the white catchfly flower blossoms exploding from cracks in the stone, a little brown and green lizard with shimmering scales, the intense blue sky kissing the red granite walls of the wadi. My step grew as light as a gazelle. I touched the feathers in my hair and smiled so wide my face hurt. *This is what it feels to be loved*, I told myself. I began to worry about how little I gave him in return for his boundless affection.

We stopped for the night near a spring but found no pasture for the flock in the barren wadi. I prepared a gruel of wheat, water, and date paste. When I called the men to eat I did not join them. I could not force myself to swallow anything while the flock went hungry.

"You must eat," Moses insisted.

He put his hand on my arm. The flesh tingled all the way to my heart. I did as he asked.

As we lay down to rest, the moon peeked in and out of the crooked mountains on either side of us and cast strange shadows over the wadi. Moses sat up late staring at these giant forms as if they spoke to him.

What did I know of this man? I knew him to be modest about his strength, humble about his wit, and respectful of Father's leadership. I knew nothing of his past and little of his heart except that he wished to bind it to my own. I wanted to know more of him.

I held my hand out to him in the dark. He kissed my fingers, the hollow of my hand, my wrist. I stroked his cheek. He rubbed his hand against my breast. We lay together near Father without touching more than that.

"You should be covered with lapis lazuli and gold." I savored each soft word as it struggled to make its way from his mouth.

"Were you once a man of wealth?" I asked of the man who did not wish to discuss his past.

"I am only what you see now," he insisted. He held me tight and I drifted off to sleep. I dreamt that he whispered to me with the smooth voice of a god.

Destiny turned on me like a false lover. We will console each other.

The next afternoon we began to climb. For five days we worked our way higher and higher. Rock pools hidden in the granite provided water. The flock found enough scattered pasturage for sustenance. During daylight Father, Moses, and I continued to position ourselves at the front, middle, and back of the flock. At night we took turns sleeping. When Father had the watch Moses and I lay together, but he dared take no more from me than a kiss. We kept each other warm with the heat of desire waiting to be fulfilled.

On the last morning in the mountains I heard Father warn Moses that we had reached the most difficult part of the journey—the Sikh pass and the steep, narrow path that leads out of it. Every year we lost at least one animal to the rocks below. Father always led the descent. This year I determined to lead, to show Moses my courage and skill.

We entered the pass as the sun climbed toward its peak. Little air penetrated the narrow fissure between two high granite walls. I coaxed the reluctant donkey forward and the flock followed, two abreast. We moved with labored breath.

When the sun reached its zenith we came to a stone depression filled with water. From here the trail turned to the south upward, along a steep and very narrow ridge. The next campsite and pasture lay in the uplands of the Hisma, a vast wilderness on the other side of the mountains.

We rested by the water for a while. The animals drank their fill, but we had no food to satisfy their growing hunger. Moses and my father ate some dates and almonds. I stayed by the water with the flock to make sure every animal had a turn to drink. The two men became so engrossed in their conversation that I found myself able to slip away with the flock before they noticed. I heard Father calling my name in the distance. I blocked his voice from my ears with a hymn to the Goddess. I knew the way. I could lead as well as any man.

The path climbed over boulders and small rocks above a deep ravine. The four-legged creatures walked single file with no room to stray to the side. As we snaked around a series of jutting walls, I often lost sight of the group behind me. To avoid growing dizzy or fearful, I kept my eyes fixed on the ground ahead. The trail wound down and then up again to a treacherous spur. Though I knew the Goddess did not dwell in these fearsome, barren lands, I sang a hymn to Her.

I reached the edge of the spur and looked out over the Hisma just beyond. No matter how many times this strange landscape came into my view, it always took the breath from my nostrils.

As I stared out at the yellow and black stone forms rising from the red sand like giant fingers and horns, I wondered if this sight could bring Moses to worship Sinn. The Hisma inspired many of the moon god's followers as they approached his sacred mountain.

I grasped the donkey's lead and began the perilous descent. I glanced behind several times to make sure the animals followed my lead; they moved with caution at a steady pace. Moses and Father remained far behind on the winding trail.

A deep rumbling from beneath the mountain startled my voice into silence. At once I understood that the harmony of god and Goddess was not meant to happen here, on Sinn's own sacred ground. I felt Sinn's trembling hands reach through the bowels of the earth, seize my ankles, and hurl me down the steep slope. He laughed in a voice as harsh and painful as a goat shrieking under the sacrificial knife. He did not want the

Goddess in his land after all.

As jagged rocks battered my flesh and grim laughter filled my ears, I saw the yellow-belted man's eyes peering at me from the top of the slope.

"You sent him to rape me!" I accused the god.

You violated my cave, Sinn replied.

"In the name of the Goddess I curse you and your followers!" Did I say the words aloud? I knew it did not matter. The moon god heard me either way. Either way he would not let me live to invade his sacred land again.

I awoke on a soft bed of yellow sand. Water droplets trickled down my face from above. I could smell the flock nearby and another, alien scent. My eyes fluttered open and I saw Moses kneeling over me, his water skin in one hand. Even after days of travel, he seemed as fresh as an almond tree in bloom. But his face held no tenderness.

The earth trembled again. My ankle throbbed with so much pain that I feared I might not be able to stand. My head ached. My flesh stung.

"She is awake," Moses called out.

"The shadows grow long!" Father complained.

"Your father called for you to wait," Moses said, his voice filled with disappointment.

I nodded. The earth rumbled and several sheep cried out. A kid wandered away from the group and nuzzled at my ear. I prayed to the Great Goddess to make me strong for Her sake.

Moses sent the kid away with a little nudge and lifted me to my feet. As I tried to walk my right leg collapsed. The world spun around me. When I looked down I saw my ankle had swollen to twice its size. Moses prodded and pushed at my foot and leg. The pain was such that I bit my tongue to keep from crying out.

"I do not feel a broken bone," he said.

How did he know?

"We must hurry!" Father called out.

"She will have to ride the donkey."

"Hurry then, the god grows restless for his sacrifices."

Moses lifted me onto the donkey. He avoided my eye.

"Your father gave you life. He gave me a new life. We must show him the respect of obedience."

Moses spoke with kindness, but as his heavy tongue labored over each word I began to doubt him. Had I been fooled? He had tamed the bull for Sinn's thanksgiving offering, listened with reverence to every word Father uttered, kept me from serving the Goddess in Her temple. Allatimm would have laughed at me. I could hear her even at that moment. *Sinn sent this beautiful man, a creature in his own image, to woo you from the Goddess, and you did not see the trick!*

My ankle knocked against the donkey's flank and I gasped. I felt ashamed for not hiding my pain. I slumped over the donkey's neck. Moses stroked my arm and offered me more water. I turned my head away from him. He took the donkey's lead and did not speak to me again that afternoon.

When we arrived at the well of Ber, Moses helped me dismount. My head no longer throbbed, but I still could not walk on my right foot. He urged me to sit with my injured leg propped up on a stone. I refused to do as he suggested.

Moses watered the flock while I sat in the shade of an acacia tree. He took the bag of provisions from the donkey and laid out food for an evening meal. I could not eat. I closed my eyes and listened to the men speak about the route of our journey and the danger of the hostile Amalekites who roamed the area. Father described the thunder deep in the earth as Sinn's hunger for the sacrifice. Later I woke to the sound of a lamb crying out under Father's knife. I hoped this would appease the moon god until we reached his mountain.

By morning my entire body ached from bruises; my ankle remained swollen and painful. But I determined to reveal nothing of my discomfort. While the men still slept, I watered the flock and took the animals in the direction of the nearby trail, where I knew they might find bushes and tufts of fine grasses for grazing.

I always welcomed this part of the journey—the flat track and reliable water sources—but never more so than now. In two days we would turn into the Wadi Dama toward the metalworkers' settlement of Dophka, where Father always stopped to have the sacrificial knives sharpened. After one more thirsty day across the wilderness of Sinn and the black stone fields we would reach the abode of the moon god, a different world from ours. Here our animals refreshed themselves on the morning dew and we gathered sweet manna on the tamarisk trees. Father often caught migrating quail and roasted them over the campfire. Closer to the mountain of Sinn the fertile plain blossomed with a thick growth of perennials and the animals drank from wide pools of clear, fresh water. None could help feeling awe at the sight of the moon god's sacred mountain rising from its flat-topped perch on the grey table mountain of Tadra.

Father and Moses arrived with the bull and the donkey.

Moses rushed to me. "Your ankle?" he asked. His soft eyes grew wide with concern as he waited for my answer. But I had no affection left for the man who would have me be obedient to Yitro the high priest and his god. I told myself that I would never permit him to touch me again.

"I am well," I lied and limped away from him.

We began the day's journey with Father leading the way. Though I followed just behind him, I soon lagged. Moses walked at the back of the flock with the bull. I felt his eyes upon me, but I did not turn to look at him as I redoubled my efforts to keep pace.

In a short time Moses called out to Father, asking him to stop. Father brought the donkey back down the trail and the two men conferred in whispers. Then Father removed one of his knives from a bag tied to the donkey and handed it to Moses. He gave Father the bull's lead and ran back toward Ber. He soon returned with a sturdy branch of an acacia, about as thick as my arm and stripped of all leaves.

"To help you walk," he said as he handed me the stick. "May your feet bring you back to me."

On the tenth day of the third month, the month of Sinn, we crossed the plain of sharp black stone fragments and arrived at the abode of the moon god. The sheep and goats scrambled to quench their thirst in the low, rain-filled pools of the valley and to satisfy their hunger on the abundant green plants. Father knelt on the altar site and offered a prayer. I watched Moses from the corner of my eye to see if he would follow. But he only stood and gazed up at the mountain with curiosity. After a few moments he approached me, still leading the bull.

"Have you climbed it?" He pointed to the mountain and then placed his free hand on my head and stroked my hair. I flushed with confusion. For three days I had been sure that Sinn had sent him to prevent me from worshipping the Great Goddess. For three days I had promised myself that I would never be a wife to him. But now his soft voice, gentle hand, and foolish question broke my resolve.

"We are forbidden to touch the holy mountain," I replied. I offered my eyes to him like a shameless whore. Though Father stood nearby Moses bent down to kiss me full on the lips.

Each year Father rebuilt and destroyed the sacrificial altar for fear that if it remained standing one of the desert dwellers might make an improper sacrifice and incur the god's wrath. So on our first full day at the mountain, Moses and Father rolled large boulders to the base of the mountain, twelve in all, one to signify each new moon in a year. Father spent the rest of the day carving a picture of a bull with large crescent horns on the stone that designated the month of Sinn.

Over the next two days many pilgrims arrived. They pitched their tents around the altar until the camp grew to be larger than the town of Qurayyah. They came from all over Midyan. Some lived in the great red desert and others in the settled areas of Qurayyah or Tabuk. Amalekite men arrived from as far as Jerash in the north and Najran in the south— they formed a group five thousand strong. I stayed with the sacred flock on the edge of the valley, far from the gathering of the clans. Some brought their own sheep to graze nearby, but these men knew to leave Yitro's daughter alone. Those clans who had no fixed camp—as we did at the oasis of Madyan—came with their women and children. But I did not mingle with them either.

Moses stood above all the men in height and bearing. What little he revealed of his wit I knew to be superior. Yet he seemed to be a man without pride. He cast his eyes down and refused all marks of honor men offered for his association with Yitro. He accepted no gift, asked them not to bow, and walked with quiet steps wherever he went. He waited on Father during all the visits of the clan leaders as if he was Father's servant, devoted to no greater calling than his master's comfort. When Father knelt all night at the altar, Moses remained by his side.

I never understood how Father knew when the sun approached each of the two yearly points where daylight and darkness came to be equal. Such secrets of the priesthood could not be revealed to any woman. But on the third evening after we arrived at the mountain of Sinn, the full white moon rose over the hills and Father announced that the season of the rising sun was upon us. He instructed each clan to slaughter a lamb in thanks for Sinn's blessings over the past year.

Father shared a lamb from Sinn's sacred flock with those who did not have their own. Men and women smeared blood on their foreheads to show their allegiance and gratitude to Sinn and to protect them from evil spirits who lurked around the edges of the camp under the full moon. They roasted the lambs and ate them.

On the following morning Father began the preparations for the fertility sacrifices. He used lamb's blood to mark a different sign on twelve kids from the sacred flock. He also marked each kid's mother and a skin for her milk with a matching sign. Then he instructed me to gather milk from the goats for the sacrificial stew. This would be offered to Sinn to ensure the fertility of the flocks and the people in the coming year.

I did not care if Sinn knew the difference, if the success of this offering depended upon cooking each kid in its mother's milk. Sinn conspired with Father to keep the women of Midyan from their Goddess, the true granter of fertility. We owed Sinn nothing. And so I took care to confound every skin.

When I finished this chore, I sat beneath a date palm and closed my eyes to rest. In the full heat of the day, even the cool Valley of Gaw can be too warm for anything more than sleep.

I awoke with a start to the laughter of a group of men leering over me.

"Pretty, pretty thing!"

"Why are you hiding from us?"

"Have mercy and give us a taste."

They were Amalekites, known for their cruelty to women and strangers. I cowered from them and they began to laugh. One of the men squatted down and touched my breast.

Though my ankle burned with pain, I flew like a small mouse being chased by a hawk. I turned toward the camp to hide in the swarm of people. As I lost myself in the crowd, I slowed down to catch my breath and began to look around. Many men sat in groups talking. A group of women gathered near the altar where cooking pots stood ready to boil the kids in milk. Some called out for me to join them. I ran from their voices as if Father's knives chased me.

The tents thinned out and I reached the edge of a desolate black plain. A man stood just ahead of me, his face hidden in a long head scarf. The setting sun cast shadows around him. He wore a long black kuttoneh and a yellow belt. His feet seemed to hover just above the ground.

I cried out and turned to run from him, but my ankle gave way and I fell. I begged the Goddess to save me this time. I called upon Sinn to have mercy on me. Then I rolled into a ball so tight that no man could invade me. And even when I knew I was safe from the demon, when people of my own clan gathered above me and called my name, I did not dare move.

At last I felt a familiar hand upon my shoulder.

"Tzipporah?" Moses whispered.

Tears of relief flooded my face. I sat up. I looked into his beautiful eyes and thickening black beard. The Goddess had heard my distress and sent him to rescue me.

My wet eyes filled with all the love I felt for the Goddess. She wanted me to give myself to this man, here on Sinn's own hallowed ground.

Moses carried me to our tent on the other side of the camp. He laid me down and stroked me with the tenderness of a ewe licking her newborn lamb. He touched me everywhere until I yearned to be one with him. My body ached from the pleasure he gave me.

Later that night, after the sacrifice of the bull and the goats, Moses returned to me in the tent. I knew from his wet clothes and damp beard that he had washed himself after helping Father. I could still smell the blood on his hands. I kissed them anyway.

ELEVEN

Tzipporah

THE day after the sacrifices, Father and Moses broke up the altar. Father blessed the pilgrims in the name of Sinn and prepared to depart with them. Moses and I remained to keep the sacred flock in the cool green uplands of Midyan as was our custom during the hottest months. Here, in the shadow of Sinn's mountain, I came to know happiness.

During the day I watched the flock while Moses explored. On his wanderings he gathered ripe figs, sweet dates, and almonds. In the evening he laid these offerings before me and described all the wonders he had beheld—caves and streams, white oryx and gazelles, wildflowers and sand dunes. My pleasure in these tales became his delight. Sometimes it seemed as if he sought these sights for no other reason than to tell me of them.

Even after a long day of walking and climbing, the lust of ten men burned in the loins of my lord. His thirst seemed unquenchable. Sometimes he laid his head upon my lap and let me stroke his hair. Sometimes his lips flew over my face and arms. But it always ended the same. He taught my flesh to yearn.

He called me a wild bird, but I soon grew tame for him. As dawn brings the glow of light upon the world, so did the darkness of spirit begin to lift. My night demon fled and returned no more. In Moses I found my missing self. He made me whole again.

I believed that our love erased the past and that each day must be our only future. Every evening when I sang hymns to the Goddess, Moses told me my voice was the most beautiful he had ever heard and that I brought him more peace than he had ever known. I smiled upon my beloved and imagined that he wanted nothing more in this life than to wake each morning with me at his side.

I should have noticed the fire that smoldered in his eyes. I should have felt the restlessness that pushed him to wander. I should have heard the longing that sometimes carved a hollowness in his voice.

But my heart admitted only what it wanted to know.

For many weeks fear and sorrow became strangers. But one evening Moses did not return. I prayed to the Goddess. I wept. I wandered among the sheep and goats but found no comfort.

The long night passed. At first light a thick mist rose over the land. I stood on the edge of the valley near our tent, more alone than I had ever been in all my life. Though I remained as still as a stone altar, my heart pounded with more force than Baal Zephon's own thunder.

I saw serpents and scorpions and vultures swirling in the murky shadows. Then at last the mist parted and a man emerged.

I cried out with relief and joy. I ran to him and threw myself into his arms. After a moment Moses confessed that he had climbed the forbidden mountain. He had not turned back soon enough before sunset. When he could not find his way in the cloudy, moonless sky, he had taken shelter beneath an almond tree and waited for morning.

I felt my face grow pale as he spoke. He had taunted Baal Zephon by entering the sea without a sacrifice. Now he had trespassed upon Sinn's sacred ground. How could one man tempt the anger of our most powerful gods without punishment?

"You are under the protection of some godly being," I whispered. "I thank him for returning you unharmed."

Moses smiled and shook his head. "No god takes such an interest in me."

"You must believe it," I insisted. "One day your god will reveal himself to you. When he calls, you must be ready to answer."

His lips fell open with surprise and his eyes turned upon me with fear. "How can you know?"

I had no good answer. "I know only what I feel."

I watched his love for me flood back into his eyes. He brushed his fingertips on my lips. He felt my face like a blind man. He touched my neck and my hair. He took me into the tent and removed our garments that we might feel our bodies become one at every point.

Later, we sat under a tamarisk tree to watch the flock. I saw that something troubled him. I stroked his arm and a fleeting smile broke through his furrowed brow. He laid his head in my lap. He closed his eyes to rest. But I saw that he struggled in his heart and could find no peace.

He did not move for a long time. At last he sat up to speak.

"When I fled Egypt, I told myself to forget the past."

Fled? I should not have been surprised. I should have guessed that a man who appears with no more than a thin garment on his back and nothing in his hands must be a fugitive. But I did not care. Whatever he once was, whatever he had done, I loved him now.

"I will never ask you to remember it," I promised.

Moses took my hand and gazed upon me with a tender eye. "You see too much for me to hide."

"I see only you," I whispered.

"You see within. I have tried to forget. But the memories crush me."

"Then ease your heart and speak," I urged.

"My tongue is heavy."

"Your voice is soothing to me, like a gentle sea washing over the sand."

He squeezed my hand. He took a deep breath and began the story of his life.

He told me of his people and his beloved sister Miryam. He spoke of the princess who had raised him, how he had come to be burned on his mouth, his training as a military man, and his favor in the eyes of the pharaoh. He described prince Merenptah, who had fed his ravenous jealousy with a baseless suspicion that Moses plotted to usurp the throne. In words more painful and halting than usual, my beloved confessed that during his last hours in Egypt he had killed a man for beating a laborer. The princess had warned him that Merenptah planned to use this as a pretext for arrest and execution. Moses had fled without a word of farewell to his family. He had followed the southern trade route out of Egypt. Ten days later he had rescued me at the well.

When at last his lips grew still, the sun hung low in the sky. He turned his piercing eyes upon me as if to ask whether I saw a different man.

I studied his handsome face. Once he had lived as a prince. He had commanded armies and enjoyed the pharaoh's favor. Everyone had known him to be destined for greatness. Now he sat in the fragrant grasses of Midyan with my hand in his. I loved him no less; I could not love him more.

I laid my hand upon his. "I am sure your sister understands. I am sure she did not want you to risk your life or hers for a final word."

His brow relaxed and his eyes softened. I rejoiced that I could ease his heart.

He took me in his arms. "One day you and she will embrace as sisters."

"May the gods will it so," I replied. But I would have stopped time itself to live in that moment forever.

I could not prevent the changing of the seasons. The days grew cool and the soaking rains fell over the land. Father expected us back in camp. And so, after five moons with only ourselves for company, we returned to the Madyan Oasis.

During daylight I shared Moses with others, but at night he belonged to me alone. Though Father favored his company over that of all other men in the camp, Moses walked with his eyes cast down and spoke little. If men came to him with complaints about Father's judgment, or to seek advice before presenting a dispute to Father, Moses shrugged and insisted that he was only a simple shepherd. He helped with labor whenever asked, clearing terraces for planting, skinning a sheep, finding a stray animal. He gave his boundless energy and strength with generosity to whoever needed him. But he never initiated these efforts or suggested any improvements. He seemed content to follow.

Moses did not hold himself over me in the way that some men ruled their women. As long as I honored Father's rules, he gave me leave to do what I pleased. But I continued my secret worship of the Goddess. I no longer dared to enter the cave lest ugly memories take possession of me once again. But I placed an offering bowl on the ground beneath the cave, against the rocky face of the escarpment. I prayed for the day when I might chant to Her again. The Goddess urged patience. She told me I would know when the time for Her return drew near. I left Her many offerings outside the cave, but Her answer never changed.

The coldest period of the year passed and the period of warm rains came. When warmer nights brought fog, the earth spirits danced in the gullies and over the jagged rocks. I heard them flee from me when I fetched the water in the early morning. Moses laughed when I told him. He insisted it was only the wind whistling over the rocks.

Later I asked the spirits to forgive him. "He still knows little of our land," I said.

The woody plants and grasses grew strong. Flowers bloomed—vibrant pinks and yellows burst from the black earth. So too did new life gather in my womb.

As lambing time approached only the Goddess knew what lay beneath my kuttoneh; I hid the truth lest a demon try to snatch the child away. Each day I prayed to the Goddess for Her protection. I prayed that my baby would be born healthy and bring joy to his father.

The first three ewes gave birth with no trouble. Moses and I watched as they moved apart from the flock and circled in a grassy area. They began to complain and settled down on the ground. After their lambs emerged, they bit the cords and licked the little creatures clean. The lambs latched on to a teat right away.

Moses expressed surprise at the ease with which the mothers brought their offspring into the world.

"For women as with ewes, after the first it becomes easier," I explained.

He took a lock of my hair and wound it around his finger. My spine tingled with pleasure.

"May your first be as if it is your second," he said. "May it be a son."

My face grew hot and my eyes stung.

He laughed at what he supposed to be surprise. More words stumbled from his mouth. "Even a blind man can tell when his woman is with child."

I stared at his joy. He knew I carried a child, but he knew nothing. I could only pretend to be the woman he imagined.

Early the next morning, as the first light crept over the grey granite hills on the east side of the escarpment, Father summoned me. One of the ewes lay in distress with a stalled delivery.

I stopped in Father's tent to take a knife, a jug of olive oil, and a thin stick I used to clear the nostrils of a newborn lamb or kid. If the lamb died in partial delivery, I would need to cut off the head and pull the rest of the body from the mother, limb by limb. Over the years I had done this bloody, terrible job a number of times. On each occasion the mother had survived to give birth in the next season.

Though I knew what to expect, my heart tore when I reached the ewe and saw her lamb's swollen head protruding from the birth passage. The creature's dull eyes bulged and its head hung like a wilted flower. The mother whimpered with pain. I prayed to the Goddess to save the lamb and be merciful to the ewe.

Father held a torch, fashioned from slow-burning rimt wood. I motioned for him to stand close. I wiped the lamb's head with the hem of my kuttoneh and probed with two fingers around her neck. I felt a faint pulse.

"Come help me," I called to Moses, who hung back behind Father. "Can you lift her hind legs off the ground and tilt her forward?"

He did as I asked with such ease that the ewe might have weighed no more than a jug of water. I poured oil into the hollows of my hands and spread it over my fingers and forearms. Then I slid my right hand through the birth canal and into the ewe's womb. As I worked I hummed a hymn to the Goddess. If I saved the lamb Father would not object.

"Tilt her to the left," I ordered. Again Moses followed my direction without complaint or question. I found the lamb's left knee, bent and locked against the pelvis. Over the next minutes I eased the leg further back into the womb and worked the hoof through the birth opening next to the head. Dawn began to climb over the horizon.

"Shift her to the other side." I took a deep breath. Sweat drenched my head and garment like a soaking rain.

The ewe began pushing again and I gave her gentle assistance with my hand around the lamb's neck and leg. A dark, wet animal emerged into my arms. I held the lamb's back legs up over my head and gave her a little shake. Still she did not breathe. I lay her on the ground, wiped her face, and probed her nostrils with the stick. Fluid poured out and she sneezed. I cleared the nostrils once more and the lamb lifted her head.

As the mother came to lick her baby clean, I felt my lord gazing upon me. Covered in blood and fluid from the lamb's delivery, large with my own child, I was not a delight to the eye. But when I looked up at him, his expression filled with wonder and admiration. He bowed to me.

"You have saved a life." Moses turned to Father. "I did not know her great skill."

Father nodded. "She learned from me and her grandmother, but surpassed us both at a young age."

A cloud passed over my lord's eyes and he put his arm around my shoulders as if to shelter me. He led me to the well in silence.

Moses poured water over my hands and arms. He soaked the front of my kuttoneh and tried to scrub away the stains by rubbing the cloth. As he worked, he promised to find another garment for me so I might have a clean one ready at all times. Even my father, high priest of Midyan, did not own two garments made of wool. But Moses spoke with such kindness that I did not wish to expose the foolishness of his words.

After he finished washing me, Moses doused his own hands and face with water. He bent his head and exposed his neck, flushed red.

I reached out to touch the hot skin. I did not know what troubled him.

He raised his head to look at me. "How could he send you away? You who have such a gift."

I turned from him and began walking back toward camp. But he laid a hand on my shoulder to stop me.

"Explain what I can not see," he insisted.

I felt big with the child and weary in all my bones.

"I am not what you imagine me to be," I replied.

"You are a woman who renews life." He put his arms around me.

My face grew red with shame and sorrow. He had told me everything about his past. I had told him nothing. "Father said no other would have me," I whispered. "Not only for my witch's eyes, but before I went to the temple…"

I broke off. His eyes looked with such tenderness upon me. "A man took me by force."

I said no more. I could not tell him the rest.

As the day wore on I felt the baby drop low in my pelvis. Moses sensed my discomfort. At twilight I insisted that he leave me in the tent to rest while he kept watch over the new lambs with Father. I promised that nothing would happen until morning and asked that he tell no one so I could rest without the women hovering near me.

The full moon rose so bright that I did not need a torch to see. I took

Father's small knife from his tent and made my way toward the cave without fear. I knew the Goddess looked after me with a loving eye. I imagined myself a shadow in the cool light, an earth spirit flitting over the escarpment.

When I reached the rocky wall below the cave I lay down in the dust. I began the opening chant to the Goddess as I used to when a woman lay in the early stages of labor. Pleased with my voice, She called back to me. I floated up like a seed borne on the wind. The stars came down from the sky.

The waters rushed through me. I chanted with each wave of pain until a cry rose in my throat. Her sweet voice came to comfort me.

Tzipporah, Tzipporah.

You will make My star burn bright.

I felt Her arms embrace me. Her smile warmed my blood. At dawn I squatted to push out the baby.

I named my son Shalim after Her son. The Goddess sang to me with joy and gratitude for my devotion. I felt Her voice remain inside my own. I cut his cord with Father's knife and wrapped him in my veil. I promised Her an offering of sweet cakes as soon as I could prepare them. I promised Her my continued devotion. I promised to return Her to the women of Midyan.

I rested with the baby cradled against my breast. Whenever I looked down upon him I saw his father in his beautiful face, so tiny and so perfect. I told the baby how much I loved him. I sang a song about a bird rising through the heavens to the golden throne of the Goddess Herself. I closed my eyes.

When I awoke, the sun sat high in the heavens. I knew that Moses and Father must be looking for me. I tried to move with speed, but the baby grew heavy in my arms and my legs lasted only a few steps, to the well.

Several of my sisters soon found me, and while Seri ran for Moses the others tried to take the baby from me to wash him. I clung to him as if to my own life.

Moses did not come to me in anger, as I had feared. Instead he bowed with reverence before me and kissed his son. When Father appeared, Moses took the boy and raised him high over his head. I cried out. Moses laughed and returned him to my arms.

"I name him Gershom—driven here." Moses announced. "For I was driven here and Yitro welcomed me as a son."

No one told him that by our custom women alone named the children of their womb. But his heart overflowed with such joy that I could not object.

TWELVE

Tzipporah

MY son grew to be strong and beautiful like his father. He roamed the camp with the other children of the clan and came to be a favorite with all my sisters. Each time I looked upon Gershom my overwhelming love for him recalled my mother's love for me.

Moses had a deep well of patience for Gershom and the boy brought a soft light to his eye. As Gershom grew older he often stayed near his father. When I saw the two together hand in hand my heart overflowed with happiness.

My lord's devotion to me continued steadfast and unwavering. Our passion did not fade. He came to me with the thirst of a man who had crossed the great desert. Desire for him burned inside me like lightning on the escarpment. After he had spent himself upon me, he laid his head between my breasts as I sang a wordless tune to soothe his spirit. His eyes grew gentle and tender. He whispered endearments, he pulled me close, he slept in my arms.

Our only sadness was that I did not conceive another child. Even before I weaned Gershom, Moses wanted another son. I continued to implore the Goddess, yet for five years after Gershom's birth my womb remained empty.

During this time the rhythm of our lives remained unchanged. We looked after the flock near Father's camp during the cooler months; in the dry season we moved to the Valley of Gaw in the shadow of the mountain of Sinn.

While we remained in camp I often found Moses occupied with something other than the sheep. If a task demanded strength or cleverness the men called upon him first. He never shirked a request for help. Soon my kinsmen saw that they could ask great feats of him—digging wells, moving boulders, binding broken limbs, mending weapons. When he sat up late with Father he carved throw sticks for all the children in camp. When he hunted with the men he always gave part of his portion to widows who had no brothers to provide for them. Everyone came to admire my lord.

I hid my knowledge of his past with my own secrets. But when the men went out to hunt or to track down a thief, my lord's great skills did not go unnoticed. They often asked him to be their leader on an expedition. He always refused. "I am but a stranger among you," he would say, though everyone had long since forgotten that he had come to us from Egypt.

As the years passed, Midyanite men began to forsake their small cultivated plots, their flocks, their pottery workshops, and even their hunting expeditions in favor of escorting caravans along the trade routes through our territory. The demand for frankincense and myrrh continued to grow and our clay and metalwork also found favor with the people of the north—Egyptians, Canaanites, and Amorites. "Should we sit idle while others have free use of the routes that pass through our land?" they argued. Father did not object. Soon no trader could pass through Midyan without purchasing protection from one of the local clansmen. Some of my kin joined the caravaners as traders and grew richer each year. None was more successful than Hovav, son of Father's eldest sister and lord of my sister Seri.

Hovav traveled the deserts and the mountains, the coastal plains and the wadis, trading pottery from Qurayyah and knives from Dophka. He went as far south as Tumala and as far north as Jerash. He returned with stories of other clans, the strong army of the Egyptians, and the strange dress of the Hittites. He spoke of the wondrous sights to behold in the settlements of the north, beyond the temple of the storm god Baal Zephon at the tip of the Red Sea—which he said the people of the north called the Reed Sea because of the reeds that grow at the edge of the salty water.

Hovav brought Seri many fine things—golden rings for her ears, a soft pillow for her head, a pair of leather sandals, a basket large enough to hold an infant, an alabaster jar with a sweet-smelling ointment. One day he returned from the land of Egypt with a thin, open robe made from a fabric called linen, the color of the sky on a clear morning. We had never seen anything so beautiful. Seri walked through the camp in her robe for all to admire. When she came to Moses and Father, who stood talking near the fire circle, Father marveled at the fine fabric, but Moses offered no more than a thin smile. Seri and Hovav appeared disappointed. I alone knew that such a garment must have been commonplace among the riches of the court where he spent his childhood and youth.

"What news of Egypt?" Moses asked Hovav.

"Many big changes!" Hovav spoke in a voice so loud that even those standing some distance away could hear him. People drew closer. Hovav loved an audience.

"The Pharaoh Rameses has passed from this world. They say he ruled more than sixty years and now he is a god. His son Merenptah rules the land and his own sister Istnofret is his first queen."

Throughout Hovav's explanation I watched my lord's face. I saw the fire kindle in his eyes.

"What of the foreigners in the land?" Moses's voice did not waver.

Hovav pursed his lips as he searched his memory.

"They say the alien residents are pressed into more labor than ever before. This pharaoh builds with greater extravagance than his father."

Moses bowed to Hovav and excused himself from the group. He disappeared from my sight before I could follow. I searched the wells, the crop terraces, and the tents of all my cousins and sisters. When I could not find him anywhere in camp I knew that he did not wish to share this burden with me. As the afternoon turned into evening, a great sadness settled into my heart.

He returned to our tent late that night and fell asleep in my arms without speaking. I begged the Goddess to help me bring him relief.

Soon after Hovav's news we returned to the mountain of Sinn for the yearly sacrifices. When Father and the other pilgrims departed from the mountain, Moses began his daily wandering. He often took Gershom, who rode on his father's shoulders. They came home with colorful stones and tales of brown-and-black-striped sand vipers and shiny blue lizards. The boy was happier with his father than with me and the sheep. But when Moses found himself drawn to the mountain, he left Gershom behind.

One cool morning, among our last in the Valley of Gaw for that year, Moses set off without Gershom. The boy and I spent the morning counting the sheep and goats. We milked a goat whose kids had run straight to pasture. After we drank our fill, I brought the skin to the tent. As I set it down on a cool corner I felt the earth spin beneath my feet. In the darkness behind my eyes I saw a pillar of fire shoot into the heavens.

Afraid, I ran from the tent to look for my son. Smoke came to my nostrils on the air from a faraway place. I saw Gershom in the valley, wandering among the sheep and goats. Though he appeared to be safe, I called him to me.

We huddled the rest of that day in the shadow of the tent. As the sun moved across the sky, my fears increased. I imagined many terrible things. The smoke came from a hostile band of men who had attacked Moses and killed him. They would soon find us, slaughter our son, and seize me and the flock for spoil. Or perhaps a leopard had torn the flesh from his legs. Maybe he had eaten a poison root, or drunk from a contaminated pool. Our clan lost men to such fates every year.

When the evening star appeared in the pink sky I gave Gershom some milk and told him to rest while we waited for his father to return. I crouched in the entrance of the tent to watch and pray.

Moses returned as twilight faded into night. I saw him rise up from the dark valley like a spirit crossing from one world into the next.

I rose to greet him, my feet light with joy.

"Thank the gods you are safe!" I called out.

He did not reply. He did not even appear to see me but kept his eyes focused on a place beyond our tent, past the pilgrim campsite into the black wilderness of Sinn.

Had a demon sucked away his spirit? As he drew closer I saw that his face radiated with a light as painful to look at as the sun. I raised my hands to shake his strong shoulders, to break the spell that held him. Instead, I embraced him. I pressed my flesh tight against his and hoped that the man who loved me would return.

He pulled away.

"Did you see a fire?" I asked.

Moses cast a stranger's eyes upon my face and began to speak. The words came out with even more difficulty than usual.

"He called me from the flames. The fire burned inside a bush and yet the branches were not consumed."

"Who called you?" I whispered. My heart shrank with fear and dread.

"My God. The God of my father, the God of my ancestors Avraham, Yitzhak, and Yaakov. Yahveh is His name."

"He called you on Sinn's mountain?"

Moses nodded. "It is Yahveh's sacred mountain now."

His voice came to me like an echo between the high granite cliffs. He turned his face upward and stared into the night. Whatever visions filled his eyes passed before me as if I was blind. I felt alone.

He stood outside the tent and continued to watch the heavens. His body began to tremble, but when I brought a skin to wrap around his shoulders he dismissed it with an irritated shrug. I sat nearby in the uneasy silence and waited.

I waited for his spirit to return to him. I waited for a loving word or a gesture of affection. I waited for him to explain.

I waited while the stars moved across the sky, while the moon slipped behind the red mountains of the west and streaks of pale blue appeared in the east. When at last he spoke, I still did not know him.

"Who am I that I should bring the Children of Israel out of Egypt? Words stumble from my lips. They do not know me as one of their own. No one will follow me."

"Your God asked you to do this thing?" I whispered.

Moses turned to me. In the early morning shadows I did not recognize his face.

"Miryam knew I would be summoned. You knew."

I shook my head. I knew nothing. Once, long ago, I had sensed that his destiny had not yet called him. But season upon season of our love had buried my premonition in a long-forgotten corner of my heart. I would have left it there forever, hidden among the bones and dust.

He said no more. But as we lay down in each other's arms it seemed that we did so for the last time. I held back the flood of my tears until he slept.

I left my lord and son asleep in the tent and went to tend the flock. Soon Gershom came running to me across the valley. His short legs could not carry him fast enough.

"Father is asking for you! He says to hurry!"

I scooped up my son and rushed back toward the tent. Moses met us halfway.

"We leave at once!" he announced. His eyes blazed, his nostrils flared, his hands quivered.

Fear flooded my being. I did not recognize this madman.

Moses seemed to sense my hesitation. He looked down at me with a glimmer of the old tenderness in his eyes.

"Come." He held out his hand. "Your sister in Egypt waits. She will be dearer to you than those of your own blood."

In the days and nights that passed on the journey back to the Madyan

Oasis, my eyes remained fixed on Moses with fear and fascination. I watched his firm step, his proud posture, his resolute jaw, the tight grip of his hand on a staff that he had brought down from the mountain. All his boundless energy seemed directed to one purpose. When he spoke of his mission to bring the Israelites out of Egypt, his lips healed and the words flowed like water. He did not touch me. He did not lift his son upon his shoulders. Day by day he grew more distant.

We came to the sea on the afternoon of the fifth day. The sun hung low in the sky. We looked down from the cliff and watched bands of red ripple across the water. Moses pointed to the mountains in the distance.

"Egypt," he said.

"Across the water?"

"We will reach it around the water's edge to the north."

I continued to stare. Somewhere beyond those mountains lay my lord's destiny. But what of my own mission? When I gave birth to Gershom, the Goddess had asked me to make Her star bright. For five years I had waited to return the women of Midyan to Her worship. Yet nothing had changed. She had sent no sign for me to resume birth chanting or to lead the women in evening prayers; Father remained set against Her. And now Moses planned to take us far away to serve his God.

When would Her time come?

We reached the oasis of Madyan just before the evening meal. Father expressed surprise at our early return but asked for no explanation as he embraced Moses and welcomed him home. Moses took the place of honor next to Father and spoke little. During the meal I spied on my lord from the women's side of the tent. I saw by his furrowed brow that he doubted himself. In the darkest corner of my heart I hoped that this would put an end to his plans. Even then I knew that his God asked too much of him.

Gershom ran off to spend the night with his cousins. I remained in the tent and listened to all that passed between my father and Moses after the other men left.

"You have returned early for a reason," Father began.

Moses took a moment to reply. When he spoke I heard no uncertainty in his labored words.

"I owe you my allegiance, Yitro. Yet news from Egypt has turned my eyes to the north. I wish to see how my brethren fare. I will return in two moons or three."

He said nothing of his encounter on the mountain, nothing of his people's God, nothing of his true mission.

Father sighed. "We will look for you again before lambing time. May the gods protect you."

"I leave the woman and her son in your care."

My chest grew tight. *Leave me? Leave me alone in Midyan?* My heart tore. Darkness fell over my eyes. For six years we had clung to each other. Did his God wish to rip us apart?

Moses kissed my father. I ran after him as he left the tent. I fell at his feet.

"What have I done that you should cast me off?" I wept. "What have I done?"

Moses looked down at me with a stern expression. "I do not know the situation in Egypt. I will not risk the child's life."

"Then take me," I begged. "Do not leave me in this place."

"You would abandon your own son?" A spark of anger flew from his eyes.

"You are abandoning us both!" I cried.

He offered no comforting touch, no tender words. He drew himself up like a proud warrior.

"You have told Father nothing of the truth," I hissed. "Has your God made you less than a man of honor?"

"*You* object?" Moses whirled around to me. A grim expression distorted his beautiful face. "You who have nothing but loathing for your father? You who never speak a word to him?"

His unexpected rebuke stung like the tail of a scorpion. I felt my face grow pale as if all my blood had drained away. So many things I had not told him. And he had spoken of his life in Egypt only once. For six years we had lived together as if the past did not exist. Now we did not know each other.

"You do not understand," I whispered.

He did not seem to hear me. My heart stood still.

Father gave Moses a donkey for the journey, two warm lambskins, and some clay bowls to trade for other supplies. Moses packed these things with our tent, a cooking pot, a water jug, a skin bag with dates, and another with clotted goat's milk. I stayed inside Father's tent and prayed to the Goddess.

Do not let his God take him away from me! Do not let him go without me! Great Goddess, I beg You, by all You hold sacred, restore us to each other.

My prayers proved useless. Moses left without even a word of farewell.

When my sisters came to begin the day's cooking, I fled the tent for the animal pen. But the flock, too, had gone. Father had taken them to graze without me. I climbed the escarpment to scan the track below for signs of Moses. It was too late. He had left soon after dawn and now midday approached. How long before he returned?

What if he never returned?

I could not endure a life without him. My weakened spirit was sure to lure the demons forth to take possession of me. Already I felt their claws sinking into my flesh. I heard their laughter deep inside my skull.

The Goddess had filled my heart with love for Moses. She had cast my destiny with his. I had no choice—I must take my son and follow his father. I must face his past to save our future. However great his anger at my disobedience, he could not send me back. I would find a way to help him with his mission. My heart grew light with relief.

During the hottest hours of midday, while Father sat in a far wadi with the flock and everyone else slept, I walked through the camp gathering all that I needed. I took two water skins, a basket with four handfuls of almonds, a flint box, a sheepskin, and the smallest of father's sacrificial knives. I pulled a dark veil over my head and wrapped it around my face so that only my eyes showed. Then I gathered my son from a sleeping mat in Seri's tent, purchasing his silence with a date cake.

We followed my lord's tracks north throughout the rest of the afternoon and into the early evening. As the sun set I saw light from the night encampment in Saraf.

Saraf had no well or even a shallow drinking pool. But many traders camped here because of the junction at Haql, about half a day north. At Haql the route from the east through Qurayyah crossed with the north-south track through Midyan. Many traders from the south, the land of frankincense and myrrh, camped in Saraf. From Haql they could continue north and east to trade their wares in Egypt or west and north to Moav and Canaan.

All the tents—perhaps fifteen—sat pitched in a rough circle around the fire ring. I heard the laughter of men and knew that they were gathered by the fire for company. I held Gershom's hand tight and skirted the outer edge of the tents. I did not want to walk through the camp and reveal myself. If my lord was not among these men I would be in great danger.

Gershom began to complain of the cold. I led him to a rocky area beyond the tents and sat on the ground behind a boulder. I took him on my lap and wrapped the sheepskin around us. While Gershom dozed, I waited for the men to sleep.

I saw night demons swirling in the darkness around us like the thin pink threads of sheep intestines pulled hand over hand from a slaughtered carcass. My heart flung itself against my chest and took the breath from me. Sweat pooled on my forehead, under my arms, in the small of my back. My limbs grew rigid and my eyelids would not close.

I pulled out the flint knife for protection and looked up toward the sky. The star that Moses called Canopus, harbinger of the soaking rains, sat on the horizon. This was the time to gather large quantities of ripened dates, to pull the thickened root vegetables, to prepare for the coldest months, to lead the rams to the ewes. Yet I journeyed far from all that into a strange land where my lord planned to rescue an entire people from the tyranny of the most powerful ruler in the world at the behest of a God who had spoken to him only once.

I closed my eyes from weariness. As I slept, doubt circled me like a wolf with red eyes and an empty stomach. I heard the pads of his paws caress the stones and felt the tension mounting in his jaw. I fled from the creature toward the other tents with the knife in my hand. A man appeared in the hollow of an open door flap, his teeth whiter than the stars above. He untied the yellow belt around his waist and moved to strangle me with it. I lifted the knife above my head but did not have the strength to bring it down upon him.

I cried out as I woke. Gershom's eyes flew open and the sight of the knife in my hand drew a cry from him too. I soothed him with little kisses on his face and held him in my trembling arms.

"Shhh," I crooned. "Everyone else is asleep. Let us go find your father."

We rose and I tucked the sheepskin under my arm. I kept the knife in one hand and squeezed Gershom's fingers with the other.

The camp lay silent. A half moon hung bright in the sky and lit our way as we wandered from one tent to the next. At last we came upon our donkey tied to the stake beside one of the tents.

"Father is inside," I whispered to Gershom. My heart pounded. How would I explain my disobedience?

I can not live without you.

The Moses I loved would hold me close.

The Moses I loved would not have left me in Yitro's charge.

I would have to begin again with this new Moses, as he had begun with me.

I lifted the tent flap and Gershom ran in. "Father! Father!" he called out. I smiled until my son's shriek pierced the silent night.

Moses lay shaking in the grip of a monstrous two-headed puff adder. The creature's black and orange scales shimmered in the moonlight. One mouth swallowed my lord's head, arms, torso, and hips. The other swallowed his feet and legs. Only his male parts remained exposed.

At once I saw what I must do, what his God asked of me.

"Stay in the corner!" I called out to Gershom. I grasped my lord's foreskin and pulled it as far down as it would go. Pinching it between my thumb and finger, I sliced off the flesh that hid the tip of the organ beneath. As blood flowed over my hands, the snake released his legs. Yet even as the creature's other head still held Moses's head and torso, the first head slithered toward my cowering son. I beat off the adder with my bare feet and lifted Gershom's kuttoneh. I fought back the vomit that rose in my throat. The boy screamed. "Be still!" I begged him, but he could not. I folded his arms over his chest and sat on them.

His foreskin had not yet separated. And so I peeled it back with my own hands and cut him. I dabbed the blood from my knife on to his thigh and on to the thigh of his father.

Moses could not walk among his people as one of them if he and his son remained uncircumcised.Once Miryam had saved his life by concealing his identity. On this night I saved him by revealing it.

"Now you are both protected by the blood of circumcision!" I proclaimed. "May you serve your God Yahveh and bring honor to His people."

The adder shrank into a worm and then shriveled into a thin stick. My son continued to scream inside the hollows of my ears. Moses rose as I broke the stick into a hundred pieces. Each one gouged my flesh with splinters. I begged him to cut off cut my hands. He took me in his arms and kissed them instead.

"You have made me pure for Yahveh," he whispered. "I will never leave you again."

PART

III

EGYPT

THIRTEEN

Miryam

W HEN Moses fled, my heart withered. The world grew dark and sour. I lived without purpose, without hope, without God.

How did I survive?

I sealed my hollow chest with iron doors. I closed my ears to the grief of others lest it remind me of my own. When I looked upon another's joy I saw only imperfections.

My market friends shrank from the bitterness of a woman who had given up the love of a good man for nothing. My family came to fear my harsh voice and exacting ways. None dared express their disappointment in the prophecy I had brought from God. I did not permit myself to recall it. I flinched whenever the name of Moses came to their lips until it came no more.

I did not like what I became. But I could not help myself.

How did I survive?

By the work of my hands.

I cooked. I cleaned. I tended Elisheva when she bore her children. I helped her raise them. I cared for sick parents. I buried them. I fed the poor. I assisted Aharon in the management of the vineyard.

The sockets of my eyes grew dry from tears that never came.

In the seventh year after Moses left, Istnofret's brother Merenptah came to the throne. As was customary, he gave amnesty to those who had committed crimes under the previous reign. But he forsook all other mercies. He called the Children of Israel to build for him long before they finished the first harvest. He could not wait to glorify his name with magnificent temples and feasting halls. Like his father he continued the exemption for vintners whose wine pleased him. But he did not extend this privilege to those who labored in the vineyards. When the men went to work for Pharaoh, the women of Israel gathered in the crops of the fields. Elisheva and I helped Aharon with the grape harvest.

I found the work dirty and unpleasant. The sun beat down on us. Sweat soiled my dress. Grapes stained my hands. Dust lodged between my sandals and toes. I longed to be back in my clean, cool house.

Elisheva saw my unhappy face across the row of vines. She threw a grape at me. When I objected she threw another.

"Shame!" I scolded my brother's wife. "You are the mother of four sons! You are a matron of the community!"

She threw her head back. She laughed like a young girl. Even at the age of thirty-six she remained pleasing to the eye. Aharon's lust for her had not faded. I slept in the room farthest from theirs so I would not hear them in the night.

"Let us enjoy this fine day!" Elisheva said. She turned to wave at her two younger sons, who ran up and down the rows of vines without restraint. At home I kept the boys in order. Here, in their father's vineyard, I did not interfere.

I frowned at Elisheva's exuberance, at her pleasures. I returned to my work without another word to her. She knew better than to try my patience further.

When the sun reached its zenith I asked Aharon's leave to return home with the little ones.

I called for Ithamar and Eleazar. I bribed them with promises of fresh figs. We departed hand in hand.

When we reached the house I told the boys to wash. After they ate their fruit, I sent them to their room to rest. I scrubbed myself. I changed into a clean sleeveless dress. Then I set to work on the evening meal. First I mixed dough for flat bread. I sliced figs to cook in wine with pistachio nuts. I made a stew of lamb, onions, dates, and the first pomegranates of the harvest. While the stew simmered in the courtyard I scrubbed the kitchen.

After I finished I stepped outside the courtyard gate to dump the dirty water into the canal. The sun grew low over the capital in the distance. Soon Aharon, Elisheva, and the two older boys, Nadav and Avihu, would be home for the evening meal. As I turned back to the house, I saw two figures leading a donkey laden with little more than a tent and a few baskets. Such poor desert dwellers often came begging in Goshen.

The bearded man carried a shepherd's staff. A young girl walked behind him. Both covered their heads with dark cloth that matched their shabby black sleeveless kuttonehs. Neither wore sandals or a cloak. When I looked closer I saw that a little boy rode on the donkey.

What could I give them? We had extra wheat meal and figs from the recent harvest. No doubt they would appreciate a watermelon. Aharon might part with one or two old kilts and long skirts. I had a cloak for the boy and some sandals the girl could grow into.

As they drew close enough for me to see their faces, the man raised his hand. He held himself in a familiar way.

My feet knew him before my eyes. I was already running when his name came to my lips. He broke away from his companions to meet me.

We held each other in a tight embrace. He towered over me as he had since the age of fifteen. I could feel his bones through the filthy rag he wore to cover himself.

"You have come back to me!" I said it over and over.

He pulled away to gaze into my eyes. His own blazed with fire. He held my hands. The words stumbled from his mouth with difficulty as they always had. "It is good to look upon you, Sister."

A thousand questions came to me. A thousand recriminations. A thousand words of relief. A thousand songs of jubilation. Everything became tangled in my throat.

Why did you leave? I longed to cry out. *What have you done these past years? Where have you been? Can you imagine how much I have suffered?*

"So many years," I whispered. "Not a word."

"This life was dead to me. I tried to build another."

I looked at his gaunt face, his weathered skin. "You were never dead to me," I said. Bitterness oozed at the edges of my voice.

Moses offered a sad smile. "Our parents?" he asked.

I bit my lip and shook my head.

He buried his face in his hands.

After a moment I broke the silence. "Aharon and Elisheva are in good health. They have four sons now. Ithamar was born after you left."

"This is my son." He pointed to the little boy on the donkey. The child wore a frayed black kuttoneh too wide and long for his thin body. His feet were bare. He looked as if he had never bathed in all his life.

Moses lifted him down. "His name is Gershom. He has seen six harvests."

My eyes widened with surprise. This boy, only a year younger than Aharon's round and smiling son Ithamar, looked no more than half his age. I gathered the neglected child in my arms. He smelled like animal dung. I would have to bathe and feed him at once.

I turned my eyes on Moses again. I felt my stiff lips curve up into a smile. Once Moses had been my whole life. Now my life had returned to me. My heart beat strong and steady in my chest. I wanted to run through the streets shouting with joy.

Through Istnofret I would help him regain his influence at court. God's prophecy would soon come to pass. I would give his son a mother's loving care. Soon my brother would have many more fine sons from his wife, the Princess Maat-Hor-Neferure.

"Your old tutor is now the pharaoh. Istnofret is his first queen."

A flush of anger spread over his face. A shadow darkened his heart. I could not believe my eyes.

"Imagine the influence you will..."

He raised his hand to cut me off. The shock, confusion, and pain after his flight rushed back to me. I recalled Istnofret's refusal to see me, to explain. Even the princess's messenger knew more than I. What I later learned from the marketplace gossips made no sense. Even after all these years I needed to know. I could not help bring God's prophecy to fruition if the truth remained hidden.

"What happened at court that day?" My voice sounded harsh to my own ears, too accusatory. I could not help myself. "Why did you leave without a word?"

Moses put his hand on my shoulder. "Later." He spoke in a firm yet quiet voice. The words came with more difficulty than I remembered. "We have much to discuss."

I felt a flicker of disappointment.

He motioned to the girl who hung behind him. As she stepped forward I decided she must be a servant or a nurse for the child. Her long, thick black hair shot out in matted tufts from her head. Patches of light brown skin showed through the streaks of dirt on her sinewy neck. Her feet, encrusted with mud and sand, looked like the hide of a hippopotamus. The skin on her face stretched tight over her skull. Her unusual eyes, large and blue as the sky in the dry season, stared at me without respite.

I grew uncomfortable under her gaze. What did she see?

"This is Tzipporah," my brother said.

The girl looked as if she awaited a greeting. I glanced at Moses. He also looked at me with expectation.

I put the child down. I stepped closer to the girl. She smelled like rancid meat.

"Welcome," I said. I could not bring myself to touch her. I did not know if she understood our language. "Have you traveled far?"

"From Midyan," she replied in a strange accent. "Nine days."

Her voice, low and sweet like the call of the hoopoe, surprised me.

"Tzipporah is the youngest daughter of Yitro, high priest of Midyan."

The girl kept staring as if she expected something more from me. Did she imagine I would be foolish enough to believe whatever story she had told Moses about her parentage? I knew that the daughters of priests dressed as well as any princess. They walked with great pride through the city. This girl appeared poorer than the poorest beggar I had ever seen.

I remembered how Moses had always taken the part of mistreated women. No doubt he rescued this girl from someone who had meant to do her harm. We could offer her food and clothing before sending her back to her people.

"I have found a home these seven years in Yitro's camp. He gave me his daughter." Moses slid his arm around the girl's waist and pressed his lips to the top of her head.

The words and gesture took my breath away. I looked from the boy to the woman. I refused to believe she was his mother. My brother deserved better for a stable servant. I could not believe that he had spent the years away from me with this filthy concubine. I could not believe that any priest would have such a daughter. What backward people he must have lived among!

Once Moses and I had walked through the land of Goshen together. Now I needed to have him to myself again, to talk of the future without the burdens of his exile.

The concubine followed Moses as he took his donkey to the stable. She tried to fill her water skin in the trough.

"No!" I cried out.

The woman startled and shrank away from the fouled water.

Moses laughed. He guided his concubine to our large water urns. Her big eyes grew even wider when he rolled away a lid to reveal the water within. She did not use the wooden drinking cup hanging from the urn. Instead she raised her skin with a questioning look to me. I nodded. She dipped it into the water. She called the boy to drink. But he clung to my leg. I carried him to the edge of the barrel. I showed him how to use the drinking cup.

"Look, Father!" he called out in an accent like his mother's. His delight in this small thing made me smile.

I led them inside. The concubine touched the walls as if she feared they might prick her. She stopped to feel the carpets and stare at the hangings of painted papyrus. I swelled with pride. I supposed our house was the finest she had ever seen. I did not imagine that it was the only house she had ever seen.

I served them some bread and juice of the citron sweetened with date sugar. Moses urged the concubine to drink, but she took only a little bread.

"The two boys are asleep upstairs," I said. "I will wake them to play with their cousin. Everyone else is at the vineyard. They will return soon. Would you like to wash?" I longed to see the old Moses—my Moses—with his clean-shaven skin and fine court garments.

Moses nodded.

"I will heat the water."

"Do not take the trouble," Moses said.

His formal words came to me as if to a stranger. It seemed that my heart sat in a chariot drawn by wild horses. One moment I knew exultation, the next moment dread. I wanted to shout in his ear. *I am Miryam, your beloved sister! Do not hold yourself aloof from me!*

"It is no trouble," I replied after a moment. "A man raised at court can not wash in cold water."

Moses shook his head. "I am no longer that man."

I heard only resignation in his voice. No regret, no determination to regain the influence he had once had. After all these years why did he come back if not to fulfill God's purpose? I studied his face. Did I still know him? I could not be sure.

"Why did you leave us?" My heart cried out with all the sorrow of the lonely years. "The death of one lowly foreman was nothing for the pharaoh's most favored general to fear. And Istnofret seemed so scared. What happened?"

Moses shook his head. "When Aharon comes home I will speak to you both."

I bit my lip. I glanced at the girl. Her strange large eyes remained fixed on me as if she could see through my skin.

Moses returned to the kitchen much cleaner after his bath. He wore the clothes I had put out for him—a linen kilt and an open robe. But he had not taken the time to use the shaving knife. With the beard, long hair, and hair on his chest, he still looked like a wild man of the desert.

I told myself to be patient. What did it matter if he waited to shave, even until tomorrow? He had returned to me, safe and whole. I fell into his arms.

I sent the concubine to the washing room with the hope that Moses and I might have a chance to speak alone. She stayed away for no more time than it took me to repeat how much I had missed him. She did not don the clean dress I had left for her. When she made no move to wash her son, I scooped him up. I announced that I would see to his bath at once.

While Moses and his concubine rested beneath a palm tree in the courtyard, I carried hot water into the tub. When I plunged the boy into the water he squealed with delight. I washed his hair and scrubbed his skin. He did not complain until I reached between his legs. He cried out and pulled away from me. When I looked closer I could make no sense of what I saw—a fresh circumcision wound. Our people performed this rite soon after birth. Others did it at the beginning of manhood or not at all. Why had they put him through such an ordeal before a long journey?

"Does it hurt?" I asked. "I have a soothing ointment."

The boy nodded. "Mother did it in the night," he said.

"Your *mother* did it?" I repeated with horror.

"To Father and to me."

Bile rose in my throat. "My God!" I muttered under my breath. What sort of woman could do such a thing?

I pressed my lips to the boy's head.

"In this house we will take good care of you," I promised.

I watched the joyous reunion between Moses and Aharon with great pleasure. All my worries and disappointments vanished as the two brothers embraced. Aharon cried. Elisheva danced around the courtyard with her sons. Of the four boys only the two eldest recalled their father's brother. I watched Moses greet each of his brother's sons. I felt proud of the boys as they stood before Moses. Were they not my sons too? I had raised them side by side with Elisheva. They looked upon me as a second mother.

The concubine hung back from all the commotion. When at last Moses introduced her, she did not move to join the group. My beloved, generous Elisheva stepped forward to throw her arms around the filthy woman, the strange woman who had circumcised her own son.

My brother had much to explain.

During our meal Moses showed no inclination to speak about himself or where he had been. He asked after our parents' passing. It took little time to tell of Father's short illness and death, and how Mother had followed him soon after. After that he resumed his habitual silence. The concubine neither ate nor spoke. I could not wait for the meal to end.

The moment everyone finished eating I sent the elder boys out of the room to take care of the younger ones. I called Elisheva aside. When I suggested that she do something about the concubine's hair, her face lit up with enthusiasm. I went to my kitchen cupboard for a jug of almond oil.

"Use as much as you need to comb it out." As I handed Elisheva the oil I leaned close to her ear. "See to her feet, her face, and all the rest of her," I whispered. "I want no lice in my house."

Elisheva returned to the table. She put her arm around the concubine's shoulders. She kissed her unwashed cheek. I looked away, unsettled by her easy intimacy with the woman.

"Let me show you our washing room," Elisheva said.

The concubine looked to Moses for guidance. He nodded.

When the two women left, Aharon and I both turned to Moses with expectation. He could no longer hold his silence.

"I have heard our people do not fare well under Merenptah," he said.

All my plans spilled forth from my mouth. "If you win back your position at court and your wife, you will hold much influence to ease the situation for us. Your wife is the pharaoh's sister. Your adoptive mother is queen now. They will not refuse your requests. Our people will be saved!"

I saw that Moses did not look with favor on my words. I leaned forward on the edge of my chair while I waited for him to explain.

"Our future is not in Egypt," he announced. His firm voice allowed no room for disagreement.

It seemed as if all my breath would rush out of me. For twenty generations our people had worked to build a home here. Was that not our Creator's plan? For what purpose had I been given the gift of revelation, if not to save our lives in Egypt?

"You always take things too far!" I cried. "With you as our leader we can lighten our burdens."

Aharon touched my arm to calm me. I brushed him away.

Moses took a breath. He touched the scar on his lips. He pulled at his long beard. Then he began to speak. "Sister, Egypt crushes the body and spirit of our people. It is you who taught me to love justice. We must take action."

"Why not work through the court rather than against it?" I asked.

"I fled because Merenptah wished me dead. He claimed that I plotted to usurp his throne. Istnofret's affection for me became a danger to her. I belong with my own people now."

I sat speechless before this revelation.

"But Egypt is a mighty power," Aharon said. "What can we do?"

"The God of our fathers came to me. He has seen the affliction of His children."

I looked into my brother's copper eyes. They glowed with the pure light I had seen at the hour of his birth. I could almost feel that light enter my heart again.

"This God came to you?" Aharon asked. He leaned toward our brother with excitement.

Moses nodded. "His name is Yahveh."

"His name?" I echoed. "He revealed His name?"

"Yahveh," Moses repeated.

I rose to my feet. I could not contain myself. The words that had remained buried in my heart for so long rushed out.

"This God came to me the year before your birth. He said our mother would have a son who would rescue our people. He showed me how to save you, with the basket. I did not tell you of the prophecy because I knew God would call you in His own time."

I paused for a breath. The years of sorrow filled my voice again. "After you left, I did not know what to do."

Moses took my trembling hand. His eyes grew moist. "Yahveh came to me two weeks ago on the mountain of the moon god Sinn in the wilderness of Midyan. Flames rose high from a bush that did not burn. I drew close. A voice called to me from within the fire."

"He came to me in light!" I exclaimed. "I saw it again in your birth room. We all saw it—me, Aharon, Elisheva." I looked to Aharon for confirmation.

Aharon nodded.

"What did He say on the mountain?" I asked.

Moses did not answer at once. It seemed that he took extra care in formulating his reply. When at last he spoke the words stumbled from his mouth with the usual difficulty. Resigned to patience, I sat down and folded my hands in my lap.

"He called on me to free our people. He will lead us to a spacious land—the land promised to our forefathers—where we will live with righteousness and justice in His name."

I looked around at my orderly kitchen as if I had never seen it before. I looked at my brother. How blind I had been! My kitchen, my cooking pots, my washing room—none of it mattered. The truth rose in me now like my own spirit. At last I understood. Our God, Yahveh, had called upon me to keep my brother safe. I had delivered him to the princess.

He had called upon me to teach my brother about justice. I had taught him about justice. He had called upon me to sacrifice my love for Nunn. I had made that sacrifice. He had called upon me to endure long years of uncertainty. I had endured. But never until this day had I understood what had begun in the olive grove—the birth of a new nation in a new land.

My face grew radiant with joy. I turned back to Moses.

"Will you join me?" he asked. "Will you help lead our people to freedom?"

I knelt at my brother's feet.

"I will stand by you until my last breath."

I heard a noise in the doorway. I turned to look. The woman Tzipporah appeared before us in a dress as blue as her eyes. Elisheva's necklace of lapis and gold beads hung around her neck. A cascade of black hair fell thick and smooth from her delicate head to her tiny waist. Her fresh young skin was the color of bee's honey. Her feet, too small to fit into my sandals or Elisheva's, remained bare. She was the most beautiful wild creature I had ever seen.

FOURTEEN

Miryam

I WANTED to take action at once. I did not see the value in long deliberation. While Aharon talked about summoning the elders to a meeting, while Moses planned to trick the pharaoh, I longed to spread Yahveh's message at once, that very evening.

"Why wait?" I interrupted my brothers with impatience. "Our course is clear. We have a message of hope. General Moses has returned. He was born an Israelite. Yahveh protected him at birth so he could lead us to the Promised Land. If we tell the people now they can begin their preparations for departure."

"We must first get the people to accept the plan to leave their homes," Aharon said.

"That will not be hard!" I felt the words dance off my tongue. "Our people do not wish to remain enslaved. Everyone will be eager to go."

Aharon laughed. "Not everyone will be as easy to convince as you."

Moses agreed. "We must tell them in stages. Begin with word of Yahveh and my return."

I frowned.

Aharon turned to me. "Consider the wisdom in this approach. From the time of your prophecy you knew to expect it. Others will be suspicious."

I forced myself to take a deep breath. "When do we tell them? When do we leave?"

Moses tugged on his beard. "Our men can not abandon the work sites without permission. Merenptah will send his armies after us."

This obstacle seemed impossible to overcome. "What can we do?"

Moses raised the corners of his lips in a slight smile. "We will seek his permission."

Moses told us his plan. In the morning Aharon and I were to spread word of his return among the Israelites. We would reveal the truth of his parentage. We would say that he came with a message from the God of our fathers. Aharon would request a gathering of the elders. Once Moses won their support he and the elders would petition Pharaoh for a seven-day leave to make a sacrifice in the wilderness—three days for the journey, one day for sacrifice, and three days to return. Just before our departure we would tell the people of our true destination and the glorious future that awaited us. We would flee to Midyan before the Egyptians realized that we did not intend to return. The Egyptian army—with its horses and chariots—would not be able to pursue us deep into the rough terrain of Midyan.

"And if Merenptah does not grant us leave to go?" I asked.

"Yahveh is with us." He offered this assurance and no more.

Only later did I realize how much Moses had held back from us that night.

The next morning I jumped from bed even before the first hint of dawn. My feet glided over the floor and my flesh tingled. I could not stop smiling. All the weary years fell away from me as if they had been but a single unhappy moment, a short prelude to this day—the day I could bring God's glory to my people. I would move among them like a queen, tall and proud with the crown of Yahveh's favor upon my head.

As I went to draw water in the courtyard I rehearsed what I would say in the marketplace. I envisioned the excitement of the women and their gratitude that Moses had returned to rescue us from Pharaoh's tyranny. I could not wait to begin.

When I passed the stable I noticed that the door stood open. I checked it every night before we retired, lest an animal escape. Had I neglected it the night before in my excitement? Had an intruder slipped in among us?

I crept toward the door. I peeked inside. In the dim light of early dawn I saw Tzipporah asleep on the filthy straw between the donkeys. My stomach churned for the ruined dress, for Moses, for the boy, and even for her.

I filled a bucket with water. I hurried back to the kitchen, where I began to prepare a simple morning meal. What would I tell Moses? He had brought the woman to us. Surely he did not want her to dishonor our home. If she could not accept my hospitality he should send her back to her people.

Moses soon joined me in the kitchen. For a moment I forgot everything but my joy in his return.

"It is so good to lay my eyes upon you!" I threw my arms around him. He returned my embrace with a gentle squeeze. We pulled apart. I motioned for him to sit at the table. As I laid a tray of cheese and fruit before him, the image of Tzipporah in the straw came back to me.

"I hope you slept well after your long journey," I said.

"I thank you, Miryam," he replied. "I woke refreshed."

"And Tzipporah?"

Moses shrugged. He began to eat. He said nothing more.

Did he not care about the woman after all? Except for a long glance when she had appeared in the doorway wearing the blue dress, he had paid the concubine no attention. Surely she must be a burden to him.

No one would dispute that our leader should choose a wife from his own people. Once I had been the best matchmaker in Goshen. Surely my skill remained with me. I would find a suitable wife for Moses among the fine young daughters of Israel. A trade caravan could take the concubine home. As for the boy, I would raise him myself.

"I saw her in the stable this morning."

Moses did not appear surprised. "She is fond of animals."

I drew my lips together and knit my brow. Clearly he did not understand. I would have to be more explicit.

"I saw her asleep in the stable."

Moses continued to eat. In a few moments he glanced up at me.

"It is the custom of her people. They watch their animals at night."

The custom of her people? What sort of people lived by choice in filth? Surely he could have accepted their hospitality without embracing their squalid ways. But even if he could permit such a habit in the woman who cared for his child, I could not. Not in my house.

"Brother, I work day and night to make a clean and orderly home, to set a good example for the children."

Moses turned his eyes upon me. They stared with such penetration that I felt as if I stood naked before him. For a moment I faltered. Had I been too blunt?

"You have changed, Miryam."

I felt my face grow red with anger and embarrassment. All the words I held back from the night before flew out my mouth. "When I see a wrong I want to right it," I replied. "You have brought a stranger into our midst. She wallows in filth."

I paused for a moment to collect myself. I did not wish to annoy him further. Nor could I keep him from the truth.

"She has done a terrible thing to her own son!"

Moses held up his hand to cut me off. The color rose in his neck and cheeks. I stood tall. I was not afraid to challenge my own brother. I too knew Yahveh's grace.

"Of what do you speak?"

"Last night when I bathed the child I saw the circumcision wound. He said his mother had done it to him. I see how he avoids her." I did not mention what Gershom had said about the woman taking her knife to Moses too.

Moses shook his head. "I lay in the grip of a creature Yahveh sent to test my resolve. She rescued us. She purified us. She brought us into the House of Israel."

The heat of embarrassment swept across my face and burned my ears. How could I have been so wrong? He was not indifferent to her but grateful, and with good cause. He could not claim to be an Israelite without a circumcision. He could not claim to be an Israelite if his own son went uncircumcised. Now he was willing to tolerate anything from her, allow her to do as she pleased, for the sake of the service she had rendered him and his son.

I bowed with remorse. *Let him live with whatever woman he chooses*, I said to myself. It mattered little to his mission.

Aharon and I left as soon as the sun rose full in the sky. He ran from workshop to workshop, building site to building site. I began in the markets. I gathered the Israelite women around me. I whispered the truth of my brother's parentage. I made them promise to keep this secret amongst our people. Some of the older women, my mother's friends, claimed to have suspected from the beginning. Others expressed great astonishment. When they asked how he had survived I saw no reason to keep the story of the basket and the princess from them. I told them that my brother was destined from birth to rise up as a leader among us. I explained that Yahveh had chosen him to relieve our suffering. I filled their weary hearts with hope.

As I spoke to groups of women, in the markets and courtyards of our neighbors, I felt the voice of my youth return to me. I delivered my message with confidence. My audience took heed. Word of my news spread and people gathered around me. I rejoiced to regain my place among the women. Yahveh's grace blessed me with a new authority. It elevated me far above the position of respect I had once enjoyed.

A few women followed me as I moved from the market into the neighborhoods. I called on poor Israelites who dwelt in little more than mud huts and the wealthier families who lived in two-story houses like ours. At each stop the group grew larger. Everyone marveled at how I had saved my brother's life. They asked for the story of the basket over and over. At last I confessed that I, too, had received a calling from Yahveh, a visitation that had directed me to save my brother, to assist him with our people. They came to see what I had always known, that I had a special purpose in this life, that our God intended me for something other than marriage and motherhood.

The women began to call me Miryam the Prophetess. I felt like a bride on her wedding day.

The elders announced a meeting for that very evening. I wanted Moses to stand before the people as the noble man they knew him to be. So on my way home I stopped at the sandal maker and the wig maker. Neither craftsman would accept payment. I supposed that all of Goshen believed in my brother and stood ready to help him.

When I reached home I heated the bathwater. I sharpened the iron shaving knife. Then I sought Moses in his room, where he sat with Aharon. I reported on my successes. I handed Moses the wig and sandals. I directed him to the bath.

Within moments Moses appeared before me in the courtyard, dressed in his tattered black kuttoneh and head cloth. His beard remained in place. He held his filthy shepherd's staff.

"You must get ready!" I urged.

"I am ready."

"You can not go before our people dressed as a poor man from the desert!"

"Sister, I am a poor man from the desert."

"You are a general!" I objected. "You are Yahveh's chosen one! Your appearance should command respect."

Moses smiled like an indulgent father. He took my hand and motioned for me to sit. "The elders must hear the message—not the messenger."

"They will be more ready to believe the messenger if he looks like a prince."

Moses rested his hand on my shoulder. "The people will choose to follow me for the sake of Yahveh and our future. Surely you know this better than I."

I sighed and threw up my hands. I could do nothing more to convince him of his mistake. He seemed at once more humble and more stubborn than the brother who had left me seven years before. Yahveh would not let him fail on account of his poor appearance.

Our custom had always prevented women from attending the assembly of elders. But such rules could not apply to me. I imagined taking my place beside my brothers on the speaker's platform. I thanked Yahveh for His many blessings.

I went to the kitchen with last-minute instructions for Elisheva about feeding the children. By the time I returned to the courtyard, Moses and Aharon had left for the meeting. Did they imagine I preferred to stay home to wash dishes? I had waited too long, sacrificed too much to keep myself hidden behind the courtyard gate like other women.

I ran to follow them.

"Miryam?"

The concubine's voice called after me. She stood in the stable near my brother's donkey. I wanted to cry for the straw, dust, and mud streaks on the fine blue linen. I wanted to scold her for damaging one of Elisheva's most precious dowry items. For my brother's sake I held my tongue.

"I must go," I called back as I opened the gate. "Elisheva is inside."

When I turned to close the door I almost ran into Tzipporah, who had come up behind me without a sound. I understood she meant to accompany me. The sun grew low in the sky. I did not have the time to argue with her.

As we walked along the canal I noticed how she moved in her bare feet like a cat, smooth and silent. We turned at the pumping station next to a rivulet near the field where the meeting gathered. Two sweat-drenched men operated the chadouf, a difficult job even in the cool evening air. One filled the huge water skin in the river and let the stone counterweight up. The stick to which the skin was attached moved to higher ground. The other worker swung the skin around and emptied it into the canal.

Tzipporah paused a moment to watch. "We must hurry!" I insisted. "We will be late."

The elders had chosen a field far from any temples or army outposts. Columns of tall torches illuminated the front, where a speaker's platform stood. Many younger men of Goshen gathered with the elders. Before I could warn Tzipporah to stay back, she joined the crowd. "They do not allow women to listen to the assembly of elders here," I whispered to her.

She fixed her strange, piercing eyes on me. "It is the same everywhere," she replied.

Through the crowd we saw Aharon speaking to Moses. I made my way to the front. Several men objected to my presence, but others—no doubt informed by their wives—greeted me as Miryam the Prophetess. I took my place next to Aharon. For a moment he seemed surprised to see me. Then he offered an affectionate smile. He squeezed my hand.

Moses mounted the platform, wooden staff in hand. He stood erect. He looked so majestic that I forgot the shabby kuttoneh and long beard. The men grew silent.

"Elders of Israel and others!" my brother called out. The words rose from him with ease.

I felt Tzipporah next to me. She rose on her toes to whisper in my ear. "His God smoothes his tongue so the words glide out like oil over flesh."

Envy of her years with my brother hardened my heart against her even more. I did not answer or even look her way in acknowledgement. What could she know of Yahveh?

"Elders of Israel!" Moses repeated.

The crowd fell silent.

"Once our people were honored and revered in Egypt. Our ancestor Yoseph held the highest position in the land."

He paused while people murmured agreement, while the contrast settled into their hearts.

"Now we labor like slaves! Our sons learn Egyptian ways in the street. They wear Egyptian clothes. They marry Egyptian women. The Egyptians have taken our future from us."

An angry murmuring rose from the crowd. My brother's words rang true in their ears.

"I am sent to you from Yahveh—the God of our fathers, the God of Avraham, Yitzhak, and Yaakov. He appeared to me and said 'I see and have seen what is being done to you in Egypt.' He will guide us to our future."

Korach son of Yitzhar son of Kehat leapt upon the platform.

"By what authority does this man exalt himself?" Korach cried out. "Moses son of Amram was raised in Pharaoh's court. He ran away from Egypt. He knows nothing of our suffering!"

Everyone began talking.

My brother's eyes blazed. "I have commanded armies. I have crossed deserts. With Yahveh's help I will lead you to a future that belongs to us, the Children of Israel."

Korach continued his assault. "Are we to follow any fool who claims a god has sent him? He has seen no god, unless it be the god of wine!"

Laughter rose from the crowd. Moses drew himself up even taller. He threw down his staff. It landed at Korach's feet. A deadly black-necked cobra rose from the platform in its place. At first I did not believe what I saw. When Korach cried out I knew it was real. I turned to Tzipporah. Her eyes remained fixed on the snake; I could see from her surprise that she had known nothing about it.

Korach jumped from the platform. My brother seized the cobra by its tail. It wavered in the air. It spit. He shook it hard. The men nearest to the platform cowered. In moments the snake became a wooden staff again. Moses lifted it for all to see.

"Do any still not trust in Yahveh?" he cried out.

The people murmured in wonder.

"A trick!" someone shouted.

I scanned the crowd for the accuser. I could not guess who he might be, but I saw that he had seeded uncertainty among the people. Angry words rose to my mouth. I wanted to leap upon the platform and tell the doubters to remain behind in Egypt if they preferred slavery to freedom.

Moses held his right hand high above his head. Then he thrust it inside his kuttoneh to his chest. When he removed the hand it was covered with the white scales of tzaraat, a dreaded skin disease.

The crowd gasped. I covered my mouth in horror.

Again Moses put his hand inside the kuttoneh. He pulled it out unblemished.

My knees grew weak.

"Now do you hear and believe that Yahveh is with me? He is with all of us!"

"Another trick!" Korach shouted.

This time few echoed him.

Moses seemed ready to offer more proof. He held his water skin upside down to show that it was empty. "Who will fill this?"

A handsome youth leapt to the platform. When I recognized Hosea son of Nunn my heart began to pound. I saw much of his father in him—the sensitive mouth, the high brow, the strong legs, the wide shoulders, the eagerness. Could I have given birth to such a fine son? Did my face ever pass before Nunn when his wife served him a meal, or helped him bathe?

I closed my eyes and shook my head. *Forget the past*, I told myself. *A glorious future has arrived.*

"Allow me, my lord," Hosea declared, "for I hear and believe."

Hosea grabbed the water skin and ran to the canal at the edge of the field behind us. The crowd turned to watch him. He plunged the skin into the water. He ran back to Moses.

Moses took the water skin and poured its contents on to the dry earth before the platform. I could not believe my eyes. A cry went up.

"It is turned to blood!" they shouted. Word spread throughout the crowd. Everyone pushed forward to see.

Aharon climbed upon the platform next to Moses. I followed.

"We must hear and believe!" Aharon declared to the crowd. "Have faith in Moses our leader and the mighty God Yahveh, who will deliver us!"

"Deliver us!" everyone cried out.

"We believe!" Aharon shouted. He threw his arms into the air.

"We believe! We believe!" the crowd clamored. They swung their hands back and forth from their hearts to Moses. "We believe, we believe…"

My spirit filled with pride for Moses and love of Yahveh.

Aharon turned to Moses and bowed low in homage.

All the men bowed. I bowed.

From the corner of my eye I surveyed the crowd before me. Tzipporah alone remained upright.

FIFTEEN

Miryam

MOSES and the elders agreed to meet in front of the palace gate at midmorning. My brother did not doubt that Pharaoh would grant him an audience. More than that he did not say. Nor did he wish to talk about the plans and preparations that must follow once we secured the pharaoh's permission. "Let us rest tonight, Sister," he said when I broached the matters of adequate food for the journey and transport for the ill and aged among us. "Yahveh will show us the way when the time comes."

I knew that Yahveh did not occupy Himself with the details of how a thing is accomplished. We would have many preparations to make for the comfort, safety, and security of our people before we departed. Still, I held my tongue. I saw how much my brother needed rest. Perhaps Yahveh did not intend to trouble Moses with these matters because He knew I stood ready to take care of them.

I rose before dawn, certain of our success. Pharaoh would grant our request. We would leave our bondage behind for a glorious future. I thanked Yahveh for bringing the day of our liberation. I stood by the window. *O Yahveh, come to me once more*, I prayed. *Let me know You as my brother does.*

I heard frogs singing in the canal. I heard a jackal howl in the distant wilderness. I heard the leaves of the palm rustle in our courtyard. As each of these sounds passed into my ears I listened for His voice. I had waited twenty-seven years to hear it again.

I knew He must be near. I felt Him all around me. Still, His silence continued.

I stood by the window until the first light of dawn crept over the courtyard walls. Others in the house began to stir. I washed my hands and face at the basin. I told myself not to be disappointed. Yahveh could reveal Himself at any moment. The time and place would be of His choosing, not my own. Whether He came to me today or in a week did not matter. He dwelt in my heart.

As I walked down the stairs I wondered how to pack all our goods for the journey. We needed both donkeys and at least two carts to carry everything. I hoped our new house would be closer to a riverbank suitable for washing clothes. I imagined Yahveh's temple nearby, grander than all the palaces of Egypt, with doors of pure gold and floors tiled in precious stones. Yahveh's throne rose in my imagination. I saw a silver chair with a high back and pictures of the earth's bounty in relief—figs, wheat, vines laden with grapes, pomegranates, olives.

Never had hope for the future so infused my spirit.

I found Elisheva and Tzipporah in the kitchen. The concubine sat at the table while Elisheva combed her hair. I watched Elisheva's long, gentle strokes. Her face held a look of contentment. For a moment I envied the ease with which she forged attachments, her blindness to flaws. She did not see the disrespect Tzipporah showed in refusing to eat my meals and sleep in my house. Elisheva would not care that Tzipporah had held me back from taking my place beside my brothers at the assembly or that she had remained upright like an unbeliever while everyone else bowed.

Elisheva saw me standing in the doorway. "Good morning," she sang out.

I smiled. "You never rise before me," I replied.

"We could not sleep. We were afraid of what would happen when they went to Pharaoh," Elisheva replied.

"Afraid of what?" I had no fear for Moses. He walked with Yahveh.

"That Pharaoh might hurt him," Elisheva said.

"Merenptah would not dare harm the adopted son of his queen and the lord of Rameses's daughter Princess Maat-Hor-Neferure."

Elisheva paused mid-stroke. Tzipporah turned her wide eyes upon me. She had not known.

I shrugged. Did she believe he could do no better than her for a wife?

Tzipporah rose from the chair. She left the room without a word.

Elisheva looked at me with reproach.

I threw up my hands as if to say the matter was out of my control. "Moses could not keep this secret forever."

I saw no forgiveness in Elisheva's eyes. She rebuked me as she never had in all our years together.

"We must be kind to her. She is far from her home. Her family showed your brother great kindness."

I turned away and began to gather ingredients for bread. I refused to feel remorse for telling the truth.

At the appointed time I stood with Moses and Aharon in the square before the palace that was built with the blood of our people. A group of elders gathered around us in silence. Aharon stepped forward to address the group.

"Today is Pharaoh's receiving day. People come from all over the kingdom to pay homage. But we do not bear gifts to exalt him. We exalt none but our divine master, Yahveh."

The elders nodded with approval.

"What will you say to him?" I asked Moses in a low voice.

"Yahveh will put the words in my mouth."

I glanced behind me to hide my envy. I saw that many of the elders hung back. After a few more steps I turned again. The men continued to drop off from the group. Anger rose in my heart.

"Cowards!" I hissed under my breath.

Moses did not look back until we reached the palace gate. When he saw that we stood alone, a shadow passed over his face.

Aharon touched his arm.

"Do not be too harsh on their fear. They have seen their sons fall by Pharaoh's hand and can not help themselves."

Moses nodded. "They have not yet gathered the courage of free men," he said.

Moses turned to face the soldiers who stood guard at the gate. He announced himself and stated his purpose. Despite his changed appearance they remembered him. Several moved to bow before they recalled that he was no longer a general over them.

After the soldiers checked to make sure that we came without arms, they let us pass through the gate with a single soldier as an escort. As we moved across the enormous courtyard, word of my brother's return spread throughout the palace. A crowd gathered to watch him. When they called his name, he bowed. A servant flung herself at his feet. He helped her rise. As they spoke I learned that he had once rescued her from a beating. I supposed that many such people still lived in the palace.

Another group of soldiers stood guard outside the long reception chamber adjacent to the audience hall. As we crossed the threshold I heard musicians playing inside the throne room. I could distinguish a harp, a double flute, a lute, a hand drum, and the clicking beads—the menat necklace said to delight the goddess Hathor. The musicians' skill filled the silence. I looked around at the luxury of the reception chamber—blue, red, and yellow glazed tiles with hieroglyphics, wall paintings of birds and marsh reeds, tables and chairs made from fine wood and alabaster. Yahveh's temple would be finer, built with the loving hands of devoted worshippers rather than by the toil of slaves.

The chamberlain rushed toward us from the door to the throne room. He stared with disdain as if he could not believe the rough man before him could be Moses.

"He tells the truth," I insisted. I forced my eyes to remain focused on the red glazed tiles beneath my feet. "The guards recognized him."

The chamberlain nodded to me. He whispered words to a messenger, who ran into the throne room. When the messenger returned, he spoke into the chamberlain's ear.

"The pharaoh will see you when the others have gone." He allowed us to move into the doorway.

We waited a long time. I watched the young female musicians. Beyond them, Pharaoh sat on a gold throne, perched on a platform high above the floor. My eye caught the glint of his thick gold armbands and gold breastplate. Polished white stone stairs led up to the throne's platform. The side of this staircase was decorated with relief figures of peoples enslaved by the Egyptians and, at the top, a royal lion in the act of devouring a man.

Rameses's thirteenth son had begun his reign at the age of sixty, after spending twelve long years as his father's heir apparent. How many years before that had he fixed his eyes on the golden throne? One by one his older brothers had died. Then Rameses had died. Now, at last, Merenptah wore the blue cobra crown of Upper and Lower Egypt. He held the heka scepter and nekhakna flail in his hands. As I caught my first glimpse of the shriveled old man with his long, beaklike nose and small, close-set eyes, I recalled his many cruel acts toward us. I recalled Istnofret's fear of him. The gossips whispered that he had hastened the deaths of any who stood in his way. As I looked upon him now I had no trouble believing them.

At last all the visitors left. The chamberlain instructed us to remove our sandals before we stepped over the threshold. As we approached the throne, an attendant rushed forward with his hands extended to receive the customary gift offering. When Moses shook his head, the man frowned.

The chamberlain announced us. "Moses son of Istnofret with Miryam and Aharon of the Israelites."

Moses moved to the foot of the throne and bowed. Aharon and I followed.

"Son of Re," Moses began.

A shrill laughter startled me. I could not believe such a sound had issued from the mouth of the man who ruled all of Egypt. I looked around. The attendants cowered. The musicians stopped playing. Moses alone stood without fear.

Even before Merenptah uttered a single word I realized the danger of the situation. It did not matter that he held the throne. He hated Moses. He would relish doing him harm. Moses must have known this even before he returned to Egypt.

Merenptah rose from the throne. He pointed the heka scepter at Moses. "You did not lose your heavy tongue in exile!" he called out. His voice sounded like that of an old woman. He laughed again. His savage eyes glittered as if he had no greater pleasure than to degrade my brother. "Israelite trash! You are no son of Istnofret. Let none dare use her name again in association with yours."

My brother's face burned red with anger. He held his fists at his sides.

Pharaoh began to descend the stairs. As he spoke his voice deepened, his tone grew more menacing.

"From the day I first put a sword in your hand I saw your murderous ambition. My sister did not see it. My father did not see it. I alone knew the truth! I heard the soldiers call for you to follow my father to the throne. I remembered those men well. Have you returned to join them in death?"

Guards stepped forward, spears in hand.

Aharon and I looked at each other in terror. We backed away. Merenptah walked up to Moses. Moses prostrated himself. We followed his example.

The old man laughed again, shrill and loud. "So the great General Moses falls."

I looked up. Merenptah stood over my brother in silence, as if deciding between life and death. His mouth turned down in disgust.

I could not help myself. "Please spare him!" I cried out.

The pharaoh glanced at me. I lowered my gaze.

"Who dares to speak in this traitor's favor?"

My body shook. But my heart remained defiant. "I am his sister."

The pharaoh turned back to Moses. He pointed to me. "Will you betray her too? My sister loved you like her own son. She loved you more than me! My father held you on his knee. He favored you with everything. Nothing was enough for you. Now you are less than nothing."

The echo of his triumphant laughter died away. The room grew silent. Moses did not rise. I closed my eyes to pray.

Lord Yahveh, You have not brought him here for death. Protect Your servant! Do not let the people believe that a mere pharaoh holds more power than You!

I opened my eyes to look upon my beloved brother. I waited for Yahveh to answer my prayer as I knew He would.

Merenptah drew close to Moses.

"You may live, dog. Live so I can laugh at what you have become." He poked my brother's chin with his slippered foot.

"Istnofret is mine now. I have had your wife too."

Moses did not respond.

"Speak, you mouse! Why do you dare show your face in this court?"

Moses lifted his head. He rose to his feet. When he stood erect he towered over the pharaoh.

"I am sent by Yahveh the God of Israel. He says, 'Let My people go that they may celebrate a feast for Me in the wilderness.'"

Pharaoh looked at him in disbelief. He stamped his foot. "Who is Yahveh that I should grant His request?" His eyes moved from one attendant to another. Each shrugged in his turn.

"I do not know this Yahveh!" he shouted.

Aharon moved forward. He prostrated himself before Pharaoh. He rose again. He began to speak in his gentlest tones.

"If it please Your Majesty, the God of the Israelites demands a sacrifice from us. I pray Your Majesty, ruler of the two Egypts, beloved of the great god Amun-Re, allow us to journey three days into the wilderness to make the sacrifice lest our God meet us with pestilence or sword. We promise to return to our labors in a week. Our God will surely reward your generosity."

Aharon completed his speech with a bow. He walked backwards to join Moses.

Pharaoh turned from them. He rose to the throne with slow, deliberate steps. When he reached the top he pointed the heka scepter at Moses.

"Your silver-tongued companion can not help you or your people! Get to your labors!"

The throne attendants and soldiers moved toward my brothers in a threatening manner. Moses whirled around and marched away. Aharon paused to offer a trembling bow. He walked backwards to the chamberlain.

A group of the elders and some of my women followers from the previous day waited for us at the gate. Moses ran ahead without speaking to them. Aharon shook his head.

Only I stopped to report on the encounter. The elders and the women turned away from me in disappointment.

When we reached home Aharon went to tend the vineyard. I tried to talk with Moses. I found him sitting on the mattress in his room. I sat down next to him.

"What must we do next?" I asked in desperation.

Moses turned his eyes upon my face as if he did not see me. "Yahveh will guide us." His abrupt reply left no room for further conversation.

Once Moses used to unburden his heart to me. Now he would not let me in.

I rose to leave. He made no effort to detain me.

I began to prepare the evening meal, but I took no pleasure in the work. The sound of children in the courtyard grated on my ears. I could not go about my household tasks as if nothing had happened. Did Yahveh want me to sit idle under the cloud of my brother's failure?

No. He expected me to act with strength and courage.

I would go to Istnofret. I knew that in her love for Moses she would not turn me away. I would ask her to influence Merenptah in our favor.

I filled a basket with things for the princess—cooked fruits, a fine linen cloth woven from thread that Elisheva spun , a jar of skin ointment made from my own recipe. I donned a large black cloak and a thick veil.

By the time I arrived at the palace the guards at the gate had changed. Those who I now approached did not recognize me. They checked my basket. I told them that I came with gifts from the priestess of Heqet. At last they summoned a young palace messenger to lead me to Istnofret's quarters.

He took me through a maze of passageways and courtyards. I saw colorful walls painted with animals and flowers, tiled fountains with running water, and enormous gold and silver statues. We passed laborers wearing only an unbleached piece of linen to cover their loins, guards in full military dress with helmets and weaponry, priests in high headdresses with papyrus scrolls tucked under their arms, royals in rich linen robes and thick beaded collars, bare-breasted servant girls with no more covering than a short apron tied around their hips. Everyone seemed to have a purpose. Few people lingered to gossip.

We turned into a covered court where acrobatic dancers were practicing a routine. I watched the young men and women leaping and twirling. They intertwined their almost naked bodies to form strange shapes.

At last we reached the private quarters of the Princess Istnofret. A servant took me into a reception room that held more furniture than our entire house. Chairs and low tables rested on glazed floor tiles decorated with pictures of blue lotus flowers and green acacia trees. Papyrus paintings of birds, frogs, and cobras covered the walls.

"I have come from the priestess of Heqet to offer this gift and greetings," I said.

The servant held out her hand to take the basket. "I will convey your message."

I clung to the basket. "My lady insisted that I alone place it into the queen's hands."

The servant smiled. "That is not possible."

I reached into my cloak for a pair of gold hoop earrings wrapped in cloth. Once they had decorated my mother's ears. I handed the package to the servant. "She did the priestess's brother a great service. The priestess wishes her servant to offer thanks in person."

The servant unwrapped the earrings. I saw at once that my bribe had worked.

"Wait here," she said. Her eyes did not stray from the gold circles resting in the hollow of her hand.

I walked up and down the room several times. I scanned the paintings on the walls without interest until I came upon one that depicted a basket hidden among reeds. I gazed at the papyrus, startled by Istnofret's boldness.

I heard a rustling behind me. I turned.

She stood before me in a rich gold-embroidered gown and a wig strung with lapis lazuli, carnelian, and pearls. The years since our last meeting showed on her face—her eyelids drooped, her once clear brow puckered with wrinkles, fine lines decorated the flesh around her mouth. She had grown heavier. Still, she remained more beautiful, more majestic than any woman I had ever seen.

I bowed to her. She embraced me. We clung to each other for a moment as sisters mourning for time and hope lost.

"How is he?" she whispered.

How could I answer such a question? The truth would take all night to tell. "Much changed; much the same."

Our eyes met. For a moment neither of us could speak.

I broke the silence. "I never gave up waiting for him to come back."

"Nor I. But you take too great a risk in coming here. You must go. Merenptah trusts no one."

"They say you are the pharaoh's favorite."

"It would not save me from the executioner."

I handed her the basket. I drew close to her ear. "He needs your help," I murmured. "He seeks to relieve our people from the heavy oppression of your brother's rule."

Tears streamed from her eyes. After a few moments she spoke in a fierce whisper. "Speak no more! Save yourself; go from this place and do not return."

"Consider my request, Istnofret. For the sake of an old friend, for the boy you raised to be a good and just man. I may know little of your life here. But this much I do know—women always hold more influence than they realize."

She shook her head. She backed away from me. "You must understand, I can do nothing."

Early the next morning a messenger ran to us with news that Pharaoh had issued a new order to the Egyptian taskmasters. They would no longer provide the straw needed to make bricks. The Israelite workers must gather it themselves, even though the quota of bricks remained the same.

The Israelites took to the fields. Moses helped them. The hot sun parched their weary bodies. They spent the entire morning gathering stubble.

By the end of that day, the production of bricks fell far short of the quota. The workers did no better the following day. Moses saw the taskmasters beating the workers. He could not stop them. When people cried out against this oppression, the taskmasters smote them harder. On the third day, some of the Israelite women came to help their men. The taskmasters grew even more thirsty for blood. They beat workers at random and preyed on the weak. A pregnant woman lost her child at their hands. When some workers tried to run away, the Egyptians caught them and broke their arms and legs. The Israelites suffered as never before.

The foremen of the Israelites sought an audience with Pharaoh. Moses did not dare accompany them. While we waited in the square, Hosea followed the foremen into the audience hall. When the meeting ended, he rushed from the palace with a look of great distress on his face. I uttered a quick prayer to Yahveh.

Hosea stood silent for a moment to catch his breath.

"Tell us," I urged.

"One of the foremen spoke for all," he began. He took another breath. "They blamed Moses. 'He does not represent us,' they said. They begged Pharaoh to return our burdens to what they were, but the pleas did not move him. He shouted at them. 'Slackers! You are slackers! Go work! No straw will be given to you and you must provide the quota of bricks.'"

"The man is a monster!" I exclaimed.

Aharon seized my arm and looked around. "Quiet, Sister, lest his agents hear you."

I glanced at Moses, who seemed unaware of all that Hosea had said. He gazed up toward heaven and tugged at his beard.

"Let us return home," Aharon suggested.

As we turned away from the palace, two soldiers approached.

"Why do you not work, Israelites?"

"I am Aharon the vintner. This is my brother who owns the vineyard with me. We provide wine for Pharaoh's table."

"Then get you to your vines!"

"Dogs!" the other one muttered.

Moses's face turned deep red. His body stiffened. I feared he might lash out at the soldier.

Aharon and I each put a hand on his shoulders.

"Let us go and avoid trouble," Aharon whispered in his ear.

"Come, Brother," I added.

We urged him forward until his fists came unclenched and he no longer looked back at the soldiers.

On the way out of town we paused at a well. After we refreshed ourselves, we rose to walk home. A group of Israelite foremen blocked our way. They glared at us with sharp eyes and curled lips. Someone hissed.

"Curse you and your God!"

"It would have been better for us if you had never returned to Egypt!"

"Korach was right to suspect him!"

The spokesman raised his hand for silence. "Moses and Aharon, may your God see you and judge you for making our scent stink in Pharaoh's nostrils."

Moses buried his head in his hands. Aharon and I looked at each other. For once, neither of us knew what to say.

SIXTEEN

Tzipporah

IVE days after we arrived in Egypt, I stood outside the gate to Miryam's house and looked down the road in the direction from which we had come. In this land of walls and water I could not breathe. Without a flock to care for, without work as a birth chanter, without my lord's desire or my son's need, I had no place in this world.

I recalled how Moses had marched us into Egypt with the determination of an entire army. I had difficulty keeping pace. At first I mourned the sweetness of our life in Midyan. But soon I realized that Yahveh's calling would make Moses the great man I had always imagined him to be. My heart swelled with pride for my beloved.

When at last the lush land of my lord's birth came into sight, I gasped in wonderment at all the green. Never had I seen such a rich land. The fields, the huts and houses, the size of the sheep and goats—everything surprised me. No one seemed to live in a tent or to move with the changing seasons. Everyone we passed looked as well-fed as Allatimm. Moses laughed when I marveled at the volumes of cloth the people wore.

"The gods have blessed this place," I said to Moses.

"We are more blessed." He leaned in to me and our lips met for the first time since our departure. I closed my eyes and saw a white oryx.

"I am glad to have you at my side," he said in the old, tender voice.

And so hope for the future came to ease the longing for what we had left behind.

But nothing came to pass as I had anticipated. Miryam loathed my presence and I grew so uneasy in the shadow of her dislike that I could not utter a word when she stood nearby. Yet my son clung to her as if he had found his true mother. My lord's audience with Pharaoh had brought only more suffering upon the Israelites. Distracted and silent, Moses neither shared his woes with me nor sought comfort in my arms. He seemed as distant as the red mountains of Midyan. I found refuge only in the company of Elisheva.

"Tzipporah?"

She must have called my name several times from the gate. I turned my gaze from the road to her soft eyes and fluttering long eyelashes. Her sweet face had a wide brow, high cheekbones that swooped to a delicate chin, and a long nose. Black hair, straight and shiny, fell almost to her waist. I marveled at her light skin, which she must have kept hidden from the sun all her life. What a contrast to tall, stern Miryam! Miryam's heart held fierce attachments: Moses, Elisheva, Aharon, Aharon's sons. By the end of our first evening, her rough hands and unyielding eyes grew soft for Gershom, too. But Elisheva blossomed with love for every living being. I never knew a woman so generous. She could have given birth to a hundred children and lavished equal affection upon them all.

"You will grow weary standing at the gate alone!" she insisted.

I shook my head. I was used to long hours of stillness and silence. I craved the calm they brought to me. I sought the Goddess in these quiet moments.

"Pharaoh must end the punishment of straw gathering," she said. "Now that he has shown us the full force of his power, I am sure he will relent and grant us permission to go into the wilderness for the sacrifice. I am sure they will return today with good news."

I could not reply. A man who rules by his own will and takes no council does not change—that much I knew from my father. But I did not wish to sour Elisheva's hope.

"Are you keeping watch?" she asked.

I shook my head.

"Then you must be dreaming of your people."

My father's face flashed before me and I heard a baby's scream echo deep inside my ears. My fingers felt sticky with blood that did not purify. No, I did not dream of my people. I dreamt of the red cliffs and the yellow sand, the kurta cat and the oryx, a falcon swooping across the golden sky at sunset, my fingers sinking into the warm black wool of a ewe about to give birth. I dreamt of the song of the Goddess. Her silence in this land made me grieve. And I dreamt of the days when Moses and I had lain together in our tent on the plain of Gaw in the shadow of the mountain of Sinn, when he had rested his head in my lap as the sun went down, when he had held himself too removed from the affairs of men to lead them.

I answered Elisheva with tears. She began to stroke my hand. Her sweet, silent sympathy, her loving nature, made me want to reveal my heart to her.

"I did not know about the other wife." The words that tumbled from my throat were few. But I saw that Elisheva understood all that they signified—a full confession of my disappointment and longings.

"He chose you, Tzipporah, to bear his son. Princess Istnofret arranged the other marriage. Moses never asked for it; he fled the morning after the ceremony. Miryam should not have said anything."

"Miryam," I echoed. Did Moses not see that his beloved sister despised me?

"Do not heed her rough ways," Elisheva urged. "She helped me though all four childbirths and none had a gentler touch. When Moses disappeared she lost her way. Now he has returned a changed man. Once he was a general, a prince in manners and education. Men gathered around him to curry his favor. Now they curse him. Nothing has gone as she had hoped and expected. She does not know what to do to help our situation and so she grows irritable."

I drew my breath in through my teeth. I felt my chest rise. I pictured Miryam—a tall woman with a round face, brown hair cropped at her chin, and the austerity of a warrior. Tough as a man, she was ready to lead the people herself. But Yahveh had not called her for that task. Perhaps she wished He had.

Elisheva continued. "She does not see how much you mean to him. She does not understand how much a man says in a single gesture."

"A gesture?" I did not understand.

Elisheva blushed. "I saw Moses this morning before they left. The way he looked at you and kissed the hollow of your hand."

Elisheva's words lightened my heart. I recalled how much I had admired Moses that morning. With his flowing black locks, full beard, and dark kuttoneh, he had stood before me as a figure of majestic beauty, strength, and vigor.

A warm breeze rose over the canal and kissed my face. I heard a chiming in the distance and watched a small yellow bird land on some reeds at the edge of the canal. The Goddess hovered nearby. I felt Her presence; Elisheva had brought Her back to me. How could I have been so blind to all that my friend saw with such ease?

"The Goddess is with you," I told Elisheva.

"The Lady Atirat?" she asked. "That is our goddess."

"No—the Great Goddess, Asherah."

"I do not know her."

"But you do," I insisted. "She brings all good things to women. She is gentle and kind."

Elisheva toyed with her earring for a moment. "Is she a goddess of the desert?"

"She dwells wherever women gather. Before my lord came to Midyan I was a birth chanter in Her temple."

"Like a midwife? My grandmother was a midwife."

"I help women in ways the midwife can not, to ease their pain. You did not become a midwife too?"

Elisheva shook her head. "I did not have the skill for it. But I went to many births with my grandmother. That is how I came to meet Miryam and Aharon—when their mother carried Moses. I was at the birth."

"Do you remember?" I wanted to know everything.

"I was young. But I will never forget. The room blazed with a brilliant light. I had to shield my eyes. Miryam knew it signified that God had marked her brother for something special. She devoted herself to him from that day forward. She gave up everything for him, even Nunn."

"Nunn?"

"They were going to be married. Nunn, who is now father to Hosea. Everyone said that they loved each other and that Miryam turned away from him."

We stood together a moment in silence. I tried to imagine Miryam yielding her heart to another, folding herself into the arms of a man. It seemed impossible.

"She will come to love you as I do," Elisheva promised.

I wound my arm through Elisheva's. Whether or not her wish for Miryam came to pass seemed less important than her desire for it.

"I want to make an offering of thanks to the Goddess for your friendship," I said.

"What does one sacrifice to her?"

"Oh no!" I exclaimed. "She prefers sweet cakes and offerings of song and dance."

Elisheva's face brightened. "Miryam and I sing and dance with timbrels when the grape harvest begins."

I gazed into Elisheva's eager eyes and saw that she would serve the Goddess well. I took her by the hand.

"Come, let us show Her."

Elisheva sent the boys to play by the canal and to keep watch for the return of Moses, Aharon, and Miryam. She ran into the house to find the timbrels. I went to the stable.

My hands trembled with excitement as I knelt down in the straw and unwrapped my pink feathers from the cloth in which I had hidden them. I laid them on a stool deep inside the dark stable away from the stalls.

"O Great Goddess, may I never stray from Your path. May I please

You in all my ways. May I worship You with my flesh and spirit."

My body filled with warmth. The back of my neck tingled. I touched the inside of my arms and desire throbbed between my legs. She would bring Moses back to me.

Elisheva joined me with the instruments in her hand and a shy smile on her face. She handed me a timbrel—a lambskin stretched over a circular wooden frame—and showed me how to rap it with my fingertips. My fingers danced over the skin as if they had been released from bondage. I began to chant and twirl. Elisheva followed me. We danced to the Goddess and knelt before Her.

"May we worship You with our body and spirit," I chanted.

Elisheva echoed me.

Tzipporah, Tzipporah! I heard Her call deep in my heart. My flesh burned. I lifted the blue dress over my head. I took my hair out of the braid so it caressed my back.

"If we dance for Her now, our lords will be filled with desire tonight and they will take pleasure from us unlike any they have ever known."

Elisheva hesitated. She had helped me bathe, now I helped her undress. Though she had given birth to four children, she had the body of the Goddess. Her full, round breasts shimmered white in the dim stable. Her wide hips narrowed into a small waist. Her treasures lay hidden inside strong thighs and a soft mound of black hair. I averted my eyes, for she was not mine to admire. She belonged to the Goddess.

I tapped the timbrel and turned. My heart pounded and my flesh sang. From the corner of my eye I saw Elisheva lift her arms high and sway in a dance of her own. I saw pleasure on her face and in her quivering hips. I heard it in her breath and in mine. I hit the timbrel to keep time with my racing heart and I twirled, faster and faster. The Goddess sent Her voice pulsing through me and my song was sweeter than any I had sung before. I was a gazelle, a panther, an eagle floating over the black cliffs.

When I came back into myself, I lay on the stable floor like a newborn lamb. I stretched my limbs, rose, and slipped on my dress. Elisheva, already dressed, knelt before the feathers as if in private prayer.

"You must lie with your lord tonight," I instructed. "Tomorrow morning we will bring Her an offering."

She turned to me with wonder in her eyes. After a moment she spoke. "You do not serve Her in the temple," she said. "But surely you will Her priestess among us."

Elisheva called the children inside to share a large pink melon in the kitchen. The sweet, wet flesh tasted better than anything I had ever eaten. Though my hopes for Miryam had crumbled like a ruin, my friendship with Elisheva blossomed like a wadi after a warm soaking rain. She was the sister Moses had promised me. Through her I would lead the women of Israel to the Goddess.

I looked at Gershom as he ate his melon, so solemn and neat for a child his age. Already Miryam's mark lay too much upon him. So I spat a seed in his direction. He laughed and spat one back. The other two boys joined him and soon the seeds fell everywhere.

Elisheva threw her head back and clapped her hands.

"Someday you will see the beauty of my land and the freedom of living in a tent," I told her in the midst of our merriment. "A tent can not be scrubbed clean."

"Miryam's tent would be scrubbed clean," Elisheva insisted. Her mouth turned up in the smile of a mischievous child. We laughed together.

In the wild flurry of seed spitting and laughter none of us saw Miryam's tall figure in the doorway. When Elisheva's face froze in fear, I knew the mistress of the house had returned.

The room grew quiet. Elisheva began to apologize, but Miryam held up a hand to silence her. She remained standing on the threshold, speechless. The room flashed before me as she must have seen it—three boys with wet faces and stained clothing, sticky black seeds all over the table and the floor mats, two women encouraging the children to destroy a hard-won order. I should have felt remorse. I should have felt sympathy for the woman who, by Elisheva's account, had lost so much. But when I saw her resentment I felt my heart stiffen.

"Go wash yourselves," Elisheva whispered to the boys. They filed out of the room without daring to glance at their aunt. I rose from my chair and started to pick up the seeds on the floor. Elisheva grabbed a little ceramic bowl from a shelf and joined me.

Aharon came up behind his sister. He looked down upon us with a grim expression. I knew then that the meeting between the foremen and Pharaoh had not gone well.

"Pharaoh does not relent," he announced. "The Israelites must continue to gather their own straw."

Miryam sat down at the sticky table and leaned her head against her hand as if she had suffered a blow. Elisheva rose to embrace her.

"What happened after the audience today?" Elisheva asked Aharon.

"The people blame Moses for the situation with the straw. They doubt the power of our brother's God."

Miryam banged her fist on the table. "He is *our* God! He is the God of our forefathers. Do not doubt, Brother. With His help Moses will save us from Pharaoh's tyranny. This I have known since before his birth."

She rose to her feet and dipped a rag in a pitcher of water to clean the table. She scrubbed the surface with all the strength of her faith. As she moved from one spot to another, I almost expected to see holes worn into the wood.

When we finished removing the seeds from the floor, Aharon offered Elisheva his hand to help her rise. I saw their touch linger and their eyes exchange a loving gaze. Elisheva adjusted her dress and ran her hands over her hips.

"My lord is tired and in need of rest," she said. "I will attend him."

Miryam waved her hand. I looked away to keep from smiling.

Moses did not appear that afternoon or later when Miryam served the evening meal. Elisheva, ravenous from the pleasures of the afternoon, asked after him with her mouth full of meat.

Miryam threw up her hands. "He sits in his room and despairs while his people wait for him to take action. He should have more patience. Did I not wait eighteen years for him to reach full maturity and another seven while he lived as an exile?"

As Miryam spoke I recalled how Moses had rescued me from the shepherds at the well and offered me protection. In all our years together he had looked after me as the cherished wife of his bosom. Six days could not take away those years. I remembered Elisheva's words— *He chose you, Tzipporah.*

Perhaps he would return to me if I returned to him. Perhaps I might yet find a way to help him.

I rose from the table, took a clay bowl from the shelf, and filled it with bread, cooked wheat, chick peas, and a piece of duck. I bowed and left the room.

The narrow stair frightened me. I, who danced over granite cliffs and deep into sandstone wadis, feared those plaster walls like the jaws of a panther. And I hated the little room where Moses sat, deep in the bowels of the dark house.

I had not been there since my first night in Egypt, when Moses stayed up late talking with his brother and sister. Elisheva had taken Gershom to sleep with her younger sons and had escorted me to this room. Standing in the doorway, I had watched her climb onto the strange brick platform piled high with mats and blankets. She had called it a bed and urged me to rest on it. When I had asked the purpose of the wooden cradles at one end of the structure, she had expressed astonishment that I did not know. She had shown me how to lay my head upon the cradle and had insisted I try sleeping in that uncomfortable position.

But after she had wished me a peaceful rest and closed the door, I had not remained on the bed. I had known I could not sleep shut away from the stars. Rather, I had paced the dark room and chanted a hymn to ward off night demons. When I could no longer bear to stay in that box, I had fled to the stable.

Bowl in hand, I tapped on the door and did not wait for an answer. Moses sat on the bed platform with a single oil lamp for light. His shoulders curled inward and his head hung low. When I entered and closed the door behind me, he did not look up.

"I have brought you something to eat," I began. My throat grew tight and I could say no more.

Moses turned to gaze at me. Though his eyes seemed dull and desolate, a smile flickered over his face. He patted the bed to indicate that I should sit beside him.

I handed him the bowl and climbed onto the platform. He took a bite of the bread and set the bowl down. I cupped his face in the hollow of my hand.

He took my hands in both of his and clasped them in his lap.

"Miryam is desolate," I said.

Moses nodded. "I should not have returned."

His voice sounded too familiar. His determination and fervor had drained away. I did not want the old Moses, a defeated Moses.

"But Yahveh chose you," I said. "You can not deny your calling." *No more than I can deny my own.*

I pulled his head into my lap like the days of old when we dwelt in the Valley of Gaw. I stroked his long hair and held him close to me. After a few minutes he began to speak.

"Five times I refused Yahveh when He told me to free the Children of Israel. 'Who am I that I should go?' I asked. 'What if they refuse to know Yahveh? What if they do not believe me?' I have never been a man of words. I begged Him to choose another. I was right."

I remembered the day that the Goddess had called me to Her. I had answered without hesitation or fear. She had entered me as sweet perfume comes into the nostrils. She had brought joy in Her presence and had asked for nothing but my devotion. My lord's God asked too much of him. But he had no choice. And I could not stand by while he allowed his destiny to escape from him. I could not stand by while he fell prey to weakness and fear, while his bones turned to dust in the sands of despair.

"Yahveh has chosen a man who loves justice and hates tyranny. You will not forsake your people as a lesser man would."

"Then why has He forsaken me?" Moses cried out as he sat up. The scars on his lips seemed to grow red and angry as he spoke. The words rang out in labored bursts.

"He warned me about Merenptah's hard heart. He promised to stretch out His hand and strike Egypt until Pharaoh let us go. But now the Children of Israel suffer even more! We should pack our donkey and return to your father's camp."

I looked at my lord's beautiful face, twisted with pain and disbelief like a woman giving birth.

I stroked his arm. "I long for nothing more than to return to Midyan with you. But in triumph, not defeat."

I watched his grief give way to tenderness. He kissed my hand.

"Seek Yahveh's guidance," I urged.

"How? He came to me unbidden."

"Can you not hear His voice in your heart?"

Moses closed his eyes. For many minutes he did not answer.

"I have not heard Him since He called me from the flames in the wilderness."

"Then you must seek Him in the wilderness. He will heed your supplication on the edge of the desert."

Moses gazed into my eyes as if to question how I knew what to do. I could not say, for the words had come to my lips as if placed there by Yahveh Himself.

"Go now," I whispered.

I watched him march through the door like a general, with no uncertainty in his steps.

SEVENTEEN

Miryam

AT first I did not believe what my eyes saw. Melon seeds covered the table. Dark stains spread from chunks of wet melon on the reed mats that covered the floor. The three boys dripped with juice from their faces to their clothing. Elisheva looked as wild as the other one, with her hair flying in all directions and her dress sliding off one shoulder. The woman that Moses brought into my house laughed like a witch at the disorder she had incited. Did she know what pain it caused me?

My beautiful kitchen lay in ruins. The women had become children, the children had become animals. Aharon spoke as if his faith in Yahveh waned. Moses shut himself into a room with hopelessness for a companion.

I refused to despair. I cleaned the kitchen. I prepared the evening meal. When Moses did not come to the table I tried to remain calm. Yahveh did not intend our quest for freedom to end like this. I would maintain order in our household. I would pray for Yahveh to show me how I could inspire the renewal of Aharon's faith and prevent Moses from abandoning his purpose.

When everyone had retired, I sat on the edge of my bed for a long time. I did not know what prayers might be pleasing to Yahveh. I could do no better than give voice to the stirrings of my spirit. *Let me sing to Yahveh, for He is the most exalted. Who is like You among the mighty ones, Yahveh?*

The prayer renewed me. I made my requests.

Let me be an influence for the good with both my brothers. Let me show them faith and perseverance.

I heard a faint noise in the courtyard below. I ran to the window. In the moonlight I saw Moses take a drink from the water jug. He turned toward the gate. I moved through the room to follow him. I wanted to know where he went, what he did. I wanted to be a part of all that happened. Of what use could I be in my bed?

I did not get further than the door to my room. As I reached for the handle I realized that wherever Moses went, he had chosen to do so alone under cover of darkness. I told myself not to intrude.

I lay back on the bed. I repeated my prayers. I closed my eyes to recall the day Yahveh had come to me, so long ago. I tried to grasp anew just a glimmer of His light in the olive grove. I tried to summon the girl I had once been. As always, she eluded me.

The next morning at dawn I met Moses in the courtyard. I watched him pour water from the dipping cup into his hands. For a moment irritation took hold of me. Why could he not use our washing room? I grieved that one who had grown up in a palace with lavish facilities—heated water and attendants to keep his body clean—should allow himself to fall so low.

Moses looked up. When he smiled at me, my spirit lifted. I reached over to pick a piece of straw out of his hair.

"Where did this come from?" I laughed.

He answered me with a faint smile.

As I gazed upon my beloved brother I realized that his strange appearance now seemed familiar. The hair flowing onto his back—much longer than my own—his full beard, and rough clothes exuded strength and vigor.

I forced myself to look into my heart, to peel away the layers of fastidious habit that had come to be like a second skin to me in the years of my brother's absence. I saw that in truth it did not matter whether he used the washing room or not. More important concerns occupied us now.

I felt as if a veil had lifted from my eyes. The world around me seemed brighter. I gazed at my brother. How much I had overlooked! His brow had cleared of anguish. His jaw set firm with determination. His eyes glimmered with Yahveh's light.

"I will return to the pharaoh later today."

"Will he agree to see you?" I asked.

"He will see me. I will return until the tyrant succumbs to the signs and portents of Yahveh's strength."

"Signs and portents?"

"Yahveh will stretch out His hand with severe punishments. He will deliver us from their midst. All Israel and Egypt will know of His greatness."

I knew I should be glad for whatever Moses told me. Yet that did not prevent a hundred questions from forming in my mouth. I wanted to know everything that had transpired between him and Yahveh in the night. What signs and portents would Yahveh send? What punishments? How long would it take?

Moses turned toward the stable, where the concubine rose from the filthy straw.

I frowned at her intrusion.

Moses glanced back to me before I could change my expression. My face grew hot with embarrassment.

"She is good with animals." He labored more than usual to say these words, but they reached my ears without a hint of reproach. "Does Elisheva's brother Nahshon still keep a flock?"

"A small flock," I replied. "Some sheep and two goats. Our milk comes from him."

"Perhaps Nahshon needs help."

I sighed with relief. She loved animals, she belonged with the animals. Let her spend her time with sheep and goats rather than hovering about my home like a silent shadow or taking Elisheva away from her children and friends. "I will speak with him this morning."

My brother's smile rose wider than I had seen since his return.

I made the arrangements at once. When I told Tzipporah that Nahshon wished her to look after his flock, happiness flooded her face. She even brought herself to thank me aloud. I did not object when she ran inside the house to don her old kuttoneh. It had been the filthiest garment I had ever washed and had dried to the color of our donkey.

Late in the morning Moses, Aharon, and I set out for the palace. We walked in rapid strides. Moses carried his shepherd's staff like a scepter. As we reached the palace gate he urged me to have patience.

"Each day brings us closer. Yahveh will deliver us in His time."

I nodded. Who could not believe a man with such fire in his eyes? My spirit lifted to the heavens in his very presence. I could see Aharon felt the same way. Moses would soon regain his influence among the Israelites. So, too, would I regain my place among the women.

Aharon's Egyptian kilt and robe, clean-shaven face, and ease of speech made him our best spokesman with the guards at the gate. They assigned us an escort. As before we waited in the audience hall.

Morning passed into afternoon. At last the chamberlain called us. I moved forward with my brothers to the foot of Pharaoh's golden throne. Aharon and I bowed. But Moses did not show the same respect. His proud demeanor revealed the truth to me. Yahveh did not wish His prophet to bow down to Pharaoh, the false god of Egypt. I vowed never again to bow to the tyrant or his like.

"Why have you come again?" the pharaoh called from his throne. A ray of sunlight pierced a high window and struck the pharaoh's golden crown. For a moment it seemed as if flames rose from the tyrant's head.

"Do you seek death?" Merenptah asked.

Moses spoke without ceremony. His tongue did not stumble over his lips. The message to Pharaoh rang out in a powerful voice as if Yahveh Himself spoke.

"We come to show the might of our God." He handed the wooden staff to Aharon. "See Yahveh's power and keep us from sacrificing to Him no longer!"

Moses turned to our brother. He motioned for Aharon to throw the staff down on the floor. The stiff wood sprouted brown scales and the hooded head of a cobra. The hissing creature slithered toward the foot of the throne. Its head reared, as if to threaten Pharaoh himself.

Pharaoh's face remained impassive. He raised his scepter.

"Summon my lector priests from the temples of Seth and Thoth," he commanded.

I knew of these men. The lector priests kept the sacred scrolls. They performed rites of magic in the temple precinct. It was said they communed with the world of the gods as no others could. These men lived according to strict laws of purity. They shaved all the hair from their bodies, including eyelashes and brows. They washed twice each day. They took no more than one wife. After relations with a woman they submitted to a ritual bath before they trod again upon the sacred temple grounds.

We did not wait long for the four priests. Each wore a fine linen kilt and a long, transparent overskirt pinned at the navel with a gold scarab. Leopard-skin stoles draped over their shoulders. Like Moses, each carried a wooden staff. They hurried to their places on either side of the stairs leading up to the throne. The cobra had not moved. Again Pharaoh raised his scepter.

When the tyrant's hand sliced through the air, each of the priests threw down his staff. Each staff became a cobra. Moses closed his eyes. He moved his lips as if in soundless prayer. Aharon and I shrank away from the venomous snakes.

Pharaoh's high-pitched laugh rang out. "My priests are as powerful as this Yahveh!"

A wind blew through the open audience hall. The room grew silent with expectation. The cobra that had sprung forth from my brother's stick lunged at the others. One by one it swallowed them all. I looked from one astonished face to another. I dared to look up at the pharaoh. He met my eyes with a stare of displeasure.

Everyone turned to watch Moses. He strode forward without fear. When he seized the snake by its neck, the scales turned back into bark. The snake's body stiffened. Once again my brother held his wooden staff. I did not doubt what my own eyes saw, what my spirit knew. Yahveh stood with us.

The priests looked up at Pharaoh with fear.

"Child's play!" he shrieked. "I have no interest in child's play! Be gone, all of you."

As we left the audience hall Moses stopped to embrace a passing soldier, a man who had once served under him. I could not hear their exchange of words.

When my brother returned to us, he did not speak of the conversation. "Tomorrow we begin," he said.

"Begin what? What will happen?"

Moses squeezed my shoulder. He said no more.

Later in the afternoon I complained to Aharon about our brother's secrecy. My temper flared. "He should trust us! Are we not partners in the liberation?"

Aharon urged me to have patience. "We must show our brother trust. I am sure we will have our part to play when the time comes."

I looked into Aharon's sweet face. He smiled at me. I could not deny the truth of his words. We each would have our part to play. I would have to wait for mine.

I worked hard that night to complete the day's neglected housework. Not long before dawn I fell asleep.

Neither Moses nor Aharon roused me when they left. I woke to the sound of the courtyard gate opening and closing. I leapt from my bed. I threw a cloak over my nightdress. I did not stop to wash or eat. I ran after my brothers as if my very life depended upon catching them.

I did not reach them until they stopped beside a low wooden platform built along the riverbank opposite the palace gate. I had walked so fast my chest heaved for want of air. Moses did not seem to notice me. He stared into the water as if someone spoke to him from its very depths.

"Why did you leave me behind?" I felt tears gather in my eyes. Was I of so little use to them?

Aharon put a finger to his lips. "We did not wish to wake you." He smiled with concern. "You work so hard."

His words reassured me. My pounding heart grew calm. In the silence I noticed that river traffic had ceased. People in festive clothing began to gather on the banks. Many of the women carried baskets of fruit and dried flowers. A group of lesser priests moved toward us with fifteen or twenty goats in their charge. The people gathered to sacrifice to Hapi, the Egyptian god of the Nile.

The palace gate opened. A long procession emerged. Half-naked acrobatic dancers flipped and turned in time to the flute and lyre players who followed. Behind them marched two rows of soldiers wearing long wigs, fine linen kilts, and gleaming swords. Each held a large ram's horn in his hand. They raised the horns to their lips and blew a stirring fanfare, loud enough to shake heaven and earth.

Pharaoh's ebony litter, held up by four strong servants, passed through the gate. Behind him four priests carried another litter, upon which rested a life-sized wooden idol of the blue river god, with his big belly and pendulous breasts. The figure was decorated with a gold breastplate, necklaces, and wristbands. A white linen cloth hid his loins. I could not look upon the strange creature, neither man nor woman, without revulsion.

A group of palace men and women followed the idol. I searched for Istnofret among them. At last I saw her. She seemed like a prisoner surrounded by attendants and soldiers. Our eyes met for an instant before she pulled her veil over her face. I longed to run to her.

The procession split to make way for Pharaoh. The gold cobra on his crown looked down on the people with malice. Moses and Aharon did not move. Priests gathered at the edge of the platform opposite my brothers. The ritual slaughterer stepped forward. A foul smell rose from the cluster of animals.

As the litter bearers stopped at the edge of the platform, Moses stepped onto the slaughter site. He faced the ruler of all Egypt and raised his staff high over his head.

"Yahveh, God of the Israelites, has sent me. He said, 'Let My people go that they may worship Me in the wilderness.' You have not listened. Thus says the mighty Yahveh, 'By this you will know I am Yahveh!'"

Moses turned away from Pharaoh to face the water. He brought the staff down hard upon its smooth surface.

A cry rose up from the crowd. The river had turned to blood.

EIGHTTEEN

Miryam

PEOPLE rushed to the riverbank. Several men lifted the polluted water to their lips. They spat it out in disgust. Fear spread through the crowd. Women began wailing as if for a lost child.

"It is a trick!" someone shouted. "He has drained the blood from the sacrificial animals into the Nile."

But the priests shook their heads and held up their hands. They had not yet taken the knife to a single goat.

A woman screamed as she uncovered a jug that she carried; the water in it had also turned to blood. I prayed that Yahveh had spared the waters of Goshen.

Pharaoh commanded his lector priests to match Yahveh's power.

"Let them call upon the river god to change it back!" several people cried. Pharaoh did not heed them.

We followed Pharaoh's litter and all his attendants to a stream near the temple of the frog goddess Heqet, where I had first met Princess Istnofret when I was a girl of thirteen. It seemed that a generation had passed in a single afternoon. I looked down at my worn, chafed hands. Once they had been young and soft. They had cradled baby Moses, smoothed the cloak of my beloved Nunn, tended to my ailing mother. So many losses! Over the years my heart had grown as thick and rough as my hands.

I frowned at myself for dwelling on the past. My people's future lay before me. I had been called to serve them with my brother. I would not look back, I would not rest until we reached the Promised Land.

The priests struck the surface of the stream just as the blood spread from the central branch. The Egyptians did not seem to understand the ruse.

Pharaoh laughed with scorn. "The God of the Israelites is no more powerful than my own lector priests!"

We returned home without permission to worship Yahveh in the wilderness. I held my breath as the canal in front of the house came into view. It, too, had turned to blood. A large group of Israelites stood waiting for us outside our gate. They ran to Moses with questions and pleas. They told him that all our water, even that already set aside for household use, had become putrid.

"Should I address them?" I asked my exhausted brother.

He looked from me to Aharon and back.

Can you not see I will make the better spokesperson? I said in my heart. *I will turn the crowd to our purpose while Aharon will do no more than offer sympathy for their suffering?*

Moses smiled at me. He knew that I understood what to do without instruction, without prompting.

"Miryam will speak," Moses announced as he and Aharon continued to move toward the house.

I stood silent while the crowd continued to gather. For a moment the task seemed too great. My heart pounded against my chest.

Someone brought a donkey cart for me to stand on. Several men helped me climb up. As I looked out across the crowd, I saw many women I had known in my youth from the markets. I saw some who had turned away from me after Pharaoh had failed to reduce the burdens of their men. I saw neighbors, craftsmen, and laborers. *These are my people*, I said to myself. *These are the people Yahveh means for me to serve. They need my assurance and guidance.*

My heart filled with love for the Israelites. Calmness fell over me. The words began to flow from my tongue with such ease that it seemed as if I had drunk too much of Aharon's sweet wine.

I called the people to order. I told them of the snakes in Pharaoh's throne room the day before and the events at the river that morning. I explained that the contamination of the water came from Yahveh.

"On this day our God has shown Himself to be more powerful than any other in the land. He has defeated Hapi. He has challenged Pharaoh. His purpose is our freedom from tyranny and oppression. We can not let our faith slacken. Even in difficult times we must stand firm!"

"When will He restore our water?" one woman cried out.

"We will die without fresh water," another added.

A clamor of fear and anger rose from the crowd.

"Have faith," I urged. "Tell your men to have faith. Tell your neighbors. Pray to Him."

I saw that the people trusted me. Many of the women fell to their knees to offer prayers to Yahveh. Some of the men followed. My spirit soared as if Yahveh Himself lifted me. Yahveh did not want the people of Goshen to stand by without acting.

I raised my hand. A hush fell over the crowd. "Let each able-bodied man join with his neighbors to dig wells in the sand along the river where it enters Goshen. By sundown we will have water for everyone."

The men set to work at once. The water that filtered through the sandy soil became clean enough to drink. The people rejoiced and praised my wisdom.

Only later—when Elisheva carried home our ration—did I realize that we could not bathe, clean the house, or scrub our clothing. I forgot my own words to the people. I forgot my own sense of duty and sacrifice.

"How can I run a household without water?" I cried out. "Yahveh asks too much of us!"

Elisheva comforted me with soothing words. She brushed my hair. I allowed her to rub a salve into the dry, cracked skin of my hands.

"Perhaps Yahveh took away our water to give your skin a chance to heal," she smiled. "I am sure all will be well, just as you have told our people."

That night I thanked Yahveh for Elisheva's love. I thanked Him for His trust in me. I prayed for Him to grant me ongoing faith and forbearance.

The next morning I ran to check our water jugs, the canals, and the rivulets. The water remained polluted. The terrible stink of dead fish hovered over the land. They littered the waterways. They piled up in the reeds and on the riverbanks. None could stand the stench.

Pharaoh's heart hardened against the suffering of his own people and ours. He cared for nothing but his imagined triumph of will over Yahveh. He would not relent.

So Yahveh's afflictions continued.

Every evening at sunset Moses went before the people to assure them that Yahveh did not forget us. He urged the people, as I had, to remain steadfast in their faith. He spoke of a glorious future. Still he did not mention the Promised Land.

I watched over those who supervised the wells. Together we ensured that the water distribution remained fair according to each family's needs. Women lined up each morning for the day's allotment. Moses agreed that under special circumstances—a birth, death, or serious illness—the family could have an extra portion. Those who wished to petition for more pleaded their cases to me. I knew how to look a woman in the eye to see if she told the truth. I could read her heart by the way she held her body. I shamed those who tried to trick me. I exposed those who offered bribes. All of Goshen soon knew that I could not be fooled or corrupted.

The distribution of water occupied me all day. Caring for my family filled the evening. I did not lament my exhaustion. Instead I gained strength from walking among the people, from receiving their ever-growing respect.

Several days after the water turned to blood Tzipporah became ill with the fever. Elisheva summoned me to examine the concubine who lay in the stable, drenched in her own sweat. I knew the signs of the fever well—chills, delirium, weakness. Mother had suffered from recurrent bouts for many years. The illness was all too common in Goshen. "Give her myrrh for the fever and keep her wrapped in blankets," I advised Elisheva. "Make sure she drinks enough."

"How will I know if it is not enough?"

I rattled off the signs of dehydration. "Sunken eyes, cracked lips, headache."

Elisheva's eyes grew wide with fear. I saw that she wanted me to stay and help her nurse her friend, but I had too many other pressing chores.

"She will be better in a day or two," I said. I left to prepare the evening meal.

Later Moses came to me in the kitchen. His face grew red with anger as he struggled to spit out a few words.

"You did not summon me."

I looked at him with confusion.

"Tzipporah is ill," he added. "You left her in the stable."

"That is where she prefers to be," I said with too much sharpness in my voice. "Elisheva was with her."

Moses frowned. He opened his mouth as if to object. Then he shook his head, turned, and left.

Tzipporah's health returned in three days. The river cleared a week after Yahveh had turned it to blood. I rejoiced by spending two days cleaning and washing. On the eve of the second day I stood back to admire all I had accomplished. The house sparkled inside and out. The fresh-swept ground of the courtyard looked like a finished floor. Even the donkeys and their stable glistened.

I took a drink from the fresh water in one of our large jugs. As the cool water passed through my lips, I felt my brother's hand on my shoulder.

"Peace, Brother, and Yahveh be with you."

"And with you," Moses replied. "Your home is a model of cleanliness and order."

I should have taken pride in this compliment. But my spirit plunged. I wanted Moses to admire me for my part in our mission, not my skill with the scrubbing brush.

"What more can I do to help our people?" I asked. "The women pay special heed to what I say."

Moses bowed to me. "Tomorrow in the morning we go again to Pharaoh. After that you will know what must be done."

My face flushed with pleasure. I embraced my brother. My heart offered a silent prayer to Yahveh. *May I never forget that I dedicate my life to Your work.*

On the following day we stood before Merenptah once again. Once again Moses delivered a message from Yahveh.

"Thus says Yahveh. 'Let My people go that they may worship Me. If you refuse to let them go I will smite Egypt with frogs. They will come into your house, your bed, your servants' houses, your ovens, and your kneading bowls.'"

Pharaoh dismissed us with shrill laughter on his lips. "I am more mighty than this Yahveh! I do not fear Him."

By the time we reached the palace gate word of Yahveh's next affliction had begun to spread among the people of Egypt. A growing crowd followed us to the river. Piles of dead fish still remained on the riverbank. I pulled my veil over my nose to keep out the stink.

Everyone waited in silence to see what Moses would do. But I could not believe my eyes when he handed his staff to Aharon.

"Hold out your hand over the water," he ordered. "Bring out the frogs upon the land of Egypt."

Aharon seemed afraid of the staff. But he did as Moses asked. As he held it over the water, the wood pulsed in the sunlight like a creature that struggled to regain its own life.

Aharon did not have the strength to hold the stick still. He grasped it with both hands. His face turned white. He looked at Moses in panic. Moses took the staff from him and held it out with a single steady hand.

The frogs came forth.

They teemed over the land, more numerous than Pharaoh's soldiers. Away from the water that nourished and hydrated them, they died. One could not walk anywhere without frogs underfoot. Their yellow guts spilled over the ground. Flesh and sandals became sticky with the foul matter. As my brother predicted, the frogs recognized no boundaries. They entered palace and hut alike. They crawled into beds. They infiltrated kitchens. I found them in my baking bowls.

That afternoon I closed myself into the small, dark grain storage room in our house. My spirit cried out to Yahveh. *If we are Your chosen people, why do You subject us to such an abomination?*

He did not answer. I grew desperate.

In the silence I heard my own heart reply. *Our people must take the afflictions of blood and frogs as a warning to separate our ways from the Egyptians. Only then will Yahveh be able to make a great nation of us. We must not worship their gods. We must not oppress others as they have oppressed us. We must care for the needy. We must never build monuments to death at the expense of neglecting the living.* All this I would convey to our people.

What of my own anguish? My longing for Yahveh's voice, his light, his love—when would these return to me?

The odor of dying frogs reached my nostrils. I heard the creatures hopping outside the storage-room door. For two days I had cleaned our house. Now Yahveh sent frogs to destroy the order and cleanliness that I cherished.

Perhaps I cherished it too much.

In that moment my own weakness lay before me. Yahveh would not come to me if I put my comfort before the well-being of His people.

I rose to return to Yahveh's work.

I found Elisheva in the kitchen surrounded by frogs. She stood weeping, unable to move.

I kicked the frogs away from her. I held her in my arms. In a few moments she caught her breath enough to speak.

"A crowd gathers outside our gate," she said. "No one can find Moses."

I took her hand. "Come with me."

I climbed onto the donkey cart to calm the crowd. I told them how we must show ourselves independent of Egyptian ways. I assured them that Yahveh would offer rewards far greater than the riches of our oppressors if we chose to dedicate ourselves to His service.

The people hung on to my words as if they were more precious than gold. They promised to honor Him all of their days.

As I stepped down I could not help wondering if I would have done better with the stick than Aharon had. Did Moses not see the difference between us? Aharon was much beloved for his gentle ways and sweet nature. But I was born to be a leader.

When the crowd dispersed I enlisted Elisheva's boys and Gershom to catch all the frogs they could find. I promised a special almond cake to whoever captured the most. By the end of the day we had cleared the kitchen and washing room. We placed open water troughs as traps around the edges of the rooms. Elisheva's older sons took turns at the windows.

As I prepared a meal, Elisheva approached me. I felt an unusual hesitation in her step and apprehension on her face.

I put down my work to give her my full attention. "What troubles you?"

"Nothing troubles me." But the pitch of her voice told me otherwise.

I grew impatient with her reluctance. I shrugged my shoulders. I turned back to the onions. She did not move. After a moment she spoke.

"They promised in fear," she whispered. "What good is a promise to honor a god if it is made in fear?"

I studied her expression. In her eyes I saw that the challenge did not come from her own pure heart. She betrayed our God with the words of an ignorant shepherdess.

My face flushed with anger. My tongue lashed out at her.

"Who asks this question?" I did not expect an answer.

For the second time that day Elisheva began to cry. This time her tears did not move me.

"You may tell your friend this. Love alone does not gain respect or grant authority."

The next day, soon after dawn, three messengers arrived from the palace in chariots. They brought a summons for us to appear before Pharaoh without delay.

As we flew through Goshen on the dusty road I clung to the side of the chariot with both my hands and all my strength. The houses and people passed in a great blur. I feared my spirit would separate from my body. Toward the end of our ride I felt steady enough to glance at my brothers, each in a chariot beside me. In that exultant moment I knew we had strength enough to overcome any obstacle in our pursuit of Yahveh's way.

We stood before Pharaoh's throne room. A multitude of servants rushed around the tyrant himself, plucking frogs from the floor, his throne, his person. I felt repulsed and triumphant at the same time.

Merenptah rose to his feet. His shrill voice rang out.

"My queen, the woman who called herself your mother, is sickened by how you have turned against her people!"

She is sickened by your lies and cruelty, I said to myself.

A frog landed on Pharaoh's shoulder. His face winced with disgust. He removed the creature with his thumb and forefinger and threw it at one of his lector priests.

Pharaoh turned back to Moses. For a few moments he stared hard at my brother without moving or speaking. Then he frowned and began to speak, as if with great reluctance.

"Ask your God to remove the frogs from me and my people. Then I will let your people leave to make offerings in the wilderness."

I smiled to myself as Merenptah acknowledged Yahveh's existence. From his tone and manner I could see that his pride had suffered.

Moses stepped forward through the frogs as if he did not see them.

"You must let us go seven days hence to make our sacrifice in the wilderness."

Even then I heard disbelief in my brother's voice. Merenptah would not let us go. Not yet.

"Call them off now!" Pharaoh bellowed.

"As you wish," Moses replied. "The frogs will retreat from you, your servants, and your people. Thus will you know Yahveh's might."

We followed Moses to the river, where frogs continued to stream from the water. The courtiers and priests gathered around him. My brother lifted his arms. "O Yahveh, hear me!" he cried out. "Let the frogs return to the waters."

I waited for a sign. In the first minutes nothing happened. I looked to the ground. I looked to the heavens. I closed my eyes to shield them from the sun. A breeze kissed my cheeks. Then it died away. I felt Yahveh's presence in the stillness. He heard my brother's prayer.

The frogs ceased their relentless croaking. Many returned to the water. Those on the land far from the river died out as the sun rose. A lingering odor settled in the houses, the courtyards, and the fields. The servants of Heqet hid themselves in shame.

The Children of Israel cheered Moses as a hero. They listened with admiration as he spoke to them of faith and perseverance. Yahveh's afflictions had convinced them of His might. My brother's ability to summon Yahveh had caused the elders to revere him as a prophet.

The Israelites began to keep vigil outside our courtyard gate. They waited in growing numbers for Yahveh's prophet. When he appeared they sought his advice and wisdom. They sought me too—for comfort, advice, and words of faith.

I, who had never given birth to children of my own, found that Yahveh blessed me with many.

Pharaoh promised to let us go. He did not. Before we began to gather our animals for sacrifice, he ordered additional soldiers to patrol all roads that led to the wilderness. He called the Children of Israel back to their brick making and temple building.

Yahveh sent more afflictions. But now He kept them far from Goshen. In this way did the Children of Israel begin to know Yahveh's favor.

After the frogs, Yahveh sent gnats. They swarmed over man and beast. Throughout the capital city, in the fields along the main waterways of the Nile, all the dust of the ground turned to biting gnats. The lector priests warned Pharaoh that the wrath of a mighty God fell over the Egyptians. Yet still Merenptah's hardened heart did not change.

"Pharaoh shows us how one act of evil leads to another," I told the people. "Do not fear. Soon we will exchange the bondage of our service to Egypt with service to Yahveh."

Two weeks later came the flies. They gathered in great clouds to attack people and animals. The bites festered into oozing wounds. Again Pharaoh promised to let the Israelites go if Yahveh removed the afflictions. Again Pharaoh did not keep his word.

As the season of Akhet fell away toward the shorter, colder days of Proyet, Moses went before Pharaoh once more. Pharaoh remained unmoved. Yahveh sent a heavy pestilence upon the Egyptian livestock.

Those who traveled into the city returned with terrible tales. Horses with swollen eyelids and necks fell in the roads struck by fever. Sheep, goats, and cattle bled from the nostrils. Their foaming mouths turned blue. They died with great suffering.

The Egyptians lost much of their livestock. Pharaoh's own stables stood depleted. His priests warned him that their power could not equal that of our God. Merenptah did not heed them.

Our protection from gnats, flies, and the death of our animals did not reduce the suffering of the men enslaved to Pharaoh's taskmasters. As the weeks wore on the people began to whisper of their desire to flee Egypt forever. One day the elders met with Moses to ask if Yahveh could find our people a new home, far from Egyptian tyranny.

At last Moses revealed Yahveh's plan to lead us to the Promised Land. He impressed upon them the need to keep this secret from the Egyptian people, who would rather see us destroyed than free.

Word spread throughout Goshen in hushed tones. The people held their tongues lest an Egyptian overhear. They expressed their joyous anticipation to me with smiles, embraces, and gifts.

I marveled at my brother's wisdom. I had wanted to tell the people of the Promised Land on the day of his return. Now I saw that a dream risen from their own midst brought more hope and determination than one imposed upon them.

One day in the Egyptian month of Ka-Hr-Ka, four months after the afflictions began, Moses asked Hosea to fetch a bucket of soot from the kiln of a local potter. Two weeks had passed since the last report of fallen livestock. We were to return to Pi-Ramesse that afternoon.

Many longed to accompany us. Moses warned them to remain home lest new afflictions fall upon them. Only Hosea and a small group of fearless young men followed us.

We found Pharaoh near the river in his litter. Once more a gathering stood ready to sacrifice to the god of the Nile. Moses took the bucket of soot from Hosea. He walked to the platform. The crowd made way for the Israelite whose fame grew greater than in the days he had commanded Egypt's army. Moses reached his hand into the bucket of soot. He tossed fistfuls of the powder into the heavens. The powder filled the air until a fine dust settled over the land.

Soon shrieks of horror rose up from the people. Great welts of pustules erupted on their legs and feet. Fever struck them down. I fled from the city. As I ran, I heard someone call out that even Pharaoh's high priest had a blistering boil on his leg.

When I reached our house, I wanted nothing more than to clean myself of any lingering soot. My hands ached for water. I ran to our washing room.

I stopped before the closed door. A beautiful voice filled my ears. It chanted without words. The lovely song soothed me. It sounded like a heavenly being.

Who could it be? I pulled open the door just enough to peek inside.

I saw Elisheva and Tzipporah dancing like two foolish young girls with the timbrels we used for the vine harvest celebration. They had removed their clothes.

I opened the door a little wider. The two played at their game alone. Tzipporah appeared lost in her song. I could not believe that such a beautiful voice came from her mouth.

Elisheva noticed me in the doorway. She flushed with embarrassment. She motioned for Tzipporah to stop.

As the two women stood in uncomfortable silence before me I saw what they had kept hidden from me beneath their loose clothing.

Each woman carried a child in her womb.

NINETEEN

Tzipporah

MIRYAM'S devotion to Yahveh seemed to grow with each new affliction. She worked day and night to increase those who followed her God, but she did not see how fear of Him spread like a skin-wasting disease among the Egyptians and Israelites alike. As her faith grew, her compassion wavered and died. Even Elisheva—who never uttered an unfavorable word about anyone—complained that when I was sick with the fever Miryam had not come to my bedside.

She spent long hours away from home. Released from her stern eye, Elisheva and I felt free to enjoy each other's company. We sought the Goddess for respite from the darkness around us. We prayed to Her for the well-being of our unborn daughters. We thanked Her for bringing us music and dance. Then we played with the boys and ate simple food from the kitchen storeroom.

On the day Miryam interrupted our worship, she stood in the doorway of the washing room and stared at our swollen bodies as if the sight offended her. All my disappointment in her turned to pity. Whatever Moses had once imagined, whatever I might have hoped, Miryam could never be my sister; in her fervor for Yahveh she had lost the spark of the Goddess that graces every woman at birth. Once it had flickered and glowed in the presence of Elisheva and her children. Now it lay dead in her empty womb.

As we left the washing room, Miryam stooped to whisper something in Elisheva's ear. My friend's eyes opened wide with surprise.

"You have no cause to doubt," she murmured.

Miryam drew herself up to her full height. Her harsh gaze fixed upon Elisheva's sweet face. "I will find out for myself." Her voice seemed colder than a desert night in the season of soaking rain.

Elisheva's cheeks flushed. She looked down and shook her head.

When I asked her what Miryam had said, she refused to repeat it. I told myself I did not care. But curiosity lodged in my heart like a splinter too deep to remove.

Later Moses came to the stable and stroked my cheek to wake me. I felt his breath on my face and reached out my arms to pull him close. Since the evening I had gone to him, he had joined me almost every night. Each time he went to the capital or spoke with his God in the wilderness he returned a broken man. But when we lay together I imagined that Yahveh's burdens fell away from him and he became the simple shepherd who lay with the woman he loved.

He touched the swell of my stomach. "Will it be another son?" he murmured.

I did not tell him that the Goddess had promised me a daughter. Instead I stroked his head in silence.

"Miryam asked if I knew of a baby coming. 'Welcome news and long awaited,' I told her."

Miryam asked. Her question hovered like a scorpion between us. All at once I understood her exchange with Elisheva. She suspected that the child had a different father.

I whispered the name of the Goddess to banish the chill of Miryam's demon spirit from the warmth of our embrace.

Moses did not return to Pi-Ramesse for a month after the affliction of the boils. He helped in the vineyards and wandered in the wilderness. The Egyptians called this the season of Proyet—the time of bringing forth—

because the barley came into the ear and the flax bloomed. For me it was the season of lambing.

As word of my work with Nahshon's flock spread, many sought my help. Most families in Goshen kept at least one goat or sheep, but no one seemed to care for them. They fed their animals too much or too little and they did not offer enough water on hot days or proper shelter during cold nights. They knew nothing of birthing. When a lamb presented breech or its hoof lodged inside the mother's pelvis, they made no effort to save either mother or child. They lost many animals for lack of knowledge and skill.

Thus I kept as busy during lambing time in Egypt as I ever had in Midyan. I ran from house to house, field to field. But when the evening star rose in the sky I always stopped to pray. I knew the Goddess heard me, because no animals died in my care.

I received many gifts in gratitude for my service, including something I had never dreamt of in Midyan—ten lambs of my own. And so Egypt brought me many blessings: Elisheva, a new child, the beginning of my own flock.

One afternoon toward the end of lambing season Elisheva summoned me home from a neighbor's house.

"Come," she urged. "They have gone to the capital and come back again."

I finished examining a healthy newborn kid and ran back to the house. Outside the courtyard gate Miryam told the gathering crowd of the latest confrontation with Pharaoh. She stood with her shoulders back and her head high. Her face glowed like a woman whose heart was filled with love. I did not know her.

"He stood firm before the tyrant," she announced. "He spoke with the might of Yahveh."

"Tell us everything!" one of the elders cried out. "Spare not a word!"

"He spoke of Yahveh's mercy," Miryam continued. "For by now

Yahveh could have stricken Pharaoh and his people hard enough to send them from the land."

"He is more mighty than any Egyptian god!" a man called out.

The people murmured in agreement.

Miryam nodded and flushed with pride. "He promised a new affliction if Pharaoh did not let us go to worship." She paused while the crowd grew silent with anticipation. She seemed to relish the moment.

"At this time tomorrow, Yahveh will send a heavy hail, such as has never been seen in Egypt since the day of its founding. Every man and beast that is not gathered into the house will die when the hail comes down on them."

I looked at all the worried faces around me. Miryam must have seen them too.

"Do not fear!" she called out. "Yahveh will keep the hail away from Goshen. But do not travel into the city tomorrow."

I wondered how much longer the afflictions could continue. They seemed to go on without reason or purpose. The people of Egypt and Goshen already feared Yahveh's power and Pharaoh only grew more stubborn.

I waited all night for Moses, but he did not come to me. Did Yahveh keep him through the long hours of darkness or had he fallen asleep in bed? I crept up to his room and opened the door just enough to peak inside. In the darkness I could see that he hovered near the window with his head bowed in prayer. I could not intrude between him and his God. I returned to the stable with regret.

At dawn Moses appeared with Miryam and Aharon in the courtyard. I hid in the shadows while they prepared to depart for the city. My lord took a drink of water. He grasped his staff and stood erect. I wanted to leap out and embrace him, but he seemed so far away.

Miryam had warned us not to travel into the capital. I did not care. Perhaps today Pharaoh would relent. If I followed them I could be a witness to my lord's triumph. I could offer my praise and admiration for his success as it happened. He would catch me in his arms. Moses the leader and Moses my lord would become one.

The walk to the capital skirted the edge of a single waterway that grew wider and wider. Footbridges spanned the small rivulets that often cut over our path. Soon it seemed as if we stood on an island, for another rivulet began to close in from the east. Everywhere I looked I saw vast expanses of water. Boats of different sizes floated by.

The tall white buildings of Pi-Ramesse rose on the horizon long before we reached the city. I could not have imagined the size of the palace walls, the gate, the endless rows of statues each taller than twenty men. Soldiers marched back and forth before the palace gate as people streamed in and out. Women carried baskets of dates on their heads and oxen pulled carts laden with water jugs. A crowd gathered on the bank of the Nile.

Everyone made way for Moses as he approached the riverbank. Some of the men bowed low and tried to touch the hem of his black kuttoneh. He swept past without pause as if he did not see them. Then he raised his staff to the heavens. Everyone grew silent. Even the people carrying wares into the palace stood still. When he spoke, his voice rang out like thunder across an empty plain.

"Thus says Yahveh: 'Hold out your arm toward the sky that hail may fall on all the land of Egypt.'"

A strong, cold wind cut through us and the sky grew dark as night. People began to run in every direction. Many forced their way into the palace gates. The soldiers who tried to stop them fell to the ground, trampled. Thunder cracked across the sky and fire streamed from the heavens to earth. Moses, Miryam, and Aharon stood firm in their place at the water's edge. I took cover beneath an abandoned wagon with several Egyptian women. We crowded close together.

The hail began to fall from the heavens. Balls of hard white matter as large as the hollow of my hand struck without mercy. Two people dropped

before me, battered and dead. An ox and several pigs fell not far away. The
air filled with shrieks and shouts. Soldiers fled inside the palace compound
for shelter. As the stones fell they formed a cold, slippery white layer over
the ground. It soon rose to be as high as my knee.

I do not know how long the hail pounded us. The morning passed into
afternoon with no relief. I saw nothing but white wherever I looked. It
seemed as if I had gone blind.

I shook with fear and grief. My limbs felt as brittle as dry twigs from
being so cramped. After many hours, four men carrying a covered chair
emerged from the palace gate. Though the hailstones did not penetrate the
cover, the porters slipped on the white ground. They stopped to set the
chair down and lifted their arms up to shield themselves. But one by one
they fell dead to the ground.

"Pharaoh himself sits inside the sedan," one of the women next to me
whispered. Her voice quivered with fright. "If he does not give in the God
of Israel will destroy us."

The other woman agreed. "Our gods can not protect us against their
God."

"Moses of Israel!" Pharaoh called out, shouting to make himself heard.

I craned my neck to see the place where Moses still stood at the river's
edge, his brother and sister on either side. The little patch of ground
beneath their feet remained untouched by Yahveh's hail.

"Your God is in the right and I and my people are in the wrong. Plead
with your God that He may end the thunder and hail. I will let you go.
You need stay no longer."

Moses drew himself up to his full height. His long hair fluttered behind
him in the wind. No one who looked upon him doubted that he was a man
destined to lead. He spoke to Pharaoh with proud disdain.

"As I go out of the city I will spread out my hands to Yahveh. Thunder
and hail will fall no more. You will know that the earth is Yahveh's. But I
know that you and your courtiers do not yet fear Yahveh."

With that he turned and walked away. Miryam and Aharon followed.

The hail soon stopped. The skies cleared and soldiers ran out to escort Pharaoh back into his palace. I crawled out from under the wagon.

The dead fallen on the road in front of the palace gate numbered many more than the fingers on my hands. I ran to the edge of the river and vomited. When I looked away from the water I noticed another body, that of a little girl, lying face down in the reeds. She could not have been more than six or seven years old. What had she done to deserve such a punishment?

The sound of whimpering came from beneath the still body. I turned the girl over and released a young, frightened dog. The girl must have held him close in her arms to shield him from the hail.

His paw bled. When I picked him up his heart pounded against the hollow of my hand. His large, soft eyes begged me to protect him.

A cry tore through my body as if I was at once the mother of the girl, the orphaned dog, and the ravaged land.

How can my lord be the agent of such cruel punishment? I asked the Great Goddess. *How can Moses, who loves justice more than his own life, serve this terrible God?*

TWENTY

Tzipporah

A S I examined the dog's injury the sun came out and began to melt the slippery layer of hailstones on the ground. I tore a bit of cloth from the bottom of my dress to bind his paw.

Soldiers emerged from the palace to collect the corpses that littered the riverbank. People searched for missing loved ones. Cries of mourning and despair rose all around me. I wished I could fly away on the wings of a hawk and never again fill my eyes with such death and destruction. But I had only my own unsteady feet to carry me through the ruined landscape.

I saw trees stripped of their leaves, small dwellings collapsed under the weight of the hailstones, flax and barley transformed into broken stalks and stubble. I saw the corpses of cattle and men in the fields. I began to run as if a demon pursued me. Yet I felt no relief when I crossed into Goshen, where the land remained whole and the people unharmed. Instead I grew more frightened. Yahveh seemed no different from the god Baal Zephon, who sometimes sent violent storms that struck one part of Midyan while another remained untouched. Like Yahveh, the storm god destroyed the innocent along with the guilty. My own mother had perished in a flood of his making, though she had never neglected a sacrifice due to him.

I knew that gods of great strength and power did not remain constant. Today Yahveh favored the Israelites. But what about tomorrow? How could Moses and Miryam be so sure that Yahveh would not turn His wrath upon them and their people?

As I drew close to the house, I saw a large crowd gathered at the courtyard gate. Miryam stood before the people. She spoke of the great hailstorm and Yahveh's anger at Pharaoh. She remained so absorbed in her tale that she did not notice me slip past with the dog.

I found Elisheva sitting in the room that Miryam used to receive guests, opposite the kitchen. She reclined against large wool cushions woven from fine yarn that she had spun. Though the baby would not come for at least two moons, she looked as tired and swollen as a woman about to deliver. When I showed her the dog her face brightened.

"He ripped a nail from his paw. He had no collar so I brought him home." I said no more—I had seen enough tragedy for both of us.

Elisheva took the little dog from me as if she handled a delicate treasure. "Maybe he is hungry; what can we feed him?"

"He will drink some milk."

Elisheva nodded. She handed me the dog and rose with great difficulty. She held my arm to steady herself as we walked to the kitchen.

We fed the creature drop by drop on the edge of my thumb. Elisheva summoned the boys to watch. As each took his turn holding the dog he seemed to gather strength. Soon he stood on all four legs and pranced from one set of hands to the next. Everyone laughed with delight. But when Miryam walked into the kitchen the little creature squatted to urinate. Fear stabbed the pit of my stomach. Miryam's face grew red and her hands tensed into fists. I braced myself for the explosion of her fury.

Everyone watched in wonderment as she exhaled with a gentle sigh. She closed her eyes. Her lips moved as if in silent prayer. After a moment she met my eyes with nothing more than a mild frown.

Relief flooded me with a desire to speak. I wanted to tell her of how I had come to rescue the animal. I wanted to describe how it had revived Elisheva's waning spirits. I wanted to say that we must cling to whatever life the gods left us whether it be animal or human, broken or whole.

I imagined how my words might bring Miryam's face to soften with understanding. But still my lips remained sealed in her stern presence.

I gathered the dog in my arms and took him to the stable.

I borrowed a small skin trough and stuffed it with straw to make a bed for the little creature. When Moses came to visit me I did not confess that I had followed him into the capital. Instead I told him that I had found the dog in some reeds along the canal.

"Drawn from the reeds like me," he laughed.

We lay together in the straw. Moses hinted that Yahveh would send even more afflictions before Pharaoh would relent and allow the Israelites to leave.

"I am sorry for the Egyptians." I said this and no more, for I feared that a direct criticism of Yahveh would arouse my lord's wrath. But how could a man who loved justice not regret the suffering of innocents whose only crime was to live in Pharaoh's realm?

Moses sighed. "The Egyptian people must come to see Yahveh's might and urge Pharaoh to let us go. I am sorry it is the only way."

His regret made me bold.

"Yahveh is a harsh God."

Moses stroked my head. "A god who rescues his children from oppression is not harsh."

"And when they come to oppress each other?" I whispered. "Will Yahveh rain His afflictions upon the Promised Land?"

His answer came without hesitation. "In the Promised Land no man will oppress another."

I could have cried for my beloved's innocence.

I wound my arms around his neck and kissed him on the lips. I felt his passion for me rise.

I will be one with you always, my whole body told him. *I will be your comfort and your home*. For I knew his vision must fail. No god, however fearsome, could control the human heart.

The next two afflictions followed fast upon the hail. While the land around the capital remained wet from the storm, Moses went to Pharaoh again. Soon after he returned we felt a strong east wind in Goshen. It blew all the rest of that day and all night. In the morning the air filled with a strange and frightening drone. It grew so loud that I felt my head would burst.

By midday swarms of yellow locusts darkened the sky like clouds gathering for a storm. Yet they did not drop upon the land of Goshen. They laid their eggs in the wet, sandy soil of Pi-Ramesse and stripped what little green remained on the land. The fruit of the trees and the grasses of the fields disappeared.

Pharaoh soon summoned Moses to ask for Yahveh's mercy. Once again he promised to let the Israelites go. But after Moses called upon Yahveh and a strong western wind blew the locusts away, Pharaoh refused to honor his word.

The Israelites began to despair.

"Pharaoh will never relent," they murmured. Miryam assured them that Pharaoh's downfall approached. She offered words to inspire all those who doubted, to bring them back into the fold.

"Our victory will be sweet," she said. "The Promised Land awaits the faithful."

One afternoon, a week after the locusts, Moses sought me in a pasture where I watched over Nahshon's flock. I felt my face blossom with pleasure to see him. A fleeting smile stole over his serious expression. He sat down a little further from me than I liked. I began to shift myself closer to him, but he held up his hand in a gesture for me to stay in my place.

"Another affliction comes," he said. "A darkness man can feel."

"When will it all be over?" I asked.

"Pharaoh's heart is hardened. The afflictions will end only when he loses what can not be replaced."

The prophecy flowed from his tongue as if it did not touch his heart. I did not know what to say to this instrument of Yahveh. I did not know him.

"How much longer?" I asked after a silence.

"You will see the granite cliffs of your childhood after the next new moon. We will sacrifice to Yahveh at the mountain of Sinn. Then He will lead us into the Promised Land."

I studied the new creases in the corners of his eyes and on his brow. His hair and beard were streaked with white. In the six months since we had come to Egypt he had aged ten years. I thanked the Goddess that his heart still yearned for what comfort I could give him.

I slid closer to him and raised my hand to stroke his hair as I knew he liked. But instead of taking me in his arms, he pulled away. The words stumbled from his scarred lips.

"That must be over between us." He gazed into my eyes for a moment and then turned away.

I looked at him with confusion. Had Miryam convinced him that the child belonged to another? Did he mean to divorce me?

"But..." I faltered. My eyes filled with tears.

"You have committed no offense," he said in a low voice.

"Then why do you cast me off?" I wept.

He looked at me with great weariness. "I do not cast you off. You are the mother of my sons. But He requires me to be pure when I go to Him. He might call me at any time."

"Is there no other way?" I whispered.

Moses shook his head and rose to his feet. "We can not touch. We can not be alone together. The temptation is too great."

My heart fell away from me into a dark well. Words flowed from my mouth without reason or consideration. "The Goddess will be angry."

Moses turned back to me. I sought a tender eye beneath his stern brow, but his gaze remained unyielding.

"Let your goddess seek her worshippers elsewhere. I direct my service to Yahveh alone."

I wept until I had nothing left to weep, until the night shadows crept across the ground and filled my hollow chest.

While everyone slept I prayed to the Goddess. I promised not to forsake Her. In return She brought me hope that the separation would last only until we left Egypt, or perhaps until I gave birth. But She could not soften my anger toward Yahveh. It took root in me and spread like a disease. Each time my lord greeted me in passing, each time he spoke to me from a careful distance, each night I spent with the dog in my arms, the well of my hatred for Yahveh rose.

Elisheva watched my transformation. But her health remained fragile and I feared the truth would upset her. I told her only that I felt Yahveh asked too much of Moses and that I feared he grew old before his time. I deceived her only in what I omitted. She did not press me further.

The ninth affliction came the day after Moses severed our bond of the flesh. In the middle of the afternoon a cloud hung on the horizon toward Pi-Ramesse. Messengers soon brought word of a large sandstorm. It swept across the capital and all the surrounding land. For three days people could not travel in or out of the city. Never before had a storm of such ferocity struck Egypt. When at last the winds settled and the storm departed, a thick layer of sand and dust covered everything in Pi-Ramesse. Piles of sand taller than a man blocked the doorways of huts and fine homes alike. The courtyards and gardens of Pharaoh's palace lay buried and ruined.

Again Pharaoh summoned Moses. Miryam reported that this time he granted permission for the Israelites and their children to leave for seven days if their herds remained behind.

"Moses insisted that we must bring the cattle in order to make the proper sacrifice." She stood at her usual post on the donkey cart in front of the courtyard gate. "He demanded an additional gift of sacrifice from Pharaoh himself."

She paused to take a drink of water from a skin someone handed up to her.

"Merenptah flew into a rage," she continued. "He banished Moses from his presence forever, upon threat of death."

"Then we will never be free to go," someone cried out.

"Have faith," Miryam replied. "Yahveh has not done this much only to abandon us."

I knew that Moses often spoke with Yahveh. He went into the wilderness at dusk and sometimes remained away for half the night. Whenever I saw him he looked tired and worn. But on the morning after his final audience with Pharaoh he appeared in the kitchen full of purpose and energy. He called for the Israelites to meet him in the assembly place, a fallow field with a speaker's platform. All of the household, even the boys, went to hear him.

"Children of Israel!" he began. "Soon Yahveh will defeat Pharaoh. We will be free of Egyptian tyranny. Our future awaits us in the Promised Land. Great joy will be felt in our midst."

The fire in my lord's eyes and breath inflamed the heart of every person in the field that day. For a few moments even I believed in his mission as if it were my own. My grief and anger gave way to pride, for all my lord intended to accomplish, for his mighty courage.

He lifted his hand and waited for silence before continuing. "Today Yahveh asks you to borrow precious objects from your Egyptian neighbors—gold, silver, jewels, and cloth. These are to glorify our sacrifice to Him. In seven days I will give you instructions for our departure."

After Moses left, Miryam ran from group to group. She told people to use the name of her brother when asking for the items. "He is esteemed among Pharaoh's courtiers and the people of Egypt," she said. "Borrow whatever they have of value."

I alone among the women of our household did not call upon our Egyptian neighbors. I did not understand Yahveh's greed. For what did the people need such riches?

Miryam and Elisheva returned to the house late in the afternoon. Elisheva wore chains of gold and silver around her neck and golden horses in her ears. Miryam, who I had never seen adorned in any way, had golden hoops in her ears and nose. When they uncovered their baskets I saw fine robes of bleached linen and a heavy cloak of yellow-dyed wool. They seemed surprised that I had acquired nothing.

"You have many acquaintances to ask," Elisheva said. She knew that I often attended the animals of Egyptians who dwelt in Goshen.

I looked at her face flushed with pleasure, her gleaming eyes, the long chains that grazed the top of her big belly. She had been my friend these many months and I loved her gentle heart. But at that moment I turned from her in disgust.

"What is it?" Elisheva implored.

I whirled back to face her. The truth spilled from my mouth. "I do not see why we should take these things. Why does this God not tell the people to seek what they need for a journey? Without water skins and tents, clothing to shield against the sun, donkeys, and foodstuff, we will perish. What use will all the gold of Egypt be to us then?"

Elisheva's mouth hung open. Tears pooled in her eyes.

Miryam heard me and came forward. She grabbed my wrist and her sharp eyes stabbed into me. "Do you dare question the will of Yahveh?"

"He is not my God," I replied.

"If you have no faith in my brother's leadership," she hissed, "you should go back to your own people."

I pulled my arm out of her strong grasp. "You will be of little help to your brother or your God if you confuse the two," I whispered.

Miryam raised her hand as if to strike me. I did not cower. What blow could be worse than the loss of my beloved's affection?

Elisheva pushed herself between us. "Please stop," she begged. "For the sake of Moses and Aharon, for the sake of our unborn daughters, we must love each other as sisters."

Miryam lowered her hand to her side. She buried her head in the hollows of her hands and walked away.

TWENTY-ONE

Miryam

I WITHDREW to my room in anger. Of course I did not take my brother for a god. What god would have chosen her for a companion?

I opened a chest to sort through clothing for our journey. I formed two piles—items to give away and items to keep. The task did not calm me as I had hoped. My troubled heart dwelt on Elisheva's distress. Why had I not restrained myself? I already knew that Tzipporah did not put her faith in Yahveh. I held no power to change that. But Elisheva hated discord. I should have avoided the confrontation for her sake.

I left my sorting to offer Elisheva an apology. I found her in the receiving room with all three little boys.

I sent the children to empty the chamber pot from the washing room into the canal and to draw water for the evening meal. When they left I sat down beside her.

"I am sorry that I caused you distress."

Elisheva offered a weak smile. I saw hesitation in her eyes and in her parted lips. Sorrow washed over me. Once we had shared everything. Now she kept secrets. She no longer opened her heart to me. Tzipporah stood between us.

"Tell me," I urged.

She bit her lips. She bowed her head to remove the gold and silver chains. She took the earrings from her ears. She pressed the jewels into the hollow of my hand.

"I myself can not explain why we took these things," she whispered. Her eyes grew large and fearful, as if she expected me to turn upon her in anger. When had she become afraid of me?

"To pay for the labors of our men," I said. "And as compensation for the bribes."

"The bribes?"

"When the soldiers came..."

I could not continue. Memory sealed my throat with grief.

"When they took bribes from the mothers," Elisheva recalled. She pressed her hands against her unborn child. Tears filled her eyes.

"Our children will soon be safe." I had dedicated myself to this purpose so many years ago at the river. For this purpose alone did Yahveh still breathe life into my nostrils.

I wanted to show Elisheva that my anger had passed. "Tzipporah did not know about the bribes. I should have explained. On the matter of the tents, clothing, and water skins, she is right. We must not delay attending to these essentials."

I kissed my beloved sister. I rose to my feet. I had much to do for our people's departure.

A week later, at the beginning of the Egyptian month of Renwet—the time of the ripened barley—Moses called us to accompany him to the palace once more. "This is the last time," Moses promised.

"Pharaoh has threatened to kill you if you appear before him again."

Moses smiled at me as if I had raised a minor concern.

On our way to Pi-Ramesse we passed men harvesting the rich fields of Goshen. When we crossed into the district of the capital city the ruined fields lay empty. The huge statues of Rameses at the city gate stood half buried in sand and garbage. Dust had turned the high stone walls from white to brown. Inside the palace many people still labored to clear sand from the courtyards. The beautiful gardens lay in ruins.

Moses had said that this audience was to be the last. But month after month Pharaoh had watched the destruction of his land yet remained unmoved. What more could Yahveh do?

I could not imagine what horror lay ahead for the people of Egypt. I did not guess that Yahveh's justice would bring such retribution for our suffering.

When we came before the tyrant my knees grew weak. But as Moses stepped forward Merenptah did not seem to recall his promise to execute Yahveh's prophet.

They locked eyes in angry silence. Once they had fought together as comrades on the battlefield. Now they faced each other as bitter enemies.

Moses spoke first. "I bring a message from Yahveh."

Pharaoh folded his scepter and flail over his chest. "I am son of Amun-Re, beloved of Seth and Thoth. The gods ridicule this Yahveh and His thick-tongued messenger."

Moses did not flinch. He stood tall and noble. He delivered Yahveh's message in a strong voice with no hesitation.

As he spoke, the faces of Pharaoh's courtiers, priests, and guards grew pale with fear. Only Pharaoh remained unmoved. I felt my eyes grow wide with shock. I turned to Aharon who looked no less surprised by Yahveh's new threat and Pharaoh's continued refusal. A leader should feel the suffering of his people as if it were his own. Yet Pharaoh seemed to care more for the dirt under his feet than those whom his gods entrusted him to protect.

"Go from me!" Pharaoh shouted. "Take care never to come before me again, for the day I see your face you will die."

"You have spoken well," Moses replied in a cold voice. "I will not see your face again."

The next morning Moses stood before the community in the field of meeting. He gave instructions about the Passover offering and described how to mark our doorposts with blood so Yahveh would pass over our homes as He brought the final affliction. After my brother spoke, I walked through Goshen to make sure that everyone understood what Yahveh asked of us. I also told them the names of all the craftsmen who, at my request, had stockpiled tents and water skins and kuttonehs and head coverings made of linen. I asked the wealthy to help purchase these items for the poor amongst us. Groups of men and women gathered to hear me. Some had not been at the assembly, others had not heard well enough in the crowd.

I held each detail of the Passover sacrifice like a jewel on my tongue. I delivered the instructions as a gift from Yahveh. "We stand at the beginning of history," I told everyone with great pride. I knew that long after my bones had scattered into dust our nation would remember this day.

"On the tenth of this month each household will single out a yearling ram. On the fourteenth day at twilight you will slaughter this ram as the Passover offering. If your household is small, two households should join together."

"What do we do with the offering?" An eager voice always interrupted.

"Roast it over fire and eat it with unleavened bread and bitter herbs. Eat it in haste. Any left over must be burned. Be ready to leave when word comes." I paused to make sure they listened with care to the instructions that followed. "This you must do to protect the lives of your children. When you slaughter the ram, take a bunch of hyssop. Dip it into the slaughter basin. Apply the blood to your lintel and the two doorposts. Yahveh will go through the land of Egypt to punish our oppressors. With the blood as a sign He will pass over our houses."

When I returned home at twilight I threw my arms around Moses.

"We are already on our way!" I exclaimed.

He laughed at my exuberance. "Did you walk among the people?"

"I have done nothing else this whole day."

"Do they understand what is required of them?"

"They understand. They await their deliverance with joyful hearts."

Moses bowed. "Your devotion to the people is Yahveh's glory."

I felt my face blossom into a smile. Our eyes met. "I am blessed in my purpose," I replied.

I bent over the water jug to take a drink. As I reached for the cup I heard the courtyard gate open. At the sound of many hooves and bleating lambs I turned.

Tzipporah led a small flock of lambs. They scampered after her in a close group.

The boys came running from the house. Elisheva followed with laborious steps. She paused to smile at the small black animals. I moved to give her my arm.

"Where are they from?" I asked Elisheva.

"The lambs she was promised. From the people she helped."

"I did not realize..." I began. What had I not realized? That anyone would find enough value in Tzipporah's service to offer such generous payment. I left my sentence unfinished. I did not want to shame myself in Elisheva's eyes any further.

Elisheva laughed at Gershom as he tried to catch a lamb. After a moment she turned to me. "I am glad to see Tzipporah happy again."

"Has she been unhappy?" I asked with surprise.

"Have you not noticed?"

I shrugged. Tzipporah's spirit never seemed to dwell among us. Her affections, her desires, her hopes—all remained as alien to me as they had been on the day of her arrival.

"Perhaps the pregnancy tired her," I said.

The next day so many people stopped me on the way to market that I did not reach my destination until midmorning. Everywhere I turned another women begged a moment of my time. When the sun reached its zenith, one woman noticed my basket, still empty. She offered to shop for me. I hesitated for a moment. I knew that no one could hold a merchant to my exacting standards. No one had as sharp an eye for a tender chicken, a sweet melon, a crisp lettuce.

But Yahveh had called upon me to guide the people. They needed me. To serve them well I would have to put aside my pleasures.

I handed the woman my basket.

All day the women of Goshen had asked me what food and supplies they should pack. I replied that we could not carry the burdens of Egypt with us in our possessions. I promised to advise them in greater detail the following day after I had consulted with Moses.

When at last I returned home I did not find my brother in the house. Elisheva had not seen him. She suggested I ask Aharon.

I walked along the canal toward the vineyard. But something drew me into the olive grove instead. White blossoms covered the gnarled branches. Beams of sunlight filtered down through the thick crowns of the trees.

I walked between the rows until I saw my brother's black kuttoneh. I drew close enough to see his face. He swayed back and forth with his eyes closed. His imperfect lips moved without sound in perfect prayer.

I waited for my brother to notice me. A gentle breeze kissed my cheek. The trees rustled. The delicate scent of olive blossoms filled my nostrils. I thanked Yahveh for His many blessings.

When at last Moses opened his eyes, he expressed no surprise at my presence.

"Peace," he said.

I bowed. "Forgive me for intruding upon you."

"Sister! By the grace of Yahveh and your strength I have reached this day. It was you who rescued me. It was you who filled my spirit with a yearning for justice. I should bow before you."

The light in his eyes seemed as bright as the moon on a cloudless night. I felt a pinprick inside my cheek. It grew sharp and painful. The pain spread down my neck. My brother's beautiful words, his gratitude, his recognition—none of this was enough for me. My spirit cried out for more. I, too, knew Yahveh. I, too, sang His praise. Why did He not come to me as He came to my brother?

"Sister, are you ill?"

I shook my head. "Only a little tired."

"You work night and day."

I smiled at him. "The women of Goshen are asking what to bring on our journey. I fear some plan to carry too much. What essentials might I tell the people to prepare for our departure other than a tent, water skins, and proper clothing? What foodstuff?"

Moses kissed my hand. "Our people rely on your good sense!"

He pulled on his beard for a moment. "Skins to carry a day's water for each person and his animals. Blankets for cool nights. Food for seven days; only what will not spoil in the heat and can be eaten in haste. A dish or two for cooking and serving. The gold and silver they have taken from their neighbors. They must take care not to burden themselves or their donkeys. The journey is arduous."

I bowed again. "I will make sure our people are ready," I promised.

Three days later the Children of Israel gathered to observe the ritual of the Paschal Lamb. We donned the clothes we would wear for our journey—simple kuttoneh robes like those that Moses and Tzipporah wore, made of cool linen rather than dark wool, and veils or head cloths to protect us from the sun and dust. I welcomed Nahshon and his family as they brought a lamb to sacrifice in our courtyard. Moses held the lamb's throat over a bowl to catch its blood. His hands worked with speed and skill. While he skinned the animal, Aharon sprinkled the doorposts and lintel with a stalk of hyssop dipped in the blood.

I watched the proceedings with awe. Yahveh had commanded the Children of Israel to observe this ritual for all time, to tell our children and our children's children the story of the first sacrifice and our departure from slavery to freedom. Next year I would serve the ritual meal in the Promised Land. One day the sons of Aharon's sons would sit at my table, and—should Yahveh grant me a long life—their sons too.

I roasted the lamb in our courtyard. The little boys kept the fire burning. The men sat together over a jug of Aharon's wine in the kitchen. Tzipporah, Elisheva, and Nahshon's wife helped me prepare other foods. When Elisheva pointed out that we ate the flatbread and bitter herb for the Egyptian festival of the barley harvest, I frowned.

"Yahveh does not ask us to adopt the customs of our enemies," I said with scorn.

"Perhaps the familiarity makes it easier," Tzipporah suggested.

I did not grace her foolish comment with any recognition.

The full moon rose high before we finished our preparations. Aharon helped me carve the lamb.

Because Yahveh instructed us to eat in haste we did not set a table or sit together as was our habit for family celebrations. We gathered in a circle and without sitting we ate the unleavened bread with garlic and lettuce as Yahveh had instructed. Then everyone ate their fill of the lamb. When no one could manage another bite, we burned everything that remained of the lamb.

While I attended the fire I waited for a sign of Yahveh's presence. The stars glittered in the sky above me. The house grew very quiet. Everyone waited. No one spoke.

The first shouts startled me awake in the middle of the night. Voices cried for us to open the courtyard gate.

A crowd of Egyptian men and women gathered before me. Their faces twisted in pain and fury. The women tore their dresses and moaned. Even before they spoke I knew that Yahveh had carried out His threat to Pharaoh.

"Our firstborn sons!" one woman shrieked. She clutched at her chest and collapsed to the ground as if stabbed by a knife.

Another woman flung herself at my feet. "My only son," she wept, "Bring him back to me! Bring him back!"

A priest with a shaved head and fine linen robe pushed himself forward.

"Your God has destroyed us!" he cried. "He left us nothing but a little wet grain, little enough to feed our eldest sons and the firstborn cattle. Now He has taken our precious ones from us. His hand has touched every house with death. We beg you. Tell your God to have mercy on us. Whatever you ask, we will give it to you!"

The priest prostrated himself before Moses. The crowd's lamentations intensified.

As Moses opened his mouth to reply we heard the rumbling of an approaching horse. A royal chariot flew down the road toward us. It stopped in front of the crowd. Pharaoh's high chamberlain stepped down.

The Egyptians turned upon the chamberlain in a rage. Hands tore at his robes and flesh. In the moonlight I saw bloody welts rise on his cheek.

"Stand back!" Aharon cried out. "Let us hear what decree he brings."

With reluctance the crowd heeded my brother's call and drew away.

The chamberlain took a moment to adjust his clothing and wipe his face. He pulled a scroll from his sleeve. He opened it and began to read aloud.

"Prince Seti, Pharaoh's first son and heir to the throne, is dead."

A gasp rose from the crowd.

"Thus says the son of Amun-Re. 'Arise, Israelites! Go out from among my people as you have said. Take even your sheep and your oxen and go! And may you bring a blessing on me!'"

As Moses listened, I saw the deep furrows on his brow give way to relief for the first time since he had returned to Egypt. He stepped forward to address the Egyptians. He spoke in a low voice.

"Return to your homes. May you never forget Yahveh's strength— neither you nor your neighbors, nor your pharaohs in the ages to come."

Several of the women flung themselves at his feet. "Please ask your God to bring our sons back to us! We will give you whatever you wish."

Moses looked upon them with pity. He shook his head. They turned away from us, numb with grief.

Inside the courtyard Elisheva brought out the timbrels. Moses put his hand on her arm to stop her from playing. We gathered around him.

"We can not delay. Pharaoh will not remain steady in his promises to us. Let us summon the Children of Israel to flee now, by moonlight, while the House of Egypt is in mourning."

Aharon and I enlisted our neighbors to help spread the word that the time for our flight had come. By the next watch every Israelite was to gather with his family and cattle in the field of assembly.

I ran from house to house. I knocked on every bloodstained door. I asked others to pass on the message. I felt myself filled with the strength and energy of five women.

The people poured into the streets. Wherever I turned I met the joyous commotion of liberation and hope. I reminded everyone to thank Yahveh for our deliverance.

When I reached the fields that divided Goshen from the district of Pi-Ramesse, I turned back to join the assembly. But as I passed our house I hesitated. Something called to me.

I pushed open the gate and stepped into the courtyard one last time. I cast my eyes from the stable to the brick walls of the upper floor to the kitchen door. My home, the only home I had ever known, stood silent in the darkness. I bowed my head in memory of my beloved parents. *May your spirit remain with us*, I prayed. *May we bring honor to your names.* So, too, did I bow my head in tribute to a dimmer memory of myself as a young woman whose heart flew on the wind to the man she hoped to marry. That girl would remain forever in the shadows of Egypt.

The gate creaked. I heard the rustling of linen robes.

"Are you sad to leave your home?" a familiar voice asked.

She had guessed that we intended to leave forever. I was not surprised.

"I have waited all my life for this moment."

"May you be rewarded with what you seek."

"May you also be so favored," I replied.

Istnofret stepped forward from the shadows. "I bring you a parting gift." Her hands emerged from her cloak with a small rectangular box. In the moonlight I could see fine rosewood inlaid with ivory.

I lifted the lid. Inside lay the long lock of black hair cut from my brother's head on the day of his tenth birthday.

I had to offer something in return. I fingered the thin gold chain around my neck. For seven years I had worn the golden fly that Istnofret had sent to me after my brother's departure. Now the time had come to return it to her.

She removed her veil. I lifted the necklace over her head. Our eyes met. Her tears glistened in the moonlight.

She reached out to embrace me. As we held each other she whispered in my ear.

"Even after the death of his son, Merenptah does not fear your God enough to restrain his greed and anger. He will soon learn of your intentions and send the army in pursuit. But I have a plan to delay this."

"How?"

"I will get him out of Pi-Ramesse. If he is upstream it will take longer for messengers to reach him with word that you do not return and longer for his order to get back to the army. I will bribe a horoskop to say that the stars show he must accompany his son's body upstream to the embalming site. How much time do you need?"

"Seven days. In seven days we will reach the Reed Sea."

"I can buy you two days, perhaps three. "

I held out my hand. Our fingers touched.

"May your God remain with you," she whispered.

I raised my hand in farewell. She slipped away into the night.

PART
IV
FLIGHT

TWENTY-TWO

Miryam

WE assembled by the light of a full moon—twenty thousand strong and as many cattle. Not every Israelite joined us. Some preferred to live in comfort under oppression rather than risk the unknown. Some who had married into Egyptian families no longer considered themselves Israelites. I did not grieve for those who lacked the courage or foresight to choose freedom. I grieved for their children, condemned to a life apart from their people, their God, their home.

In the confusion, a number of non-Israelite slaves and other foreigners conscripted into labor escaped with us. I feared the influence of these people in our midst. Moses did not listen to my objection.

"Let all who wish to be free of tyranny come with us!" he proclaimed.

I did not challenge him on the matter. He marched in Yahveh's footsteps with a fixed purpose in his eye. He saw only our glorious future. I determined to follow his example.

At first I walked between my brothers at the front. The well-worn road provided easy footing. Soon I moved back among the people to urge them forward so we could cover as much ground as possible. But a group of twenty thousand people can not move with great speed. I prayed for Istnofret to succeed in her plan to win us a few more days.

We walked for twelve hours without stopping. Long after midday we reached the town of Succoth, near Lake Timsah, where the Egyptian army kept a garrison. Moses presented himself to the commander. He offered Pharaoh's scroll as proof of permission to travel three days into the wilderness. The soldiers let us pass through without incident.

After the fort we passed an ancient temple of Atum, the Egyptian god of creation. I gazed at the pictures of the god carved into the stone wall. Atum sat on a curved serpent surrounded by a solar disc, holding the ankh of life in one hand and a staff in the other. He wore the double crown of Upper and Lower Egypt. I rejoiced that I would never have to look upon it again.

The canal flowing into Lake Timsah offered more than enough water for us to refresh ourselves. Those at the back of the main group did not reach the water until long after those at the front had taken their fill. The weak and the sick took much longer.

As the men built fire pits and gathered wood, the women hauled water and prepared flatbread. I showed several groups of women how to cover the baking stone so the flour and water mixture crisped without burning.

Moses paced up and down the shoreline, impatient to continue. When I called him to our meal, he ate standing.

"The water here is plentiful," I observed. "How long until we find another source?"

"We pass no certain water until we reach the sea."

An old man who sat near us overheard our exchange. "What route do we go by?"

"The desert road to the Reed Sea," I replied.

The elder objected. "The Way of Horus is better. It will take us into the land of the Canaanite. The road is easy and water abundant. Why not settle in the new land first and then send a party to worship at the mountain?"

Moses pulled at his beard as if he pondered the elder's suggestion. But I knew he would not change the route. He gave the appearance of consideration to show respect for the man. I would not have been so patient.

"The Way of Horus is too well guarded," Moses replied after a moment. "We have permission to travel into the wilderness for three days. If we take the Way of Horus along the Great Sea and away from the wilderness we will be killed or captured long before we reach the Promised Land."

The elder showed no impatience as my brother struggled to get the words out of his mouth. When he finished, the man nodded. "We are in good hands with you, General," he said with admiration.

"I have no name but Moses," my brother corrected him. "We are all equals in the eyes of Yahveh."

In all the days of my life I had never left the Nile valley. Succoth seemed even greener than the land of my birth. I knew that like me most of the Israelites could not imagine life without abundant water. Would they take care to ration their supply? I voiced my concerns to Moses and Aharon, who agreed we must remind all the people of our upcoming hardships.

Communication among such a large group required many dedicated messengers. I assembled Hosea and forty others to assist me with this task. We walked among the people all afternoon.

"Be ready to resume the journey this evening by moonlight," I said. "Take care with your water. We must travel by sun and by moon, seven days to the sea. We will find very little water before then. Do not grow weary in body or spirit! Let your hearts remain fixed on the Promised Land and your legs will not grow weary."

As I passed through the groups settled on the shores of Lake Timsah, I met numerous old friends. I acquainted myself with many Israelites I had not known in Egypt. I took special pleasure in admiring the children. People sought to grasp my hand or touch my kuttoneh. They asked for my blessing. The women continued to call me "the prophetess." Their affection filled me with energy and purpose. With each step I felt my heart grow large enough to love them all.

During the hours that I walked among the people I prepared myself to face the one person I did not want to see.

Nunn and I had avoided each other these many years. An

unacknowledged glance, a figure in the distance, a back in the doorway—
our acquaintance had become no more than this. But I could not avoid
him forever. Surely I would have to face him during the course of our
journey. What would I say when he stood before me?

I would compliment him on his fine son. I would thank him for allowing
Hosea to assist Moses. I would ask after his wife and other children. I
would present myself as an old family friend and no more.

But I did not see Nunn that day. I thanked Yahveh for sparing me from
the discomfort of a meeting with him.

As we resumed our march toward the sea, the land soon turned arid.
We took only a short rest on the morning of the second day before Moses
called for us to move on. My nose and throat grew dry. My eyes stung for
lack of moisture. I willed my spirit not to shrivel with the scrub.

We labored up a gradual incline for many hours. The rocky ground
tore at the feet of those without sandals. Hosea and I did what we could
to aid the elderly, the ill, and the young. I gathered a group of men to
seek out able-bodied people riding donkeys and ask them to share their
animals with people in greater need.

The long afternoon stretched into evening. My patience grew thin.
Too many of the strong cared nothing for the weak. Did they not see the
injustice of riding in comfort while others could not put one foot in front
of the other? As I lifted a small child up to a wealthy farmer I tried to
convince the man to let the child's mother take his place on the donkey for
a short time. "Look upon her as your own daughter," I said.

"I have taken the child," the heavy farmer grumbled. "You should be
grateful for that."

Before I unleashed my fury at the man, Hosea came up and tapped
my shoulder.

"I have seen a young woman too ill to walk. Her family can not be found."

I looked at Hosea, so dedicated and energetic. His youth shone with
exuberance and earnest devotion to our purpose. If ever a man had lived

without an evil inclination in his heart, it must have been Nunn. In this as in so much else Nunn's son followed his father's ways. He was the child I would have wanted, a son worthy of Yahveh's grace. I had hurt Nunn when I left him. Now I would offer what recompense I could by looking after his son.

"May Yahveh bless you," I murmured as I followed him to the sick woman.

She had collapsed on the road. When I raised her head to give her some water I saw that she could not have been more than fifteen. She expected a baby very soon. I looked around for a donkey. "She must ride," I insisted.

As Hosea and I tried to raise her from the ground, a clean-shaven man in an Egyptian kilt and open robe came to our side. His strength exceeded my own many times over. He lifted the woman into his arms. I rejoiced at this act of kindness.

We walked for a long time to reach the front of the procession, but the man did not grow tired. When we reached our donkeys I saw that Elisheva rode upon one and Gershom and Ithamar on the other. I asked the boys if they could walk for a while. They jumped down at once.

The clean-shaven man eased his charge onto the donkey. I gave her some water.

"Thank you," she whispered.

I patted her arm. "What is your name?" I asked.

"Teye."

An Egyptian name. "Where is your lord?"

She shook her head. She seemed too weak to utter another word. I assured her I would return later to help find her family. I asked Elisheva to look after her.

I stood for a moment to catch my breath. As I drank from my water skin, the tall man came up to me.

"I am grateful for your help," I said.

"I am honored to be of service to you. My name is Bak."

I liked his expression of face, serious but not dour. He wore his straight black hair cut short at the chin. He had a long nose, high cheekbones, and almond-shaped eyes. His muscular arms suggested that he was a man who worked with heavy stone.

"I am Miryam."

"Who among us does not know of you?"

Despite hunger, exhaustion, and the burden of many people yet in need of assistance, I felt my spirit lighten.

"Can I guess that you were a stone worker?" I asked the man.

He smiled. "A sculptor. I carved wood and stone statues of the gods. I also did gold work on them. My father is an Egyptian. My mother was an Israelite."

A man of mixed parentage who served the Egyptian gods—I did not know whether to be disappointed by his past or happy that he had abandoned it to join us.

His eye caught mine. He smiled as if to say his eye found me attractive. I blushed. I looked away.

"I am glad you are here," I said.

As we spoke I found my pleasure in his company increasing. I learned that he had married an Egyptian woman in his youth and that she had died in childbirth. They had no other children. He had never remarried. I marveled at how fine he looked for a man of five and forty.

All the rest of that afternoon and evening Bak helped me organize the efforts to attend those in ill health. Near sunset I made my way from the back of the group to the front with Bak at my side. When I reached my family I saw that Teye seemed much better.

"I believe she is alone," Elisheva whispered to me.

"Let us wait until tomorrow to question her," I suggested.

When Gershom caught sight of me he jumped into my arms. I lifted him into the air. As I kissed my favorite, I noticed a question flit over Bak's face.

"My brother's son," I explained. I put the boy down.

Bak smiled as if he saw all the beauty of the world in my eyes. A pleasant shiver passed from my neck to my fingertips. My feet grew light.

We reached the crest of the Tih plateau soon after nightfall. As I walked with Moses and Aharon, a breathtaking sight came into view far in the distance—a great, glowing column of fire rose from the earth to the heavens.

We stood in awe. I had felt Yahveh's loving embrace in the olive grove. I had seen His light at my brother's birth. I had witnessed His might in the afflictions that devastated Egypt. None of these compared to what I now beheld.

"He shows us the way," Moses proclaimed.

Word spread among the people. Everyone rushed to the top of the plateau. Moses led us in prayer. We thanked Yahveh for freeing us from Egypt. We thanked Him for the beacon of hope.

That night we camped on the exposed and windy plateau. I watched the column of fire for many hours. Bak sat with me apart from the others. We shared stories about our lives. He spoke in a rich, deep voice with elegant court language. He seemed to hide nothing from me. My own heart opened with a flow of words. I described how I had helped to save my brother's life. I spoke of the difficult years while Moses lived in exile.

Bak listened with his eyes rapt upon me. I felt a twinge of guilt. Yahveh had not come to me so that I might raise my esteem in the company of men. *Where is the damage?* I argued with myself. *I do not make a habit of boasting. I have told him nothing more than the truth.*

In the last watch before dawn Bak suggested I sleep, to refresh myself for the following day.

"I should rejoin my family," I said. "Thank you for your help today."

He took my hand. I did not pull it away. He pressed his lips against the tops of my fingers. Feathers danced over my flesh.

I woke as the dawn rose over the mountains far in the distance ahead of us. When I opened my eyes I saw that the column of fire had turned into a column of white cloud.

While people gathered to look at the cloud I checked on Teye. She sat near Elisheva, much improved. I prepared some flatbread over a small fire. After Teye ate and drank, I asked about her lord.

"I am not wed," she confessed. "I was a slave in the palace of prince Seti, grandson of the pharaoh. I worked in the kitchens." She paused and then resumed in a halting voice. "Late one night he roused me from sleep. A group of men sat drinking wine. He gave me to them."

She pointed to her belly and began to cry.

"I do not know who did this," she whispered.

Elisheva embraced the poor girl. I knelt down next to her.

"You wish to remain among the Israelites?" I asked.

The girl dried her eyes. "I do. You have been kind to me."

I liked the way she attended to my words. I liked the courage she showed in running away. I admired her truthfulness.

"You can help me with the food for our family. You can help me tend to others until your time comes. I ask one thing in return."

"I will serve you with all my heart," she said.

"It is loyalty to Yahveh that I require."

"I will pay allegiance to Him and no other," she replied. Her eyes filled with gratitude and joy.

I accepted her promise.

We traveled night and day over the rocky limestone plateau. By midmorning the sun burned us without relief. We rested at midday and again in the middle of the night. During this time I discovered the majestic stars above us, too numerous to count. The bright moon cast shadows on the hard ground and rocky formations that rose from the landscape. When we stopped for a few hours before dawn, Bak and I found a quiet place to sit. We talked about the day's events and our hopes for the future until we grew weary. On the second night we fell asleep as we sat side by side. No one cared. Propriety seemed irrelevant in the wilderness.

By day the column of cloud showed us the way. At night we followed the column of fire. Moses posted guards to our rear, on our flanks, and ahead of us at a distance. He feared the Egyptians had already begun their pursuit. As we drew closer to the sea he pushed us harder. When I longed for water to wash, a fresh garment, or a thick loaf of wheat bread, I found solace in Yahveh's guiding presence. I continued to help people who grew weak in body or spirit. To those who complained of the pace, I stressed the urgency of our flight.

I began to hear talk of desert spirits and night demons circulating among the women. I asked Elisheva if she knew of such stories.

She hesitated to answer. After a moment she spoke. "Tzipporah has lived in the desert all her days," she began.

I did not need to hear more. "She turns the women away from Yahveh with these tales!" I pointed to the column of fire. "That is all we need see in the dark. If we follow Him we have nothing to fear."

Elisheva apologized. I took no comfort in her contrite words. No matter how much leniency I showed Tzipporah, the woman gave me no ease.

On the third night we arrived at Nakhl. The animals drank from a brackish pool in a shallow limestone depression. People who attempted to follow their example spat out the water with disgust. I heated some of it in a small pot and used it to wash. But I knew my hands and face would not remain clean for long. I feared that I might never be clean again. As I poured the water over my fingers, I looked forward to the time when we could pitch our tents to keep the dust away from us at night. I laughed at myself, for I had never imagined that I—whose spotless house was the envy of the neighborhood women—would one day yearn for a simple tent over my head.

Elisheva came upon me as I washed my face. "Bak is looking for you," she said, her voice lilting in a strange, singsong tone. I looked up at her.

"He likes you."

I waved my hand to dismiss her foolish talk. "Bak is a friend. That is all."

"He wishes to be more."

"My head has more grey hairs than black. My disposition is not soft. It is too late." *I belong to Yahveh in body and spirit.*

Elisheva kissed my cheek. "It is only too late if you make it so, Miryam."

On the fourth day our surroundings changed. The hills closed in around us. They shone in bright hues of purple, yellow, and grey. Fissures appeared in the earth. Whenever we came upon such a canyon we posted guards to make sure no child or animal would stumble into it. As the fissures grew wider and deeper, I prayed to Yahveh to keep the people safe. Yahveh remained with us. We lost neither man nor beast.

On the afternoon of the sixth day we reached a place called Naqab, the end of the Tih plateau. The view over the edge took the breath from my nostrils. Far below lay the vast Sea of Reeds, shimmering red as the sun set. Jagged mountains on the distant shore also shone red. Yahveh's cloud rose high into the sky behind them. Black mountain peaks towered over the land to the right and left. We could not see what lay at the bottom of the drop down to the sea.

"The water is turned to blood like the Nile!" the people called out with fear as we congregated on the edge of the plateau.

Tzipporah stood like a stone as she stared across the blood-red sea.

"We will never find fresh water!" Elisheva lamented. Her voice seemed to summon Tzipporah back to us.

"The water is not blood," she said. Her eyes remained fixed on the sea.

Moses came up behind me. "It is a reflection of the red mountains on the other side," he said. "This is the region of Etham."

Tzipporah gazed for a moment upon the father of her children. He seemed to be a stranger in her eyes.

"When will we find fresh water?" Bak asked.

"We come down a steep road into the Wadi Masri," Moses replied. "Across the wadi, we will find water in the great marsh at the edge of the sea. Tomorrow we will camp there, at Pi ha-Hiroth between the watchtower known as Migdol and the sea, opposite the temple of Baal Zephon."

As Moses spoke to Bak, I glanced from one man to the other. I realized that my brother looked upon the sculptor with approval. My face flushed with pleasure. I grew confused. Why should I care how my brother felt about this man? Could Yahveh mean to share me with another once we reached the Promised Land?

I looked into my heart. I saw that it was not impossible.

TWENTY-THREE

Miryam

AFTER six days with little rest even the most vigorous among us grew weary. But at dawn on the seventh day we stood above the sea with renewed strength. Moses had promised abundant fresh water by the afternoon. From the plateau we could see the wide gulf below and the mountains of Midyan on the far side of the water, where safety awaited us. The column of Yahveh's cloud, also across the sea, reassured us of His presence. The smell of freedom filled our nostrils.

We began our descent to the beach at first light. The rocky trail twisted in sharp curves. It fell so fast that every step jarred my knees. I feared for those who could not hold themselves steady on their feet—the elderly, the sick, and expectant mothers. Children might be separated from their families if they ran too fast. Even the most cautious person could lose his footing on the crumbling, rocky trail.

I held my veil high above my head, a signal to my messengers. Within moments they began to flock to me. I voiced my concerns and scattered them among the people. They reunited children and parents, they assisted those who could not make the descent on their own, they helped maintain order.

I posted myself at the bottom of the trail. Moses sent word that we would proceed no further until everyone had gathered on the beach. He asked me to notify him as soon as the last group arrived. They reached me at midday.

I scanned the beach for Hosea, who had promised to stand ready to deliver a message to Moses. I saw him some distance away with a small group. He gestured for me to join him. I did not see his companions until I had drawn too close to turn away.

Nunn bowed. "Peace, Miryam."

My face and hands grew hot. My heart swelled against my chest. I felt pleased to see him. I felt embarrassed. I wanted to turn away at once. I longed to embrace him.

The years had softened his flesh and carved fine lines into the corners of his eyes. But I knew him still. The sweet, handsome face, the clear and trusting eyes, the energetic manner—all remained unchanged.

What did he see when he looked at me? Miryam—tall, round, and plain. The freshness of my youth had weathered into middle age.

I opened my mouth to deliver the speech I had rehearsed many times. But my tongue grew so heavy I could not utter a single word. I stood before the man I had once loved, who had once loved me. A sea of tears could not fill the vast distance between us.

Nunn spoke. "You have met my wife Ahata?"

I turned my gaze to the woman by his side; I had not noticed her.

Her delicate beauty remained vibrant. I tried to tell myself that I did not envy her. But no part of me could believe this untruth.

Nunn raised his hand to caress her shoulder. The gesture struck me like a blow to the chest.

"Hosea has told us everything you do for our people and how you look after him when he attends Moses. We thank you. The Children of Israel owe you a great debt of gratitude."

I looked into Nunn's earnest admiration. My spirit did not rally.

Why, I asked Yahveh, *could I not have given myself to him and to You?*

My anguished heart knew the answer.

One can not be Ahata and Miryam in the same lifetime.

Hosea and I set out along the water's edge at a rapid pace in search of

Moses. But I soon heard someone call my name from behind. I turned and saw that Nunn had broken away from Ahata to follow us. We stopped to wait for him.

Hosea's father reached us so out of breath that he could not speak. He held up his hand to apologize for the delay. He turned to his son.

"Give us a moment," he asked.

Hosea did not object, though we did not have time to spare. He bowed and walked further up the shore, to wait where he could not hear us.

I turned back to Nunn. He took both my hands in his. His eyes glistened.

I smiled at him with the affection of a sister.

"I wanted to say…" He broke off.

Remorse filled my heart. I did not wish to change places with Ahata. I did not regret the choices I had made so long ago. But I had hurt the man I loved and his pain remained.

"I am so sorry," I whispered. I shook my head.

"I wanted to say I understand." Nunn spoke with a tenderness that made my arms ache for him. "For a long time I could not understand, but now I do."

"Thank you," I murmured. I squeezed his hand and pulled away to find Moses.

Moses and Aharon stood with a group of elders at the water's edge. The elders made way for me and Hosea.

"Are all assembled on the beach?" Moses asked.

"All are assembled," I confirmed.

Moses turned to fix his eyes on the column of cloud rising from the mountains across the water. "Let us move forward across the Wadi Masri to the marsh. Tonight we camp at Pi ha-Hiroth toward the head of the gulf."

"We should sacrifice to Baal Zephon," an elder suggested. "I have heard that the storm god unleashes his fury upon travelers who fail to make an offering to him at the sea."

My brother stared in silence at the cloud. Before he responded, the answer came to me.

"We have seen proof of Yahveh's might over all the gods of Egypt. He is with us wherever we go. Let us not pay homage to another god lest it give Yahveh reason to doubt our faith."

As I looked from face to face I saw that my words did not inspire the men. Many of them frowned at me. Several seemed almost resentful. I felt anger rise in my chest. My face grew hot. Yahveh had revealed Himself to me long before He spoke to Moses. I had devoted my life to His service. I had given up everything for Him. The women called me a prophetess. How could these men doubt my authority?

Moses turned back to us. He put his hand on my arm.

"Miryam is right. We will cross the Wadi Masri twenty thousand strong in His name. He will protect us."

His words soothed my wounded spirit.

Moses raised his hand to issue instructions. "We will travel northeast along the coastline, over the wadi that divides the beach." He pointed to a sloping ridge ahead of us.

How could he allow us to turn away from Yahveh's beacon?

"If we go north the cloud will fall behind us," I objected in a low voice.

My brother, lost in his own reflections, did not answer. His furrowed brow and unyielding eyes rekindled dread in my heart. As I looked out across the calm surface of the water I could feel Merenptah's hatred drawing closer. Imaginary hoof beats echoed in my ears. How many extra days had Istnofret won for us? Did we have time to camp for a night?

"Would it not be more prudent to continue as fast as we can until we reach safety in the mountains of Midyan?"

"I follow Yahveh's explicit instructions," Moses replied. He did not explain why we must turn away from Yahveh's beacon.

I opened my mouth to ask, but Moses shook his head.

An old bitterness rose in my throat. However much I pressed Moses he would say no more. He defended my place as a leader among the people, but Yahveh spoke to him alone.

The Wadi Masri cut across the land from the north and ended at the edge of the sea. As we climbed over the top of the ridge I saw the whole sweeping curve of the gulf. From here I understood what Moses had not explained. We had turned away from Yahveh's cloud to follow the shoreline around the tip of the gulf into Midyan. Once we reached the tip of the gulf we would turn back to face the beacon in the south.

As we descended to the beach, patches of fresh water reeds appeared at the shoreline.

"They are fed by underground springs," Moses said to me. He pointed to a marshy expanse above the beach. "It is all fresh water."

People waded into the marsh with abandon. A group of women gathered around me; I led them in a prayer of thanks to Yahveh for His precious gift.

While the people drank their fill, Moses invited me to walk with him along the sandy mouth of the wadi. Bak and Hosea followed after us. When Bak came up to me I avoided his eye. I scolded myself for all that I had allowed to pass between us. Surely Yahveh had not turned me away from Nunn only to let another take his place in my heart.

East of the marsh another sandy wadi cut into the land. The mouth of this dry riverbed spread so wide we could not see from one end to the other. Moses told us that this wadi, known as the Arava, spread north into the land of the Canaanites.

A sheer wall of dark stone defined either side of the Wadi Arava. The twin walls rose steep from the ground. It seemed that Yahveh had sliced down the center of a single mountain range with a knife to create the separation. An abandoned watchtower loomed over the sea on a high peak to the east toward a place called Etham.

Hosea pointed to a structure ahead of us at the tip of the sea. It had three walls made from large stones and stood about as tall as a man. The side that faced the sea remained open, as did the top. The structure stood so close to the edge of the sea that water rushed in and out of it. Several large boulders sat clustered in the center of the open space. The stark formation looked unwelcoming, even menacing.

"What is that?"

"The shrine of Baal Zephon, the god of storm and sea," Moses answered. "But the area is named Pi ha-Hiroth," he added.

"After the cow goddess?" Bak asked.

Moses nodded.

"Why?" Hosea asked.

"The copper mines are not far to the north," Moses answered.

"She is patron of the mines," Bak explained to me. "When I was young I made a life-sized figure of her for Pharaoh. We dressed her in our finest metalwork and jewels. I often wondered how a stone figure made by our own hands could grant him favor."

"A truth spoken for all the gods of Egypt," I observed.

Bak shrugged. "I have left all that behind."

I smiled at him. If I could not be his wife I would still hold him dear to me as a brother.

Late that afternoon we made our campsite on the beach. But by Moses's instruction we did not set up our tents. He asked Hosea to post guards halfway up the descent from Naqab and also in the watchtower at the Wadi Arava. By these preparations I understood that my brother believed the Egyptians could pursue us from either side.

"How can they reach us through the Arava?" I whispered to him.

"If they drive their chariots north from Succoth, where a flat wadi connects to the Arava, and then turn south to cut us off here."

"Would Yahveh permit this?" I asked with great alarm.

"Yahveh will not abandon us."

I felt my brow wrinkle with displeasure. "That much I have known since before your birth."

I walked away to wander among the people.

The days of travel had taken their toll. People suffered from raw feet. Their eyes became swollen from the dust. Some knew how to care for themselves; others begged me to find them relief. Over the course of the afternoon I gathered a group of men and women adept at healing. We set aside an area at each end of the camp for those in need. I organized supplies and made sure that all who needed attention received it.

At dusk Bak brought me a small, fresh melon. I gazed at the fruit as if it were a miracle.

"Where did you find such a thing?" I asked with great wonder.

He shrugged his shoulders. "You spend all your time caring for others," he said. "Not everyone takes your selfless efforts for granted." He placed his hand over mine for a moment.

A pleasant warmth filled me. I felt my flesh weaken.

I took a knife from my cooking kit, but before I could open the melon, loud horn blasts echoed from the east and west. Bak and I leapt to our feet as messengers from both directions converged upon us.

"Egyptians! Egyptians! They come on horseback down the pass from Naqab!"

"And on chariots from the Arava ahead!"

Panic spread among the multitude. As darkness began to fall, people gathered their families and belongings to flee. But we were trapped against the water. Cries of terror filled the air. Brave men drew their weapons. Others insisted that we should surrender at once, even if only to save the lives of the women and children.

A furious throng gathered around Moses. Korach stepped forward.

"Was it for lack of graves in Egypt that you brought us to die here in the wilderness?"

"We put our lives in your hands!"

"Your god has tricked us!"

Moses raised his staff. His eyes flashed like lightning over the people. "Do not fear!" he bellowed. "The Egyptians will know Yahveh's full might, and so will our people. Stand steady and be quiet!"

A hush fell over the people. Everyone stood so still that I heard only the sound of people inhaling and exhaling. The ground trembled from hoof beats in the distance. Moses stood on the edge of the sea and raised his staff over the water.

A mild breeze came up from the east. It caressed my cheek and ruffled my hair. Clothing rustled and a baby's whimper floated away. Soft ripples moved across the water. I felt Yahveh in my heart and all around us.

The gentle current of air rose into a steady wind. In moments it blew strong enough to bend the tops of the date palms set back from the beach and push children off balance. Soon it filled the air with the deafening blast of a thousand ram's horns. Fragments of household items, refuse, and firewood flew by. Dense clouds of sand turned twilight into night. Everyone pushed toward the shore where I stood at Moses's side.

I used one arm to shield my eyes from the blowing sand. With the other I held Gershom against my chest. I turned toward the churning sea. High waves soaked us with a steady spray. The moon broke over the rough water in bands of shimmering white light. Across the sea Yahveh's column of fire blazed high into the dark heavens.

"Yahveh! We await your mercy!" I cried out.

Even as I fixed my eyes upon the bands of moonlight on the choppy water the dark sea swallowed them. A rush of water and wind rose to drown the screams around me. People drew away from the edge of the sea. They tried to crouch as they clung to their children and possessions. Someone nearby shouted that the storm god meant to devour us.

Under the glimmering moonlight water rose before me, sucked upward in a body as vast as the sea itself. The water rose higher and higher without dropping or moving forward toward the shore. I craned my neck to follow its movement as it met the heavens above. Water and sky became one.

Moses held his staff steady. The towering wall of water before us began to split, yet the water remained suspended high into the heavens against all sense and understanding. As the two walls of water pulled apart, the moonlight illuminated a clear path across the dry sea floor. I stepped forward into the wind and raised my eyes to the sheer walls on either side. I reached out my hand to touch one wall; the force of the water's upward rush stung my fingers.

"He has parted the sea!" I called out in triumph. "He has parted the sea so we may flee from the Egyptians!"

I saw Moses shouting but I could not hear him. With his free arm he gestured for people to move forward. One man ventured onto the path between the walls of water, but the force of the wind beat him back.

"Link arms!" I cried out. "Link arms! Huddle close together! The weakest on the west side, away from the wind!"

The people fell into formations spanning the width of the path between the walls of water. Mothers pressed young children close to their chests. Men prodded their animals forward with sticks. As more rows of people pushed closer together they began to make slow progress.

I watched Aharon and his family pass in a group with Bak and Teye. When Tzipporah came with her lambs she opened her arms out for Gershom. But I clung to the child and gestured for her to move forward with her dog and her flock. I believed my own strong arms could brace the child against the wind better than hers.

"I will return him to you on the other side!" I shouted. "I will keep him safe!"

I could not hear her reply. She stared up at the walls of water with fear in her eyes. I called for several people to link arms with her. They carried her forward into darkness with all the others.

I stood at the edge of the sea through the night with Hosea posted across from me. The blowing sand obscured the beach in the distance so

I could not see if the Egyptians approached, though I knew they must be near. We urged the people forward. We found help for those in need. We offered encouragement. We praised Yahveh.

As the first streak of light appeared over the eastern mountains, the last of my people stepped between the walls of water. I turned to make sure that no one remained. Moses still stood nearby with his staff extended over the sea.

Behind him I glimpsed dark clouds that formed over the beach. Why did Yahveh drive this heavy sandstorm at our backs? Something glinted inside the vortex of swirling sand. I strained my eyes and caught a glimpse of rearing horses. Chariot wheels, soldiers, armaments, more horses! They could not reach us through the sandstorm. Yahveh had beaten back the entire Egyptian army while we had crossed the sea to safety.

"Go now!" Moses cried out to me. "I will follow you."

I held Gershom tight with one arm. I linked the other arm through Hosea's. Together we plunged into the wind between the miraculous walls of water.

TWENTY-FOUR

Tzipporah

THE Goddess called to me across the sea, from the high cliffs of my homeland. I heard Her just before I began the descent to Pi ha-Hiroth.

Tzipporah! Tzipporah!

Her voice floated over the water on rippling red bands. After months of silence it washed over my withered heart like a steady, soothing rain.

Tzipporah! Tzipporah!

I had not fulfilled my promise to spread Her worship among the Israelites in Egypt. Only Elisheva had come to know Her. But the Goddess understood. As long as Yahveh's afflictions threatened, as long as flight seemed imminent, as long as Miryam filled their ears night and day with Yahveh's name, the women of Israel could not open their hearts to the Great Goddess.

I renewed my promise. *I will teach the women of Israel to honor You. I will win my lord back into my arms.*

As I stood on the edge of the sea I cried out to take my son with me. But Miryam pretended not to hear in the onslaught of the furious wind. She clung to Gershom as if he were her own and she pushed me into the grip of men who hurled me into the demon's mouth.

Sand and spray blinded me. I strained my ears to hear my lambs, but the wind sucked all sound away. My feet began to sink into the soft sea floor and my knees grew weak. I folded my arms over my womb to protect the child within. The men carried me across.

When I reached the other side I gathered my lambs around me and held the little dog close like an infant. I watched the others behind me emerge from between the two walls of water. I waited all night for my son.

As the first rays of sunlight glinted over the mountains of Midyan, Miryam reached the shore with Gershom in her arms and Hosea at her side. My son broke free of her and ran to me. I scooped him up into my arms. When at last I looked up I saw Moses at the edge of the sea. He stood with his back to us and held his staff out toward the water. The sandy path between the two walls looked much wider than it had seemed in the shadowy moonlight. The parted waters held steady in the wind and I could see the great distance we had covered across the gulf. Even with no wind it might have taken half a morning to cross it.

I sensed a blur of motion coming toward us from the other side. At first I imagined the noise to be seawater rushing forward to fill the gap between the two walls. But as it drew nearer, I and all those around me distinguished the sounds of horses and warriors. The Israelites, so sure of their safety, began shrieking. The Egyptian army followed so close behind that it seemed we would all be slaughtered.

I flung myself into the mass of Israelites that surged across the beach and climbed to higher ground. From the ridge we paused to glance at the scene below. At the edge of the marsh on the opposite shore of the gulf we saw wheels of abandoned chariots stuck in the mud. But a swarm of horsemen and foot soldiers advanced into the sea. So many men! It looked as if Pharaoh had sent his entire army.

Some of the Israelites turned to flee. Miryam bellowed for everyone to remain calm. She called upon Yahveh to protect us. I could not take my eyes off Moses, who remained on the beach at the water's edge with his back to us. He stood as still as a rock with his arm yet extended over the sea. As the cloud-filled sky grew lighter the Egyptians advanced at a rapid pace. But Moses did not falter.

We watched for a long time. I could see no more of Moses than his back, his flowing hair, and his raised arm trembling with the staff in his hand. I knew he gathered strength through his God, but the will to stand with such courage under such strain came from within his own heart.

As the first Egyptians drew within an arrow shot of Moses, the last group entered the sea. A beam of light broke through the clouds and bathed Moses in a golden halo. An Egyptian bowman drew his weapon and aimed toward my beloved. All around me the Children of Israel screamed. With one swift movement Moses lowered his staff. In the space of a single breath the wind ceased. The walls of water collapsed and with a single gulp the sea swallowed the entire army, horses and men. The churning waters hurled their cries into the air. The waves grew still. Then the clouds parted and the sun sparkled over the glittering blue surface. A single wooden bow floated toward the shore, all that remained of Pharaoh's mighty army.

Cheers of joy broke the silence and proclamations of victory rose up around me. I did not join them. I stood still with my son and my flock and gazed after the fallen. So many dead in Yahveh's wake. I feared that their cries would echo in my ears forever.

We descended back to the beach, but I turned away from the waters like a widow from her lord's corpse. The men and women had separated themselves into two groups. Aharon stood before the men and proclaimed Yahveh divine warrior and king. The men knelt and repeated his words. A vision came to me as real as anything I had ever seen—a crown of flames rising from their midst. It hung in the heavens and scorched the morning star.

I whispered to my children, Gershom in my arms and the unborn in my womb. "Moses buys their freedom at a heavy price. Yahveh's killing will never end."

Too young to understand my fear, Gershom scanned the beach until he saw his cousins. I raised my hand to Elisheva and let the boy run to her sons. But as I started toward my friend a timbrel caught my ear. I moved with my lambs toward a cluster of women.

The timbrel grew louder as I drew closer to the group. Miryam's voice rose in song. The women repeated her words, sentence by sentence. They held their arms high and swayed their hips. Their feet twirled with joy as they chanted.

Sing to Yahveh: He has triumphed.

He has flung horse and charioteer into the sea!

Yahveh is our strength.

He is our deliverance

Let us exalt the God of our fathers

Yahveh, the Divine Warrior!

Though she celebrated Yahveh, Miryam's song called to me. The rhythm of her hand upon the timbrel's taut skin seized my legs, my torso, my hands, my heart.

I felt her gaze upon me as I joined the dance. Our eyes met. We smiled at each other.

Later, when everyone sat down to a feast of thanksgiving, I felt the soft breath of the Goddess brush my cheek.

Go to Moses, She urged. *He is in need of you.*

Whenever the Goddess came to me I saw the desert bloom, I tasted sweetness in bitter herbs, I felt the moon kiss my skin. She gave me life. But each time Moses encountered his God, each time he served as Yahveh's arms and voice, I saw his strength and vigor drain away. Now I would look after my lord and win him back to me.

But I could not find him.

I followed a set of prints—three people and one donkey—along the edge of the shore. I saw a black tent rising from the sand in the distance toward the foot of the black and red mountains of my homeland.

Hosea and Bak stood guard outside the tent, stiff as Pharaoh's soldiers at the palace gate. I looked from one to the other.

Hosea hovered on the cusp of manhood and loved Moses better than his own self. Short yet powerful in body, handsome, bearded, and energetic, he did not seem aware that he could have any woman of his choice. I had seen the temple women bare their breasts and brush their hands against the loins of youths far less desirable than Hosea—pimpled, slight boys— to win the privilege of being first to show them the pleasures of the flesh. Had Hosea's father brought him to the temple, the high priestess herself would have taken him. But he seemed to have no use for women. He slept with his sword and served my lord day and night.

Bak, with his round eyes and sharp nose, reminded me of a falcon. Almost thirty years older than Hosea, he was tall, languid, and furtive. His shameless wooing of Miryam did not prevent him from eyeing pretty young Teye. Poor Miryam; neither she nor her brothers saw how Bak sought a place for himself within my lord's inner circle. I held my tongue. Miryam would learn for herself soon enough. And I would not interfere where the Goddess might gain a foothold. If the falcon softened her into a woman, he deserved whatever reward he could glean from his nearness to Moses.

I raised my hand to open the tent flap. Bak moved to block the way.

"He asked to rest alone." The falcon spat as he spoke.

"We have seen to him," Hosea added with kindness. His eyes asked me to forgive the refusal.

I bowed to the two foolish men who knew nothing of life in the wilderness. They did not yet realize that protecting the occupant of a tent required guarding it from all four sides.

I put my lambs in the care of a woman I knew to be gentle and kind with her own animals and I walked with the dog away from the sea toward the mountains. Because Hosea and Bak had set the tent flap to face the water and stood together on that side, they did not see me as I crept along the beach behind them.

I dug into the soft sand at the back tent wall and slid underneath with ease. I gazed upon the man who had brought a nation out of tyranny, who loved me well enough to keep me from the temple and make me the mother of his children.

At first I took him for dead. He lay still on his back, his open eyes unseeing. His skin looked as blue and dull as that of a stillborn infant. The powerful arm that had held back the sea for hours lay limp by his side. His long fingers had shriveled into desiccated twigs.

Hosea and Bak had raised the tent for shelter yet neglected to lay mats on the ground or provide any other comfort. My lord lay in the sand without so much as a water skin.

I lifted his head and poured a few drops from my water skin into his mouth. He turned his eyes to me. Where fire once burned I saw only ashes. He raised a hand to touch the locks of my hair that brushed his shoulder. I sang a soft song of love and held his head on my lap. He drank more water; then he slept.

In the morning Hosea lifted the tent flap and gasped when he saw me inside. The sun flooded across my lord's face. He opened his eyes.

I smiled upon him. I bent down to kiss him. Out of the corner of my eye I saw Hosea withdraw from the doorway.

An expression of confusion passed over my lord's face. He pushed away from me and sat up. I looked at him with disbelief. He had aged ten years in a single night—his black hair had turned white and deep furrows lined his brow.

"Why are you here?" he demanded.

I shrank from the lashing of his tongue.

"Hosea!" he shouted.

The young man appeared at the tent flap.

"I wanted none to enter."

"We kept guard all night!" Hosea insisted.

"I came to care for you," I murmured through my tears. "You were not well. I gave you water."

I rose to my feet and fled.

When I turned back I saw Moses step out of the tent. Miryam rushed to him with a bowl of food and a thousand questions.

"Tzipporah!" he called out as if to appease me. His voice lodged in my heart like the point of a sharp sword.

He came toward me, a majestic figure risen from the dead, until an arm's length remained between us.

"I thank you. But you know it can not be."

Terrible words rose in my throat. Yet I feared Yahveh too much to curse Him. I walked away in silence and did not open my mouth for the rest of that day.

Moses led the people down the beach toward Haql on the sea, where I had circumcised him on our journey to Egypt. As we drew near to that terrible place, darkness and dread fell over me. I stood outside the camp while people raised their tents and settled down for an evening meal.

As the sun fell away from the land, Yahveh's cloud turned to fire and my hands began to tremble. I felt a demon flow through my body and I shook so much that I could not hold myself upright. The dog broke into a frantic bark. I felt the creatures of the night circle around me, laughing and moaning. They cast visions before my eyes—an infant girl with a broken neck left for carrion on a high rock, the man with the yellow belt stained red from a wound, a cobra head in place of my lord's face. The demons meant to hurl me into the deep well of madness and I could not cling to this world much longer.

I cried out to the Goddess, but She seemed to have no power in that place. Desperate, I turned to the God of the Israelites, the Divine Warrior.

Yahveh, have mercy on the unborn child of Your servant Moses and save us.

I awoke on a mat in the tent I had once shared with Moses. The Goddess hovered over me and wiped my brow with a wet cloth.

"You are sick again with the fever! I have made you a poultice."

"My daughter?" I whispered.

"You have none but the child you carry. She still awaits her time."

"My daughter?" I asked again.

"Should I summon Moses from the meeting of elders?"

I looked up and saw Elisheva in the flickering lamplight, her sweet face filled with concern. I shook my head and wept.

The demon left me at daybreak. I rose from the ground and held my hands high toward the roof of the tent. My head grew light as I felt the creature depart through my tingling fingertips. A shadow crept across the floor and I heard a breath behind me. I turned. Moses stood in the doorway.

"You are better?" he asked.

I stared at him. I tried to see the shepherd who had given his heart to me at the mountain of Sinn. But the man who stood before me faced his destiny alone.

I heard Miryam calling. Hosea appeared.

"Thank the gods that the fever moved through her in a single night," Elisheva said.

Moses bowed to me and left.

I gazed at Elisheva. I had lost Moses, but I still had her. Neither god nor man could break our bond.

We embraced and I kissed her cheeks. She glowed like the full moon.

We began the walk to Saraf too late in the day. Moses was called upon to settle several disputes and to dissuade the elders from sacrificing to Yahveh before they reached the mountain. When at last they agreed to delay the tribute, the sun sat high in the heavens above us.

The scarce water in Haql went to those who needed it most—women nursing infants, young children, the infirm. In the great heat, those who had not conserved their water began to complain of thirst. When they learned that our next campsite would have no water at all, fights broke out. Accusations of stolen water skins flew from person to person and some lamented their decision to leave Egypt.

My heart turned away from the Israelites that day. Even the youngest child of my clan knew to conserve water and share it with those in need. Yet the Israelites came to blows after one day without a water source. They were a greedy and selfish people—not worthy of my lord's pity, let alone his life.

Moses led us away from the sea into the mountains deep into Midyan. As we climbed the granite pass onto the plateau of my homeland, I guided my lambs to a patch of saxaul plant. "You will have bean caper and white rimt at Saraf," I promised them. I gazed ahead at the column of cloud still in the distance. My father's face flickered in the white plumes. Did Moses imagine Yitro would accept Yahveh in this land, permit worship of Him at Sinn's mountain without objection? Their bond, like ours, would not withstand Yahveh's dominion.

I closed my eyes and willed my father's face away. When I opened them he was gone.

We reached Saraf and made camp. As darkness fell I sought no food or water but rested against some boulders with my flock around me.

I do not know how long I slept before Elisheva woke me, breathless and upset.

"Teye's labor is upon her and she suffers!"

I roused myself and followed her.

Teye lay inside a cramped tent. A gathering of women waited outside. Only the midwife attended her. A small oil lamp gave no more than a thread of light.

"Her hips are too small," the midwife announced.

Teye's eyes widened with terror. Fear did her no good.

"She is no smaller than my six sisters," I said. "Each has given birth with ease."

"Six sisters?" Elisheva repeated with surprise.

I had never spoken to her of my family. "You are my only sister now," I whispered to her.

I knelt next to Teye as she shuddered and screamed. The midwife bent over her.

"Where is Miryam?" I asked Elisheva. I knew she had planned to attend her favorite in childbirth.

"I could not find her. She must be walking with Bak."

Teye's cries grew more desperate.

I began to chant in a slow and steady rhythm. I took Teye's hand and called upon the Goddess to heed a young girl's cries, to ease her pain, to let the child come with no more suffering.

Teye fell into a light sleep. I took a moment's breath.

"The baby is in the wrong position," the midwife whispered.

"Turn it around," I spoke with impatience. The midwife held up her big hands and shrugged. "It is beyond the power of a midwife to do such a thing."

"Do you have some oil?" I asked Elisheva.

"Miryam has precious little olive oil remaining," Elisheva replied.

"Give it to me."

I swathed my hands and arms in oil and resumed chanting in a low and steady monotone. I signaled for the midwife and Elisheva to hold Teye's knees open.

I must have turned a lamb in its mother's womb a hundred times. But this proved far more difficult. Even my small hand would not fit all the way inside Teye. I massaged and manipulated from the inside and out. Teye cried in pain and tried to struggle.

"Focus on the chanting," Elisheva urged her. I worked hard to keep my voice from following the effort of my own labors.

At last I felt the baby's head slip into place. I told Elisheva and the midwife to lift Teye, one on each side beneath her arms. After this the midwife seemed to know her task. She urged Teye to bear down and push. I chanted words of comfort and inspiration. I chanted to keep Her presence with Teye and with me. I did not want to stop.

As I rode on the wings of my voice into the stars, I left Moses far behind, a small stone on the ground. Somewhere in another world I heard a newborn cry. The past fell away from me. My voice soared in jubilation.

A harsh cry brought me back too fast. My flesh quaked. Tears bled over my cheeks.

I opened my eyes.

Miryam stood among us.

TWENTY-FIVE

Tzipporah

MIRYAM'S wounded heart filled the tent. She did not pause to admire the baby or to congratulate Teye before she lashed out at us.

"You knew I was needed here. Why did no one summon me?"

Elisheva apologized in a small voice. "We could not find you."

"Then you did not look."

She turned to Teye and her face softened. She knelt by Teye's side to kiss her. "I wanted to be here for you."

Teye offered her hand and a weak smile.

"I am sorry for the noise and disorder," Miryam added. She waved her hand in my direction.

"But Tzipporah saved the baby!" Elisheva objected. "She summoned the Great Goddess Asherah for Teye and eased the baby's way."

Teye nodded in agreement.

Miryam looked at Elisheva with a spark of fury in her eyes. "You gave birth to four healthy sons with prayers to the Lady Atirat alone. The women of Israel called upon Atirat at the birth of Moses. We have not fled Egypt and her gods so that we may submit ourselves to the gods of yet another people!"

"I do not understand—why can we not have both?" Elisheva whispered.

Miryam looked from me to Elisheva with anger and resentment. She shook her head and bit her lip. After a moment she spoke with measured control. "I expected the granddaughter of Shifra to honor her memory."

Elisheva's face crumpled. She buried her head in her hands and wept.

This is how it will be, I said to myself. *Miryam will forbid the women of Israel to worship the Goddess. Day after day she will find ways to demand that Elisheva choose between us.*

I looked up at Miryam. Her jaw remained firm, her sharp eye stayed focused. In a tent where the breath of the Goddess yet lingered, Miryam's splendor was that of a man—great physical strength, resolution, merciless in the face of the enemy.

This is how it will always be.

I recalled Moses shrinking from my arms as if I meant to poison him with my love. A great weariness pressed against all my bones. The baby kicked.

I am too tired to fight them any more. Goddess, forgive me but I can not.

Miryam followed me out of the tent into darkness. Neither of us held a lamp, but even though I could not see her expression I felt her anger.

"This is an Israelite camp, wherever we travel." Her words came to me as a warning.

The clouds parted to reveal a bright crescent moon. For a brief moment Miryam's face flashed white before me, like death. Then the moon slipped back behind the clouds and we stood hidden from each other once again.

I understood what I had to do. It did not come to me as a sudden revelation; it came to my heart like a sorrowful song I had always known.

I returned to the tent to sit with Teye and Elisheva. The new mother smiled at her infant. I bent down to kiss him.

"He has good color in his face," I observed.

"And plenty of air in his chest!" Teye laughed.

As if to prove his mother right, the baby began to cry.

"Have you chosen a name?" I asked Teye.

"Miryam told me that if I had a son I should call him Yadiavu—may the Divine Father know us all." Teye paused. "But I want to name him

Asher, in honor of the Goddess."

Both she and Elisheva looked at me with uncertainty in their faces. They did not wish to anger Miryam. I did not blame them. And a name to honor the Goddess would mean nothing in Miryam's camp. The Goddess would not dwell where women could not welcome Her with an open heart.

I chose my words with care.

"Yadiavu is a good name for a boy," I agreed.

Elisheva smiled with relief as she took the baby from Teye. "Rest now, while you can."

Teye closed her eyes. In a few moments she slept. I felt as if my spirit had left my body to roam over the land without me.

Elisheva's hair shone bright in the flickering light. I looked into her face, soft and full of compassion. Her beauty would grow wild in the wilderness like generous clusters of pink flowers emerging from the yellow sand.

After a few moments of silence, her voice came to me halting and filled with regret. "I am sure Miryam did not mean to hurt you."

Only to exile me from my beloved Goddess, and from you. "Do not worry," I said aloud. *I am weary from a hundred woes.*

"Would you like to hold the baby?" she asked.

I took the little creature in my arms. His perfect sweet face—the tiny nose, eyes, lashes, mouth—filled me with warmth and sorrow. I stroked his ear and held him close to me. "In Midyan a baby born without a father is not permitted to live."

The words slipped out with my tears. I could not take them back.

Elisheva's eyes widened in disbelief. "Why?"

"A child without a father has no clan," I whispered. "No people."

The baby grew restless from my tight grasp and I handed him back to Elisheva. I felt her eyes upon me, waiting for me to continue.

He dashed her head against a rock. Flesh of his flesh, blood of his blood. My skull smashed with hers, my heart stopped beating inside her scream. I died with her. The vultures ate my flesh where I lay exposed.

Until Moses rescued me. And now that has come to an end.

I would not tell her. I would not soil the purity of her heart with any of it.

But Elisheva surprised me. She read the truth in my heart.

"Tzipporah." She laid the baby down next to his sleeping mother and put her arm around my heaving shoulders. She wiped the river of my tears. "Did this terrible thing happen to you?"

The months of our friendship fell away. Soon it would be over. She would return to Miryam and Miryam to her.

"I did not know who he was," I rasped. "I told myself that the Goddess sent him to me. But She did not."

She held me for a long time.

"You have been a good friend to me," I whispered. But she did not hear the finality in my voice.

The baby cried again. I watched her help Teye gather him to her breast. Soon I would have another child. I prayed to the Goddess for a daughter to replace the one I had lost.

At dawn I woke resolved to carry out my plan. I told Elisheva that I would remain behind with the new mother and child. "A day or two until she is recovered enough to travel by donkey," I said. "The large group does not travel fast and we will catch them with no trouble. I will ask Miryam to leave a man with us for our safety."

Elisheva's eyes widened with concern. "I can not abandon you!"

"Even in my homeland women do not rise the morning after giving birth to walk an entire day. Someone must stay with her and I know the wilderness better than any among us."

I left the tent to search for Miryam. She knelt over a fire cooking flatbread.

I bowed to her. She asked after the child and I responded that Teye and the baby were well.

"Miryam?"

She looked up, her gaze as hard as the rocks behind me. But I spoke without fear.

"Teye can not walk or ride. She will need two days to recover. I can stay with her. Perhaps you can leave a man to escort us."

Miryam smiled and offered me a piece of warm bread. "It is good that you do this thing. We must leave the foolishness of last night behind us."

I nodded. *You will have your way*, I said to myself.

Thus began my farewells.

I sought Gershom among his cousins in the tent where they lay sleeping. As I bent down to kiss him I knew this would be the most difficult parting. But Elisheva's children were his stars and Moses his moon. Miryam watched over Gershom with loving devotion as she did all her family. He would grow to be strong, brave, handsome, and loyal. He would walk in his father's footsteps. I could not tear him away from this life; I could not give him anything better. I had served my purpose and it was time for us to separate.

His eyelids fluttered. I bent down close to his ear.

"I love you, my beautiful son," I whispered.

He smiled and fell back to sleep.

Elisheva's smile tore my heart.

"We will not remain here long," I promised, careful to tell her no untruth.

She kissed my hands and my eyes.

I dared not linger. "I must return to Teye now," I said. *May the Goddess find a way into your birth tent.*

I said nothing to Moses. If anyone else informed him that I remained behind I did not know it—he did not come to wish me a safe journey. I told myself it did not matter. His God had claimed him from me.

Miryam brought us a donkey, food, and some extra water. She sat with Teye for a few moments to admire the child.

"You have chosen a future of hope and righteousness for him," she said as she held the baby. "I am proud of you."

Teye's face reflected all the happiness in her heart.

I walked from the tent with Miryam. "I know you will watch over my son," I said before she turned to join the stream of Israelites on the road to the oasis of Madyan. "He loves you like a mother."

The lines of her brow softened. "He reminds me of his father as a child."

I left Teye and her baby in the tent and took my lambs to the top of a nearby ridge. For several hours I watched the procession. They would reach my father's camp before nightfall. Yitro would embrace Moses.

I was glad that I would not be present at this reunion. The people of Midyan were not my people. Nor were the Children of Israel. Had my eyes been as dark and clear as Elisheva's, my manner as direct and unforgiving as Miryam's, and my nature as innocent as Teye's, I would still not belong to either people. Like my mother I was born to serve the Goddess in the temple. To the temple I would return. No one would follow me. No one would object. The Israelites had their purpose and I had my own.

I looked away from the road below to the rocks around me. I watched my dog romp among the lambs. Instead of finding joy in the sight I felt pain for my parting with my son and Elisheva, for the loss of my beloved.

When I went back to check on Teye I saw a man's footprints in the dust. I approached the tent with caution, berating myself for leaving her. But as I drew close I heard laughter. I peered through a crack in the tent flap. Bak sat next to Teye with his long legs folded under him. He watched her nurse the baby. She did nothing to cover her breast and Bak looked on without shame.

For Miryam's sake he would keep Teye safe and bring her back to the Israelites. But I could not sit in the same tent with him, even for a single hour.

I stayed with the lambs and my dog in the shelter of a rock. Just before dawn I set off away from the column of fire, back toward Haql, where the road across the wilderness merged with the incense route to Egypt.

I traveled fast enough to reach Haql in the early afternoon. I turned away from the sea into the mountains and then back toward Yahveh's pillar of cloud on the western track. Though the terrain grew rough in the high mountain pass, I did not stop for rest. I climbed and descended, climbed and descended. But as the sun sank over the mountains into the sea I still did not reach water. I stopped for the night and huddled with the lambs for warmth. I dreamt that I lay with Moses in our tent in the Valley of Gaw. His arms held me close.

I woke under a bright moon, weeping and cold. I wanted to curse the God who took my beloved from me. But I held my tongue for fear for my child's safety. As I rose to resume my journey, I did not fear the night demons in the shadows or crevices or in the broken rock beneath my feet. I sang to the Goddess and felt Her presence watching over us.

Late the next morning I reached the well at Gaser, where the black granite mountains gave way to brown sandstone. The sheep took long, deep drinks from a skin bucket left at the site. I drank and replenished the small supply I could carry.

I found a little grazing for the sheep in the area surrounding the well. As I sat down to watch the animals I closed my eyes from exhaustion and fell asleep.

When the sun sat low in the sky the dog licked my face to wake me. I felt stiff and cold. The baby inside me cried out for nourishment. I did not have much food—a handful of almonds and a few dates. I saved the almonds and shared the dates with the dog.

The following day I came to the end of the Shifa mountains. I lost track of the trail markings scratched in the sandstone and traveled south instead of east. I realized my position by the shadow of the sun and backtracked, but this cost so much time that I did not reach the next water spot, the spring at M'salbam, before nightfall.

When I woke at dawn the baby sat low in my pelvis. I did not know how much further I could go before the baby came. I prayed to the Goddess to protect me. I promised to dedicate my daughter to Her service.

I pulled myself to my feet. The pressure of the baby bearing down made my legs unsteady. I closed my eyes and tried to imagine the faces of those I loved—Elisheva, Gershom, Moses, my mother. My memories spurred me on.

I came down from the mountain pass into the wilderness in the full heat of midday. With relief I gazed upon the nafud—the bright yellow sand—of the Hisma desert. My feet sank into the soft, warm granules. If I did not linger, I could reach my destination the following evening.

I paused with the animals at the M'salbam well. I saw from tracks in the sand that a small group of travelers—five men with donkeys and a ram—had passed through the area in recent days. A single ram meant a sacrifice. And so I came to recall that the time of the yearly sacrifice to the moon god approached. At the next full moon Midyanite men would gather around the mountain to sacrifice to Sinn.

Far to the south the Israelites were making their way across this same wilderness. They approached the mountain of the moon god, with its tall cone rising into the mist. Why did Yahveh send the Israelites to gather beneath the looming mountain at the same time as the Midyanites? Did He seek a battle on Sinn's hallowed ground?

I knew the weakness of my lord's people. They softened at the lack of water for a single day. They could not defend themselves against the most ruthless Midyanites. True, Yahveh had saved them from the Egyptians and protected them from the storm god Baal Zephon. But did He have the power to occupy the sacred site of another god? I looked ahead of me toward the mouth of the Wadi Ndjeli, the final stretch of my journey. I turned my gaze south toward the ever-present column of cloud, the smoke of a thousand campfires burning in the heavens.

Would Yahveh be afraid for Himself or His people?

I knew the answer. *Yahveh knows no fear.*

When I reached the outskirts of Qurayyah the next evening I kissed the ground to thank the Goddess for Her guidance. As I rose, a tight cramp rippled over my lower abdomen. I willed myself to walk across the town to the temple I had left long ago.

In my memory, the temple of the Great Goddess rose as a shining palace high over the surrounding mud dwellings and workshops. But memory failed me. The dull mud brick walls and the sanctuary building looked like all the other structures I had passed in the town—no alabaster columns, no majestic halls and porticoes, no bright limestone walls. In Egypt I had seen a hundred minor temples grander than this hovel. My spirits sagged. I fell from a cliff into darkness.

I awoke with a mat beneath me. I smelled a familiar musty odor. I opened my eyes.

I was in Allatimm's chamber near the sanctuary. Two women sat with me—Ahatel and Thabis.

Surely I am dreaming, I said to the Goddess.

Thabis smiled down on me. I looked at her and the other woman through Miryam's eyes, for I saw their tangled hair, smudged faces, and kuttonehs that had not been washed in many months.

"She is awake," Thabis said.

I tried to rise. I tried to speak.

"Shh..." Thabis eased me back down upon the mat. "You are having a baby soon."

Warm fluid rushed between my legs. The baby would not be long now. Fear rose in my chest.

"Take me to the sanctuary," I begged. "I must deliver my baby there, to dedicate her to the Goddess."

"Allatimm would not allow that!" Ahatel objected.

I drew upon all my will and strength to lift myself to my feet. "I must go."

Neither woman tried to prevent me. They followed close behind.

I stopped just inside the sanctuary to catch my breath. Allatimm lay across the stone altar. A white robe fell away from her withered body. The breasts that had never suckled a child hung low. Her white skin looked as thin and colorless as rainwater and fell in plump folds. I approached the statues of the Goddess before the altar and lowered myself in obeisance. Allatimm climbed down from the platform.

The old woman embraced me. She felt stiff and cold as a statue of Pharaoh. "I knew you would come back to me." Her soft voice echoed in the sanctuary and filled the air like a demon in a cave. "From the moment I set my sight upon you, I knew you were destined to serve Her here."

An intense spasm of pain wrenched every fiber of my body into a small, tight knot. Allatimm saw but took no pity. She looked at me with hungry eyes and pointed to my swollen womb.

"When *that* is gone you will show men Her power." She licked her lips.

"Gone?" I whispered.

The high priestess laughed. "Did you imagine you would keep a child here? We will sell it for good profit. Now remove yourself from this place." She glanced over her shoulder toward the altar.

"Let me pray to the Goddess here," I begged.

"She wants none of your birth fluids contaminating the sanctuary."

I knew better. The Goddess loved women in birth and death, on the altar in Her temple and at the washing stone by the well. If Allatimm did not understand this, she understood nothing.

I looked at Allatimm's wrinkled face and at the gold hoop in her nose, her gold earrings and the rings that covered plump fingers. I loathed the soft, bejeweled hands that worked only to lift food to her mouth.

"You do not know the Goddess," I whispered.

"Go now." The high priestess dug her nails into my arm. "A supplicant is coming for me."

I fell back onto the ground. I cried out with pain.

A man emerged from a door near the altar. I heard his heavy footsteps and caught a glimpse of his open white robe, a ritual garment identical to Allatimm's.

"Go now," Allatimm raised her voice. "Go without looking at my worshipper."

"*Your* worshipper?" My whisper of outrage became a cry. I drew up my kuttoneh and began to push. The baby would not wait.

Allatimm ran across the sanctuary to the man and urged him to leave. He shoved her aside and walked toward me. Between waves of pain I saw the grizzled old face draw near.

It was Yitro, high priest of Midyan, my father.

PART V

THE MOUNTAIN OF GOD

TWENTY-SIX

Miryam

E passed through the walls of water, a nation reborn. Our sorrows and hardships drowned with the enemy. We had endured four hundred years of living under alien rule. Now I could taste the Promised Land on my tongue, as sweet as a bite of honey cake soaked in milk.

I stood on the eastern edge of the sea with these reflections. I imagined that our glorious future lay just a few easy days' walk from where our enemy lay defeated. I had not met the enemy within.

I endured many disappointments in those first days of our journey through Midyan. Yahveh's chosen people grew quarrelsome and greedy. They hoarded scarce water while children thirsted. They looked no further into the future than their next meal. They lamented the comforts they had left behind. Most surprising of all, some even attributed our victory to Baal Zephon and Lady Atirat of the Sea. I had no patience for those who could not see the hand of Yahveh in all that had brought us out of Egypt.

Even Elisheva disappointed me. When Teye's time came, I was walking at the edge of the camp with Bak. Anyone could have found us. I had seen Elisheva through the births of four children. She knew my skill with a newborn child exceeded that of the midwives. She knew I favored Teye and Teye favored me. How could she have called for Tzipporah instead?

But I could not bear to see Elisheva grieve over my anger and I forgave her that very evening. I told myself that she did not have the strength to resist Tzipporah and her bewitching goddess.

When Tzipporah apologized she spoke to me with humble respect. All my life I had taken pride in seeing the truth before my eyes. I believed none could tell a falsehood in my ear without detection. As I left Tzipporah behind, I congratulated myself for having tamed the wild creature at last.

I was blind and deaf. I understood nothing about her.

We climbed into the mountains. When I walked with Moses I did not mention Tzipporah's absence. It did not matter to him if she stayed behind a day or two. I cared for him a thousandfold more than she did.

The people grew restless in the heat. Water supplies ran low. Moses promised water sweeter than the Nile at our next stop, the Madyan Oasis. He had lived there for six years. As we climbed, he spoke well of Yitro, high priest of the moon god Sinn.

"He is a good and honorable man. I owe him my life."

I admired my brother's gratitude and loyalty. I looked forward to thanking Yitro myself. I pictured him as a majestic figure, like an Egyptian high priest.

Hosea and I comforted the weary travelers all afternoon. We urged them on with my brother's promise of sweet and plentiful water.

As we drew closer to the oasis of Madyan the land remained dry. We passed several small planted terraces; their crops rose from the rocks brown and stunted. I did not see a single dwelling place. After all our days in the dust I was eager to fill my eyes with green. I thirsted for cool handfuls of fresh water. My ears longed for the sound of birds in the trees.

At each turn of the track I expected the land to blossom before us. But it did not happen. When we came upon a wide escarpment with several wells dug into the barren ground, I did not recognize it as an oasis. The only trees seemed to be a single stand of seven date palms. Dry, thorny plants sprouted from the rocks. The high cliffs pressed against us. The sun beat down without mercy. Disappointment brought weariness. We had been walking for ten days, but it seemed like months.

I stood back as people pushed toward the wells. Everyone clamored for a turn. I spoke to Moses with alarm.

"We must impose some order or they will kill each other in the crush."

Moses approached the crowd. "Hear me, Children of Israel!" he called out.

I waited for the people to turn their attention to Moses. They did not. We heard angry shouts. Several elders pushed through the crowd to confront Moses.

"What have you done to us?" one of them cried. "You promised sweet water, but this is more bitter than donkey urine!"

The man shoved a skin bucket into my brother's hands. Moses brought it to his lips. He took some of the water into his mouth. He spat it out.

"Yahveh's wind has carried the seawater into the wells."

"What will the people drink?" Hosea asked.

"You and Miryam must walk into their midst. Tell them Yahveh will purify the water."

Moses walked with purpose to a nearby acacia tree, dead from lack of moisture. He pulled a dry branch with all his force until it snapped. He broke the branch into four pieces.

I followed him to the wells. The restless crowd made way for us. I told the people not to fear. "Yahveh will send us pure water," I promised. "Trust in Yahveh, who brought us out of the land of Egypt."

When Moses reached the wells, he threw a piece of the branch into each one. He spoke before all the people.

"We will call this place Marah because the water is as bitter as tears. Pitch your tents while we wait for Yahveh's miracle."

When the sun hovered over the western cliffs, Moses drew some water from the first well. He passed the bucket to the elders. One by one they drank. As soon as the first elder swallowed, he fell to his knees to thank Yahveh. The others followed. Word spread throughout the camp. Moses was right. The water tasted sweeter than the River Nile.

Before nightfall Moses and Aharon set off to pay a visit to Yitro's camp with a gift of a lamb. The elders felt that they, too, should pay their respects to the high priest of Midyan, but Moses urged them to wait until the morning.

"They must have word that our group passes through the land. But if too many go to greet them they will suspect a raid on their flocks."

"Who will lead us in your absence?" one of the elders asked.

My brother answered without hesitation. "Miryam."

My spirit filled with joy.

Elisheva joined me as I sat outside my brother's tent beneath the evening sky. She spoke of her baby, which she expected to deliver in the next few days. She mentioned concern for Tzipporah and Teye. I assured her that Bak would return them to us soon.

"Tzipporah has lived through difficult times," Elisheva said.

"So have we all."

Elisheva looked deep into my eyes. "But she more than others."

"In what way?" I asked without much interest. I did not want to spend my precious hours as leader of the people in women's gossip. I scanned the camp laid out before me and wished that someone would call upon my authority for help. *Four thousand tents,* I said to myself. *Not a single dispute among them. Not even a complaint about a stolen goat.*

I rebuked myself for wishing discord. A peaceful camp did not make me any less worthy as a leader.

I realized that Elisheva had not answered my question. I saw that she squinted in pain.

"Are you ill?"

She shook her head. "A little cramp." She ran her hands over her swollen belly.

"The baby?"

"Not yet. But I will go rest."

I left my post to help Elisheva lie down in her tent. Nadav, Avihu, and

Gershom played nearby. I instructed them to stay close.

"Summon me at once if she calls," I said.

As I walked back to my brother's tent, I saw that Aharon and Moses approached.

"You have returned soon," I observed. I did not conceal my disappointment.

"Yitro is gone to Qurayyah," Moses explained.

"I am sorry you missed him. I know you looked forward to your reunion."

"We will meet at the Mountain of God."

"Surely Yitro will not come to sacrifice to Yahveh," I said.

"The people of Midyan sacrifice to Sinn every year at the full moon after lambing."

His news alarmed me. "If we sacrifice to our God at the same time, will they be angry?"

Moses put his hand on my arm. "They have named the mountain after Sinn, but Yahveh dwells there now. All the people of Kush—the Midyanites, the Yoqtanites, the Amalekites, the Mushri—will come to know of Yahveh's glory."

As we set off the following morning, a group of women from Yitro's camp arrived with a gift of roasted meat and fruit. All but one wore plain kuttonehs woven of black sheep's wool, just like those of Moses and Tzipporah.

"Where is Tzipporah?" Moses called out to me after he welcomed the women, each by name. "Tell her to come greet her sisters."

"She is not here," I began. I explained that she would soon follow with Teye and Bak.

Moses grew angry. "You allowed her stay behind in her condition?"

"The woman is one to do as she pleases," I pointed out.

Moses paused. His brow cleared. "When are they to rejoin us?"

"A day or two."

"We will press south to Elim, where the water is more plentiful. We will wait for them by the sea."

We reached the oasis at Elim in the late afternoon. The people's spirits lifted in this place, more lush and tree filled than any we had seen since Lake Timsah. We rejoiced in the flowing springs and plentiful grazing. Many families, hungry for meat, slaughtered a sheep or a goat. I feared they would deplete their flocks too much if this continued.

I walked down to the beach. Moses stood alone. He stared out over the water.

"It is beautiful here," I said as I walked up behind him. He held a pink feather in his hand.

He did not take his eyes from the sea. He did not acknowledge my presence. He stood lost in a place of memory or dreams.

Resentment crept into my heart. I wanted him to return to me, to our mission.

"If the people continue to slaughter their cattle they will have none left for flocks in the Promised Land. They will have none for sacrifice to Yahveh."

Moses turned. His expression was empty, as if he did not recognize me. Had he heard what I had said? Did he find my intrusion unwelcome? I stood before him in uncomfortable silence. After a moment he seemed to come to his senses.

"Tell them to refrain from slaughter until we reach the mountain. They should await instruction from me in this matter."

We talked of practical matters for a few more minutes until a shout from the cliff above interrupted us. Aharon waved with great urgency. He called out and gestured for me to return to camp.

Elisheva's many friends gathered outside our tent. They had set up altars to the Egyptian goddess Heqet and the Lady Atirat. I nodded to the women as they made way for me, mother of the people.

"Give her our prayers and blessings," they called to me. Several tried to press wooden Egyptian birth charms into my hand—a cow, a frog, the hippopotamus goddess Taweret, a copper ankh.

I refused the objects. "Yahveh will be with her."

"What can He know of childbirth?" they giggled.

I had no time to answer. One day they would know Yahveh as I did— the Creator of all things.

"Be ready with hot water in a pot and a swaddling cloth," I said. "I will need some salt and oil."

The women scurried off to do my bidding.

In the tent a midwife stood ready to help my sister. I thanked Yahveh for bringing her into labor before Tzipporah's return. I had always been Elisheva's comfort during her birthings. I did not wish to share this one with another.

Elisheva labored in great pain all night. The effort of bringing her fifth child to light seemed greater than that of all the others combined. I insisted that the midwife burn some of her precious supply of terebinth resin, to speed the labor. But the sweet, smoky substance did not seem to help. The midwife confided her fear that the child might be too large. I called for another midwife. She knew no more than the first. I held Elisheva's hand. I massaged her feet. I placed cool cloths on her forehead. I prayed to Yahveh.

Yahveh! Worker of Wonders! Do not take our dear one from us! Let her child live. Send grief from Your sight. Fill the camp of Your chosen people with rejoicing this night. Awesome One! Hear my prayer.

At dawn she began to push. As her time grew near I called to those who kept vigil outside the tent to bring me all that I had requested.

Elisheva delivered a beautiful little girl. The child's strong cry and good color showed that the long labor had done her no harm. I cleaned her with warm water. I rubbed her soft flesh with salt and then oil. After I swaddled her she settled into a light sleep. When I looked down upon the infant's sweet face, every feature so small and perfect, my heart swelled with love for her. I prayed for her to grow up beautiful and gentle like her mother, practical and productive like me.

I set the child next to Elisheva. She took the bundle into her tired arms and covered the little face with kisses. "What should I name her?"

"Elyah," I said without hesitation. My God is Yahveh.

We waited at Elim for two days. Moses said nothing more about Tzipporah's absence, but I knew he did not want to move on without her. The people did not press him to continue. They had water to drink, trees to rest beneath, and ripe dates for nourishment.

Moses spent his days sitting in judgment. Many men came before him to argue about stolen property. Several disputed bride-price agreements. A few brought claims of slander. Accusations of theft ran rampant throughout the camp. The people looked to Moses to resolve their conflicts.

Each afternoon I oversaw a group of women who walked through the camp to help those in need. We brought food and water to widows. We comforted the sick and sent healers to those who needed them. We made sure that all the expectant mothers found midwives to attend them. We sent Nadav and Avihu to help a woman bury her father. We urged those with animals to refrain from further slaughter. I spoke often of Yahveh's might over the gods of Egypt. I encouraged people to offer Him prayers of thanksgiving and praise.

Everywhere I went the people greeted me. Women offered me food from their precious stores; I refused with gratitude. They tried to give me gold and silver. "Save your riches," I cautioned. "Our journey is not over."

"We love you, Miryam!" they called out. I believed that Yahveh spoke to me through them.

On the third day Bak and Teye appeared on the track from Marah. Teye and her baby looked to be in good health. I took the child in my arms. I stroked his cheek.

I felt Bak watching me. I looked away from the baby to smile at my friend. I could not deny my pleasure in seeing him again. Did he feel the same way? His manner seemed subdued and unfriendly. My spirits sank.

"Tzipporah," he began.

I looked down the track. "Does she linger with the sheep?"

Bak shook his head.

I glanced at Teye. She did not look me in the eye. "We tried to find her," Teye said. "We even began to walk back to the campsite we stayed at before I had my baby..." Her voice trailed off.

Bak continued. "She disappeared the first night. I spoke to a merchant who saw a woman alone with a small flock heading east toward Qurayyah. It is a long journey and we could not follow her there. She took food and water. She must have planned it."

Teye's eyes filled with tears. "I do not know why she left us. She did not even bid us farewell. Elisheva will be heartbroken."

Tzipporah's parting words echoed in my ears. *I know you will watch over my son. He loves you like a mother.*

How could I have mistaken that for a simple apology?

In all the days of my life I strove to do good, to put others before myself. I tried to be worthy of Yahveh's favor. I guarded against the evil inclination that preys on every human heart. Until Tzipporah. I had wronged her. I had made her feel unwelcome. I had turned her away from those who loved her.

"I am to blame," I whispered.

Bak tried to comfort me with his arms. I pushed him away.

"Who will tell Moses?" Teye asked.

"I am to blame. I should be the one to tell Moses."

I found my brother sitting outside his tent with a circle of elders around him. He rose to greet me. I asked to speak with him alone.

At first I remained silent. The words did not come. I led him toward Teye and Bak.

"She did not stay with them," I said. "They had word of her on the route to Qurayyah."

Moses stopped walking. "How could they let her go?" he asked with disbelief.

"She left in the night." I glanced away. I buried my face in the hollow of my hand. After a moment I summoned the courage to continue. "It is my deed. I was angry with her. I did not mean to make her feel so unwelcome among us."

Even as I uttered words of remorse I remembered how I had rejoiced in leaving Tzipporah behind, in her contrite spirit. A veil of shame covered my face.

My brother's lip twisted as if it burned anew. He turned to look at the pillar of fire, now to the east of us. For a long time he stood in silence.

"What is in Qurayyah?" I ventured after a while.

"A temple to the goddess Asherah. Tzipporah once served there."

"Brother, forgive me," I whispered.

He raised his hand in a gesture of finality. "Do not speak of it again. We are each responsible for our own actions."

I did not mention it to anyone. When Elisheva heard the story from Teye, I repeated my brother's pronouncement. "She chose to abandon us." I left Aharon to comfort her.

I buried the guilt deep within my heart.

From Elim we continued along the Reed Sea coast. We camped that night at the shore. The place offered neither fresh water nor food. We rose before dawn to begin our trek east over the red Shifa mountains. We entered the Wadi Tiryam, a dry and desolate place. We climbed upward through a narrow pass. The steep trail grew too dangerous for people to ride on their donkeys.

We made slow progress throughout that long day and into the night. With Yahveh's beacon ahead of us we continued to walk by moonlight. No one stopped to rest. I walked with the weakest, who struggled to keep from falling even further behind. Bak carried a weary child on his back.

We reached the crest of the mountain pass at daybreak. I paused for a moment to look at the strange and frightening land below us. The red mountains gave way to yellow sand. I saw a plain of black rock in the distance. Sandstone shapes rose from the ground like weathered versions of Pharaoh's obelisks. This was the wilderness of Sinn.

We hurried to meet the others who had been waiting since dawn at the bottom of the descent, where the Wadi Sadr began. With few trees for shade and no water to drink, the people cried out to continue.

We walked along a track into the wilderness of Sinn.

The column of cloud lay to our east. How much closer it seemed! I felt Yahveh's presence in all my bones. My fingertips quivered with exhilaration. My feet rejoiced.

But others did not share my excitement. We walked with empty stomachs and parched mouths, in the full heat of the sun. By mid-afternoon a large group of men and women clamored around Moses.

"If only we had died by the hand of Yahveh in the land of Egypt!"

"Return us to the fleshpots! Let us eat our fill of meat and bread before we perish!"

"You have brought us into the wilderness to starve our people to death!"

Moses pulled at his hair with frustration. He fled from the people's grumbling. I tried to follow as he continued south along the track. When he felt my presence behind him he turned to wave me away. "Stay with the others!" he commanded. "Though Yahveh knows they do not deserve you," he muttered.

Why can I not stand by his side as he seeks You? I asked Yahveh in my heart. A wind swept down from the mountains behind me. The column of cloud rose in the distance before me. Yahveh sent no other answer.

We waited through the afternoon. Men began to pitch tents in the sand. Bak and I helped where we could. Some turned their hostility on me. They wanted to know when my brother would return. They wanted to know how he would find us food and water in this barren wilderness. I had no special knowledge. I had only my faith that Yahveh would protect us.

As the sun began to sink behind the mountains to our west I caught
a glimpse of Moses descending toward me from the east. Where had he
been? Had he walked back from the south through the hills? I would
never know. He did not speak of his encounters with Yahveh.

His skin glistened with sweat. I ran to him with a drink of water. He
walked into the middle of the haphazard camp and climbed onto a large
sandstone rock. Everyone gathered to hear his words.

"This evening you will eat flesh! In the morning you will fill yourself
with bread. By these gifts you will know Yahveh your God."

As soon as Moses finished speaking we heard a noise from the east. The
flapping of wings filled the air. The sky grew dark.

Everyone rushed to catch the birds as they landed in our midst.

"Quail!" they sang out.

The women gathered brush for fuel. The men dug several great fire pits
to roast the birds. No one slept hungry that night.

We rose late the next morning, after the dew had cleared. We emerged
from our tents to a miraculous sight—a flaky white substance fine as frost
and round like coriander seed covered the surface of the ground.

Gershom ate it first. "Sweet as honey and rich as cream!" he called out.
The people rushed to eat their fill. Nothing I ever cooked tasted as delicious.

Moses climbed on the rock and warned the people not to hoard. The
manna, he explained, would come from Yahveh every morning. Each
person must gather his fill. Those who tried to keep more than their
portion would find it infested with maggots. He went on to describe a
single exception. On the sixth day we must gather a double portion and on
the morning of the seventh we would awake to find the manna edible. For
the seventh day was to be a day of complete rest—Yahveh's Holy Sabbath.
As Yahveh rested on the seventh day of creation, we too would rest each
week in memory of His glorious works. Moses told the Children of Israel
that Yahveh's Holy Sabbath would link the generations for all time.

I sent my messengers throughout the camp to make sure the people
understood these instructions.

I will never forget the first Sabbath, celebrated in the wilderness. It came to us as a day of great rejoicing. People cast aside their grumbling and discomforts. Friends visited from tent to tent. We ate sweet manna together. We sang hymns of praise to Yahveh. We danced in His name. We spoke of soon reaching the Promised Land.

We continued south along the trade route through the wilderness of Sinn. Our pace quickened on the flat ground. By early evening the great fire furnaces of Dophka rose before us in the distance. The people of Dophka mined and smelted iron. Moses offered them gold for the use of their water supply. We camped nearby without incident.

From Dophka we moved on to Alush, where water ran too meager for our great numbers. Moses apportioned it to the weak, expectant mothers, and the very young.

After Alush we turned east into the wilderness toward the column of cloud. As the day's journey progressed, black mountains came into sight in the distance. I walked for a time with Bak. In the late afternoon we reached a campsite at Rephadim, an arid plain dotted with gnarled sandstone formations and huge boulders. Hosea and Aharon went in search of water.

I leaned against a large rock to rest. Tired and thirsty, I could not summon the energy to speak.

"You take too much responsibility for the people upon yourself," Bak said.

I looked into his weathered face. His age showed more with each day.

"They are like my children. I can not turn my back upon their needs."

He touched the flesh of my forearm, dark and dry from the sun. "What if you had your own child to care for?"

His question made my heart pound. My own child! Could Yahveh yet open my womb? I knew women of forty who had given birth to a child. Why not Miryam sister of Aharon and Moses? Bak saw that I felt the same longing as every woman. He had seen me hold Elisheva's and Teye's beautiful children. He understood the secret yearnings of my heart.

Bak looked at me with expectation. If I gave a favorable answer he would speak to my brothers about a marriage. They would not object.

A child of my own! I could almost taste Bak's lips upon mine. My whole body tingled in anticipation of pleasures I had never known.

I felt my face flush with embarrassment. I shifted my gaze away from him. The corner of my eye caught Yahveh's column of cloud. I felt a slight tremor in the earth beneath my feet. I had dedicated my life to Yahveh and His people. I had set myself apart from the concerns of women. If I became like the others, would I ever walk side by side with my God? I had waited almost thirty years to feel His pure light and heavenly voice enter me again. How could I give that up now? Had I forsaken Nunn for nothing more than Bak?

My eyes met his. I wanted so much to be the woman he saw. I wanted a child, a family of my own.

But I wanted more than that.

I prayed for Yahveh's help. *O Lord, what am I to say?*

The answer came to me on Hosea's swift feet. "Come!" he shouted. "We can find no water! A terrible thing is happening!"

We followed Hosea toward a gathering crowd. Moses stood on a rock above them with Aharon at his side. He tried to calm the people. They did not listen.

Men held stones in their hands. They shouted at their leader.

I gathered strength in my anger.

"Have you already forgotten Yahveh's miracles?" I shouted. I pushed my way through the crowd to join my brothers. I climbed to the top of the rock.

"Have you already forgotten the victory at the sea and Yahveh's promise to heal you?"

"Yahveh is not with us!" one cried.

"Get down from here, Sister," Aharon whispered to me. "Do not expose yourself to this."

"I will not be moved from my place!"

Moses looked over the crowd. He took the staff of Yahveh from Aharon.

"You brought us here to kill us with thirst!"

"Our cattle and children will die because of you!"

"Kill him!"

Moses raised his hands in supplication to the heavens. "Yahveh!" he shouted. A hush fell over the agitated crowd. "What can I do with these people? They will stone me to death!"

A wind came up. It raised great swirls of sand and dust around us. It swallowed all the cries of anger and doubt. Darkness enclosed us. Aharon clung to me. I clung to him. We crouched low on the rock to protect ourselves. Moses remained standing. He did not shield his eyes. He did not lower his arms. I saw a pinpoint of light penetrating the darkness to meet his upturned face. My eyes filled with dust and tears. I could not see. I pulled my veil over my face.

I do not know how long the sandstorm continued. It seemed an eternity. But in truth it came and went with great speed, like a passing rain shower.

When the air cleared, Moses called for the elders to follow him. He leapt from the rock. Aharon and I slid down to join him. As I stood next to Moses, the leader of our people, my spirit filled with pride for his courage and fortitude.

While the elders gathered around I began to wipe his face and beard with my veil. He brushed my hand away.

I stood alone in the midst of a multitude. I longed for water to wash my smarting eyes. I knew they would sting and swell for many days. I cursed myself for not turning sooner from what I was not meant to see. I cursed myself for not being Yahveh's chosen.

Moses led the elders to the smooth brown rock that Bak and I had stood against before the sandstorm. It loomed taller than Moses and wider than fifteen men standing side by side.

A subdued crowd gathered behind the elders. Moses raised his staff high above his head.

"In Yahveh's name!" He brought the staff down upon the rock with the full force of his strength.

A crack formed where the staff hit the stone. I held my breath as the fissure spread downward with the sound of a thousand breaking bones.

"Stand back!" Moses called.

The split grew wider. I saw drops of water glisten on the rock face like beads of sweat. We moved back.

"Further...further!"

A tide of cool fresh water rushed at us. Those who had doubted Yahveh renewed their faith in the water's purity and abundance. So, too, did I see an answer from Yahveh in the severed rock—Bak and I were not to be united, at least not yet.

TWENTY-SEVEN

Tzipporah

WHEN I was thirteen I gave birth to my first child alone in a tent at the mountain of Sinn while Father watched the sheep. Until that day no one knew the truth of what I concealed beneath my loose kuttoneh. In the early months I had feared discovery because I knew the fate that awaited a child with no father. But I learned that people never see what they do not expect to see.

When the pain started, it washed over me like waves on the sand. I sat at the edge of the valley and waited for my mother's Goddess to gather me into Her arms, to carry me to Her dwelling in the stars and ease the baby from my womb with Her gentle hands.

Nothing happened as I had imagined. The Goddess showed me no special favor. The pain worsened as the day progressed. When night fell, Father took his turn guarding the sheep and I withdrew to our tent. In the dark I tried to remember my mother's face.

The baby came to me at dawn like the morning star.

I had so little time to hold her.

In those days, before I went to the temple, I knew no safe haven. Father and I dwelt at the mountain alone during the hot months. I could not call upon a sister or cousin to pretend the newborn had sprung from her own womb. Had we camped closer to the trade routes I might have sought a passing merchant willing to keep her for his own profit. Even that would have been better than the destiny of her birth.

Our clan—as all the clans of Kush—took swift action against any man who fathered children on an unmarried woman. If he had no wife, her kin would demand marriage. A man already married risked death if he did not flee. The paternal grandfather assumed all responsibility for the child of such a union and paid the violated woman compensation for the strain on her womb.

But a child with no known father had no people. And one can not live without a people.

When Yitro found me with the child I told him that the baby had come to me as a gift from the Goddess. He drew his knife and threatened to kill me if I did not reveal the father's name. I confessed I knew nothing of the man and never saw him again. I did not tell the truth, for the man lurked in every shadow, at every abandoned well. He tormented me in the night like a demon.

Father tore the infant from my arms. He held her by the legs like a chicken going to slaughter. The child wailed. I begged him to spare her. But the rules of my clan did not change for the high priest's daughter. He took her away into the wilderness.

I tried to run after them, but I was still weak from the birth and my legs gave way. I cried out to the mountain. *Sinn, save my child!*

He answered with the piercing echo of her scream. Then silence.

Yitro returned with her blood on his hands. I turned away from him. As he silenced my child, so too did I vow to be silent in his presence forevermore.

When my labor for Gershom began, I hid from Yitro. He had no reason to take the son of Moses from me, yet still I feared.

My third child came to be born in the sanctuary of the Goddess. Thabis held a cool cloth against my brow. Ahatel chanted, and though she started too late, her voice eased the worst of my pain. Afterwards I held her hand and offered words of appreciation. She smiled at me with gratitude. I felt happy that once again we could be friends.

I had returned to the temple in anger and despair. In anger and despair I had told myself that I belonged inside these walls, in the bosom of the Goddess, and nowhere else. Yet neither the Goddess nor Her high priestess had sustained me. Thabis and Ahatel had been my support. Now, with the baby at my breast, I yearned for others whom I held dear in my heart—Elisheva, Teye, Gershom, Moses.

How had my mother devoted herself to the Goddess with so many people to love?

Perhaps her devotion had wavered.

Perhaps she had made offerings in the cave only when required, in the season of warm rains, at the birth of her children, and when she wished to implore the Goddess for help. Perhaps these and no more.

As for birth chanting, any chanter knew that her voice served the mother far more than the Goddess.

And so as I lay in the sanctuary of the Great Goddess I saw how little my devotions mattered.

I gazed at the infant in my arms, more precious to me than anything. He had his father's face—the wide brow, high cheekbones, slender nose. With my finger I traced the baby's full lips, his father's perfect lips before the burning coal had touched them.

My heart blossomed with tears for my sons and their father. If I abandoned them now, I abandoned myself.

My friends helped me to a small room near the sanctuary; they did not leave me for a moment.

Yitro's face softened at the sight of the infant.

"You and the little one belong with his father," he pronounced with a tenderness I had never known from him.

I opened my mouth and uttered my first words to him in many years. "Father, you speak the truth."

Traveling merchants had given Father word of the Israelite's exodus and their victory over the Egyptians at the sea, but he knew little else. I told him how Moses had defeated the Egyptians with the help of his ancestral God, a divine warrior named Yahveh, and how this God required a sacrifice at the mountain of Sinn. I waited in fear for his anger to rise.

Instead he smiled. "An ambitious nature will not be restrained for long."

My father's words surprised me. Though I knew my lord's restlessness too well, I had seen no purpose in him until he had heard Yahveh's call.

I shook my head in disagreement. "He was never ambitious."

"He tried to convince himself that he wanted no more than a little food, a woman, and a tent over his head. But he shunned leadership with too much vehemence."

I recalled how Moses had appeared as a god to me when I had first laid eyes on him. Only a foolish girl would imagine she could keep him—beloved of Yahveh—for herself.

In two days I recovered enough strength to leave. Allatimm urged me to take one of the Goddess statues from the sanctuary.

"She will bring you back to me again, next time to stay."

I shook my head and held up Thabis's hand. I spoke in a quiet voice. "This is what I will take with me."

Yitro laughed at my boldness.

"Set her free," I urged, " in the name of the Goddess, whom she has served these many years."

Allatimm hid her displeasure with a smile. "She is worth no more than a lamb."

And so I bought her freedom with a lamb from my flock.

We traveled south along the flat plateau of the Hisma on the well-worn caravan route between Qurayyah and Dedan. As we walked, the column of cloud remained before us in the distance. I told Father and Thabis how Yahveh had led His people forward with this constant sign of His presence. I told them of Yahveh's afflictions in Egypt and the death of the Egyptian firstborn.

With each story Father's admiration for Yahveh's power grew. As the light of day faded into twilight we watched Yahveh's cloud turn to fire. Father stared with surprise at the fiery column. After a long silence he spoke.

"Soon after you were born I made a double sacrifice in your name."

"Grandmother told me the story many times."

Father nodded. He took a deep breath. "I saw things I told no one. Not even your mother."

My heart beat faster; I drew closer to him. I had long suspected that a secret lay hidden in those sacrifices. Some believed that Father allowed me to live for my mother's sake. But I had always hoped that he had seen something special in my destiny—a spark of the Goddess—that he did not dare extinguish.

Father turned toward the column of fire. His eyes looked away from me into the distance as if to say that he had foreseen Yahveh's fire.

"You saw the fire? What else?"

He turned his gaze back to me with his lips curved up. "Signs do not reveal themselves like a story waiting to be told. When I make the sacrifice I call upon Sinn to inform my vision."

"Did he speak to you of Yahveh's fire?"

Father shook his head. "Nothing. Never before or since has a portent come in such silence."

I drew in a deep breath through my nostrils; it lodged in my throat like brittle, dried twigs. Why had my father allowed me to live?

Father continued, his eyes still fixed on the column. "A fire alone indicated nothing. Sinn's silence meant death. Everyone waited for me to give my pronouncement. Would Reema's witch-eyed child live or die? I moved my lips in silent pleading. For your mother's sake I begged the god to save you. When he remained silent I laid my hands upon my eyes."

He covered his face with the hollows of his hands as if to recreate that moment.

"I implored any god to come forward with a sign. That is when the vision came to me. The fire I had seen in the sheep's entrails rose high into the heavens. It shed a holy light over all the land."

Father lowered his hands to gaze upon me. "I knew then that another God had taken your part. It was a God of fire and light. Now you have told me His name. His power is vast."

All night I pondered Father's vision. Before Moses had come to me I had lived in the world of men as I found it—grim, forbidding, cruel. I took what happiness the Goddess gave me without hope for a better day. Even when I had lain with Moses in love I had never turned an eye to the next sunrise.

But twenty years ago Yahveh's holy light had risen before the high priest of Sinn for my sake. For my sake He had granted me the life that had brought me to this day and would bring me to another, and another after that. For what purpose had He given me a future?

I saw only one.

The next morning I resumed the journey with light feet. When Thabis helped me carry the child, I told her that she was a free woman. Free or not, she said, she would never leave my service.

As we drew closer to the city of Tabuk we heard rumors of a people who traveled through the wilderness, twenty thousand strong. Still, none of the travelers we met had seen the Children of Israel with his own eyes. On our fifth day we turned into the mountains at Raes and stopped at an oasis for the night. Here at last we had direct word of those we sought.

As darkness fell and the fiery column rose, we sat by our own small fire to eat. A stranger approached with his donkey and even before he could ask to join our company Father urged him to sit with us and share our salted meat and bread.

"From where do you come?" Father asked when the man had eaten.

"From the west across the mountains and south. I stopped at Dophka for fine knives to sell in the far north. Where do you go, sir?"

"To the mountain of Sinn," my father answered. "We have business with the Israelites. Did you hear word of them in the south?"

The traveler smiled. "I saw them defeat the Amalekites."

"Will you honor us with the tale?" Father replied.

The man nodded and took a drink from his water skin. "I came to Dophka on the day they left. I heard they were a peaceful group, on their way to Sinn's mountain. I caught up with them in a place known as Rephadim. But they called it Massah and Meribah because the people quarreled and tried their God—so I was told—about lack of water. Their leader, a man named Moses, struck a rock and an entire pool of water poured forth. I drank from this pool myself when I arrived at the campsite.

"It is hard to imagine the vast size of such a group, and they have many cattle with them. They seem to be rich, for their robes are made of fine cloth and all the women and young men wear gold in their ears and noses. They say they are on the way to a new home, in a land that flows with milk and honey. No one knew where this place might be—or perhaps they did not want to tell me.

"In the morning they broke camp and began to move east. The young and healthy walked in front while the elderly and sick stayed at the back. As we began to move forward, shouts came up from the back and a great confusion reigned. A group of Amalekite bandits had attacked the weakest at the back of the group and stolen their gold—an act of cowardice.

"The Israelites stopped to bury the dead. I came to the place where the leaders had gathered. I knew the leader when I saw him—a tall man with a great beard and a plain black kuttoneh. He covered his head as the people of Midyan do. He spoke with an Egyptian accent and seemed to stumble over his own tongue.

"He placed his hand upon the shoulder of another man much younger than he and addressed him before the witnesses.

"'From this time forward you will no longer be known as Hosea but as Yehoshua—Yahveh is salvation. Go among the people and pick twenty men. I will station myself on that hill. You will attack the Amalekites and kill them. Let the message be clear to all others. Yahveh will not allow the Children of Israel to be defeated.'

"As Yehoshua and his men set out, Moses stood with his staff overlooking the plain. He held the rod to the heavens.

"The Israelites crept up on the Amalekites and surprised them. The Amalekites beat them back, but none of the Israelites fell. Each time Moses lowered his arms the Israelites lost ground. And when he held them up again, they advanced against the Amalekites. People said that the power of Yahveh the Divine Warrior flowed through his arms.

"When Moses tired, a man named Hur rolled a boulder for him to sit on. Hur and Moses's brother, Aharon, held up his arms. With his arms outstretched toward the battle, the Israelites continued to prevail. By the end of the afternoon, the entire band of Amalekites, fifty men strong, lay dead.

"The people rejoiced that night. They built an altar of stone and Moses stood before them to speak.

"'This altar will be called Yahveh Is My Banner. Yahveh has sworn upon His throne that for all time He will wage war against the Amalekites who attacked our weak. He will wipe their name from under the heavens.'"

When the merchant finished his tale I thanked him with all my heart. Hosea, now Yehoshua, was a good man and I rejoiced for his success. But I feared that my lord had suffered more than anyone suspected. Only I seemed to notice that each encounter with Yahveh drained him like a slaughtered animal whose life blood flowed away. He needed me to care for him.

Just before dawn I instructed Thabis to break our camp while I woke Father and told him we must leave at once. I did not even allow him time to eat.

We traveled hard for three more days, through the mountains, down to sandy wadis, over a hard black plain. On the sixth day we saw the mountain rising before us. Smoke poured from somewhere at the top. The Valley of

Gaw lay ahead. There I hoped to find my beloved Moses with his people.

As we walked into the valley, a group of men came out to meet us. They held swords on their thighs and stared at us with suspicion. I knew none of them.

"Who are you and what do you want?" one of the men asked as my lambs ran forward to graze.

Father stepped forward. "Tell Moses that Yitro, his father by marriage, has come with his wife and son."

One of the men turned and flew across the valley on swift feet. Yet still the waiting seemed endless.

At last I saw my lord approaching. I moved forward to Moses. I wanted to throw myself at his feet and beg his forgiveness. I wanted to present his son and see the joy in his face. I wanted to be an oasis of rest and relief from his burdens.

But Moses did not look at me. He walked past me to my father as if I held no more substance than a light breeze. His eyes did not even graze my flesh. The baby cried. Yet still he would not acknowledge us.

How much better to have died in childbirth and walked the earth as a spirit, forever separated from those I loved! At least then my son would have received his due.

My knees grew weak and my eyes filled with tears. The baby wailed. I no longer knew how to comfort him. I stood at the bottom of a dark crevasse with no way out.

"Tzipporah!"

I felt a hand on my shoulder. Elisheva appeared before me, her face bright with joy at my return. We embraced. I kissed the infant in her arms.

She led me to the tent I had once shared with Moses and gave me fresh water. We lay down side by side with our babies between us so we could admire them. All my bones ached from the days of hard walking so soon after childbirth. My body seemed as dry as the bed of a wadi in the hottest month.

"I have my little girl at last," Elisheva said. "But I feared I might never see you again." She began to weep.

I kissed her hand and then her baby's cheek. How could I explain? I had never wanted to hurt her.

"I ran from demons that do not exist."

"Will you stay now?" Her tears continued to flow like a spring in the season of soaking rains.

"I promise never to leave you again," I whispered.

Thabis followed behind us with the sheep. She insisted on standing guard outside the tent so I could rest. Elisheva and I fed the children and fell into a light sleep.

I woke to the sound of argument.

"My mistress rests," Thabis said. We could see that she blocked the entrance to the tent.

"Who are you?" Miryam's deep voice demanded.

Elisheva and I exchanged glances. Thabis would soon learn that no one dared refuse Miryam.

"I am Thabis of Moav. Tzipporah is my mistress."

"We have no slaves in this camp," Miryam said.

"She is right," I called out. "Let her in."

Miryam stood before us with my son. Gershom dropped her hand and ran toward my embrace. I held him so tight he squirmed. He put his hands on either side of my cheeks. I showed him the baby. After I assured him that I would not leave him again, he ran to find his cousins and tell them the news of his new brother.

I looked up at Miryam with apprehension. I expected to see her strong, sure eyes filled with disappointment, even anger. I knew she did not want me back.

But I did not see the Miryam I knew. Instead of anger and judgment I saw remorse. And she, who had always spoken with such certainty, seemed unable to find words.

"This is my son." I lifted the baby into her arms.

She gazed with tenderness at the infant. After a long moment she spoke. "He has his father's face."

Elisheva helped me hang a curtain across the tent so I could separate myself from Moses and yet still be close enough to attend him—if he would forgive me.

"Now you have a place of your own when people visit," she said as we surveyed our work.

She did not know the truth—Moses would not allow me to sleep near him.

We heard the movement of many feet outside the tent and the sounds of rhythmic clapping and timbrels.

"They are going to sacrifice to Yahveh," Elisheva explained. "But you should rest. I will look after the boys so Miryam can be a witness to the offering."

I put the baby down and embraced my friend. I did not want to let go. Why had I ever left her?

"I will be back soon," she promised.

But Miryam returned first. She brought me a plate of food, an oil lamp, and blankets.

"Your father helped with the sacrifice and shared a meal with the elders," she said. She paused to drape a blanket over my shoulders. "He declared Yahveh to be greater than all gods."

"My father returns the favors Moses gave him these many years past." I recalled my birth sacrifice and Father's vision, but I said nothing. "What of all the others who have come to sacrifice to Sinn?"

"Sinn may have the mountain when we leave. Yitro has said he will delay his sacrifices until we are gone. Most of his followers have stayed away for fear of the cloud."

Miryam watched me eat for a few moments. I took the plate to Thabis, who remained outside in the darkening evening.

"Why does she not come in?" Miryam asked.

"She looks out for the lambs. I will have to build a pen to hold them at night."

"I will send Bak to help you."

"Is he well?"

Miryam cast her eyes away and flushed. "I have seen little of him these past days. He fought with great bravery against the Amalekites. Do you know of our victory?"

I nodded. "And of Yehoshua."

"He is a fine young man." For a moment her gaze seemed to leave me. The Miryam I knew moved forward in bold steps and never looked back. But as I gazed upon her now it seemed that she sat lost in recollection of the past.

Elisheva brought a group of her friends to visit. Miryam sat for a few more minutes before rising to leave. I thanked her for the meal and she promised to send Bak in the morning.

After Miryam left, the women grew more lively. Their chatter became loud enough to echo into the valley below. First they gossiped about Miryam. They admired and feared her; they speculated that she would never marry Bak. Some recalled that as a young woman she had almost married Nunn, father of Yehoshua. Elisheva confirmed the truth of the story.

I knew Miryam cherished her place at her brother's side. I knew she felt more comfortable in the company of men. But that night in the warmth of the tent surrounded by women I could not help wondering—if Miryam could choose to be one of us, would she?

The women asked me many questions about the temple in Qurayyah. I told them how Thabis and I had once served its high priestess, but I said nothing of the men forced upon my friend. I told them that the women took men by choice and that like my mother, I had remained chaste. When Teye described my birth chanting, they listened with great attention. They asked if I would chant for them. I promised to help any woman who called for me in her time of need.

After that the talk turned to other matters—the rigors of the wilderness, difficulties of finding adequate food, hope for the Promised Land, children, potential matches among the young men and women, speculation on a wife for Yehoshua. Many named their own sisters, but everyone agreed that in the end Miryam would find the best match for him.

"Miryam?" I asked with surprise.

"She has already made many matches," Elisheva replied. "Years ago people often sought her help."

"She has the eye for it," Teye added. "And she knows everyone."

"She will soon have someone for you," one of the women teased Teye. We all laughed.

Teye blushed. "I am too much used and have a child by another," she objected.

"You are as fresh as a flower in moonlight," I said. "And you will be a blessing to the man lucky enough to get you."

When the women murmured their approval and agreement I felt a surge of happiness and well-being. Whether or not the Goddess sat among us, whether or not Moses forgave me, I belonged here. Here I would stay.

As the night wore on the women began to leave. I thanked each for coming and invited her to return whenever she pleased. I stepped out into the cool night air with Thabis.

Fires dotted the camp behind me. I hoped that Moses would soon return. I did not want the night to pass with this rift between us. He could divorce me if such was his pleasure. Better that than the hollow stare of a stranger.

At last I heard voices. My father spoke and then Miryam. Moses replied and my heart jumped. I lifted the baby into my arms.

When the three of them stood before me I bowed to each: Miryam, my father, and Moses. Then I fell to my knees.

"My lord, I can not let another night pass with no name for your son. As Yahveh has shown mercy to His children please show mercy to this innocent one. And if you find in your heart the will to forgive me for my sins against you, I will strive to be worthy of your trust again."

Moses took the baby from my arms. Miryam raised her lamp high so Moses could see the child's face. His own face radiated joy as it had upon the birth of Gershom. Relief embraced me like my mother's arms across the vast distance that separated the living from the dead.

Moses lifted the child above his head. "I name you Eliezer, for the God of my fathers was my help and He rescued me from Pharaoh's sword."

The child whimpered. Moses returned him to my arms. He stood in silence, his hard gaze fixed upon my own imploring eyes. Had I destroyed his love for me?

His expression softened. I began to cry.

"In the presence of this company and Almighty Yahveh I thank you for giving me a second son. May Yahveh bless you."

TWENTY-EIGHT

Miryam

IN all the months Tzipporah dwelt with us I never witnessed affection between her and Moses. I took this for indifference. Elisheva and Aharon often embraced in my presence. When Aharon entered the room, Elisheva's face always grew bright. They whispered to each other. They held hands. I could not imagine love between a man and woman without these signs.

On the evening after we defeated the Amalekites, I sat with Teye and Elisheva. Their conversation turned to how Moses fared without Tzipporah. As a rule I did not permit myself to participate in gossip or to listen when others indulged in it. Such behavior, I reasoned, did not befit one dedicated to loving all the people. But on this occasion I could not help myself.

"I do not know how Moses can lead without her," Elisheva said. "Even a man who does no more than work in the fields needs a wife who will listen to his cares and assure him of his worth."

"Perhaps a prophet of Yahveh needs no such comfort," Teye speculated.

I could not hold my tongue. "He has many friends and companions to share his burdens. He has us."

Elisheva looked at me. Did I see pity in her eyes?

"It is not the same," she said.

Over the next few days her words echoed in my ears many times. They revealed the truth hidden in my heart.

I recalled my brother's anger when I had told him of Tzipporah's departure. A man with no attachment would not have cared. I had sensed a great sorrow on the day that I came upon him at the shore with a feather in his hand. I had seen him look upon Elisheva's newborn with longing in his eye. Sometimes he scanned Gershom's face as if he sought the features of another. Before, while Tzipporah remained in camp, he sat with us for most meals. Now we never saw him in our tent.

From the beginning I had been unfair to her. I did not treat her as my brother's chosen wife. I shunned her unfamiliar ways. I judged her worth by habits that I found distasteful. I did not try to welcome her as a sister. I drove her away. Now my beloved brother suffered from her absence.

I vowed to myself that if she returned I would set things right between us.

The day that Tzipporah came out of the wilderness I thanked Yahveh for His mercy. I rejoiced in the birth of my brother's new son. I rejoiced for the return of the woman he loved. So changed was my heart that I grew angry when he did not forgive her at once. When she offered her apology to him that night my heart wept for her.

In the days that followed I observed her with fresh eyes. She, too, had changed. She watched over her infant with as much attention as any mother I knew. She showed great pride when people admired him. She slipped into Elisheva's circle of friends with an ease that surprised me. She no longer wandered by herself with the sheep night and day. The stream of women visitors to my brother's tent became so constant that the curtain Tzipporah put up did not shield him well enough from the chattering voices. He began to talk about raising a separate tent to use for meetings.

After her return Tzipporah seemed more attentive to Moses. She offered him refreshment when he sat in judgment. She served him at meals. She brought him water to wash. Yet I never saw more than a smile pass between them. They held themselves aloof from each other. They spoke little.

I tried to accept what I did not understand. But my curious eyes could not stop searching for proof that they loved each other as man and wife.

I sought information about Tzipporah from the girl Thabis, a liberated slave. She seemed a practical and capable person. I liked her at once. So much had the years of service worn her down that I guessed her age to be close to mine. In truth she had not passed her twenty-first year. When she told me that her parents had sold her at the age of thirteen, my face grew red with fury.

"The circumstances are not so unusual." She said this as if she spoke of a stranger.

I drew from her the story of the temple, its abominations, and the terrible afflictions the high priestess visited upon the women who lived there.

"Did Tzipporah…" I stopped myself. Whatever darkness lay in Tzipporah's past should not be of concern to me.

"No," Thabis replied. By her forthright answer I saw that she did not condemn my curiosity. "Tzipporah refused. She had more courage than all of us together. I owe her my life."

By her account Moses had chosen a woman worthy of him after all.

I promised Thabis a place among our people if she abided by Yahveh's way. She agreed without hesitation. With Tzipporah's permission she came to help me with the food tent for orphans and men without families. She was a skilled cook and required little instruction from me. We worked side by side as friends and partners.

The old man, Yitro, greeted Moses like a son. I laughed at myself for having imagined him as an Egyptian priest. He wore a dirty black kuttoneh like any other member of his clan. He covered his head with a long black cloth secured by a black wool cord around his skull. His weathered skin reminded me of a dried grape. His white beard fell to his chest. How little difference his appearance made when he began to speak! He commanded attention with the authority of his voice and the wisdom of his words. He listened to the story of how we went out from Egypt. He accepted the

greatness of Yahveh. He helped Moses make the first sacrifice at the foot
of the mountain that he had long claimed for his own god.

When I attended Yitro the next morning he understood that I meant to
honor him. He thanked me for the food and water that I provided.

"I will return to my people now," he said. "May you be blessed in the
north, in the land your God gives you."

"Do you not wish to come with us and worship Yahveh?" I asked.

The old man seemed surprised by my question. He did not take offense.

"I see He is a powerful God. But I can not abandon my people or
my god."

I escorted Yitro to Moses, who sat in front of his tent to judge. I
explained that on days we did not travel Moses stationed himself before
the people from morning to evening. Yitro shook his head.

When Moses finished with the men who stood before him, he and Yitro
embraced. Yitro did not waste any words.

"This thing is not right." He gestured to the crowd waiting for Moses.
"You will wear yourself out."

Moses replied, one word following another with difficulty through his
scarred lips. "People come to me with their disputes. We are one people
now. What choice do I have?"

"Seek from among your people capable men who fear your God and
will not take bribes. Divide the people and assign them to these judges.
Let the judges come to you with difficult cases."

Moses pondered Yitro's words for a few moments before his face
brightened. "It is a good plan."

I welcomed the priest's wise suggestion, for I saw how much more
practical his system would be. I wondered that I—who knew how to
apportion tasks to serve the people—had not devised it myself.

The next day I did not see Moses in the morning. Neither Yehoshua
nor Hur knew where he had gone. Aharon, busy interviewing men to sit
in judgment with Moses, did not know. I sought Tzipporah. She sat with a

group of women near her sheep in the valley, at the base of the mountain. Several of the women seemed to be many months pregnant. They greeted me with great respect. Two moved to make a place for me in their circle. I did not join them. I inquired about the health of each and their families.

I turned to Tzipporah. "Have you seen Moses?"

She pointed up toward the mountain, where a thick cloud hovered over the top of the cone.

"When?"

"He set out at dawn."

"Alone?" I asked with alarm.

"Do not worry," she assured me. "He knows the land well."

Moses returned to camp in the early afternoon.

"Summon the elders," he called out to me. "I will speak at the altar."

We gathered at the altar without delay. As I stood, I found Bak by my side. I had promised him an answer when we reached the mountain, five days earlier. I did not know how to tell him that now I could not answer before we reached the Promised Land.

He rested his hand on my shoulder. I softened at his touch.

The crowd grew silent as Moses stepped onto a boulder. He raised his arm for silence. He spoke as he always did when delivering a message from Yahveh, with no impediment.

"Israelites! You saw all that Yahveh did to Egypt. He bore you on eagle's wings to freedom. Now if you will hear His voice and keep His covenant you will become a treasure for Him among all people, a nation of priests. This you must promise."

A nation of priests! The very idea made me tremble with excitement. I answered my brother's call in a voice so loud it reverberated across the crowd. "All that Yahveh has spoken we will do!"

"ALL THAT YAHVEH HAS SPOKEN WE WILL DO!" the people echoed me.

I did not doubt their promise.

The following day Moses went up the mountain again, to tell Yahveh of the people's promise to keep His covenant. We saw the cloud that covered the cone. We felt a rumbling beneath our feet. The animals in camp grew restless. When Moses returned again, the earth grew still. He told us that Yahveh would speak with us in three days.

"Wash your clothes and purify yourselves," Moses announced. "Do not go near a woman. Be ready for the third day! We will climb the lower mountain, which flattens into a plain at the top. In the midst of this plain rises the upper mountain of God. From the plain you will hear the words of Yahveh. Do not set foot on the upper mountain. Do not touch its edge. If you violate this rule you will die by the hand of Yahveh."

I did not know whether to be happy that I would be in His presence or sad that I received no special distinction. After a few moments I put aside my uncertainty and allowed my excitement to blossom. At last I would hear His voice again!

After Moses finished his speech, he asked Yehoshua and me to make sure that the people understood. I called my messengers. We began to walk through the camp at noon and did not finish our task until sunset.

I found a large group of women washing clothes at the rock pool fed by a stream on the west side of the mountain. Elisheva and Teye worked together. Their infants lay on a blanket behind them. I noticed with a twinge of regret that Teye washed Bak's robe as well as her own dress. I reminded myself that I did not have time to attend to such matters. I could not even wash my own clothing—I had accepted Thabis's offer to do it for me.

The women chattered with excitement.

"Remember Yahveh's words," I announced. "Keep yourselves away from your men for the next two nights."

One woman, a fisherman's wife, called out to correct me. "Moses said for the men to stay away from the women, not the women to stay away from the men."

Laughter rose from every corner of the crowd.

How could they make light of so serious a matter? My stomach grew sour with annoyance.

"It is in our power to help our men stay pure," I said.

"You have nothing to worry about!" someone called out from the group of women before me.

I did not recognize the voice. It did not matter. She was not the only one who mocked me. I saw the suppressed smiles on many of the faces around the pool.

My hands clenched. My skin grew hot. I had given my life to them, I had cared for them with love and dedication. I had served them while my own womb turned to dust.

I turned away in anger and sorrow.

Elisheva followed after me. "Miryam! Wait!"

I stopped.

"They meant no harm," she insisted. "They all admire you. We rely on you."

"I do not care about their foolishness," I lied. "All I do is for the glory of Yahveh alone."

The next morning we rose at dawn to the sound of thunder in the heavens. A thick black cloud covered the mountain. Whiteness enveloped our land like a heavy fog. Ash covered our clean robes. Lightning cracked across the sky. It blazed like torches in the night. Everyone trembled in fear. The sound of a ram's horn drew us forward.

Moses led the Children of Israel up the grey mountain. The climb took much of the morning. It drew us ever closer to the thunder. The mountain shook beneath our feet. My faith in the women came to be renewed with this evidence of their great courage. No one turned back.

When we reached the top, a vast plain spread before us wide enough to hold twice the entire camp of Israelites. We saw our tents in the valley below and the mountains in the distance. The upper mountain rose from the center of the plain into the thick cloud above us.

"Do not touch the upper mountain!" Moses called out. He pointed to its blackened base. "This is Yahveh's instruction to you. Do not go up or touch its edge. If you do, you will die."

As we huddled in a single large group, thunder exploded above us. Blasts of a ram's horn seemed to herald the sound of the mountain splitting into two. Grown men could not hold their bowels for fear. Children and women screamed.

I had not expected so much noise, the odor of fear. Did He test us? Did He imagine we doubted His power over all creation? *I fear You and love You*, I whispered in my heart. *I submit myself to You.*

I resolved to hold myself steady. A single explosion of thunder shattered my skull. The world grew silent. I saw people cry out. I could not hear them. All around me men and women clutched their heads in pain, but I felt a flood of happiness wash over me like a powerful wave. Ash fell like snow.

I am Yahveh your God, who brought you out of the land of Egypt, from the house of slaves. No other gods will you have in My reign.

The voice crept into my heart through the silence. A quiet voice, no more than a whisper. I could not be sure I heard it. I looked around me. Others, too, seemed confused. Many fell to the ground, as if their legs could no longer hold them up. They twitched and jerked like crushed insects. Some men struggled to bring their wives back to consciousness. The ground began to rumble again.

Moses stood on the edge of the cone mountain, unharmed. He called out to the people below him.

"Do not fear death. Yahveh has come to test you and put His dread upon you so you do not go astray."

"You speak to us instead," a man called out. "We will hear you! If you let Yahveh continue, we will die!"

Others echoed his plea until a great clamor rose from the gathering.

Moses raised his arms as if to bless the Children of Israel. He turned to climb into the black cloud, on the mountain I could not touch. He rose to receive Yahveh's words alone.

The thunder stopped. People ran toward the path that would take them down the mountain. They slipped in the thick layer of ash. Many fell. By Yahveh's grace none were trampled. A human wave began the descent back to camp.

I alone longed to stay.

Yehoshua and I waited for Moses on the lower mountain. As the afternoon became evening Moses emerged from the cloud. We walked down together in silence. Could I have endured all that Moses did when he spoke to Yahveh? The question gnawed at me.

The people waited for Moses at the foot of the mountain. Moses spoke of Yahveh's covenant with us. He described the Ten Sacred Edicts by which we would live from that day forward. He told us that Yahveh's rule was eternal. We must promise to worship no other god but Him.

Tears of joy came to my eyes. The yearning of my heart, my desire to worship Him and Him alone, would be fulfilled by all my people. At last He had confirmed what I had always suspected. He required no less of us.

I promised myself that I would follow Yahveh's laws with all the love I had to give and more. I would dedicate my last breath to helping my people know the goodness in His way and follow the path He laid before us.

After the Ten Sacred Edicts Moses explained many other rules and edicts. The people listened in awe. Some made logical sense. Others Yahveh asked us to follow as proof of our faith. Moses finished with Yahveh's promise.

"If we worship as Yahveh asks, He will bring us to the Promised Land. He will bless our bread and water. He will take away sickness and fill the empty womb. He will make our enemies run from us."

Everyone knelt to thank Yahveh. We rejoiced that our sojourn in the wilderness would soon end. People tried to touch Moses as he passed through the crowd.

Moses retired to his tent. He did not accept the food I offered him. Later I returned to find him writing Yahveh's words onto a scroll. Tzipporah held the papyrus smooth as he worked on it. I wished he had asked for my help. Surely he knew I honored Yahveh's laws more than Tzipporah, a stranger among our people.

I watched him dip the reed into the precious jar of ink. He formed the Egyptian characters with care. No one spoke. I longed to ask a hundred questions about my brother's work, to give voice to my love for Yahveh and my eagerness to follow His laws. But I sensed that Moses required silence and so I restrained myself. I regretted that I could not read. I longed to look over his shoulder and feast my eyes upon the words of Yahveh.

Moses paused to glance up at me. Did I see a slight frown before he smiled?

"Sister, the quickening of your heart makes my hand grow unsteady."

My spirits plunged. He did not wish to have me near him. I offered a stiff bow and withdrew. But as I returned to Aharon's tent I told myself that I should not take offense. Had I been able to sit calm and unmoved like Tzipporah, Yahveh would have doubted my love.

Moses finished at dawn. I ran to collect food for a simple meal. After we ate, Moses called for Hur and Yehoshua. They left the camp to climb the lower mountain. I followed.

The mountain did not rumble. No thunder struck us from above. Heaven and earth remained quiet while we fashioned an altar from twelve pillar-shaped boulders. Then Moses instructed Yehoshua to choose twelve strong firstborn young men to assist with the sacrifice. He told Hur to help him find the bulls and sheep they needed. My messengers informed the people that a public gathering would take place. Moses also asked me to find women to collect wood and brush for a pyre.

The ceremony began at noon near the base of the blackened upper mountain. I had been a witness to the sacrifice of the Pascal Lamb. The sacrifice of young bull calves required far more strength. Many women turned away or covered their eyes as the blood flowed into basins. I watched Moses give instructions on how to handle the fierce animals. Yehoshua took the lead. I marveled at the strength and courage that all the young men showed.

When the sheep and bulls lay drained of blood, the men heaved them onto the pyre. Smoke rose up to Yahveh on His throne in heaven. Moses stood above the crowd on the altar. He asked for Yahveh's blessing to be upon the people of His covenant. He sprinkled half the blood from the basins on the twelve pillars. He held up the scroll that he had spent all night writing.

"This is the book of the covenant!" He opened the scroll. He began to read from it. For the second time we listened to the laws by which Yahveh expected us to live—one law for all people, rich and poor, leaders and followers, masters and slaves. Yahveh even required certain considerations for our enemies and their animals.

"Yahveh is just and merciful!" I called out after each law. Soon the people took up my response. They made it their own.

When Moses finished reading he handed the book to Aharon. He turned to the people. "Do you promise to follow in faith all that Yahveh has spoken?"

Cries of agreement swept through the crowd. I could see some made their promise in fear. Many more faces shone with joy. The people held their arms out to Moses.

My brother lifted a basin of the sacrificial blood. He dipped a branch into the thick red substance.

"This is the blood of the covenant that Yahveh makes with you!"

As Moses sprinkled the blood over the people, we raised our faces and hands to be consecrated unto Yahveh, a nation of priests.

TWENTY-NINE

Tzipporah

WHEN I sat among the women of Israel I no longer knew loneliness. I understood the comfort that my mother found among my father's people in Midyan. I did not love my sheep any less or forget the beauty of the land. At night my spirit traveled over the red and black granite mountains, swam in the clear rock pools of the wadi basins, and flew across the sands of the Hisma with the white oryx. Yet in the morning I always ran back to my sisters like a desert sojourner to a well. They took me in, with my silences and songs, my strange eyes and plain clothing. I held my little son in my arms and they held me in theirs.

But on the grey table mountain everyone faced Yahveh alone. His footsteps thundered over my trembling flesh and crushed my bones in the dust. His voice pierced through my head from one ear to the other. My eyes filled with ash and I could not see. Fear seeped into my nostrils like the sickening scent of rotting carcasses. It pooled in my mouth with the metallic taste of blood. Twenty thousand people shrieked for mercy. Moses spoke, but I could not hear his words. I found myself swept up in a great tide of people washing down the mountain. Gershom clung to one hand and I clutched the baby to my chest with the other. I knew Moses would not flee the terror. I turned my head for a moment and saw him rising into the black cloud.

Even after we reached safety at the foot of the mountain I could not stop shaking. The people waited in silence, but the cry of my heart exploded through me like Yahveh's voice. How could Moses continue to endure it? Seven months ago he had stood before Pharaoh as a tall and mighty warrior. Now—with his wrinkled brow, white beard, and stooped shoulders—he looked as old as my father. I served him like a loving daughter.

I turned my face to the cloud.

Yahveh! Can You not see that You destroy him? We were not made to walk with divinity.

Elisheva and Teye joined me on the edge of the crowd. We wiped the ash from our babies and sat down to nurse and restore calmness to our spirits. Gershom ran back to camp with his cousins.

Aharon sought us out and sat for a moment. He kissed his wife and child. My own lips ached at the sight.

"Miryam and Yehoshua stayed behind on the mountain," he said. I could not tell if he envied their courage, but I saw relief in Elisheva's eyes. She preferred a man who chose the way of safety.

"Why did Moses take us into Yahveh's presence?" I asked Aharon.

Aharon shook his head. He had no answer for me.

"He will die of it himself," I whispered.

"None of us have more time than Yahveh gives us," he replied.

Tears filled my eyes.

Aharon leaned close to my ear. "It is good you came back to him," he murmured.

I stayed up all night with Moses to help him write Yahveh's laws onto a parchment scroll. The next afternoon, after the sacrifice of the covenant, I sat in my tent with Elisheva. Miryam came with some flatbread. She appeared at least once each day with a gift of food or an offer of some service. I knew she meant these acts of kindness to mend the rift between us and I showed my appreciation with gratitude and warmth. Yet in truth an awkwardness remained between us.

Miryam handed me the bread but would not sit.

"What is the mood in the camp?" Elisheva asked.

"The people are satisfied with Yahveh's laws," Miryam replied.

"They seem merciful and just," I agreed. "The punishments are fair and fitting."

Miryam nodded with pleasure.

Yet one thing troubled me: Yahveh's jealousy, as boundless as His power. He forbade worship of all other gods. Lest we succumb to temptation, He prohibited depictions of objects in the heavens, on the earth, or in the waters. None who came out of Egypt with Moses could deny Yahveh's authority and power. But what of the sea and the rain, the wind and the womb, the crops of the field and the fruit of the trees? Did Yahveh care if my sheep multiplied or the starflowers blossomed? I did not dare question Miryam on this matter.

Instead I reminded myself that Yahveh's rules required compassion for the poor, the widow, the orphan, the violated woman, and the slave. He told us how to conduct ourselves with each other and in turn promised to bless us with good and prosperous lives. The gods of Egypt, Canaan, and Midyan seemed like capricious children next to Yahveh. Perhaps the infant nation could do no better than obey this stern and fearsome parent.

I turned my heart to Moses. He had received the law from Yahveh and written it in a book. The people had accepted Yahveh's covenant, sealed with the blood of sacrifice. Yet now Moses returned once more to Yahveh.

"Why did Moses go up again?" I asked Miryam.

"To seal the covenant in stone with Yahveh. Yehoshua stays on the table mountain to wait for him. He designated Aharon and Hur as leaders in his absence." She frowned and looked up toward the heavens. Then she rubbed her eyes and shook her head as if to be free of something I could not see. With a sudden surge of energy she moved toward the tent flap. "Come, let us wash ourselves and prepare a meal for my brother's return."

But Moses did not come back that night. We waited all the following day and the next. Miryam conferred with Aharon and Hur. Hur sent his grandson, Bezalel, to climb the mountain and speak with Yehoshua. As the young man set off laden with baskets of food from Miryam, alarm settled into my heart. Surely Yahveh knew that without my lord's leadership the nation must perish in its infancy. I feared, too, for Moses—the Divine Warrior did not seem to recognize the limitations of the flesh and blood that gave His prophet life.

I stood helpless at the edge of the valley and watched Bezalel walk toward the mountain until he disappeared from my sight.

Bezalel brought supplies to Yehoshua every few days, but each time he returned with the same report. Moses remained with Yahveh.

The first quarter of the moon came, the second, the third. The full moon rose over the mountain. A month passed without Moses. Miryam worked hard to keep our spirits high, but I could see that she worried as much as any of us. As the days passed the murmurs of impatience grew louder and more urgent. Some people spoke out against Yahveh for delaying our arrival in the Promised Land.

Wherever I walked women asked if I had word of Moses. Men turned their faces to me with questioning hope until I shook my head. By the end of the fourth week people no longer asked. They frowned when they saw me with Moses's sons. Even the most trusting of the women began to lose faith. Some of the men in Korach's family spread the story that Moses would never come back. Others whispered that Sinn had returned to claim his abode, that Moses had died in a battle between the two gods. Every time I set foot in the camp the cloud of tension thickened until it seemed that a fog of anger, doubt, and fear enveloped us.

At noon on the thirty-seventh day, Bezalel returned once more with no news of Moses. Word soon spread from tent to tent. We never knew who began the call, but by late afternoon a large crowd of angry men gathered in the square at the center of the camp to stand against Aharon.

"Will we be trapped in this wilderness forever?"

"We are tired of waiting!"

"Who will guide us to our new home?"

"Better to be a slave with meat in his mouth and a roof over his head!"

Miryam and I stood on the edge of the gathering. We watched Aharon grow weak in the face of their anger. One by one the elders joined the crowd against him.

"Where is Hur?" Miryam asked me through clenched teeth.

"It does not matter," I replied. Miryam and I exchanged a look of understanding. She knew that Hur could do no better than Aharon. In judicial matters the two wise and prudent men garnered respect. But their soft-spoken and conciliatory natures did not carry enough force. Only Miryam could stand next to Moses in authority and conviction.

All around me order dissolved into chaos. Men broke out into fights. I heard several women accuse others of seducing their lords or stealing from their meager supply of flour. My whole body shuddered with fear for what would follow. No one would be safe from his neighbor. Yahveh's laws would mean no more to the people than the yowl of a kurta cat. An angry rabble would rule.

Why had Moses not seen the obvious before he left? He should have designated Miryam to take his place.

"We do not know what happened to that man Moses!" someone shouted.

"He could be dead!"

"Who will go before us and lead us to the Promised Land?"

"Give us a god to show us the way."

Aharon raised his arm as Moses did to silence the crowd. The men continued to shout their demands. Moses would have lashed out in anger. Aharon turned his distress inward, as if he blamed himself for the rebellion.

"I understand your impatience," he called out. But his weakening voice did not command attention.

"Understanding is not what is needed!" Miryam groaned. She began to push her way through the crowd. When she reached the front she climbed onto the boulder next to Aharon. She drew herself up to her full height. She raised both arms toward heaven.

A momentary hush fell over the crowd.

"Children of Israel!" she thundered. "Yahveh is testing you with this long absence and delay. Will you fail Him whose covenant you accepted?"

But she spoke too late. A spirit of madness swept through the crowd. The men lashed out at her as never before.

"Go back to your kitchen!" a man shouted.

"Women should do women's work!"

They chanted against Miryam, beloved of the people. The women did nothing to stop them. Only Yahveh Himself could turn the people from their purpose now. And He did not come.

Aharon whispered something to Miryam. Her face flushed with anger. He touched her arm. She pulled away and jumped from the boulder. Bak tried to calm her without success. After she stormed off, Bak approached Aharon and motioned for a word. Aharon squatted down to listen. Though I stood too far away to hear their conversation, I saw that Bak spoke with animation. After a few moments Aharon turned back to the crowd.

"Give us a god we can worship!" the people cried. "Give us a god to show us the way."

Again Aharon raised his hand for silence. Someone threw a rock at him. Then another. He covered his head with his arms.

"Stop!" he cried out. "I will give you what you want!"

For the first time the crowd grew quiet. Aharon looked down at Bak who nodded and pulled on his ear.

"Take off the golden rings that are on the ears of your wives, your sons, your daughters. We will make a golden bull calf to bring our God into your presence."

The people murmured their approval and dispersed without more trouble. But even then I knew that Aharon's peace came at too high a price.

I sought Miryam in Elisheva's tent. As I walked up to the flap I heard the two women arguing.

"I can not tell him how to lead the people." Elisheva's voice sounded tight and high. "He knows what is right and not right."

Miryam stamped her foot. "He is a weak man and will give in to their demands."

Elisheva saw me. Her eyes pleaded for help, but I had no words of comfort to offer. Without Moses the people would betray their God and all Miryam's dreams would be shattered. My baby began to cry. I sat down to nurse him.

"You feed him too often," Miryam snapped.

"I feed him when he is hungry," I replied in a mild voice. I knew Miryam meant nothing by her harsh words. A woman of few tears had no choice but to lash out when her heart tore.

An unfamiliar young man appeared at the door. He held a basket.

"Aviram." Miryam greeted him with coldness. "What do you seek?"

"Aharon has sent us to collect your gold for the god he will make."

Elisheva fingered the gold bracelet I had given her. I knew she did not want to give it up.

Miryam's eyes narrowed into angry slits, sharper than my father's slaughter knives. Her face and neck grew red. "Get out!" She shouted. She pushed him toward the tent flap. "You may shame yourself in this blasphemy before Yahveh but not before me!"

The young man turned white in the onslaught of Miryam's anger. He clutched his basket and fled.

Miryam turned back to Elisheva. She took a deep breath. "If the women unite in their objections, the men will cease. We must be strong for the sake of Yahveh and the Promised Land."

Elisheva sat down next to me. She turned her soft, large eyes up to Miryam. "Is it so bad?" she murmured. "If it keeps them from rebelling until Moses returns, is it so bad?"

I looked from Elisheva to Miryam with dread. The Children of Israel had accepted Yahveh's Ten Sacred Edicts. We had bound ourselves to follow them with sacrificial blood. Though Elisheva and Aharon yearned for peace and reconciliation, Yahveh allowed no room for compromise.

A look of panic crossed Miryam's face and it seemed she could not breathe. I handed the baby to Elisheva and rose to see if I might help her. She fled from my sight. I searched for her in the kitchen tent and at the pool. I asked for her among the people. No one had seen her.

Aharon, Elisheva's sons, and Gershom returned to Aharon's tent for an evening meal we had not prepared. I went to the edge of camp and caught some desert mice to roast. We threw together what we could find in the tent—some dates, a handful of ground wheat, and two cups of sour goat's milk. No one enjoyed the repast, yet they did not dare complain. At first we ate in silence. Elisheva offered Aharon many encouraging looks, but I could see that Miryam's absence weighed upon him. Soon Aharon began to defend himself.

"Yahveh can not be angry if we sacrifice to Him."

"He can not be," Elisheva agreed. "Maybe it will bring Moses back to us sooner."

"The golden statue will be Yahveh's throne to sit upon and no more."

"It is what you must do to calm the people," Nadav said.

"Bring something to worship into their midst and they will cease to complain," Avihu added.

Aharon glanced at me for approval. I looked away. The self-deception of his arguments pained me. How could he, entrusted by Moses to keep the covenant, justify making a golden god? Everyone had seen proof enough of Yahveh's might. Did they dare risk His anger and their leader's disappointment? If Aharon continued with his plan of appeasement, Yahveh might abandon the Children of Israel to the desert forever.

For once I agreed with Miryam.

I gathered up the baby and motioned to Gershom. He asked if he could sleep in his cousins' tent, as he often did.

"Come with me tonight," I said.

The boy shook his head and refused to move. I took his hand and pulled him along.

As we approached our tent on the edge of the camp I sensed another person nearby.

"My lord?" I whispered.

In the darkness I saw Miryam's tall figure looming near the sheep pen.

"We must talk," she called out to me. Her voice flapped with agitation.

I sent Gershom inside to sleep and sat with Miryam under the starry sky. I handed her the baby. Perhaps he could calm her.

"I went up to the mountain to speak with Yehoshua," she said.

I should have guessed.

"He knows nothing more. He will not leave the mountain. He is sure Moses will return. We prayed to Yahveh. I wanted to go up and look for Moses."

I took in a sharp breath. Miryam replied with a short, bitter laugh.

"It is true that Yahveh promised death for anyone who touches the mountain. Do you believe this threat?"

"I have seen enough of Yahveh's might to believe," I said.

"Aharon, a leader among the Israelites, does not believe."

"Aharon is afraid. He wants peace. But he should not give in to the people's demands."

Miryam leaned closer to me. "You were right about the gold. We took it for no good purpose."

"But you acted under Yahveh's instruction. I am sure He intended it for another use."

Miryam buried her face in the hollow of her right hand. "My people need your help." Each muffled word oozed with pain.

My eyes filled with tears. "If they will not listen to you..."

"They might listen to you!" she insisted. "You are the wife of Moses. The mother of his children. Speak to the women. They can stop the men."

The night grew cold and I felt a shiver pass over my flesh. I longed for my lord's arms, for the days before Yahveh. Miryam's desperation saddened me, but I could not help her.

"I have worshipped the Goddess Asherah most of my life. I served in

Her temple. What can I say that will convince them?"

Miryam grabbed my arm. "You will know what to say. The words will come to you. Yahveh only gives us opportunities. We must use them to make things happen. My very bones cry out that this is your moment."

A vision flashed before my eyes—Moses in the jaws of the two-headed puff adder on the night of the circumcision. My moment had passed. I had returned to be near my beloved. My faith was in him alone.

The baby began to wail. "We can do nothing tonight," I said. "Let us sleep and in the morning we can decide."

I took the baby and went into the tent. When I saw that Miryam did not make any motion to leave I invited her to sleep with us. She lay down on her brother's mat. I covered her with a warm goatskin.

I nursed the baby again and drifted into sleep. But I did not rest. I ran across the valley to the Mountain of God. I climbed the eastern side away from the washing pool. I tried to tell myself to stop, but the words died in my throat like a lamb trapped in its mother's womb.

The terrain seemed much rougher on this side of the mountain. Hard black rock cut at my hands. I slipped down the steep slope several times. Every pore on my flesh oozed sweat from the heat and the effort. I paused to look up. The sun sat high overhead and yet I still did not see the top of the table mountain. A bush above me burst into flames. A river of molten fire snaked its way toward me. I realized that I had climbed too far. My feet rested against Yahveh's sacred mountain.

I felt my face and my arms to see if I yet lived. I tried to move away from the molten river, but it seemed to follow me. I began to weep for fear of being taken from my sons.

"Let me live to see them grow to manhood," I begged Yahveh. "Let me live to have a daughter as sweet as Elisheva's. Let me live to see Moses bring his people into the Promised Land!"

The sun fell out of the sky and flooded down the mountain into my eyes.

"Yahveh!" I cried out. "Return Moses to us. Only he can save the people from Your wrath."

I shielded my eyes with my hand. As the light ascended back up the hill it left a mosaic of gold and lapis lazuli in its wake, a shining path to the heavens. I heard the blast of a ram's horn and felt the mountain tremble beneath my feet. As I turned away to retrace my steps, everything went still. I heard a small voice, the voice of an echo.

Those who sin against Me will perish.

The sound of wailing children filled my ear. I tried to run, but my legs refused to move.

I pulled away from the dream vision and woke with a tremor of terror upon my flesh. I opened my eyes in the dark tent and for a moment I feared the bright light had blinded me. I soon made out the form of my crying baby. I pulled him close to me and felt the tiny face so much like his father's. My spirit had sought Moses while I slept, but instead I had found Yahveh. He had allowed me to live, to see my children again.

I would do what Miryam had asked of me.

When the baby finished nursing I peeked around the curtain. Both Miryam and Gershom still slept. With Eliezer in my arms I crept outside the tent. A faint purple light swept across the eastern horizon. The morning dew cooled my feet. Small bursts of flame dotted the mountain. The cloud hung low over the peak. Something had changed.

Those who sin against Me will perish.

The haunting voice mingled with a sound of hammering somewhere in camp. I glanced at the lambs that needed watering.

"I will be back soon," I whispered to them.

The tents remained quiet in the hour before dawn. A thin column of smoke rose in the pale sky to the west. I followed it and the hammering to the other edge of the camp.

Even before I saw Bak's face I noticed his muscular arms. He stood behind a flat-topped boulder and wore only a loincloth. He clutched a black granite rock that he used to beat a layer of soft gold into a thin sheet. On the ground in front of the boulder sat a lamb-sized acacia wood sculpture of a bull calf with rounded crescent horns.

"Miryam," I whispered to myself. With each blow of the stone Bak smashed her heart.

I glanced at the fire in a nearby pit. He must have used it for light and to melt the gold. It still burned hot enough to consume the statue.

Bak looked up from his work and grinned at me. "Flesh of the gods," he declared as he held up the sheet of gold. "That is what the Egyptians believed."

"What do you believe, Bak?"

My question startled him.

"I am an artist. I make anything possible and believe nothing."

"Then you are no more than a demon," I replied.

He came around to the front of the rock and began to fit the gold sheet onto the wooden bull calf. I remained fixed in my place and stared at him.

"Is it better for the people to rebel against Aharon and fight among themselves?" he asked. "This will calm them."

"Until Yahveh unleashes His anger."

"Amusing talk from one who ran away to the Goddess."

"Burn it, Bak," I begged. "Burn it before you destroy Miryam's heart."

His dark eyes flashed at me with anger and a mocking smile spread over his face. "She has a heart?" he asked with false innocence. "I did not know."

I ran to find Aharon. On the way I noticed that people already gathered in the square near the altar. They were dressed in fine Egyptian robes and all their remaining gold. Several men led lambs to be sacrificed.

When I reached Aharon's tent I threw myself at his feet. Elisheva and their sons crowded around me. I saw the river of molten fire surround us. I felt the mountain tremble in my bones.

Those who sin against Me will perish!

"You must not continue with it!" I cried. "It will be the death of many! Moses will return soon."

Elisheva came to take the crying baby from my arms. "Come rest with me inside the tent." She spoke to me in a soothing voice, but I would not be soothed.

"Aharon!" I called out as he walked away. He did not turn back.

I sent Teye to water my sheep and left the baby with Elisheva. Then I ran from tent to tent. I told the women to stop their lords and sons from worshipping the false god. "I am the wife of Moses!" I said. "Remember our covenant! Remember Yahveh's might!"

Some feared Yahveh but felt they had no influence with their men. I told them to gather at the foot of the mountain at midday. We would pray for Yahveh to return our leader to us.

My voice grew hoarse from pleading, but I paused only once the entire morning, when I saw Miryam near the cooking tent. She, too, spoke with a group of women. By the anguish in her face I knew that she had learned of Bak's handiwork.

"I have told the believers to meet us at the mountain," I called out to her. "To pray that Yahveh bring Moses back to us soon."

She nodded with gratitude and I moved on.

The sacrifice happened long before I finished making my way through camp. As I visited the last tents and spoke with those who hung back from the golden bull calf I could smell the burnt offering. I heard the noise of wild song rise over the camp. When I could find no one else in the tents, I turned back toward the valley to meet the faithful and find Elisheva and my baby.

On my way through camp I passed clusters of revelers. Some drank wine that they must have carried out of Egypt. As I drew closer to the square, the wild activity intensified. People danced in frantic circles. They pushed and shoved each other. I saw men grab at the breasts of women they did not seem to know. Couples lay on the ground together, mating like animals, while others stumbled over them. Hovering over the crowd, on the stone from which Moses had once spoken of the covenant, Aharon sat with his face in his hands.

I fled to the valley where Miryam led a group of two hundred men and women in prayer. I searched through the kneeling crowd for Elisheva. When I did not see her I grew frantic.

I ran back toward her tent. On the way I came upon her eldest son, Nadav, sitting with a pretty girl of perhaps thirteen. I took in the scene before me—Nadav's dusty kuttoneh and his flushed face, the girl's disheveled hair, her torn garment, her tearstained face. He had violated a virgin. A great fury rose in me.

"May you go to your grave with the shame of this day in your eye!" I cursed him.

I offered the girl my arms, but she refused me. She jumped to her feet and ran from us.

"Find her father and pay for her hand!" I hissed. "If the man does not strangle you first."

Nadav hung his head and whimpered. "A demon came into me."

I offered no comfort. We each have our demons. Those who do not struggle to resist allow them to prevail.

As I approached Aharon's tent, the sound of a crying infant—Elyah I guessed—reassured me that Elisheva yet remained inside. She looked relieved to see me. I picked up my hungry infant and tried to persuade my friend to come to the mountain. I did not trust her safety in the camp.

"Miryam is there," I said, "and many of our friends. Some of the men have come too."

Tears filled her eyes. She could not speak.

"Yahveh came to me in a vision," I told her. "He wanted me to help keep the people from harm. I fear that if you remain here…"

"No!" she shouted, whether to me or herself I could not tell. "I can not make this choice to go against Aharon."

"The choice is for Yahveh, not against Aharon," I argued.

She shook her head and looked away.

THIRTY

Miryam

IVE hundred of the faithful gathered at the base of the mountain. I stood on the outer edge of the group with my eye turned toward camp. For a moment I sent my prayers toward those who remained behind—all those who had lost faith or never known it—in hope that at least a few more would come to join us. But I could not endure the sound of wild celebration that reached across the valley. Anger throbbed through every sinew of my body. Tzipporah had told me something of the madness in camp. She had seen Aharon sitting alone, in anguish. What had he expected? Yahveh's first Sacred Edict forbade graven images. Appeasement of evil brings evil.

Despair tore at my heart. How could so many have betrayed our God? Why of all our family did Tzipporah alone stand with me? How could I have been so wrong about Bak?

I remembered the sight of Bak that morning as he had directed the ten men who carried the golden bull calf to the center of camp. His face had beamed with exhilaration. As the procession passed he had caught my eye. His careless smile had wounded me more than all the words of the men who had spoken against me. I felt a cry rise up from deep within my flesh. I had trusted him. I had hungered for him. I had clung to the glimmer of hope he had offered me, as if in reward for all I had sacrificed in my youth.

He had deceived me. Even worse, I had deceived myself.

Now I wanted to rend my clothes and smear ashes on my face like a woman in mourning.

We prayed and waited. I walked among the women to praise them for their righteousness. When the sun descended halfway between its zenith and the horizon I heard a murmur of excitement pass through the crowd. I pushed my way closer to the base of the mountain. I saw two figures making their way down the rocky slope.

"Yahveh be praised for the return of His prophet!" I cried out.

"Yahveh be praised!" the people replied. Women wept with joy and relief. Men clapped each other on the back. A few broke out in celebratory dances.

As Moses drew closer I saw two stone tablets cradled in his arms. Yehoshua stood by his side. The two men stopped above us where they could survey the group. I gazed at Moses with surprise. My beloved brother, not yet thirty, looked like an old man. Day by day I had not noticed the changes in his once smooth brow and warrior's stance. Now, after more than a month of separation, I could not help but see his wrinkled face, his hunched shoulders, his pale skin, his white hair.

Everyone grew silent. The sounds from the camp grew louder.

"Does someone make war on us?" Yehoshua asked.

"No," Moses replied. "It is not the sound of fighting that I hear. It is the sound of lawless chaos."

Everyone turned toward me. I stepped forward to reveal the sin against Yahveh that our own brother perpetrated and all that had followed from his permission to build the golden calf. My face flushed. I opened my mouth. But the words did not come. Instead I saw myself as if Moses looked at me, as if Yahveh Himself looked at me. Why had I been unable to prevent it? True, Moses had not designated me as leader. But I was Miryam, mother of the people. I should have found a way to stop them. I should have been able to prevent Bak, who claimed to love me, from making the idol. I had failed my brother. I had failed Yahveh.

Caleb son of Yephunneh came up to my side. He lowered his head in shame. He knew that all of us bore some responsibility for the transgressions of those who remained in camp.

"When you did not come down from the mountain the people rebelled against Aharon. Now they sacrifice—before a golden bull calf."

Moses looked to me to prove this report false. I shook my head.

Moses stood before us with the gleaming tablets. The inscriptions shone like polished lapis lazuli set in shining gold. My brother's return would end the madness that had seized the people. All would soon be set right in camp.

At last I spoke. "We gathered the faithful here to pray for your return."

"You have done well, Sister. Those who have worshipped at the altar of an idol will be punished."

I stepped aside for Moses to pass. "Tzipporah has stood by me," I called out after him. "She helped gather the faithful."

He turned. For a moment his eye brightened.

We followed Moses back to camp. I knew that not everyone who had remained behind was a traitor. Some wanted to protect their property. Some could not move because of illness. Some stayed from loyalty to a parent or spouse. No doubt others wanted to see the rites out of curiosity. How would Moses separate the guilty from the innocent? What would he say to our brother?

Moses halted at the low ridge between the valley and the flat plateau of the camp. We saw the golden bull calf perched high on the altar in the square. Hundreds of people without clothing flung themselves in a frenzied dance around the idol. Some lay together in lust before our eyes. I saw married men with girls who had been virgins that morning and women with boys young enough to be their sons.

My brother's body shook. His eyes flashed. His mouth twisted with the rage he could not contain. He lifted the stone tablets high over his head.

"No!" I begged him. "Do not destroy Yahveh's work! Let me keep it safe for you!"

I held out my hands to take the precious tablets too late.

He hurled them to the ground. Yahveh's work, the gift of our future, smashed into a thousand bits. I fell to my knees. I tried to gather up the pieces. They turned to dust in my fingers. I saw the futility of my labor, but I could not stop.

Tzipporah's foot appeared on the ground before me. I looked up at her face twisted with frustration and sorrow.

"Your brother expects too much," she said. "If people must be godly to receive Yahveh's gift, where is the need for it?"

I shook my head. I could not answer for my brother's action.

She gestured for me to rise. "Come, Miryam. Moses needs you by his side."

The revelers seemed oblivious to our presence and the return of their leader. When we reached the square Aharon remained as Tzipporah had seen him before—sitting on a rock with his head in his hands.

Moses looked at his brother with disgust. "What did this people do to you that you have brought such evil upon them?"

Aharon lifted his eyes. His face held an expression of pain and remorse. I waited for his apology. At last he opened his trembling lips.

"Do not, my lord, be angry. You know how the people are inclined toward evil. When you did not come back they demanded I do something to bring our God to us, to lead the way in your absence. So I said to them, 'Whoever has gold, take it off.'"

Aharon paused to catch his breath. He bit his lip for a moment. His eyes opened wide.

"They gave it to me," he continued. "I flung it into the fire, and out came this calf."

My face grew hot with rage. Only Tzipporah's grip on my arm kept me from lashing out.

"He is a weak man," she whispered. "He cares more for the people's love and your brother's approval than for Yahveh."

Her words changed my anger into sorrow.

"I had hoped for better from him," I whispered.

"He is also disappointed in himself. Shame lodges in his heart."

Moses ordered Yehoshua and some helpers to build a fire near the pool at the base of the mountain. He insisted that Bak and Aharon alone carry the golden bull calf to the fire. Many of the revelers mistook the procession for part of their festivities. They followed the calf with song and dance. Those who had sense enough to fear Yahveh remained behind.

They set the calf into the fire. The blaze roared with Yahveh's anger. No one dared approach the flames. When the fire burned out, Moses beat the charcoal and lumps of gold into dust. He scattered this dust over the water. He ordered every man to drink of the water and the women to bring water to those still in camp.

The people drank. I assigned women to fill buckets. Yehoshua and some of his men accompanied the women back to camp, where they forced every man to drink. Tzipporah remained at the pool with me.

When Yehoshua returned, Moses gathered all the men who had spoken against the calf. I counted two hundred. I saw twenty or more who did not belong. No doubt they feared exposure and punishment. I walked toward Moses to object. Before I reached him, people began to groan and cry out. They scratched at their flesh. I saw great thickened lumps emerge on their arms, legs, and backs. I checked myself to confirm that I remained free from the affliction. I looked at Yehoshua to make sure that he remained untouched. In a moment I realized that the water brought this pestilence only to the guilty. It did not mar the flesh of the innocent.

People ran from the affliction as if they could escape it. Moses spoke to the men who had sided with Yahveh. I scanned the group of brave Israelites, ready to do Yahveh's will. The sight of them began to heal my heart.

"Let every man among you put a sword on his thigh and go throughout the camp to search out those with Yahveh's mark. Let each man kill his brother. Let each man kill his neighbor. Let each man kill his kin until we are purged of all those who do not fear Yahveh!"

Tzipporah and I exchanged looks of surprise.

"Is the pestilence not punishment enough?" she whispered.

"As an example," I replied with more certainty than I felt. "Those who live among Yahveh's people must honor their promise to follow His laws."

Tzipporah shook her head. Tears filled her eyes. "But why must neighbor kill neighbor? How can Moses condone such cruelty?"

I could not answer.

Yehoshua raised his sword to lead the charge back toward our camp. Only Moses remained behind with us.

"You do not join the slaughter?" Tzipporah whispered.

He did not answer. Had he heard her question? He held his arms out for their infant son. She handed him the baby with reluctance. The child brought the light of happiness to his face.

"Why must our men kill the transgressors?" I asked. "Will Yahveh not bring the full punishment upon them Himself?"

Moses struggled more than usual to utter the words of his reply. "When Yahveh saw what the people did, He wanted to kill everyone. He wanted to start anew. I argued that He could not bring us out of Egypt only to murder us. I promised that His people would prove themselves worthy of Him."

Tzipporah lifted a hand to her eyes, but she could not stop the tears. She took the baby from Moses and turned away without a word, without a gesture to either of us. I watched her trudge toward the far end of the valley where Teye sat with the sheep.

When I returned to camp I saw before me all that Tzipporah had anticipated. Carnage replaced revelry. Bloodied bodies lay everywhere— in front of tents, in the square, at the edges of the wells. Wives wept over their lords, mothers over their sons. I wandered past them as if through a heavy fog. I could not comprehend the sight of so much death.

The fiercest battle raged at the far end of camp, away from the mountain. Here warriors pursued the afflicted men into the wilderness. Their weakened limbs could not carry them far. One man fell near my feet, and then another. Sour bile rose from my stomach. It burned my throat. I turned away from the dead to vomit.

I recognized Yehoshua in the chaos. He pierced a man's neck. Blood spurted out and stained his face. The warrior did not pause to wipe himself but swung and caught a pestilence-ridden man in the chest. I flinched. Another warrior stabbed a man who dropped to his knees to beg for mercy. My legs shook.

I knelt over the corpse of a man whose wife I knew well. Years ago I had found a match for their daughter, a good woman who now attended the sick in camp. She did not deserve the grief of this loss. I did not wish this suffering upon a single woman.

I embraced the man's rotting flesh. Blood from his wounds spilled onto my kuttoneh.

"O Yahveh, have mercy on us! Give us time to learn Your ways!"

I felt myself giving into despair and doubt. I grew afraid. What would become of me if I questioned Yahveh's wisdom? What would become of our people if I—who had dedicated my life to serving them for Yahveh's sake— did not remain strong for them?

I recalled my brother's words. Yahveh required us to prove ourselves worthy. His punishment was not without purpose. Each of us had the desire to turn toward evil. So must each of us cling to Yahveh's way that we might overcome that desire. Yahveh's laws could hold no sway over a people who did not hesitate to break them. He did not lead us out of Egypt to abandon us. If we did not honor the covenant we had made with Him, our slavery would continue—we would remain slaves to our worst inclinations.

I laid the man back down upon the ground. I looked up. Several unblemished men picked their way among the corpses. They snatched gold chains from the lifeless necks and rings from their hands. One youth began to untie the sandals from the feet of a fallen man.

I rose to my feet in a rage. "Thieves!" I shouted. "Do you dare risk Yahveh's anger to steal from the dead?"

When the men recognized me they dropped the stolen goods. They turned and run.

I walked with a heavy heart to Elisheva's tent. Aharon and all their sons huddled in the far corner. None had signs of the pestilence upon them.

Elisheva and I embraced as if after a long absence. I tried to ignore Aharon. But I could not help noticing how his eyes wandered down to his arms, as if he feared the lumps might appear at any moment. At last I spoke to him.

"You wronged Yahveh out of weakness alone."

"It is true, Sister," he whispered.

I turned my hardened eyes upon him. I made no effort to soften the harshness of my words. "Yahveh will not punish you with death like the others. He will punish you with life."

The camp grew quiet. I peeked out of the tent flap. I saw the warriors searching tent to tent for any of the guilty who hid. I heard an old woman beg for her son's life. Her screams turned to moans and weeping. I did not have to witness her son's death to know what had happened. I slunk back into Aharon's tent.

When the sun hung low over the western mountains, the warriors began to bury the dead in the sandy wilderness north of our camp. Over three hundred men had died that day.

As night fell, Moses lit a fire in the square. He blessed the warriors for their dedication to Yahveh. He called the people to him. No one refused to heed him.

"All are guilty for this thing that came into our camp. I will return to Yahveh. Perhaps I may win forgiveness for you."

The people fell to their knees. They called out to the heavens. "May Yahveh have mercy on us!"

Moses sojourned on the mountain another forty days and forty nights. During this time a pall of silence settled over the people. Women mourned their dead. I reminded myself that the loss of a lord or a brother brought tenfold more grief to them than what I felt in Bak's betrayal. I visited each woman who had lost a loved one. I encouraged the wives, sisters, and mothers of the traitors to shed their tears. So, too, I reminded them, should they teach even their youngest sons the fear of Yahveh.

Those women able in body and spirit gathered firewood each day. They cooked meals. They visited their friends. Some spun wool. Others wove it on handlooms. The men hunted for quail and other small animals. They patrolled the edges of the camp lest another clan try to raid us. They kept their swords well sharpened.

Aharon and Hur sat in judgment according to Yahveh's rules. Elisheva's circle of friends gathered around her each day. Tzipporah hid her anger at Moses in the birth tents. I did not ask what she did for the women in labor. I trusted Tzipporah now. I had my own sorrows to lose in work.

The pestilence did not afflict Bak. I supposed that Yahveh considered him no more guilty than Aharon—he had created the idol but not worshipped it. But he was dead to me. We never spoke again. He did not try to apologize, to reconcile. He knew Moses would never give permission for our union. I did not want him. This did not erase my regrets. For days I looked at expectant mothers with envy. I soothed my heart with prayers to Yahveh. I thanked Him for revealing Bak's true nature before our alliance came to be sealed.

I began to see Bak and Teye together. I tried to warn my friend about his untrustworthy character. Her response wounded my heart; she said that if I did not want him I should not try to keep him from another. After that we avoided each other.

The second time that Moses came down from the mountain all the people rejoiced. Word spread throughout the camp that he held a new set of tablets in his hands.

We ran to meet him and Yehoshua. Aharon led the way. But he stopped short before he reached our brother. A light as bright as the sun radiated from Moses's face. No one dared approach him.

While the others hung back I moved to the front of the crowd. I did not fear the light of Yahveh as the others did. Still, I shielded my eyes with my hands.

"It is your face," I explained. "They are afraid of your brilliance."

My brother's lined brow frowned with confusion.

"Look into my eyes," I suggested. "Can you see the reflection of Yahveh's light?"

I willed my eyes to stay open while Moses gazed into them. I could not stop the tears of pain from flowing. The light blinded me, but I did not care. I longed for it to come into my spirit and possess me. I longed to share my brother's glow.

"Enough," he said after a moment.

I looked away. The world seemed hidden in dark shadows behind the flashing bright spots that remained in my eye.

"Give me your veil," Moses said.

I removed my head covering. He draped it over his head so that the cloth hid his face. He asked Yehoshua to cut a slit for each eye so that he might see.

From that time forward Moses always wore the veil except when he relayed the word of Yahveh to the people. No matter how often he spoke in Yahveh's name without the veil, each time the people cowered in awe.

Did Moses remove the veil in Tzipporah's presence when they lay together in their tent? The question tormented me for days. At last I learned the truth from Elisheva. One day, when Elisheva sat admiring Elyah's beauty, I asked her if Tzipporah longed for a daughter. The question did not surprise her.

"She does. We used to talk about it."

"No more?" I pried.

Elisheva shook her head. "I do not wish to remind her of her unhappiness."

"Unhappiness?"

"Their separation," she replied as if to remind me of something I already knew.

In a moment I understood. How long had he kept himself from her for Yahveh's sake?

I rejoiced in my brother's purity—it vindicated my own. Then I realized the unfairness of my reward. Yahveh had come to me only once, when I was a young girl. Year after year I had longed for Him to return to me. Instead He had sent Bak as a test and I had failed to recognize temptation. Moses had never endured such testing. He had had two sons before he spurned the desires of the flesh. He even complained that he had never wanted to be Yahveh's prophet!

I tried to smile at Elisheva, to ease the disquiet of my spirit. *You have work to do*, I reminded myself. *Yahveh will not favor one who covets her brother's grace.*

"I will go visit the sick now," I said to Elisheva.

When Moses came down from the mountain a second time we had dwelt in that place four months. Many felt eager to move on to the Promised Land. Before we could leave the mountain, Moses told us, we must build Yahveh a sanctuary—a Tabernacle—to keep Him in our presence as we journeyed north through the wilderness. Aharon and his two eldest sons would serve as priests. This responsibility fell to them and their descendants for all time.

The announcement of the priesthood brought a fresh bloom to Elisheva's cheeks. She never blamed her lord for all that followed from the golden bull calf. But the condemnation of others—silent and spoken— had weighed upon her. Now she beamed with pride. Her friends shared this joy. Except Tzipporah.

She turned from the group of women clustered around Elisheva. Did she object that her own sons could not look forward to a similar honor? I followed her away from the gathering.

"Tzipporah!" I called out.

She stopped but did not look back toward me.

"What troubles you?" I asked when I reached her.

"They did not shun the golden calf." Darkness gathered on her brow. She spoke with her eyes fixed on the distance, as if she did not recall the past so much as look into the future. "Neither of Aharon's elder sons joined us at the mountain."

"No," I agreed in a low voice. "They remained in camp."

"I saw Nadav," she whispered.

I shuddered. I did not want to know more.

"Let us pray that they will do credit to their office," Tzipporah said.

"Let us pray," I agreed.

Later I wondered how Tzipporah could have been so distant from us in spirit and yet so close in premonition.

These are the things Yahveh required to build the Tabernacle: silver, gold, and copper; blue, purple, and crimson yarns; fine linen and goat's hair; skins of rams; lapis lazuli; oil for lighting and spices for anointing; acacia wood. The people saw that Yahveh's plan for the Tabernacle far exceeded the splendor of the false god that Bak had made. They contributed with such generosity that Moses soon had more material than he needed. At last all the items we had taken from the Egyptians were put to good use.

Moses assigned two craftsmen to supervise the work. Bezalel son of Uri son of Hur held responsibility for the wood and metalwork. Oholiab son of Ahisamach took care of the textile work. Many others helped. Bezalel took a group of men with him to Dophka to smelt the metal. Caleb and another group journeyed to the south for oil, incense, and spices. Oholiab sent his helpers on several expeditions to find enough dried acacia wood. Tzipporah, who knew the wilderness better than anyone, went with them. Elisheva assisted in spinning fine yarn. As part of their preparation for the priesthood, Moses met with Aharon, Nadav, and Avihu each night. Of all the family, only I had no role to play.

When I mentioned this to Elisheva and Tzipporah, they groaned.

"You already do more than three people together!" Tzipporah said.

I shook my head. "It is little enough."

Elisheva threw up her arms. "You feed the workers, you care for the ailing, you look after the orphans and all of us, you spread Yahveh's message of righteousness throughout the camp."

"Let us take her away from these labors to romp with the lambs," Tzipporah teased.

I tried to frown at her foolish suggestion. Instead I found myself laughing at the ridiculous image of me cavorting with the lambs. The other two joined me.

"I am who I will always be," I admitted.

"So are we all," Elisheva said. She reached out to hug us both, one on each side.

The Tabernacle and its furnishings, including the priestly vestments, took eight months to assemble. We watched the beautiful things take form before our eyes. As the months wore on the excitement gathered. Each day I surveyed the work of the craftsmen in camp and the metalwork delivered from Dophka. When an item reached completion—from the smallest copper spoon to the golden Ark to the large altar and its ramp—I stood before it with admiration.

When the Tabernacle stood completed, Moses came to tell me in the kitchen tent. I embraced him.

"Now, Sister, Yahveh has a task for you."

At last! I too had a contribution to make.

"For the dedication we need unleavened bread, unleavened cake made with oil, and unleavened wafer spread with oil. You must use pure wheat flour."

I nodded my head with solemnity. Inside, my spirit soared. I recalled Tzipporah teasing me about romping with the lambs. Would she believe the music and dancing in my heart now?

I knew what to do. First I purified myself at the pool with water from the mountain spring. I washed my clothes. I heated water to pour over the baking stones that they too might be purified. I knelt to offer prayers of praise and thanks to Yahveh. I kept all other food away from my preparation area. I found the best flour in the camp. I baked the bread, cake, and wafer with all the love I felt for Yahveh and His people.

On the first day of the first month of the second year, Moses summoned the entire camp to the dedication. Most gathered outside the Tabernacle walls. Moses invited two hundred people to stand inside between the entrance and the Altar of Burnt Offerings. The group that squeezed inside included the elders and their families, the craftsmen and their families, Yehoshua, Hur, Tzipporah, Elisheva, and me.

First Moses consecrated the priests. Aharon, Avihu, and Nadav came forward wearing linen breeches. Moses washed them with water from the copper washbasin. Then he dressed Aharon in the magnificent vestments of the high priest. The garments transformed him. I no longer saw the weak man who had given in to the people against his own better judgment. In his place stood a priest who would serve the people and Yahveh with dignity.

Moses proceeded to anoint all the objects in the Tabernacle with oil reserved for that purpose. He anointed the Altar of Burnt Offerings and its utensils seven times to consecrate it to Yahveh. After that he poured oil on Aharon's head. He dressed Nadav and Avihu in their tunics, tied the sashes, and wound their turbans. I turned to Elisheva. Tears of joy pooled in her eyes. I reflected on the strangeness of Nadav's recent alliance with the young daughter of a very poor bricklayer. Elisheva was not happy about the girl, or that her son had made his choice without consulting any of us. Aharon had refused to challenge an adult son who had already entered into a promise with the father of the girl. Now Elisheva seemed to have forgotten her disappointment. She stood tall with pride for her sons and their father.

After the offerings of a bull, a ram, and the bread I had baked, Moses concluded the ceremony of ordination for the priests. He took some of the blood from the altar and mixed it with the anointing oil. He sprinkled the mixture on Aharon and his sons and on all the priestly vestments.

"Thus are you consecrated to Yahveh," he announced. "You will boil the Ram of Ordination in water at the entrance of the Tent of Meeting. You will eat it with the bread in the basket. The flesh that you do not consume you must burn. This you must repeat each day for seven days. You must stay in the Tabernacle."

Every day for seven days we returned to witness the Elevation Offering. On the eighth day Moses called for the people to contribute a he-goat for a Sin Offering, a calf and a lamb for a Burnt Offering, an ox and a ram for an Offering of Well-being, and fine flour meal with oil mixed in. When the people brought these things forward, Moses told Aharon to make the sacrifices as an expiation for himself and the community.

We stood for many hours while the priests carried out the sacrifices. A sense of Yahveh's presence nearby prevented us from feeling any discomfort. Even I, who found nothing more unpleasant than idle hands, remained transfixed. The Tabernacle and the priests brought us close to Yahveh. They signified our purpose as a nation.

Aharon and his sons completed their offerings. Aharon raised his hands to bless the people. He stepped down from the altar. Moses and Aharon parted the Veil that curtained the entrance to the Tent of Meeting. We waited in silence while the two men prayed inside the Holy of Holies, where the golden Ark of the Covenant sat.

When they came out, both Aharon and Moses blessed the people. I looked around the courtyard at all the faces. We stood together, a people sanctified unto Yahveh. My heart swelled with love for all of Yahveh's chosen. I told myself that I must forgive all those who had ever harmed me, even Bak. I felt almost purified by Aharon's sacrifices. Now I must do my part to complete the task. I must seek forgiveness from those I might have harmed.

At the conclusion of Aharon's blessing, many people turned to leave the courtyard. I moved to join them. A moment later a great roaring filled our ears. I felt the scorching heat of fire. Flames shot down from the heavens to the Altar of Burnt Offerings. The fire consumed all of the last sacrifice that remained on the altar. Everyone fell to their faces in His presence. Except me. I stretched my arms out to Him. My feet carried me toward the altar. I could not stop myself. All my life I had waited for Yahveh to come back to me. Now I would go to Him.

I might have been blinded or burned. I might have thrown myself upon the altar if Moses had not seen me. He ran forward in my direction across the courtyard. He put his arm around my shoulder. He eased me down to the ground, where I hid my face to pay homage like all the others.

THIRTY-ONE

Tzipporah

YAHVEH'S column of fire pierced through the heavens and shot into our midst. I knelt with all the others in the Tabernacle enclosure. I hid my face from His fearsome presence. *How can anyone love a God who rules by terror?* I asked myself as I touched my forehead to the ground.

After the golden calf I lived in dread of the next transgression. I saw that others felt the same fear of Yahveh's watchful eye and merciless hand. People grew more hesitant in their steps and more cautious in their words. Many lined up to seek advice from Moses and Miryam on matters of Yahveh's law for fear that the slightest infraction would bring Yahveh's wrath upon them. Sometimes I escaped into the wilderness alone. I bathed my feet in the yellow sand and rested my eyes on the red cliffs and fixed my ears on the song of the blue roller. But even away from the mountain the world seemed scorched and silenced by Yahveh's rule.

On the night following the dedication of the Tabernacle, Moses lay exhausted and depleted on his mat. He removed his veil and I began to rub salve into his face. Only I knew what agony he suffered from Yahveh's light.

The first time he had removed the veil before me I had drawn away in horror. The bright light pierced my eyes. Through my tears I saw that his flesh blistered and oozed like a terrible burn. He grimaced in pain.

"What has He done to you?" I wept.

Moses answered me with resignation. "None who draw near to Yahveh can remain unscathed."

"But you are His prophet."

"I am only a man," he insisted.

In the days that followed I soothed his burns with a salve Elisheva had given me for the baby's skin. Each night I shielded my eyes with one hand and used the other to rub the ointment into his tender face. Because he permitted no other touching between us, I concentrated all my love for him into my hands as they tended him.

Each night, after I finished, he donned his veil and we talked. Our brief conversations did not touch upon the weighty matters of God and leadership. We spoke of the children, family, people in camp, the days ahead. But on the night after Yahveh's fiery display in the Tabernacle I did not speak at all. Moses read my heart through my trembling fingers. His reply came with the usual difficulty.

"It is better for us to live by Yahveh's laws than the tyranny of men. Unlike men, Yahveh values life more than property."

"His punishments are too harsh," I whispered.

"Would His children listen otherwise?"

I could not bring myself to give the answer Moses sought, though I knew it to be true.

Moses sighed. "The people have not learned to act with the responsibility that freedom demands. In their hearts they are still slaves. For the time being only fear of His anger will teach them the wisdom of His laws. I pray it will not always be so."

It is a vain prayer, I said to myself.

"The yoke of leadership is heavy," he added.

I felt tears pool in my eyes. Once, I might have taken his head into my lap to ease his burdens, if only for a moment. Now I had only words to show my concern. "I fear that Yahveh asks too much of you. He has already weakened you beyond repair. How much more of yourself can you give?"

Moses bowed his head. He spoke in a low voice. "I would be far weaker if I refused my calling."

A flood of pictures filled my memory—Moses at the well, our bodies intertwined in the ocean, his joyful face when he first looked upon his son. He had been my calling. Through him I had drawn my first breaths of strength.

"That is a truth I can not challenge." I spoke with a heart full of love for the man who hid behind a veil, who I could not touch. I looked upon him with longing—to see his beautiful face whole again, to gaze into his eyes, to feel his hands on my flesh.

Moses lay back on the mat. He turned on his side to sleep.

I did not want our conversation to end. I had not felt so close to him since our days in Egypt. Yet I could not keep him from what little rest he took. I turned to creep away on silent feet.

"You are a good woman," he murmured as I left. "You are a blessing to me."

The next afternoon Elisheva and I sat with a group of four other women. We took turns with the spindle as Elisheva taught us how to make fine yarn from wool. One of the women, Caleb's wife Aviela, expected her first child at any time. I had promised to ease her pains with my chanting.

Some months earlier a friend of Teye's had come to ask me to chant during her labor. Because I no longer knelt to the Goddess, I believed no harm could come of using the chants. The woman had given herself over to my voice and delivered with ease.

Word of my skill spread. I attended four or five other births. I did not refuse anyone who called for me. Why should I not bring ease to a woman when I had the ability to do so? But without the Goddess to thank or blame I began to dread the first time, sure to come, when my chanting would not be able to prevent a rough labor or even death.

I looked at Aviela, who held the wooden spindle over her swollen belly. Her innocent trust worried me. If the gods decreed that a woman's time to die had come, could I appeal to Yahveh? I knew no god more powerful. But did Yahveh take an interest in such matters? He seemed more occupied with the concerns of men.

We took turns with the spindle while Elisheva corrected us. Before it came into my hands Miryam burst through the tent flap, her body quivering with excitement.

"In ten days we are to break camp. We are going to the Promised Land!"

Miryam's smile blossomed like a pink lotus flower. I gazed up at her and saw something new in the familiar face. The high cheekbones, wide forehead, almond-shaped eyes, long nose—she resembled Moses. Why had I never noticed it? In a moment I knew the answer. Their differences had blinded me. Where Moses saw necessity, Miryam embraced Yahveh's rule like a lover. Her confidence in the people and in herself set her apart from everyone, even her beloved brother.

"The Promised Land at last!" Elisheva clapped her hands.

As excitement spread through the tent, Aviela felt the first mild twinges of labor.

"I will send one of the midwives to examine you," Miryam said. "It may be as much as a day or two before you deliver."

I regretted Miryam's harsh honesty, for I saw that it set fear into Aviela's heart.

"You will do better to walk," Miryam added as she left the tent to spread her message. "It will make the hard labor come faster. Ask if the midwife has some terebinth resin to burn—that also helps speed up labor."

After we bade Miryam farewell, I took Aviela's hand. "We will not leave you alone," I said.

The girl smiled at me in gratitude.

The midwife's exam revealed little more than what Miryam had already predicted. Aviela would not deliver soon and she should walk to make faster progress. When I asked about the terebinth resin she said that she preferred to save her small supply for more desperate cases. I did not argue.

I suggested we walk down to the valley where my sheep grazed under the supervision of Gershom and his cousins Ithamar and Eleazar. The boys, now between the ages of seven and ten, seemed old enough to entrust with the task for a few hours in the afternoon. Whenever I asked them to look after my flock they beamed with pride.

Elisheva and I stood on either side of Aviela and began a slow journey across the camp. Before we went very far Caleb ran up to us, frantic and breathless. Elisheva and I smiled at his agitated manner. We assured him that we would look after Aviela and return her to their tent long before she required the attention of a midwife.

"I am training with Yehoshua on the western edge of camp," he told us. "Be sure to send a messenger the moment…"

Elisheva laughed. "Go play with your swords," she teased. "We know what to do here better than you."

As we approached the edge of the valley, we saw smoke rising from the Tabernacle. The smell of something burning filled the air. I turned to Elisheva.

"Did they plan a sacrifice today?"

"I heard nothing of it."

We saw a group gather before the Tabernacle entrance. Elisheva and I exchanged looks of dread. We clasped hands. My breath rose fast and shallow in my chest.

"What is it?" Aviela asked.

"Perhaps an unannounced sacrifice in honor of our imminent departure," I replied. I found no solace in my story, yet Aviela seemed eager to believe it.

Elisheva glanced at me.

I understood her unspoken request to leave us and nodded. "I will take Aviela to my tent and then meet you."

"Why can I not come too?" Aviela asked.

"You have walked for over an hour. Would you not prefer a few minutes of rest?"

She agreed to rest in my tent. I kept Eliezer in my arms, though he grew heavier by the day. The dog, at my heels as usual, would have followed me to the Tabernacle. I told him to stay by the tent and watch over our guest. Aviela laughed with pleasure to see how well the little creature listened to me.

I ran to the Tabernacle and pushed my way through the people who formed a semicircle around the entrance. As my nostrils filled with the strong scent of burned flesh, I felt Yahveh's harsh hand nearby. I heard Elisheva cry out.

When I saw what lay on the ground I buried my face in my veil. But as Elisheva's shrieking filled my ears I could not keep myself apart from her. I opened my eyes and forced myself to look at my friend as she knelt between the two charred bodies of her sons Nadav and Avihu. In many places their flesh had melted away to the bone. Yet each face held the expression of an agonizing death and their clothes, the priestly vestments, remained untouched.

I handed my baby to a woman I knew and moved forward to put my arms around Elisheva. When I bent over her, she turned to me. Her eyes burned with hatred.

"Leave me!" The shout tore her throat. She waved her hand at me and the growing crowd. "All of you and your terrible God!"

"He is not my God," I whispered to her.

"You go along with it like the rest of them! You let Moses bring Him to us."

"Elisheva," I begged, "Come away from here."

The baby in her arms began to cry.

"At least let me take Elyah," I pleaded.

"No!" Her shriek fell off into hoarseness. She clutched Elyah to her bosom. "I will kill myself before I let any of you take another child from me!"

I backed away and retrieved my own baby. What could I do for her?

"Does anyone know what happened?" I asked.

"They made an offering that displeased Yahveh," someone said.

The crowd parted for Miryam, Moses, and Yehoshua. Aharon followed close behind. They stood speechless. Miryam tried to comfort Elisheva.

"You are worse than any of them!" Elisheva sobbed. As she pushed away Miryam's hands. "I never want to see you again!"

Miryam came to my side. "How can she blame me? It makes no sense."

I pointed to the bodies. "Nor does that."

Aharon did not move. He did not speak. He stared at the bodies of his sons with a blank face, as if they did not register in his eyes. Moses went inside the Tabernacle and returned with two fire pans and a small jug like those Aharon had used for wine at the vineyard.

"Who knows what happened here?" he called to the crowd through his veil.

Someone pushed a woman forward. I recognized her as one who waited upon the priests and attended to the upkeep of the Tabernacle. Her whole body trembled.

"Speak up!" Moses demanded. "What did you see?"

"They drank to celebrate our upcoming departure," she said in a quivering voice. "They drank too much. They said, 'Let us make an offering of incense to Yahveh to draw near to Him.'"

Moses clenched and unclenched his fists. "Yahveh did not decree such an offering!"

The woman pulled her veil over her face to hide her weeping. "They brought embers from outside the Tabernacle. When they dropped the incense oil into the fire, the flames..."

She broke off and could not finish.

I glanced at Miryam. Did she find death a just punishment for her brother's sons? She had loved them as her own.

I watched her face twitch as if she struggled with doubt in her heart.

Moses turned to Aharon. I could not see his expression behind the veil. I heard anger and disappointment in his voice. "They profaned the

Tabernacle with drink and alien fire."

Aharon stood silent. He hung his head in shame.

"They dishonored their position. But you must continue to serve the people. Do not bare your head or tear your robes. Israel will mourn in your place."

Aharon did not violate his brother's edict. But Elisheva was under no obligation to restrain herself. As Aharon's cousins carried the bodies out of camp to bury them, she threw her veil to the ground and rent her kuttoneh. She smeared her face with ashes from the fire pans. Her hollow wail rose over the camp. Every woman among us wept with her.

After the crowd dispersed, Aharon went to his wife, but she turned away from him in silence. Several of her friends came forward, women who had lost sons in the killing eight months before. These she leaned on. I walked into the valley where the boys watched over the sheep and told Eleazar and Ithamar to return to their tent and stay near their mother. I did not have the strength to tell them what had happened. They would learn soon enough.

Gershom and I brought the sheep into their pen. I asked him to stay with them and the dog while I brought Aviela to her own tent. I refused to answer her questions about the commotion at the Tabernacle. But the truth followed us through camp and soon Aviela knew the story from all the eager gossips.

When Aviela lay settled in her tent and the midwife arrived, I left to visit Elisheva. Aviela begged for me to stay with her, but I promised to return soon.

Many women clustered around Aharon's tent. Cries rose from different groups in turn. The women made way for me until I reached Teye, who stood guard at the tent flap. She refused to move aside for me to enter.

"She does not want you or anyone."

Tears pooled in my eyes. I loved Elisheva and she loved me. I wanted to share her grief, to lighten it if I could. I knew she lashed out in anger for her loss. But as I looked past Teye into the tent I felt my heart bleed as if from a wound of the sword.

"Elisheva!" I called out. I craned my neck to catch a glimpse of my friend.

"Go now," Teye said in a harsh voice.

I continued to look at the tent flap. I wanted Elisheva to emerge, to tell me that she needed me.

"Go!" Teye repeated.

"If I could see her for a moment..."

The flap opened a crack. My spirit leapt. Elisheva's hand appeared and flung something toward me. As the flap closed again I noticed a shiny object at my feet—the gold bracelet I had given her in Egypt.

I sought Miryam and Thabis in the kitchen tent. I needed someone to care for the baby and to look after Gershom while I helped Aviela. I needed someone to reassure me that Elisheva's anger would pass. And I needed someone to understand that I too grieved for the loss of Avihu and Nadav.

Throughout the camp women wailed for the young men. When I reached the kitchen tent I found Miryam and Thabis sitting in glum silence. Neither bothered to greet me. Miryam looked old. When had she aged so much? I could see that Thabis had been crying.

Minutes passed without words. I recalled the first time I had seen Aharon and his handsome sons returning from the vineyard. Elisheva had run to meet them, her face lit with delight. She would have been content for everything to remain forever as it had been that day. The Promised Land meant little more to her than a return to the happiness she once had known in Egypt.

At last I broke the silence. "She would not see me."

"Nor me," Miryam replied.

"She does not want the comfort of friendship to soften her grief," Thabis said.

Miryam neither agreed nor disagreed. She hid her anguish behind the sturdy shield of her stern face. But I could feel it bleeding from every pore of her body.

I did not like to see Miryam's hands idle. I handed her the baby. He awoke and began to play with Miryam's fingers. She smiled at him.

I rose to my feet. "I promised to attend Aviela," I said. "She has gone into labor sooner than we expected. Can you look after the baby and Gershom?"

Miryam nodded. "She has no female relatives. It is kind of you to sit with her."

I felt my eyes widen with surprise. I assumed that Miryam—who seemed to know everything that transpired in camp—had heard of my occasional birth chanting. I felt a twinge of guilt. Perhaps she had been too busy with the Tabernacle and the widows and orphans. Perhaps others had kept the truth from her lest she object.

"I have been singing to the women, to ease their pains."

"Indeed. You have a beautiful voice," she replied. But I could see that her heart dwelt on something else.

She put the baby on the ground to let him crawl. We watched him explore the tent until he reached the flap. Miryam scooped him up and he began to cry. She bounced him on her knees.

"You knew something like this would happen?" Miryam asked her question without taking her eyes off the baby.

I remembered back to a day I had tried to forget, when the golden bull calf had poisoned the camp, when I had come upon Nadav and the girl. But Nadav had made reparation to her as Yahveh's laws demanded. And so I had never told anyone what I had seen. Months ago, when Moses had announced the priesthood, a premonition of darkness had overwhelmed my heart. I had almost revealed all that I had seen to Miryam. She had been right to stop me. What good could come of such gossip now?

"Nothing could have changed their destiny," I whispered.

Miryam did not reply. She put the baby down. He pulled at her sandal and she lifted him into her arms again.

"Come, little man. Let us find your brother."

When I returned to Aviela she moaned with gratitude to see me. The deaths of Elisheva's sons had upset her so much that she seemed certain of her own death to follow. I tried to calm her heart with a simple song that my mother used to sing as we fell asleep. When I saw that Aviela began to relax, I took a drink of water and caught my breath.

We sat for an hour or more while her contractions gathered strength. I tried to speak with her about her hopes for the child, about her wedding in Egypt and her love for Caleb, about the Promised Land, about anything that would keep our hearts from the sadness that weighed upon us. At last, when she could no longer converse with me for the pain, I knelt by her side and began to chant.

I imagined myself a bird in the branches of a flowering almond tree at dusk. The words and melody came to me without effort from the depths of my being and flowed outward like the scent of the flowers, the rays of the setting sun, the waters of birth. I knew the world with all my senses—the fragrant leafy trees, the hard rocky ledges, the trickle of a cool mountain stream in the season of rain. I felt my voice lift on my wings to the roof of the tent and beyond. I swooped up and down, daring myself ever closer to heaven's vault and the abode of the gods. At last I spread my wings wide and soared into the vastness of the deep—higher, higher, beyond, beyond, into the golden realm.

Aviela's final push and her new baby's cry brought me back to myself. I glanced over to the midwife and saw that she held a little girl. I smiled at the two women enlisted to support Aviela as she squatted over the birth stones. And then I saw another person in the darkness beyond the open tent flap.

"Miryam?" I whispered. She disappeared. I ran after the apparition. "Miryam?" I called out.

I saw her in the shadows ahead. She stopped and turned. We stood together in the square before a blazing fire circle. Others sat in small groups nearby for warmth and companionship.

"You have betrayed my trust!"

"Let me explain..." I begged.

"You dare to call out to a goddess in *this* camp! On the day Elisheva's own sons died for disobeying Yahveh!"

"Please Miryam, believe me. It is just a song to ease the pain. The Goddess has nothing to do with it any more! I do not even hear the words. It is for the women..."

"Your lies are more poisonous than a scorpion's sting. You are an unfit wife for Moses. You are an unfit mother for his sons. You are an abomination in this camp."

She turned and ran from me. I did not follow.

Moses awaited me in our tent. My hands shook as I rubbed the ointment into his blistered skin, but I did not tell him of my encounter with Miryam. He would hear of it from her soon enough.

"How is Elisheva?" he asked when I had finished with his face.

"She will not see me or Miryam. She will not see anyone. She is destroyed." I began to cry. "Why did He do it?"

The reply came from his lips with such agony they might have been uttered by a dying man. "They desecrated the priesthood and the Tabernacle."

I found no comfort in his grief. We sat for a few moments in silence. My heart remained turned toward Elisheva.

"Perhaps you should visit Elisheva," I suggested. "She will not refuse to see you."

"I will heed your wisdom in the morning."

Moses covered his face and lay down. I moved over to my side of the tent, where the boys both slept. I tried to rest but could not banish the sight of the charred bodies from my eyes or the sound of Miryam's angry words from my ears. The smell of burning flesh filled my nostrils. Toward morning I grew cold. I had not known such misery since before I met Moses at the well so many years ago. How could I defend myself from

Miryam's accusations, soon to come? Surely Moses would send me away.

How could I endure the lonely years ahead?

I crept back into his section of the tent. I lay down beside my beloved. How sweet the nights we had once shared in this place! The desire he had taught my body rushed into me like a flood through a dry wadi. I lifted my kuttoneh and felt the warm flesh open for him. I moved my hand beneath his garment, along his leg, to his loincloth. His own flesh rose with desire for me, yet still he did not wake. I wove a circle of dreams around him with my arms and smiled. *I am a witch after all*, I said to myself.

He took me between sleep and waking, where our early days merged into the present and time vanished. We floated in the Red Sea with bands of gold shimmering over our bodies. A whole flock of flamingoes rose above us. We caught soft feathers as they fluttered into our hands. My kisses healed his lips and his tongue grew light and smooth. "My love for you is more infinite than Yahveh Himself," I whispered.

I felt his muscles go rigid as he woke. But he could not stop what I had begun. When it was over he pushed me from him with such force that I cried out.

He ripped the veil from his face and I shielded my eyes.

"Woman!" he shouted in anger. "You have polluted me before Yahveh."

I curled into a ball and held myself.

"Can a wife live with no affection?" I whispered. "Month after month, year after year. I can not even look into your eyes. How can I go on?"

I felt his anger drain away like sand between open fingers. He lay his palm upon my shoulder. He folded me into his arms. He stroked my hair while I wept against his chest.

"Hush..." he murmured as he rocked me back and forth. "Do you not know? Our separation is the hardest thing Yahveh asks of me."

THIRTY-TWO

Miryam

I KEPT a lonely vigil in memory of Nadav and Avihu. All night I wandered through the camp in darkness. I recalled every detail of their births. They brought great joy when they came into this world. I could not believe they had left so soon and with such sorrow.

I had shared Elisheva's pride as they stood beside their father to be anointed. *They are my sons too*, I had said to myself. *I raised them to serve the people and Yahveh.* Yahveh had chosen them above all others to be close to Him. He had graced them with a glorious future. Generations upon generations of priests would have followed from their seed. All this they had traded for the contents of a wine jug.

"You have slaughtered those who loved you." I whispered to them as if they yet lived. "You have made us grieve when we should have rejoiced."

I walked past darkened tents under a clear sky filled with bright stars. Sorrow, crushed hopes, and anger held every footstep fast to the ground. It did not matter that I understood Yahveh could not tolerate priests who violated his most sacred place. I hated Yahveh's justice that day. Why had he not punished Tzipporah too? Should she not at least be removed from camp? I had grown to trust her. Now she had betrayed me.

I knew I should tell Moses. I should have told him at once. But I could not face him. We had lost too much.

I went to begin the morning's work in the kitchen tent. Our supplies ran low. Two weeks earlier Moses had sent a group of men north to purchase some much needed food. If the men did not return soon we would have to ask Yahveh to send the manna again. In a year at the Mountain of God I had grown used to the hunger and the filth. I knew that Yahveh counted on me to be an example of patience and perseverance. Still, I wished for an easier life.

Thabis came to help me. She reported that Elisheva continued to refuse all visitors. Aharon and the children sat with her.

"Did you know about Tzipporah chanting in camp?" I asked.

The question surprised her. "She is always singing."

"I mean chanting at a birth."

Thabis saw the displeasure on my face. She heard the edge of anger in my voice. I saw she knew enough of Yahveh's laws to understand Tzipporah's flagrant violations. "Only a few times," she whispered.

Fury consumed me. "Why did everyone keep this secret!"

I did not wait for an answer. I stormed out of the tent to find Moses.

My brother stood with Yehoshua and a group of elders near the Tabernacle. As I drew close I caught snatches of a discussion about who would carry different parts of the Tabernacle on our journey. I did not hesitate to intrude. I knew the matter that I wished to place before him merited his immediate attention.

The men made way for me. I stood before Moses. I did not take the time to greet him.

"I must tell you of an urgent problem among the women," I said.

Moses frowned. He waved his hand as if to dismiss me. "I leave the affairs of women to you."

I stared at Moses in disbelief. The men resumed their discussion as if I did not still stand in their midst. How could they show so little respect for me? I did not run to Moses about every small problem. He should have known that if I broached a matter it must be serious.

"If Yahveh cares so little for women, why did He come to me even before your birth?"

The men stopped talking. I stared at my brother. He stared back through his veil. I hoped that I had hurt him as much as he had hurt me.

I looked from man to man. The elders would not meet my eye. I felt my face grow hot as I realized that my words, rather than injuring my brother, had caused him to suffer embarrassment on my behalf. As I turned away I overheard Moses apologize for me. "She takes the deaths of her nephews very hard."

I heard his explanation as a further slight. I stormed back to the kitchen tent. I grabbed the last loaf of bread and a bowl of cooked lentils. In my anger I knocked over several things. Thabis shrank from me in fear. I saw that the rage in my heart might lead me to push away everyone I cared about. I stood still for a moment to calm myself. After a few breaths I turned back to Thabis.

"I am going to Elisheva. I want you to deliver a message to Tzipporah." Thabis nodded.

"Tell her she must stop the birth chanting or I will see that she is banished from camp."

Elisheva did not refuse me entrance to her tent. I handed the food to Aharon. Ithamar and Eleazar tore at the bread with great hunger—they must have gone without an evening meal the day before. Elisheva looked at me with dead eyes. Pale skin hung from her face as if someone had drained away her life's blood. Elyah sat in a corner crying. No one moved to comfort or feed her.

I picked up the baby. I rocked her in my arms.

"I hate your God who took my children from me," Elisheva said.

My own anger at Moses and Tzipporah seemed foolish next to her grief. I motioned for Aharon to take the boys out of the tent that I might speak to Elisheva alone. He nodded with gratitude.

"The baby is hungry," I said after the men left. I handed Elisheva the remainder of the loaf. "You must feed yourself to keep up your milk for her."

Elisheva shook her head.

"Neglect of your three living children will not bring back the two that are gone."

Elisheva wept as she ate a bite of the bread. She took a handful of the lentils. When she put the baby to her breast I saw that she grew calmer. I had seen many bereaved mothers and widows blame Yahveh's hand for their loss. After the golden calf I had called on each one. I had learned then that I could not offer Yahveh's wisdom as a comfort to them. Yahveh understood if they preferred to blame Him rather than the wrongdoing of their men. In time they would come back to Him. He knew a woman's heart.

I sat with Elisheva in silence. After a time I took her hand.

"You must have courage," I said. I rose to my feet. "For the sake of your children and for Aharon. Do not push your friends from you. They will bring relief."

I bent down to kiss her.

Her lips began to move. I could not hear. I squatted close to her face.

"Where do you find the strength?" she whispered.

In Yahveh, I replied in my heart. *Women, too, are made in his image.*

Later that day the supply caravan arrived from the north. A man named Hovav came with it. He wore a fine Egyptian linen robe and a head cloth of red and yellow wool. He wore gold chains around his neck and gold rings in his ears. I learned that he was married to one of Tzipporah's sisters. A trader, he knew the way to Canaan. Moses had sent for him to serve as our guide through northwest Midyan and into Moav. He spent many hours talking with Moses and Yehoshua about the journey ahead and what we would find when we entered Canaan.

I busied myself with preparations for our departure. I baked flatbread. I advised Moses about how best to pack items from the Tabernacle. I supervised the organization of the kitchen tent. I told the women how to prepare for the journey. I tried to raise the spirits of those who dreaded the journey. Above all, I avoided Tzipporah. Nor did she seek me.

Early one morning while Thabis yet slept I decided to relieve her of the task of fetching the day's fresh water for the kitchen tent. I had not passed the Tabernacle at dawn for many days. As I approached it I noticed a small tent that Moses had pitched nearby on the day after the deaths of Nadav and Avihu. Yehoshua stood guard outside the flap. Before that morning I had supposed the tent to be a place for private meetings or to rest during the day.

I approached Yehoshua, who stood like a soldier at attention.

"Good morning!" I called out. "Yahveh's blessing be upon you."

"And you," Yehoshua replied.

I tried to peek into the tent. "Does my brother sleep in there?" I asked. Yehoshua nodded.

I held my lips together lest the satisfaction that burst from my heart be revealed on my face. Someone must have told my brother about Tzipporah's blasphemous birth chanting, and he had separated himself from her even more. This evidence made me feel justified in everything I had ever held against her.

Moses did not tell us the exact day of our departure. I soon realized that he did not know. He awaited a sign from Yahveh. Seven days after we first had word about leaving, a cloud came down from the mountain. It settled over the Tabernacle. Many in the camp rushed to see it. Moses stood before the Tabernacle entrance with Aharon.

"When the cloud lifts and moves forward we will depart. Be ready!"

Everyone bowed toward the cloud in fear and reverence.

We waited for three days. Each morning I asked Yahveh to heal Elisheva's heart. I asked Him to heal my anger at Him for taking Nadav and Avihu. I asked Him to bless all the Children of Israel. I asked Him to bring us to the Promised Land with speed. I repeated my prayers every evening as the cloud turned fiery in the dark sky.

Those three days seemed endless. At last, on the second new moon of our second year the cloud lifted. We packed our tents. We ran to fill skins and jugs with water. Those assigned to carry the Tabernacle took their positions at the front of our long procession.

We moved north into the land that the Midyanites called the Hisma. This time I noticed all the colors—the yellow sand, the grey sandstone formations rising in strange gnarled shapes, the red mountains to the west. We stayed on flat, higher ground for two days. Despite the recent rains we did not find much to eat in this barren land. On the morning of the second day Yahveh sent the manna to us again.

We did not move as fast as we had the year before, following our escape. After so many months of living in tents, I expected greater resilience than many displayed. The people seemed less tolerant of discomfort. Their feet had grown soft in the fertile land surrounding the Mountain of God. I tried to bring cheer to those whose spirits fell. I reminded them of our flight to the sea, of how Yahveh had defeated Pharaoh's army. As I told the tale I heard the thunder of chariots. I felt the spray of the sea. I knew terror and joy all over again. For many others the memories seemed dimmer than a dream. Like a woman who forgets her labor pains the moment they are over, the Children of Israel seemed too eager to shed their history. I promised Yahveh to make sure that never happened.

On the third day we approached Dophka. We camped near the smelting ovens. Hovav told Moses and the elders that at our current pace we must travel at least another week through the wilderness before we reached the trade route, where water and food would be more plentiful.

That night a small group of malcontents began to complain. They cried out that hunger weakened them and the entire camp. In the evening a group of twenty sought Moses in front of the Tabernacle. Their loud, gluttonous cries filled the air.

"If only we had meat and fresh vegetables to eat!"

"We used to eat fish in Egypt for free."

"With cucumbers, leeks, melons, onions, garlic!"

"Our throats grow so dry! We have nothing but manna."

Moses shook with anger. I moved my way around the group to stand at his side.

"Should I send away this ungrateful riffraff?" I whispered to him.

"Why do they come to me with this?" The veil muted his fury.

"The spirit of Yahveh is always with you," I said. I expected my reminder of his divine grace to calm him. "They believe only you can relieve their suffering."

"*Suffering?*" His anger seemed to grow rather than recede. "They suffered from slavery and oppression! From idolatry! One does not suffer for want of meat!"

He reached under his veil to pull at his long beard. He turned toward the Tabernacle. I heard him speak in an undertone, words such as I had never expected to come from the prophet of Yahveh.

"Yahveh! I can not carry the burden of this people by myself. It is too much for me. Kill me and let me live no more of my miserable fate!"

I felt my anger rise. How dare he prefer death to serving Yahveh through prophecy and leadership! *Let me be Your prophet again*, I begged. *I will never complain.*

The men shifted their weight from foot to foot while they waited for Moses to respond. Moses stood silent for a long time. The men began to grow restless. At last Moses turned back to them. He lifted his veil to expose the blinding light of his face. I held up a hand to shield my eyes. The group of men recoiled. Everyone knew that Moses only removed the veil to reveal a message from Yahveh. Had Yahveh come to him in the silence? Why had I not felt His presence, heard His voice?

Moses began to speak. "You wept in the hearing of Yahveh and said that it was good for you in Egypt. Now Yahveh says He will give you meat and you will eat. Not one day will you eat and not two days. Not twenty days will you eat but a full month of days until the meat comes out of your noses!"

The men nodded with satisfaction. They clapped each other on the back. They did not seem to recognize that my brother's words portended more than a feast of abundance. My own heart grew cold with fear at the prophecy. Those who angered Yahveh would not escape untouched.

Moses turned to Yehoshua. "Tell the people that tomorrow morning Yahveh will send them meat. Now Yahveh commands that the elders gather here before the Tabernacle."

Word of Yahveh's summons spread through the camp. I watched from a distance as the elders came before Moses. When Moses counted the men he found two absent, Eldad and Medad. He sent Yehoshua to search for them and led the others into the Tabernacle. I crept forward to the entrance, where I peeked through a crack between the entry curtain and the gold pillars that framed the door.

As the sixty-eight men stood near the Altar of Burnt Offering, the cloud above the Tent of Meeting rushed down to envelop them in a thick fog. I remembered how Tzipporah had once said to me that evil spirits dwelt in the fog but that the fog could be scared away by the presence of a fox. She told me that if I ever found myself trapped in a fog I should say, *O Father Fog, run away! The fox comes!*

I shook my head to banish the memory of her foolishness.

When the fog lifted I saw that the spirit of Yahveh had entered them. Many of the men lay writhing on the ground. Some danced in jerking movements with their eyes rolling up into their heads. Others called out strange words I did not recognize, as if they spoke in a different tongue.

Moses stood before the flock of elders with his face hidden beneath the veil. What did he say to himself as he watched those useless prophets, those weak men, overwhelmed by Yahveh's spirit? Did he long for one to rise and relieve him from the toil of leadership?

I stepped inside the curtain. I alone could help him. I had been a mere girl of twelve when Yahveh's spirit entered me. His power had not flung me to the ground or twisted my tongue into strange and incomprehensible sounds. I had the strength Moses needed. Yahveh had only to call upon me. I would show them all.

My wishes went unanswered.

One by one the men came back into their senses. As I slid back around the curtain, Yehoshua returned from camp out of breath. He did not bring the two missing elders with him.

"Come!" he cried out to Moses through the curtain. "My lord, you must come at once!"

Moses appeared at the Tabernacle door so fast it seemed he must have flown across the courtyard.

"The elders Eldad and Medad jerk their limbs and their mouths pour forth with prophetic utterances! My lord, you must stop them!"

"Are you upset on my account?" Moses asked in a calm voice. "I did not choose to bear this burden alone. I wish for nothing more than Yahveh's spirit to enter all the people."

I could not contain my objection. "You speak as a foolish man on this day. Who would not wish to have the special grace and favor Yahveh has shown you?"

He turned his veiled head toward me.

"Your words bring me no comfort, Sister," he said.

A sword could not have delivered a sharper blow.

The quail came as Moses had promised. A wind from the west carried them over the mountains into our camp, where they fell to the ground. The people rejoiced to have meat again. I watched in horror as some of the men, like the worshippers of the Egyptian god Osiris, tore the birds limbs from limb and put the uncooked meat in their mouths.

"Yahveh has forbidden this!" I cried out. They did not hear me in their frenzy.

Soon Yahveh struck those with raw meat between their teeth. Thick, oozing lumps erupted on their arms and legs. Before the sun set thirty men lay dead.

That night I felt so sick in my heart I could not bear the company of others. I lay in the kitchen tent alone, considering what Moses might have said as he stood before the men who now lay dead. He could have urged them to remain upright in the eyes of Yahveh. He could have reminded them that meat and vegetables are a small price to pay for freedom. Even the hungriest might have found solace in descriptions of the Promised Land and all its riches.

Moses could have tried to save the people. He had not. He had said nothing. He had shunned Yahveh's gift of leadership. He had even permitted a woman who spread goddess worship to remain among us.

I told myself that Yahveh could not have intended for us to stand by while one terrible thing after another brought His anger upon us. If Moses would not take action, I must do something myself.

The next morning Moses and Aharon purified the camp with a Sin Offering—a kid burned on the altar. Afterwards, I waylaid Aharon outside the Tabernacle.

"Brother!" He stopped without greeting me. I looked from his eyes, dulled by grief like Elisheva's, to a lock of graying hair that fell over his lined forehead. Moses had forbidden Aharon to tear his clothes or wail in mourning. But he could not prevent our brother's flesh from displaying the grief in his heart.

"I do not understand why Moses sets all the rules," I said. "He does not follow them himself."

Aharon shook his head. I could not tell if he meant to agree or disagree with me. It did not matter. The rush of venom poured forth.

"He allows that Kushite priestess to dwell among us! She goes from tent to tent with the incantations of a goddess upon her lips! Listen, Brother. Has Yahveh spoken only to Moses? No! He has spoken to me as well."

I meant to say more, to suggest that we ask Yahveh to let the two of us lead with Moses, to relieve him of the burdens he abhorred. But before I could finish, the cloud that hovered over the Tent of Meeting swept down to encircle me. It filled my nostrils like smoke from an uncontained fire. Every breath I took poisoned my lungs. I gasped for air. My arms jerked upward as if someone yanked them from above. My head seemed to float away without me. My eyes grew dim. I felt the ground open beneath my feet to swallow me.

As I fell through darkness a terrible sound hit my skull like the hammering of metal on metal. I began to distinguish words inside the reverberations, an echo within an echo.

If a prophet of Yahveh is among the people,
I make Myself known in a vision, in a dream.
Except for My servant Moses.
I speak with him mouth to mouth.
To him alone I show Myself.
Him alone I trust.
And you dare to speak out against him?

I tried to force my eyes open, to pull myself up from the depths of this terrible dream.

I felt the fog gather. I felt it lift away. I awoke to find myself lying on the sandy ground near the Tabernacle.

I gulped deep breaths of clear air. Relief washed over me as I opened my eyes. Moses and Aharon hovered over me. Had they heard Yahveh's reproach? I tried to open my mouth. It seemed to be sealed shut with a gritty, sandy substance. I sat up. My brothers shrank away from me. They looked upon me, their eyes filled with horror. I felt the skin of my face, thick and rough as a fish from the River Nile. I looked down at my hands, my arms, my feet—every inch of my flesh appeared to be covered with scales as white as snow. I ran my nails along my arm to scratch away the scales. Bloody welts appeared. My spirit writhed with the agony of impurity.

"Tzaraat!" Aharon gasped. As priest it fell to him to declare a person unclean, to send one stricken with this disease from camp.

"No!" I screamed. "Please, Yahveh, make me clean!"

Aharon fell to his knees.

"Yahveh! Forgive our sin committed in foolishness! Pray let her not be as one dead who emerges from his mother's womb with half his flesh eaten away."

I pulled my veil over my head. It did not shield me from the revulsion that rose in my stomach. Through the darkness I heard Moses call out.

"Yahveh! Pray heal her."

The feel of my tongue against the scales on my mouth made me gag. I lay flat to touch my forehead to the ground. *Yahveh! None has served You with more devotion! None has given up so much as I for Your sake! I am Your handmaiden!*

I looked at my hands. The scales remained.

"Do not move," Moses ordered. He entered the Tabernacle.

O Yahveh, I will never again speak ill of another if You heal me of this impurity! Moses himself has forgiven me! Please do not condemn me further!

I could hear a crowd gather around me. Aharon kept the people at a distance. I tried to curl into my kuttoneh and veil so none of my flesh remained exposed. I knew it did not matter. Word of my affliction would spread soon enough. Once beloved of everyone, I would become an outcast who inspired only disgust. My people would disown me.

When Moses returned he rendered Yahveh's verdict. I knelt before him. I bowed my head as he spoke.

"Thus said Yahveh, 'If her father spat in her face she would bear her shame seven days. So she must be shut out of camp for seven days, and afterward be gathered back in.'"

"Seven days," Aharon declared. "Let none go near her impurity until she is gathered back to us."

Aharon gave me a water skin. He led me out of camp into the lonely wilderness. He did not speak to me. I found a shady place under a jutting cliff. I sat down. I closed my eyes. I opened them to look at my hands. I wished Yahveh had chosen to take my life rather than inflict such a punishment.

I sat alone with my memories and grief and remorse.

When did I notice the black-veiled form on the horizon? It must have been late afternoon, when the sun's heat always played its cruelest tricks. The illusion reminded me of Tzipporah dancing after we crossed the sea. She had had a light step even when she was many months pregnant with Eliezer. As she had reached up to borrow my timbrel our hands had touched. I remembered her smooth flesh grazing mine. Our eyes had met. We had exchanged smiles.

I had not disdained her then. Even before that, when I first met her, deep in the recesses of my heart I always knew that she understood Moses in a way I never could.

This I admitted to myself now, too late.

The figure drew closer. The Angel of Death. I rose in fear.

Yahveh, do not gather me unto You with such impurity on my person! Even the righteous must be humble. Now I know. I wanted too much glory for myself.

"Miryam!" a voice called out to me.

"Tzipporah?" I could see she carried several bundles in her arms.

I held my veil over my face up to my eyes.

"You should not be here," I warned. "They say the tzaraat is contagious."

Tzipporah did not stop. She walked right up to me. She dropped the things she carried onto the sand at my feet. She took a deep breath.

"O Miryam," she chided. "Will you allow me, this once, to show you kindness?"

She had brought me a sleeping mat and warm skin blanket for the night. She had brought more water. She laid a feast before me, goat's cheese, almonds, wheat flatbread, fresh dates.

"These things are scarce," I objected. "I should not eat them."

"Your brothers did not mean to send you without food."

"It is too extravagant."

"Miryam, Yahveh is a harsher judge than you, and I am sure He does not expect you to add to your punishment."

"Harsh?" Her allegation startled me. "I am not a harsh judge. I ask no more or less of anyone than is reasonable."

She stared back at me. After a moment she burst into laughter.

I felt myself weaken until laughter overcame me too.

When my breath came back to me I looked at the food on the cloth. Pangs of hunger gnawed at my stomach. I let the veil fall away from my face. Tzipporah did not flinch at the terrible sight of my flesh. "I will eat only if you share the meal," I said.

She came back the next afternoon with more food and a wooden box such as we had used to keep salve in Egypt.

"Do my brothers know you have come to me?" I asked.

"They do not ask and I do not tell," she said. "You are much missed in camp."

Why had I never noticed her sweetness before? I felt my eyes begin to fill yet again. They seemed to hold a lifetime of unwept tears.

"I thank you..." I broke off, embarrassed by my display of emotion.

Tzipporah smiled to herself. She opened the box. I recognized the contents at once.

"That is Elisheva's ointment for sunburn," I said with surprise.

She dipped her fingers into the thick substance. She reached for my arm. I shrank from her.

"You must not touch me!" I exclaimed. "It is bad enough you are here. I am unclean."

"This will ease the discomfort," she said. "I trust that Yahveh will not afflict me for bringing you relief."

She rubbed the ointment into all of my flesh. It soothed the itching. While she worked she sang a beautiful song about a bird soaring past the vault of the heavens in search of God's golden throne.

"Where did you learn it?" I asked her when she finished.

"The song is almost the only thing I recall of my mother. She was a birth chanter too."

Tzipporah grew very quiet. She paused in her work.

"I am sorry you lost her so young," I said after a few moments.

Tzipporah nodded. She began rubbing ointment into my feet. After many minutes she spoke again.

"The Goddess left me long ago. But I believe my mother is still with me when I sing."

I gazed upon her beautiful face. Her clear blue eyes spoke of sorrow for my suffering and all that she herself had endured. "Then your chanting is to honor your mother's memory and not to worship a goddess."

She looked at me with gratitude and love.

Tzipporah returned to me every afternoon. I awaited her visits with eagerness. On the seventh day she came at dawn. She held out a bundle wrapped in black cloth.

"This is from Elisheva," she said. "She made it for you. It provided her much distraction from her sorrows."

I had never felt so pleased to receive a gift in all my life.

"Please unwrap it for me," I asked. I did not want to touch the gift with my tainted skin.

She shook off the cloth to reveal a beautiful white linen dress and robe, a yellow cloak, and a crimson veil.

"I can not…"

"Aharon says you must burn the things you are wearing now."

"A plain black kuttoneh such as yours would be more suitable."

Tzipporah shook her head. "Everyone looks forward to your return. Should you greet them in mourning or in joy?"

I held up my hands. "I am eager to return to my work. How will I know when?"

"Surely Yahveh will make it known to you."

The sun's rays began to peek over the mountains far in the east.

Tzipporah pointed to a lone tamarisk tree atop a nearby cliff.

"Let us climb to it," she said.

"On that crumbling rock?" I objected.

"Come!" she called out as she ran to the base.

I scrambled after her with difficulty. I tried to follow her footholds. She seemed as nimble as a cat.

The climb must have taken an hour or more. By the time I reached the top, my hands and feet felt raw from scraping against the rough stone. But when I took in the view I forgot my discomfort. There, spread on the plain before us, stood our camp. I saw the tents, the fire circles, the golden walls of the Tabernacle, the people—my people—moving to and fro.

"They are not yet ready to be free," Tzipporah said. "You know that better than me."

I did not challenge her. "I always believed that I could save people from their own weaknesses," I confessed.

Tzipporah shook her head. "You are a strong woman. But even Yahveh does not have that power."

"I have learned something in these lonely days."

She looked at me with curiosity.

I embraced her with my impure flesh. "Wisdom comes from unexpected places."

We stood with our arms around each other. I glanced down at the Tabernacle. The shining walls caught a glint of sunlight. It reflected upward. The golden light rose closer and closer toward us.

"Look!" I whispered to Tzipporah.

We turned to face the light. She clung to my hand. The light spun a white web around us. My heart grew easy, my mouth quivered with joy. A breeze kissed me with lips sweeter than honey. I felt aware of every limb as if no more wondrous thing existed in all Yahveh's creation than my own being. As His spirit entered me I became more myself, not less. I turned to Tzipporah. Her blue eyes shone like the sky, her smile glittered like the stars.

He said no words to me. I needed none. When at last the light faded I saw that the flesh of my hands lay smooth across the bones again. I lifted my kuttoneh. Not a single white scale remained.

We climbed down from the cliff. Tzipporah helped me put on the new clothes and burn the old. We walked back into camp together.

EPILOGUE
MOUNT NEVO
Tzipporah

Last week I saw my reflection in the water of the River Jordan. I touched the wrinkled skin on my face in shock. When did I become an old woman?

Age crept over me as the heat of the day fades to dusk. It came through seasons of grief and joy. So many deaths—my mother, my firstborn, the men who rebelled before the golden calf and in the wilderness and with Korach, those who broke Yahveh's covenant, Nadav and Avihu, the spies who lied about the Promised Land.

So many deaths to mourn, yet none more than Miryam's. Of all the losses, this one fell upon me the hardest.

Elisheva and I try to fill the empty places in our hearts with memories. Sometimes we laugh to recall how Miryam spent her final hours, at the age of eighty, teaching Elisheva's great-granddaughters how to bake the bread of offering for the Tabernacle while she told them the story of how Yahveh brought us out of Egypt. We often cry for all the times we should have thanked her   and never did.

The people grieved at Miryam's passing like that of a mother. We mourn her still, these many months later. Her story is that of our nation. May she never be forgotten.

Night draws near. Yahveh, blessed be His Name, has called me to one last task. I must bury my beloved where no one can find his grave. He is a man, after all, and not a god. "Let the people never be tempted to worship me," Moses said. "Let my flesh return to the dust from whence it came."

This morning we climbed Mount Nevo to look across a great, mountainous desert into the Promised Land. Its riches lay before us for our children and their children after them. Yahveh's spirit dwells within Yehoshua now. He will lead the next generation into our dreams.

The light has faded from my beloved's face. At last I can look upon him again. How many times in the forty years of wandering did we violate Yahveh's demand for purity? I will not say. Let the secret of our sins be scattered over the plains of Moav. We could be no more than human.

As I hold him in these final moments, I recall my first glimpse of him, so many years ago. I saw a man of God that day at the well, long before he knew his own calling. I looked upon him with the eyes of a wounded gazelle. He healed me. I loved him.

Can I have more than that to tell?

A NOTE ON NAMES

For the sake of authenticity I have used the Hebraic form of most names. So Miriam is Miryam, Aaron is Aharon, Zipporah is Tzipporah, Jethro is Yitro, and Joshua is Yehoshua. Again, for the sake of authenticity I have retained the Egyptian form for Moses, rather than using the Hebraic "Moshe."

The Hebrew Bible does not provide vowel sounds for the name of God and this name is not spoken today. Translated, the letters form the unpronounceable word "YHVH." But the Israelites would in fact have spoken the name of their God, whom they knew as one of many gods and goddesses, albeit the only one whom they were permitted to worship. For this reason I have used the word "Yahveh" as God's name.

SOURCES

I began my research for *Seven Days to the Sea* with a few intriguing questions about Miryam and Tzipporah. Why was Miryam called a prophetess? What sort of conflict caused her to complain about her sister-in-law? What drove Tzipporah to rescue Moses in the mysterious circumcision scene? Why was she separated from Moses and when? By exploring possible answers I hoped to find a way to give these two women—who play such essential roles in the Exodus story—stronger voices. I wanted to imagine, as realistically as possible, how Miryam and Tzipporah might have been shaped by their very different worlds and how they came to cope with being thrust together.

Little did I know what an enormous project this would turn out to be! Delving into the scholarship brought many delightful surprises. Perhaps the biggest source of inspiration, other than the biblical text itself, was a wonderful book, *The Miracles of Exodus* by Colin J. Humphreys. I found his arguments about the route of the Exodus as well as the natural phenomena associated with the plagues and Mount Sinai very persuasive. Though Professor Humphreys is a world-renowned scientist, his book is written for the layperson, and I recommend it to anyone who wants to know more about how and where the Exodus story could have happened.

For details about life in ancient Egypt, the reign of Rameses II, and the Israelites in Egypt, I turned to the following sources: *Israel In Egypt* by James K. Hoffmeier, *Religion In Ancient Israel* by James Miller, *Pharaoh Triumphant: The Life and Times of Ramesses II* by Kenneth A. Kitchen, *Ramesses II: Greatest of the Pharaohs* by Bernadette Menu, *The Complete Gods and Goddesses of Ancient*

Egypt by Richard H. Wilkinson, *The Gods of the Egyptians* by E. A. Wallis Budge, *Egypt: 4000 Years of Art* by Jaromir Malek, *Life of the Ancient Egyptians* by Eugen Strouhal, and *On the Reliability of the Old Testament* by Kenneth A. Kitchen.

To learn about Arabia and the Hejaz, I turned to the following books and articles: *The Manners and Customs of the Rwala Bedouins* by Alois Musil, *The Northern Hejaz: A Topographical Itinerary* by Alois Musil, *The Rock Art of Arabia* by Muhammed Abdul Nayeem, *Arabia and the Bible* by James A. Montgomery, "Archaeological Sources for the Early History of Northwest Arabia" by Peter Parr, *Meaning in Ancient North Arabian Carvings* by Kerstin Eksell, *Canaanite Gods in Metal: An Archaeological Study of Ancient Syro-Palestinian Figurines* by Ora Negbi, *Ancient Records From North Arabia* by F. V. Winnett and W. L. Reed, *Midian, Moab, and Edom* edited by John F. A. Sawyer and David J. A. Clines, *Arabian Adventure* by Douglas Carruthers, *The Gold-Mines of Midian* by Richard Burton, *The Land of Midian* by Richard Burton, *Peoples of Old Testament Times* by D. J. Wiseman, and *History of the Arabs* by Philip K. Hitti.

For research on the goddess in Semitic cultures I consulted the following: *The Hebrew Goddess* by Raphael Patai, *Gods, Goddesses, and Images of God in Ancient Israel* by Othmar Keel and Christopher Uehlinger, *The Cult of Asherah in Ancient Israel and Judah* by Judith M. Hadley, "The Goddess Atirat in Ancient Arabia, in Persia, and in Babylon" by Edward Lapinski, and "Tamar, Qedesa, Qasdistu, and Sacred Prostitution in Mesopotamia" by Joan Goodnick Westenholz.

For general material on the early Israelites and to research questions about the biblical text I used the following: *Yahweh and the Gods of Canaan* by William Albright, *From Epic to Canon* by Frank Moore Cross Jr., *Studies in Ancient Yahwistic Poetry* by Frank Moore Cross Jr. and David Noel Freedman, *Frank Moore Cross: Conversations With a Bible Scholar* by Hershel Shanks, *Canaanite Myth and Hebrew Epic* by Frank Moore Cross Jr., *The Bible Unearthed* by Israel Finkelstein and Neil Asher Silberman, *Who Wrote the Bible?* by Richard Elliott Friedman, *Exploring Exodus: The Origins of Biblical Israel* by Nahum M. Sarna, *Semitic Writing* by G.R. Driver, and *Babylonian Menologies and the Semitic Calendars* by S. Langdon.

Throughout the project I relied on many different translations of the Hebrew Bible and accompanying commentaries. When I draw dialogue directly from the text, I use my own translations. The biblical texts I used most often in my research include those by Everett Fox, Robert Alter, Nahum Sarna, and Artscroll Publishing. Biblical and midrashic commentaries also informed my work. These included the wonderful series by Nehama Lebowitz, the ancient text of *Midrash Rabbah*, *Legends of the Jews* by Louis Ginzberg, *The Particulars of Rapture* by Avivah Gottlieb Zornberg, the work of the first-century historian Josephus, and the medieval commentary by Rashi.

For information and inspiration on the flora, fauna, and environment in both Egypt and Midyan I used the following: *Golden Days in the Desert: Wild Flowers of Saudi Arabia* by Betty A. Lipscombe Vincett, *Plants of the Bible* by Michael Zohary, *In a Desert Land: Photographs of Israel, Egypt, and Jordan* by Neil Folberg, *Celestial Nights: Visions of an Ancient Land* by Neil Folberg, *Mysteries of the Desert: A View of Saudi Arabia* by Isabel Cutler, and *Off-road in the Hejaz* by Patrick Pierard and Patrick Legros. The video *Lambing Time Management*, featuring Don Bailey and Woody Lane, educated me in the basic issues of ewe obstetrics.

Several reference books proved essential to this project. These included the following: *The Brown-Driver-Briggs Hebrew and English Lexicon* by F. Brown, S. Driver, and C. Briggs, *A Historical Atlas of the Jewish People* edited by Eli Barnavi, *The Macmillan Bible Atlas* by Yohanan Aharoni and Michael Avi-Yonah, *The Holman Bible Atlas* by Thomas V. Brisco, *Dictionary of Deities and Demons in the Bible* edited by Karel van der Toorn, Bob Becking, and Pieter W. van der Horst, *Eerdmans Dictionary of the Bible* edited by David Noel Freedman, *The Oxford History of the Biblical World* edited by Michael D. Coogan, and *Encyclopedia Judaica*.

While I relied on the work of many scholars, *Seven Days to the Sea* is a work of fiction. Any mistakes or inaccuracies are solely the product of my imagination.

ACKNOWLEDGEMENTS

Who says that writing is a lonely profession? From the conception of this book through the research, writing, and editing, I had the constant support of many talented, loving, and—above all—patient individuals.

My first and biggest thanks goes to Chris Min Park. I have been truly blessed to work with such a gifted editor. Chris often understood what I was trying to accomplish long before I understood myself. She believed in the book from the moment I first suggested writing about Miryam and Tzipporah. Her ability to see both the forest and the trees never fails to dazzle me.

The contributions of other people at Rugged Land have been instrumental. Web Stone, managing editor, offered many insightful suggestions on both substance and style. His dedication and support played a critical role in bringing the book to completion. I would also like to thank publisher Shawn Coyne and publicity director Zoe Feigenbaum for their enthusiasm. Of course, my agent, Esther Sung, deserves a huge thanks for her faith in me and for always being there when I need her.

On the home front, thanks as always to my friends—Kathy, Sarah, Gail, Cecilia, and Rabbi Edward Boraz—who offered more support than they realized. Thanks also to all those members of the Upper Valley Jewish Community who suffered through my Saturday-morning sermons on the Exodus.

Of course my love and gratitude turn first and last to my family. Thanks to my mother, Phyllis Lerman Woloshin. I hope she is as proud of this "grandbook" as she was of the last. Thanks to Daniel, Elena, and Max for their support. I have no adequate words to thank Meir, who had the unenviable task of figuring out a way to comment on drafts without hurting my feelings and who could find any book I needed anywhere in the world. Little do his students and academic colleagues know that he is just moonlighting as a professor; in real life he is my research assistant. And finally, thanks to Leah, who is my number-one fan, who has helped in many ways, and who has been asking for years, "When are you going to write about a character who has a baby?"

Well, here you are.

READING GROUP GUIDE

1. In *Seven Days to the Sea*, Rebecca Kohn relies on contemporary research that dispels a number of myths about the Exodus story, including the location of Mount Sinai (in Midyan rather than current day Sinai) and the route that the Israelites followed. In what other ways did the novel challenge your ideas about the Exodus?

2. Tzipporah and Miryam are very different in their backgrounds and attitudes toward life. In what ways are they alike? Do they undergo any changes in the novel that make them more like each other?

3. Do you identify more strongly with Miryam or Tzipporah?

4. Throughout the story a number of characters are touched directly by God or, in Tzipporah's case, a goddess. Compare and contrast the different responses to this experience. How does a divine encounter change their lives?

5. In the world of *Seven Days to the Sea* the characters never doubt the existence of gods, goddesses, and demons or the ability of the divine to influence the human realm. This is clearly a different world from ours, where scientific explanations predominate. In contrast, what, if any, similarities did you find between the world of Miryam and Tzipporah and ours?

6. Miryam chooses to give up the love of her life, Nunn. What do you think of this sacrifice? Was it necessary?

7. Princess Istnofret adopts Moses and becomes sympathetic to the Israelites. At one point Miryam, seeking her help, says, "…women always hold more influence than they realize." What does this belief say about Miryam? Do you think it is true in Istnofret's world? What about among the Israelites? The Midyanites?

8. In what ways do Tzipporah's early experiences in life before she meets Moses affect her later development?

9. Tzipporah dreads returning to the temple because she does not want to become a prostitute. But when Moses convinces Yitro to give him Tzipporah as a wife, she feels that her removal from the temple is a great loss. Why?

10. In Chapter Eleven, Tzipporah predicts that one day Moses's god will call him. This echoes Miryam's words from many years earlier. Moses is startled and asks her how she can know. In reply she says, "I only know what I feel." How is this different from Miryam's conviction? How are these differences reflected in the outcome of each woman's story?

11. At one point Miryam tries to enlist Tzipporah's help in turning the women against the golden calf. When Tzipporah expresses doubt, Miryam says, "You will know what to say. The words will come to you. Yahveh only gives us opportunities. We must use them to make things happen." What does this tell you about Miryam's belief in fate and destiny? Why does it take more than Miryam's argument to persuade Tzipporah?

12. The novel has many instances in which a person, a place, or even God is named. What is the significance of naming in the story?

13. The epilogue takes place many years after the main part of the story. As Tzipporah looks back on her life, do you think she is satisfied with how things have turned out? Imagine Miryam looking back on her life at the end. What would she have been happy about and what would she have regretted?